The Fregoli Delusion

Also by Michael J. McCann

THE DONAGHUE AND STAINER CRIME NOVEL SERIES

Blood Passage
Marcie's Murder

SUPERNATURAL FICTION

The Ghost Man

The Fregoli Delusion

A Donaghue and Stainer Crime Novel

Michael J. McCann

The Plaid Raccoon Press
2012

This is a work of fiction. All names, characters, institutions, places and events portrayed in this novel are either the product of the author's imagination or are used fictitiously. Any resemblance to actual persons, living or dead, events or locales is entirely coincidental.

This book is dedicated to my mother,
whose memories are now gone,
and to the memories of her that I still cherish
and share with her now as new stories,
to make her smile.

1

Lieutenant Hank Donaghue put away his notebook and looked at his watch, surprised to see that it was nearly noon. He rubbed his neck, trying to relieve the stiffness and cramping he felt from having kept his eyes on the ground for much of the morning.

Their crime scene was on a bike path in Granger Park, a district in northwest Glendale that was home to the wealthiest stratum of the city's population. A protected green space, it featured well-trimmed stretches of grass, an abundance of trees, and decorative shrubbery. It was a pretty spot.

The sky, he noticed as he moved his head around to loosen his neck muscles, was clear and blue. The sun was almost directly overhead, baking the air to the ninety-degree Fahrenheit temperature predicted to continue pounding Maryland for at least the next week. His shirt was damp beneath his suit jacket, and his mouth was a little dry.

He walked over to Captain Martinez, who was flipping through the pages of her notebook.

"I don't mind talking to them, Ann."

Martinez shook her head. "I've got this. Then we need to talk. Things are happening."

They walked together to the yellow tape at the edge of the crime scene. Hank gestured to a uniformed officer, who moved the small crowd of reporters back a few yards. He and Martinez ducked under the tape and stood before the small circle of microphones, cameras, and notepads.

"The deceased is a male in his late sixties," Martinez said without preamble in a high, clear voice. "He was shot once in the head. Evidence indicates he was riding on the bike path when he stopped, possibly to speak to the person who shot him. His bicycle was found upright on its kickstand a few yards away from the body. Robbery may have been a motive. The victim's wallet was found farther down the path under a bush with no cash or credit cards in it. The identity of the victim is being withheld pending notification of next of kin."

"Who found the body?" someone asked.

"The victim was found by a man who was taking photographs in the park and heard the shot in the distance."

"What's his name?"

"Is he a suspect?"

"Did he shoot the victim?"

"What's he saying? Did he see who did it?"

Martinez held up her hand. "Just a minute, take it easy. At this time he's being treated as a witness. We're still in the process of interviewing him and we'll let you know as soon as possible whatever we can. That's all for now."

"Captain Martinez," one of the journalists called out as she turned away, "can you comment on the fact that the recent outbreak of murders downtown now seems to have spread to Granger Park? Is the mayor's campaign against violent crime a failure?"

Hank stepped forward. "We're fairly certain this is an isolated incident in no way connected to any recent events in Midtown or anywhere else in the city. You can remind your readers that, statistically, violent crime is down this calendar year compared to last year, due in large part to the mayor's campaign. The people of Glendale can rest assured that the police department is doing everything possible to keep our streets and homes safe."

The journalist gave him a thin smile and shook his head.

Hank followed Martinez back to the crime scene command post behind the barriers, where Detective Karen Stainer was stripping off her latex gloves.

"I gotta take him downtown," Karen said. "He's not making a hell of a lot of sense, and his old man called their lawyer."

"All right." Hank saw a uniformed officer leading their only witness back along the bike path, away from the reporters. "He said he knew the victim?"

"Yeah." Karen glanced at Martinez. "He gave us all this yakkety-yak about taking pictures of the trees and hearing the shot and finding the vic. He said his father works for the old man. So he calls his father and waits until he gets here before doing anything. I mean, does that sound right? The guy's in his thirties and he has to wait for his daddy before he can dial nine-one-one? Give me a break."

Karen's Texan drawl, which made "right" sound like "raht" and "give" sound like "gee-uv," would be charming if it weren't coming from a mouth that looked like it might bite a chain in half at any moment. She was thirty-seven years old and a sixteen-year veteran of the police department. A Tai-kwon-do black belt with a mean streak, she was five feet, three inches tall, weighed one hundred and five pounds, and had small fists that could punch a hole through drywall without any special effort at all. Her blond hair was shoulder length, her nose and chin were somewhat pointed, and her pale blue eyes tended to fix on people in a laser beam cop's stare.

"Well," Martinez said to her, "see what you can get out of him." She looked around the scene. The bike path was sealed off for fifty yards in each direction from where the body had been found. Granger Park was a district of gated communities, mansions, and high-end developments. The bike path was used almost exclusively by millionaires and their children. She looked at the fluttering yellow tape, the yellow numbered markers identifying evidence that was still being photographed and collected by crime scene technicians, and the gurney from the office of the medical examiner that was waiting to transport the body to the morgue.

"We need to nail this down," she said. "This is a big one."

"You ain't kidding." Karen turned on her heel and headed off after her witness.

Tim Byrne, the crime scene investigation team leader, informed them his crew would be finished processing the scene in about twenty minutes. Dr. Jim Easton, the medical examiner, was now supervising the movement of the body to the gurney. An ambulance waited at the curb along Cumberland Avenue, the street paralleling the bike path. Reporters were beginning to peel away from the crowd to record and file their stories.

"Let's go," Martinez said to Hank. She led the way to her car, one of the new unmarked Ford Taurus Police Interceptor models, which was parked half a block away.

Martinez started the engine, waited for a television news van to pass, then pulled away from the curb. "You know these people."

"Somewhat." Hank fastened his seat belt and slipped on his sunglasses. "The witness, Brett Parris, I've never met. His father, Walter, I know slightly. Walter's mother, Constance Parris, is a friend of my mother. I know her fairly well. I was introduced to the victim once, at a reception or something my mother dragged me to when I was in college. It was a five-second thing. He seemed like an arrogant bastard. Billionaires don't tend to notice the teenaged sons of retired state's attorneys."

"What I mean is, you *know* these people. You know what makes them tick."

Hank looked at her. Martinez was forty-two years old, the daughter of a convenience store owner. She'd worked her way up the ladder through hard work, dedication, and a strong sense of internal politics. Hank had been her supervisory lieutenant when she was an up-and-coming detective, and now she was his captain. They trusted each other, and because of the history between them he knew she could handle whatever was thrown at her, but Hank understood her discomfort with the social circle into which this case was going to pull them.

"Yeah," he said. "I know what makes them tick."

"I need you to take the lead in this." She glanced in the rear-view mirror. "When I called the chief to tell him who the vic was, he said he wanted you working it. He told me to talk to the media to keep them out of your hair. Which translates as him wanting future press conferences at his level, I guess, with me as his second fiddle. He wants you to focus on the investigation. Stainer can work it with you as long as she minds her Ps and Qs, but given the current state of our budget and the fact that Jarvis took Carleson with him to that damned Chinatown task force, I can't give you any more help than that until I talk to him again. That's where I'm going right now. To plead our case."

"Okay."

"Start by informing the widow and getting her statement. I'll drop you off."

"No problem, Ann."

"There's more," she said, glancing over at him.

"There always is."

"Barkley's been chosen to replace Paup as deputy chief."

"I'm not surprised," Hank said.

"They've asked me to move up to acting commander of Detective Services Bureau."

Now that *was* a surprise. "Congratulations, Ann. That's great news."

"Yeah, I guess." She braked at a stop sign and looked at him. "They called me in last night. They're not going to backfill my spot. The budget, as I said, is a bitch right now. They expect me to continue running Major Crimes along with the rest of the bureau. I told them they had to move you up to acting captain to run Major Crimes for me, but the chief refused. On top of that, he said he wouldn't fill our detective vacancies." She turned the corner and shook her head. "Given the huge case just dumped into our laps this morning, I've got to go right back and ask him to reconsider. We're going to take major heat, and we need a small army to work this one."

"Good luck," Hank said.

"I'm going to need it." She looked at him. "I won't have much time to spare. I need you to run Homicide for me. It sucks they won't pay you for it, but I need you to cover my ass."

"You've got it."

"Thanks. You have no idea." Martinez slowed the car at an intersection, frowning at the street signs. "Am I going the right way? Am I getting close to Fairbanks Court?"

"You're just a few blocks away," Hank said. "Next right, then a left."

She glanced again in the rear view mirror. "Where's the cruiser? They're supposed to be right behind us."

"They're coming, Ann. They know where to go. It's their district."

"I talked to Peterson before I came over," she said, referring to Aaron Peterson, commander of Granger Park district. "He'll make sure you have whatever uniformed assistance you need on this."

"That's fine."

She sighed. "I have to get used to this."

"You'll be great."

She slowed alongside a high cement wall topped with wire and cameras. "This must be it." She pulled up to a gate. A uniformed security guard stepped out of a booth and approached the car. Martinez looked at Hank.

"I feel bad, dumping this on you."

"No problem, Ann," Hank said, unbuckling his seat belt. "This is what I do. Good luck downtown."

"Yeah, thanks."

Hank got out of the car and watched her drive away. Then he turned to the security guard and held up the leather wallet containing his badge and identification.

"Lieutenant Hank Donaghue, Glendale Police Department. I'm

here to see Mrs. Jarrett."

The security guard frowned. "Got an appointment?"

"Funny guy." Hank looked at a golf cart parked on the other side of the gate. "Do I have to drive that thing myself, or is somebody going to take me up to the house?"

2

The front door was opened by a slender, dark-haired woman who appeared to be about thirty years old. She wore a black pantsuit, oversized eyeglasses, and sensible black shoes.

"I'm Megan Winterbottom," she said, "Mrs. Jarrett's personal assistant." She had large front teeth and spoke with a British accent. "Mrs. Jarrett is with Mrs. Parris in the sun room."

Hank followed her inside. As they passed the circular staircases on either side of the grand entry hall, Hank looked at the enormous oil portraits of Herbert Joseph Jarrett and his first wife, the late Judith Wilson Jarrett. Until this morning, Jarrett had been the president and chief executive officer of Jarrett Corporation, a health care company headquartered in Glendale with annual revenues exceeding one billion dollars. Now he was just a corpse being transported to the morgue in the back of an ambulance.

The portrait revealed a small, wiry man with a slightly oversized bald head, trim mustache, solid chin, and cold eyes. He was dressed in black-tie formalwear and his left hand was shoved into the pocket of his trousers. The pose conveyed the to-hell-with-you attitude that Hank understood to have been typical of the man.

Judith had been his first wife. They had married in 1969. She was a tall, slender woman with reddish, shoulder-length hair and a kind, patient face. She wore a simple but beautiful black gown and several strands of pearls. She had passed away, Hank understood, two weeks after giving birth to her first child, Edward Wilson "Ned" Jarrett, in 1970.

As Hank followed Megan Winterbottom from the entry hall down a short passage into the sun room, he glanced at a mahogany long-case clock that was probably worth about fifteen thousand dollars. The clock told him it was nearly half past noon.

He was met at the doorway of the sun room by Constance Mercer Parris, a friend of Mrs. Jarrett. She stepped forward, embraced him warmly, and allowed him to kiss both her cheeks.

"Very nice to see you, Hank, although I sincerely wish the circumstances were different. Chrissy's over here." Constance led him across the room to an arrangement of wicker furniture and side tables.

Christine Jarrett rose to greet him with a firm handshake and a faint smile. Hank noticed that her eyes were a little red and that she clasped a tissue in her left hand. Otherwise, she presented a calm front.

"I'm very sorry for your loss," Hank said.

"Thank you."

"Walter called me," Constance explained, "so I came over to break the news to Chrissy."

"I understand," Hank said.

"I've heard about you," Chrissy said, motioning him to a seat, "and your mother too, of course. I know she and Constance have been friends for a very long time. I'm sorry we haven't met before. Would you like something?"

"No, I'm fine, thanks."

"I'll leave you two alone," Constance said, glancing at Winterbottom.

"Just a moment." Hank looked at Chrissy. "Uniformed officers are on their way. When they arrive we're going to secure the premises for the time being and control access to Mr. Jarrett's private rooms, including his bedroom and home office. We'll be getting the appropriate warrants before we search and remove anything to be used as evidence, but right now we need to make sure that no one enters these rooms until we're finished with that part of our investigation. Can I count on your cooperation, Mrs. Jarrett?"

"Of course." Chrissy turned to Winterbottom. "When the officers arrive, show them whatever they need to see."

"We'll do everything we can to minimize the inconvenience," Hank said.

"I appreciate that. Megan?"

Winterbottom left the room. Constance followed.

Hank sat down and clasped his hands between his knees. They were big hands, with long slender fingers and large knuckles. His frizzy hair was medium brown and beginning to show some gray. He had recently shaved off his quarter-inch beard, revealing a square jaw and dimpled chin. His heavy brow gave his large brown eyes a brooding look. He wore a charcoal worsted suit that was moderately expensive, a light cream shirt, and a rust-colored tie that picked up the color of his hair and eyes.

Chrissy said, "Walter told Constance that Herb was shot on the bike path. Is it true?"

"I'm afraid so. He was shot around seven o'clock. It looks like he died instantly. Was it his habit to go for a bike ride in the early morning?"

Chrissy nodded. "Every morning when the weather's good he goes out along the bike path. He's up by five o'clock, showers and has breakfast, gets some work done, then at seven or so takes an hour to exercise before going to work. In the winter he rides a stationary bike in the gym downstairs and in the summer, if it's not raining, he loves the bike path." She grimaced. "Loved."

"So this is a routine he always followed?"

"We've been married six years and, as far as I know, he's followed it every day."

"That's very impressive for a man of his age."

"He's in very good health." She lowered her head. "Was."

Hank brought out his notebook and pen. "You don't mind if I ask a few more questions?"

"Let's get it over with before the circus starts."

"All right." Hank sat back, balancing the notebook on his knee. "I'm wondering about his personal security. Didn't he have someone assigned to be with him whenever he went out?"

"I think so. I don't really know all that much about it. He owns the company that handles all his security, and I know there's a guy I can text if I want someone when I go out, but I'm not really sure what Herb did himself. Our lives ran on separate tracks. I guess I should have been more worried about kidnapping or getting shot or something, but I really didn't give it much thought. Nothing ever happened."

"What kind of household staff do you have?"

"We have a live-in staff of six people. There's Megan, a cook, two housekeepers, and two drivers. The guy who's head of security works out of the tower downtown, and I guess the people at the front gate work for him. Everything else is electronic around here. Motion sensors, cameras, intercoms."

"His wallet was found empty. Did he carry credit cards or cash with him?"

"Yes, he had a couple of credit cards. He liked to be able to pay for little things himself if the impulse struck him. You know, if he saw something in a store window when he was traveling that he thought someone might like. He didn't carry cash, though, because he hated a bulky wallet. I suppose the cards should be canceled."

"No, we'll leave them as is for now, in case someone tries to use them. I'm a little surprised, though. Did he always take his wallet with him when he went for a bike ride?"

"Probably. He never went anywhere without it."

"All right." Hank made a note and looked up at her. "Does anyone come immediately to mind who'd want to do this?"

She glanced away for a moment, looking out at the garden, then turned to him with a cool expression. "Well, I didn't. I think we should talk about that first."

"Okay. You're his third marriage. There's a difference of what, forty years?"

"You're trying to flatter me. I'm thirty-four years old, so there's a difference of thirty-four years. I was born and raised in Reno. My dad owns a hotel there. My mother died when I was young. I went to UNLV and got a degree in business administration. When I was a student I started modeling through an agency out of Los Angeles. For a while I appeared in magazines on a regular basis and I also had a couple of billboards. Just fashion and cosmetics. Everything above board. Shortly after I finished my degree, there was a lull in the action and a couple of us got this gig as hostesses at a conference at Lake Tahoe. A group of very rich people get together for a week every year with their families and have a sort of retreat. There's stuff for the wives and kids, motivational speakers, and a lot of private meetings to talk deals. I met Herb there. He'd been divorced for quite a few years. We became friendly, he was surprised that I knew something about business, and before he left at the end of the week he asked me if I'd be interested in marrying him. That's how he put it. I said probably, but could I have a week or two to think about it? He gave me his private cell number and told me to call him. I talked it over with my father, who told me to do whatever I felt was right, so I called Herb and told him I'd like to fly to Baltimore and stay there for a while. We could meet a few more times and talk it over. That's what we did. He gave me the name of a lawyer he said was hated by his law firm and told me to call her. I did, we met a few times with the lawyers, and negotiated a prenuptial agreement.

When it was done we had a quiet ceremony and that was it. We were married. It's been six years now."

Hank jotted a few notes. "Who's your lawyer?"

"Bethany Johnson."

Hank wrote it down. Hated, indeed. B-Jo was known to throw entire board rooms into an uproar just by walking through the door. "Go on."

"This year Herb decided to change his will. It hadn't gone through yet, so the old will is still in effect. That might be a motive, someone who didn't want the old will to change. I don't know. Anyway, after he made up his mind to go ahead with the changes, we had a meeting about it. He said our prenup would still be in place and I wouldn't notice any difference financially. But I'd notice a difference personally because he was changing the will so he could divest himself of Jarrett Corporation right now and retire. He was very concerned about the estate tax and what it would do to his children's inheritance. I'm not a tax expert, so you'll have to talk to his lawyer about it, but he was going to buy a place in St. Lucia and spend a lot of his time down there, and he wanted to know if I wanted to come down with him or if I'd rather stay here. I told him I'd probably spend some of the time down there with him but I'd have to talk to my friend about it. He said that was fine. It was all very cordial. That's how we were. Good friends. Cordial."

"You'd have to talk to your friend about it?"

"I should explain our prenup," Chrissy said. "You'll see a copy of it later, I guess. It paid me fifty million dollars the day after our wedding and ten million a year after that. So that's a hundred and ten million I've received into my own personal bank account as his wife, minus taxes, of course. On his death I receive this house and grounds and also the baseball team. Bethany held out for that one, because I'm a huge baseball fan."

"Baseball team?"

"The Glendale Pirates. The team here in town."

"Oh. Right." The team was a Class A affiliate of the Pittsburgh Pirates. "He owned that?"

She nodded. "So that's everything. Under the old will, as per the prenup, I'd get this place and the baseball team and nothing else, even though he's worth billions in total. It was going to stay the same under the new will. I was happy with the prenup, and still am. Who wouldn't

17

be? I'm interested in business, yeah, and I keep a close eye on my own investments, but I have absolutely no interest in Jarrett Corporation. I never have and never will. I should mention that, according to the prenup, if we divorced I'd still get the team and this house."

"You had to talk to your friend about St. Lucia," Hank prompted.

"Yes. The prenup also said our marriage would be open, so that both of us could have boyfriends or girlfriends and it wouldn't be used against the other in the event of a divorce or for any other reason. Herb was, um, kind of slowing down a bit and preferred to have things out in the open. Apparently he had a long history of infidelity in his past marriages and was tired of the trouble it caused. I didn't see any problem with it. As far as I know, there was someone at the beginning but nothing since. I didn't bother with any other relationships for the first few years, but then I met someone. We became close friends, and we have a physical relationship. I wasn't sure how he'd feel about me spending a lot of time down in the Caribbean with Herb, so I wanted to talk to him about it. Herb understood."

"What's his name?"

Her face clouded. "I'd rather not say, if you don't mind. He's not involved with this, and I don't want his business hurt by negative publicity."

Hank stared at her without expression. "I'll need to question him to verify his whereabouts this morning and rule him out as a suspect."

Chrissy returned the look, then seemed to remember she was speaking to a police officer and not a social acquaintance. She averted her eyes. "His name's Perry Crocker. He owns CrocComm, the telecommunications company."

Hank wrote it down. CrocComm generated over one hundred million dollars a year in revenue, if he remembered correctly. Not exactly the kid who comes around to clean the pool. Chrissy reluctantly gave him Crocker's home address and cell phone number.

"Just to be sure I understand the situation," Hank went on, "you've been aware of the various relationships your husband has maintained since your marriage?"

"There was just the one."

"And no current relationship?"

Chrissy shook her head.

"Did any of his relationships, either before or since you were married, end badly?"

"Well, one ended when the woman was killed in a plane crash. That was before we were married. The woman he was involved with a few years ago, though, got married later. No hard feelings. I think she lives in St. Louis."

"Name?"

"Cynthia Troy. Now Cynthia Powell, I believe it is."

Hank wrote it down. "Where were you this morning between six and seven o'clock.?"

"In bed, asleep. I usually get up at eight. Lillian, one of the housekeepers, calls me if I'm not already up."

"Did she call you this morning?"

"Yes."

"All right," Hank said, making notes. "Thanks." When he was finished writing he looked up at her. "Just to go back for a moment, you said Mr. Jarrett had decided to retire. I don't remember reading anything about it."

She shook her head. "There hasn't been an announcement yet. He was still working out all the details."

"Who knew about it?"

"Oh, a few key people, I suppose. All his senior people at the company, the board of directors, his son and daughter."

"Anyone particularly upset about it?"

"I don't really know," Chrissy admitted. "I imagine it caused quite a stir. Succession planning usually does. There was a lot to do to organize his replacement, a lot of negotiations and jockeying for position by people, and all that. But I don't know anything about it. You'll have to ask Walter. He was in charge of it."

"All right." Hank made another note, then tapped his pen on his knee. "I'd still like you to try answering the question I asked before. Can you think of anyone who'd have a reason to kill your husband?"

Chrissy stared at the toe of her shoe. Finally, she shook her head. "No. A lot of people didn't like Herb. I don't know very much about his business dealings because I didn't really care and he never talked about it with me, but I knew he could be ruthless when he wanted to be. But I don't know who'd hate him enough to actually kill him."

"What about you, Mrs. Jarrett? Have you received any threats or had any unexplained phone calls, e-mails, that sort of thing?"

"No. Should I be worried?"

"I wouldn't think so if you haven't noticed anything out of the ordinary, but until we understand the reason for the attack on your husband it'd be a good idea to be extra vigilant. Before you go out again you might want to text that guy you mentioned."

"All right, if you think I should."

Hank put away his notebook and stood up. "I appreciate your time."

"That's all right. You're just doing your job." She stood up and shook his hand.

As he turned away she put a hand on his arm. "I should probably make myself clear about something."

Hank turned back, waiting.

"It may sound like I'm just a trophy wife, bought and paid for. That's not the way it was."

Hank said nothing.

"Herb really liked me. He used to tell me that all the time, and I think he actually grew to love me, in his own way. The feeling was mutual. The marriage was, um, consummated, and occasionally we'd get together. It was always very nice. It's not what people will think. We were good friends and occasional lovers. I'll miss him terribly."

"I understand," Hank said.

"Maybe you do," she said, tears in her eyes. "After all, you're one of us. If I can say that. But other people, the public, they won't understand. The media will have a field day."

"You're going to have to ignore the media," Hank replied. "Their only motivation is to make money, pure and simple. There's nothing personal in it, even when it seems that way."

"Okay," Chrissy said. "I'm sorry. Thanks for your patience with me."

Outside in the hallway he found Megan Winterbottom waiting for him with Sergeant Richard Booth and two other uniformed officers.

"We're parked just inside the gate, Lieutenant," Booth said. "She was just going to show us where Mr. Jarrett's rooms are. He had a private gym and a screening room. You want us to secure them, too?"

"Yes." He turned to Winterbottom. "Before you show the sergeant around, I want to ask you a few questions."

"Of course."

"Did you see Mr. Jarrett this morning before he went out?"

She shook her head. "Mrs. Jarrett and I have rooms in another wing of the mansion. I was doing some work in my office until we got the call from Mrs. Parris, so I literally hadn't seen Mr. Jarrett since yesterday and had no idea what had happened."

"What was Mrs. Jarrett's schedule like today?"

"Fairly light, actually, thank goodness. Lillian called her at eight and she was free until eleven. She had an appointment with her dental hygienist, but we rescheduled it after Mrs. Parris called. We've rescheduled everything for the next week."

"All right, thanks. There'll be other detectives coming later who'll ask you for a more complete statement, so if anything else comes to mind, don't hesitate to tell them." He looked at Booth. "Are the security guards cooperating, Rich?"

"Yes, sir. No problems there."

"Good. See what they have to say for themselves."

"It's on my to-do list."

Hank nodded. "I'll see myself out," he told Winterbottom.

"Of course." She stood up and led Booth and his officers down the hallway and through a set of double doors.

Hank went back to the grand entry hall and out the front door, where he found Constance waiting for him.

"Can I give you a ride somewhere?" she asked.

"I have to go back downtown," Hank said.

"Come along, then."

They got into the back of Constance's limousine. She asked about his mother and he told her she was doing well. She recalled, as she often did, how much she'd always enjoyed his visits with his mother, retired State's Attorney Anna Haynes Donaghue, when he was a small boy. Friends since childhood, Constance and Anna would talk politics, drink bourbon, and trade investment advice while Hank dawdled nearby, playing with her collie dog.

"You were always such a polite and quiet boy," she smiled, "but very, very attentive. You never missed a thing, did you? A good quality for a policeman to have."

The small talk continued until the limousine eased onto the expressway heading south toward Midtown. She turned to look directly at him.

"I'd appreciate it very much, Hank, if you could give your

personal attention to this case."

"I will." Hank thought about Bennett's instructions that Hank assume the lead in the investigation and wondered if the chief had received a phone call on the subject before issuing his edict to Martinez. Perhaps he'd already known the identity of the victim before hearing it from her.

"I know you have a lot of responsibilities, but everyone will appreciate it if you handle things personally. Your reputation as a police officer is so excellent, it'll be comforting for the families to know it's in your hands."

"We're understaffed right now," Hank said, "and I'll be the lead investigator, but Detective Stainer will be doing a lot of the work, and we'll need others to help as well, running down leads, collecting evidence, taking statements."

"I understand. Thank you, Hank." She sighed. "Please bear in mind that Brett's actually a very gentle and kindhearted young man. He wouldn't hurt a fly. He's just ... different. You'll have to take what he says with a grain of salt."

"Detective Stainer found him pretty difficult to deal with this morning."

"It's because of his disability," Constance said.

"Disability?"

"I'll let Walter explain it," she said. "Brett's my grandson, but Walter's been the one who's had to manage things on a daily basis. Just don't judge the boy until you understand."

3

Hank stepped out of the elevator onto the ninth floor and turned left, passing the cubbyholes assigned to the Arson Unit, and on into the larger open space assigned to Homicide. Along the wall on the right were filing cabinets, a gun locker, a coffee machine that dispensed poison in brown paper cups, a pigeon-hole mailbox, and a networked printer and fax machine. Along the wall on the left were the captain's office, more filing cabinets, and the office of the supervising lieutenant which had, until a month ago, been occupied by Bill Jarvis. Now it belonged once again to Hank as it had before, several years ago.

In the middle of the open space was the cluster of desks, arranged in pairs back-to-back, that served as the detectives' bullpen. As Hank skirted the bullpen on his way to his office, Detective Jim Horvath hurried toward him, putting on his jacket.

"Home invasion, Hank. Chinatown. Peralta's waiting for me downstairs."

Horvath was in his early thirties, tall and slender, with a handsome, pleasant face and neatly combed straight black hair. He'd been with Homicide for almost two years now and was showing an aptitude for the job. His partner, Detective Amelda Peralta, was more experienced, less chatty, and a stickler for procedure. She didn't mind explaining to Horvath his shortcomings when it came to homicide investigation and Horvath, to his credit, took it with good humor.

Hank frowned. "Won't Jarvis be there?"

"I guess, but they called us, too."

Hank rolled his eyes. "No love from the watch sergeants, either? Poor Bill."

"Yeah, he's a poor dickhead, all right. Anyway, they want us over there. Maybe to keep a uniform from fragging him."

"Maybe. Give me a call if he isn't there and you need me."

"You got it." Feeling under his jacket to double-check for his sidearm, Horvath hurried off to the elevator.

The other two detectives assigned to Homicide, Kaplan and

Belknap, were currently off-duty. Hank was looking for some sign of Karen, but instead he saw Detective Maureen Truly loitering outside his office door. She moved aside self-consciously as he approached and unlocked his door.

"Hello, Detective. How are you doing?"

"I'm well, Lieutenant. You said I could drop by, so I thought today might be okay. If, um, it's okay."

Truly worked in the Cold Case Unit. She was thirty-one years old, single, short and lumpy, with wavy brown hair and unflattering glasses with narrow red frames. When she'd learned last month that Jarvis was leaving and that Hank was replacing him as supervisory lieutenant, she'd approached him about a transfer to Homicide. He said they couldn't bring in anyone new at the moment, but she was welcome to come up and talk to him about it further, if she liked. He didn't think she had the right temperament for Homicide, but there was something about her that he liked, and he wanted to find out what it was.

Unfortunately, she'd picked a bad time to show up for a job interview.

"Lou! Hang on a sec!"

Hank turned, his office door swinging open. Karen was coming up the corridor from the interview room with Walter Parris a few steps behind.

"Excuse me," he said to Truly.

"No problem."

"We're not getting anywhere," Karen said, stopping in front of Hank. "The lawyer's here, and nothing they're saying is making any sense."

Hank looked over her shoulder at Walter Parris. "You want a sidebar, Mr. Parris?"

Walter nodded. "There are a few things I need to explain."

"Come on in."

Karen pushed by him, fuming. Walter followed, eyes down. Hank glanced at Truly, hesitated, then motioned with his head for her to step inside. He closed the door behind her, sat down at his desk, unclipped his holstered sidearm, locked it in a drawer, and looked at Karen.

"Is the witness being uncooperative?"

Karen screwed up her face. "That's what I'd call it." She shifted on her chair to confront Walter. "Look, Mr. Parris, with all due respect, your son says he knows the guy he saw leaving the scene, but you and your lawyer won't let him tell me who it is. I'd like to lock the three of you up for obstruction and throw away the fucking key at this point."

Walter opened his mouth but Hank held up a hand. "Mr. Parris, just a moment." He looked at Karen. "Walk me through it."

"He says he was in the park this morning, taking photographs. Apparently it's about a ten-minute walk from his house to where he was when he heard the shot. He gets up at dawn and likes to go for a walk. He doesn't have a job right now, he says, other than this photography thing."

"He's a freelance photographer," Walter said. "I can give you the name of his agent."

"Great." Karen glared at him, then turned back to Hank. "He was busy taking pictures of trees or whatever the hell when the shot was fired. He didn't have line of sight. The path curves and there were trees between him and where Jarrett got it, so if we buy his story then he didn't see it happen. He said when he heard the shot he turned around and looked back in that direction. After a moment he started walking back toward the curve. At this point he says he saw a guy running toward a car parked at the curb. He says he took pictures of the guy. The guy saw him, ran over, grabbed his camera from him, and knocked him down. When he got up, the guy had driven away. So he walked around the curve until he could see where Jarrett was lying on the path. He walked up to him but says he didn't touch him, just saw the blood and called his father. Says his father told him to wait and not touch anything, that he'd be right there. So he waited. Took a couple of pictures of the vic with his cell phone while he was standing there. We have the thing. Expensive, naturally. He let us test him for GSR, by the way. It was negative."

The absence of gunshot residue on Brett Parris lent strength to his story and suggested they could continue to treat him as a witness rather than a suspect.

"Okay," Hank said. "What does he say about the guy he saw running away?"

"Zip," Karen said. "That's where the roadblocks come up."

Hank looked at Walter. "What's the problem?"

"I understand how serious this is," Walter said uncomfortably. "It's not that we want him to be uncooperative. It's just that there's ... context that must be understood first."

"Context?" Karen snapped. "What the hell does that mean?"

Walter sighed and ran his hand over his bare scalp. He was a short man, fifty-eight years old, and somewhat stout. His hands were small and his fingers looked like little sausages. What was left of his hair was gray stubble around the base of his skull from ear to ear. He wore a yellow golf shirt, designer blue jeans, gray socks, and blue Sperry deck shoes. He wore a gold wedding band on his left hand and an enormous ring on his right hand that featured rubies and diamonds. His watch was a Rolex. As chief financial officer of Jarrett Corporation, his annual income would make Karen's look like something you'd hand to a street person for a sandwich at the lunch wagon down at the corner. At the moment, however, he looked to Hank more like a father struggling to protect his son.

"Brett has a condition," he said finally. "We don't normally talk about it to other people because we want Brett to have as normal a life as possible. He started having difficulties as a junior in high school. He attended Jesper Logan—"

"The private school?" Karen interrupted.

"Yes, Detective. The expensive one. He wasn't athletic at all and his grades were mediocre at best and he's very introverted so he wasn't very popular. He kept to himself. He endured hazing and bullying, and we had to talk to the headmaster about it several times. Brett was very depressed that year, but we told ourselves it was just adolescence, something we all go through.

"After graduation he enrolled at the University of Baltimore to do a program in communications. He lived in residence on campus. His first year went okay but he ran into a lot of problems as a sophomore. Behavioral issues, mood problems, paranoia. He was drinking a lot, getting into trouble that way. We brought him home, and the doctors diagnosed him as schizophrenic. We were devastated. He went on medication for it, and his psychiatrist at the time suggested he go back to school, that it would be good for him to pick up where he'd left off. We compromised by getting him transferred to State so he could live at home and continue his degree here in Glendale. It went all right for a few months, then he started drinking again, skipped his medication, and went off the rails. The paranoia escalated. We were very upset and took him to a different psychiatrist. She worked with him for a year and then told us he had something called Fregoli syndrome in addition to the schizophrenia."

26

"Jesus Christ on a stick. What the hell's that?" Karen asked.

Walter spread his hands. "I was just as skeptical as you, Detective. But believe me, after ten years of living with this I understand it almost as well as Dr. Caldwell."

"Dr. Sally Caldwell?" Hank asked. "That's his psychiatrist?"

"Yes."

Karen rolled her eyes. Hank shook his head microscopically at her. Dr. Sally Caldwell was a celebrity psychiatrist who'd published several books and regularly appeared on television as a popular guest on talk shows and news programs. He'd actually read one of her books, on body language, and thought it was good, although it didn't really have anything new to say on the subject. Just the same, he understood Karen's reaction. A problem witness with a celebrity psychiatrist at the center of a murder investigation in which the victim was the fifth-richest man in the state was not a situation that would make any detective feel particularly comfortable.

"What did she say about this condition of Brett's?"

"It's a disorder in which the person believes they're being stalked by a particular individual who's disguised as various other people," Walter said. "It's apparently a rare form of what they call delusional misidentification syndrome, DMS, where the person has what she calls a disturbed familiarity with people. The area of the brain that handles facial recognition doesn't function properly all the time. There are different forms of it, I guess, but Brett has what they call Fregoli syndrome. He has a paranoid belief that a specific person is persecuting him. At first they thought it was just the schizophrenia, but Dr. Caldwell recognized a very specific pattern and realized it was this other syndrome on top of it."

"Specific pattern," Hank prompted.

"When he was in high school," Walter said, with obvious reluctance, "there was one boy in particular who picked on him. It was hard to get Brett to talk about it, but when he did it was always this same boy who was beating him up and tormenting him. We went to the headmaster a number of times, and he spoke to the boy. Several times he admitted to having bullied Brett, but on other occasions he vigorously denied the accusations. It didn't make a lot of sense. Then after Brett came back from Baltimore we noticed he talked about this boy all the time. I knew the boy had gone off to Connecticut to go to college, but Brett insisted he kept running into him here in town and that the boy continued to have it in for him. He talked about the boy stalking him, wearing disguises. To Dr. Caldwell this was the key to diagnosing his illness as Fregoli syndrome. People with this condition believe that a single person is persecuting them by following them everywhere disguised as other people. He might look at you, Lieutenant, and believe you were this boy disguised as a police officer. Then he might go outside and see a courier go by on a bicycle and decide that the boy had switched disguises and was after him again. It's exhausting."

Out of the corner of his eye, Hank saw Maureen Truly leaning against the closed door, nodding as though she knew what Walter was talking about. When he looked at her, she made eye contact but said nothing.

"So he gets this all the time?" Karen growled.

"Not exactly. It's intermittent. If he misses his medication, he gets it. If he's under extreme stress, he gets it. If there's nothing at all unusual happening, he sometimes gets it. It might go away over the course of a day or last for several days. They don't really understand a lot about it."

"Who's the boy, out of curiosity?" Hank asked.

"His name's Richard Holland. He's not a boy now, of course. He's actually a senior executive with us, vice-president of corporate and regulatory affairs."

Hank's eyebrows shot up. "He's Brett's age and he's an executive with your company?"

"He's a year older, but yes, he's been with Jarrett for several years. H.J. brought him in. Apparently Holland's father worked for H.J. a long time ago."

"Does he ever get violent when he has these delusions?" Karen asked.

"No," Walter replied emphatically, "not at all. Look, he's never hurt another person in his life. He's been beaten up before, as I said, but he never even tried to defend himself. He'd never hit another person, not even at his most agitated. And he'd absolutely never shoot someone with a gun. We have no firearms in our home whatsoever. He's not capable of shooting anyone."

"I take it we can confirm all this with his shrink."

"We'll provide you with written consent."

"And we can search his room for the gun you say he'd never use."

28

Walter frowned. "This is a sidebar, Detective, without Brett and his legal counsel. My son gave me permission to discuss his condition, as you heard, but I'll thank you not to push it too far. Entering our home for any purpose other than an interview will require a warrant."

"Okay, okay. But let me guess where you're heading with this. I'm going to go back into that room and ask him again who he saw on the bike path this morning. Now that we've had this little chat, you and his lawyer are going to back off and let him tell me, right?"

Walter nodded reluctantly.

"Okay, great. But then you're going to insist he's not a reliable eyewitness because of this Fregoli thing, right? Because he believes that a bunch of different people are the same guy, following him around?"

"Essentially, yes."

"I never went to Harvard," Karen went on, "but I bet I'm smart enough to guess who he's gonna tell me he saw. Am I right?"

Walter stared at her, then dropped his eyes and nodded. "That's right, Detective. He said he saw Richard Holland."

4

The captain's office had a television set, so they crowded inside at 2:00 P.M. to watch the news conference. Chief Bennett was at the podium making his statement when Hank turned it on.

"Good afternoon, everyone." Bennett stared into the camera with his usual arrogance. "I understand it's very warm in the room and I apologize for our air conditioning, which is being serviced as we speak, so I won't keep you very long. I'll make a brief statement, we'll take some questions, and then I'll let you go so you can make your deadlines.

"I have with me Deputy Chief Douglas Barkley of our Investigations Division and acting Commander Ann Martinez of the Detective Services Bureau." He gestured behind him, where Barkley and Martinez sat stiffly on plastic chairs. "Commander Martinez made a statement this morning at the scene regarding the shooting death of a white male, aged sixty-eight, who was murdered while riding a bicycle on the bike path along Cumberland Avenue in Granger Park. We're here to announce that the victim was Herbert Joseph Jarrett, president and chief executive officer of Jarrett Corporation. Mr. Jarrett was riding his bicycle on the path when he was met by an unknown subject. Evidence suggests that he stopped his bicycle to talk to this UNSUB and was shot once in the head from a distance of four to six feet, dying almost instantly from his wound."

Bennett paused for a moment to allow the noise to die down as the journalists reacted to the identity of the victim. "Mr. Jarrett's wallet was found about twenty yards down the bike path from the body, thrown under some bushes. The wallet contained no cash or credit cards. We're considering the possibility that Mr. Jarrett was the victim of a robbery, but we're also going to pursue the theory that Mr. Jarrett knew the UNSUB and that the wallet was a ruse to throw us off the scent."

"He's more FBI than the FBI," muttered a robbery detective standing next to Hank. Apparently Hank wasn't the only one who was annoyed by the chief's continual use of FBI terminology such as "UNSUB," slang for "unknown subject," a hangover from his days with the Bureau.

"We've interviewed a witness who was present in the park when the shooting occurred," Bennett went on. "He did not witness the shooting itself. He was a fair distance around the bend in the bike path, with trees and bushes between himself and the scene. He heard the shot in the distance and walked over to find the body. Nine-one-one was called and our responding officers arrived within five minutes. We're still talking to the witness in case he might have any further information that will be of use to us, but at this time we'll be vigorously pursuing all other leads.

"Our condolences go out to Mrs. Christine Jarrett and the rest of Mr. Jarrett's family, friends, and colleagues. That's all I have for you at this time."

Questions had erupted from all quarters. Bennett pointed to someone in the first row.

"Sarah Hume, CNN, Chief Bennett. Given that Jarrett Corporation is the seventh-largest company in Maryland, with revenues exceeding one-point-two billion dollars last year, and given that H.J. Jarrett was the state's fifth-wealthiest individual, with a net worth of more than a billion and a half dollars, is it safe to say that your department is assigning this homicide its highest priority?"

"Absolutely," Bennett replied. "I can tell you that we've formed a special task force to investigate this heinous crime, reporting to Commander Martinez. Our top investigators will be working on this case night and day until it's solved."

The robbery detective standing next to Hank grinned. "A task force, huh? Must be your lucky day."

"First I've heard of it."

On the television, the questions continued to fly.

"Have you spoken to the governor?" the correspondent from CBS was pressing the chief.

"I haven't," Bennett frowned, "but Mayor Watts has, and the governor has been assured that the Glendale Police Department will solve this case in a timely manner and bring the perpetrator to justice." It was obvious that Bennett felt miffed about not having spoken to the governor himself.

The correspondent from Fox News put up his hand. "Can you

tell us who the witness is, Chief Bennett?"

"At this time," Bennett said slowly, "we're not going to release his name."

"Is he a suspect? Do you think he shot Jarrett himself?"

"No, no. Well, let me just say that we're pursuing all leads right now."

"What's he saying? Did he know Jarrett? Did you find evidence that he might have robbed Jarrett?"

Martinez stood up and joined Bennett at the podium. The chief gratefully yielded the floor.

"To answer your question," Martinez said, "no, we found no evidence to indicate that the witness robbed the victim. He told us basically what the chief told you, that he heard a shot, walked back around the bend along the bike path, found the victim already deceased, and no, while we're actively considering all possibilities, we don't think the witness is the person who shot Mr. Jarrett. I'll mention now that he was tested for gunshot residue with negative results. We're treating him strictly as a witness, and one who may only be able to help us on a very limited basis. We're concentrating our efforts in a number of other directions."

"Have you found the gun?" asked a newspaper correspondent.

"Not at this time."

"Do you have any suspects?"

"Not at this time."

"Do you have any leads?"

Not at this time, Hank thought.

"We're pursuing several lines of inquiry," Martinez replied, "and we'll provide an update as soon as possible. That's all for now."

Bennett reclaimed the podium and thanked them for coming. The broadcast switched to a news anchor who began to summarize what had just been revealed. The murder of the fifth-richest man in the state was about to become one of the top stories of the year.

Hank turned off the television, and the crowd emptied out of the captain's office. He closed the door behind him as Karen strode into the bullpen area from the elevators.

"How'd it go?" he asked.

Karen held up her black leather portfolio. "All set." She and Assistant State's Attorney Leanne DiOrio had just paid a visit to the courthouse to obtain a set of warrants for the Jarrett mansion and the corporate offices in the downtown headquarters known as Jarrett Tower. "How did the press conference go?"

They walked back to the elevators. "It was short and sweet." Hank stabbed the button.

"The networks were there, right?"

"Yes."

"We're gonna be under the microscope."

"I imagine."

"What'd they say about Parris?" Karen punched the elevator button impatiently.

"Martinez cleared him as a suspect and said he'd be of help on a limited basis only."

"Okay," Karen said. "That's fine. There's not a chance in hell he shot the vic. It just doesn't work for me. But I think he could still be a witness. He was pretty damned sure about what he was saying."

"Maybe," Hank replied noncommittally. "We'll need to talk to Dr. Caldwell to get a better sense of his reliability."

Karen looked at him. "Can I ask you a question? And you won't get pissed?"

"Sure. Go ahead."

"What the fuck was Truly doing in our interview with old man Parris? Has she transferred to Homicide or something and I didn't get the memo?"

Hank shrugged. "She's asking for a transfer. I've told her we can't take anybody right now, but I wanted to see how she handled herself. She took it all in and kept her mouth shut."

"She's a slug, Lou. Her street experience is nil and she's got the personality of a fucking traffic cone. She wouldn't last five minutes in Homicide."

Hank said nothing.

"They're all duds in CCU," Karen went on. "Cold case, frozen brain. Look at Waverman. A complete tool."

Hank's cell phone vibrated. He took it out, looked at the call display, and thumbed the green button. "Donaghue."

"Hank, it's me," Horvath said. "We've got a big problem."

"What kind of problem? Are you still in Chinatown?"

"Yeah, we're here. But I need you to get the hell over here right away." Horvath lowered his voice, and Hank couldn't catch what he said next.

"Didn't get that, Horvath. Say again."

"I said, Peralta's had some kind of a breakdown. She's fallen apart. I called her husband and he's on the way but I need you ASAP. Jarvis is here and I don't want him talking to her like this."

The elevator doors opened and Karen stepped inside. Hank followed, caught her eye, and shook his head.

"I'll be right there," he told Horvath.

5

There was no one to give him a ride, so Hank caught a taxi. The home invasion had taken place at 1437 King Street, half a block from Columbia Street in the heart of Chinatown. He told the taxi driver to let him off on Columbia, just short of King. He walked around the corner and showed his identification and badge to officers at the wooden barriers blocking vehicular traffic.

This section of King was a mixture of tenements and small houses converted into grocery stores, tea houses, and souvenir shops. An old man sitting on the bottom step of one of the tenements watched expressionlessly as Hank walked past. A dog on the top step lifted its head, following him with its brown eyes. Next door someone parted the curtains in an upstairs window. A crime scene van trying to work its way down to Columbia blipped its klaxon to warn off the clusters of young men smoking cigarettes and talking in the middle of the street. By this time, Hank figured, the scene would be processed and the technicians would be heading back to the lab with their findings. He could see a number of police cruisers and unmarked vehicles ahead, light bars and dashboard bubbles still flashing, but it looked as though the medical examiner's office had already transported the bodies and cleared the scene.

At the yellow tape bordering the crime scene, Hank gave the leather wallet containing his identification and badge to the uniformed officer controlling access to the house where the invasion had taken place. She wrote down his particulars in the log on her clipboard and handed back the wallet. Hank had never seen her before. Small and blond, she looked young enough to be his daughter.

"I hear it's pretty bad," Hank said.

"These people are animals."

Hank put the wallet back in his jacket pocket and lifted the yellow tape. He walked up the steps onto the porch, where the front door was propped open by a black equipment case belonging to one of the crime scene technicians. The building was a duplex. Next door, the other half was taken up by a tiny grocery store with dusty bags of rice in the front window. A family by the name of Chee had lived in this half, a couple in their late fifties with two grown sons.

Hank stepped into the hallway, nodding at a uniformed officer on his way out. The first thing was the smell, a wave of vomit, excrement, and blood. Then it was Bill Jarvis, pointing a finger at him.

"Out of my crime scene, Donaghue."

"Where are Horvath and Peralta?"

"Look," Jarvis said, moving into Hank's personal space and tapping him on the chest with his index finger, "didn't you get the word? The chief's decided that all violent crime in Chinatown will now belong to my task force. Oh wait, that's right, you don't report directly to Bennett, like I do. It takes time for news to filter down the food chain."

Lieutenant Bill Jarvis was forty-two years old. He was short and a little thick around the stomach. His dirty blond hair was thin and straight, his blue eyes were narrow, and his lips were thin and tended to curl away from his teeth in a grimace he thought looked friendly but wasn't. Hank found him annoying and obnoxious, but he'd spent the first four years of his professional life with the FBI and understood how to sell that experience to the current administration.

Detective Larry Carleson appeared behind Jarvis and pointed with his chin down the hallway. "This way, Lieutenant."

"Thanks." Hank moved around Jarvis and nodded at Carleson, glancing involuntarily, as he always did, at the jagged scar on the detective's pale, shaven scalp, the result of an altercation involving a broken beer bottle and an angry drunk when he was a rookie patrol officer.

Carleson led him down the hall to a small staircase on the right, just short of the kitchen. "Down the stairs and straight ahead through the door. They're in the back yard."

"Thanks."

"Jarvis is a prick, but he's right. Didn't you get the word?"

Hank looked at him. Carleson had skipped shaving this morning, and the stubble on his pasty skin looked like grains of pepper spilled on a tablecloth. He was taller than Hank by about two inches, but much bonier. They'd always gotten along well enough in Homicide, and Hank had no reason to believe that Carleson harbored any ill will against him. He understood that when Jarvis had offered the secondment to his task force, Carleson had correctly recognized it as an important career move.

"Martinez probably found out after you sent Peralta and Horvath over," Carleson went on. "Maybe she left a message on your cell."

"Maybe." Hank went down the stairs and through the door into a narrow space between this building and the next. He walked down to the back yard, a small rectangle of dead grass and weeds littered with garbage, bicycle parts, and a rusted child's swing set.

Horvath looked relieved to see him. He stepped forward and touched Hank's arm, turning him around. They went back into the space between the buildings.

"Her husband got here ten minutes ago. Byrne cleared him to come back here; they've already processed the outside. He's talking to her now."

"What happened?"

Horvath rubbed his face with both hands. "It's a bad one, Hank, but not that much worse than what she's seen before. The old man and woman were in an upstairs bedroom, tied and gagged. They were tortured with knives. The woman was raped and they cut off the old man's dick before they shot them both in the head. Both sons were home at the time and both were shot downstairs, one in the hall and one in the kitchen. Looks like they broke through the front door, took out the two downstairs, caught the parents before they could get away, and dragged them upstairs."

"Executions," Hank said.

"Exactly. A message from the Dragon Head to anyone stupid enough to think they can disobey. Both sons have the usual Triad tatts, so I'm guessing they supported the wrong side. There's a lot of blood. The bastards used it to scrawl Chinese signs all over the bedroom wall. I don't know what they mean, but I'd say they're a pretty clear message to whoever's supposed to read them."

"Peralta," Hank prompted.

"Yeah." Horvath swallowed. "We were here, what, ten minutes, looking around, talking to the responding officers, the usual, when she walked up to me in the kitchen and threw up all over my shoes. Then she just knelt down and started to cry. I couldn't get her to stop. I've never seen anything like it before, not from a cop, you know? I finally got her outside into the back yard here and tried to get her to calm down. Nothing I said made any difference. She looked at me and said, 'I can't do this anymore, Jim,' and I said, 'Sure you can, A.P. You're a tough sonofabitch.' It was the wrong thing to say, I guess. She shut down on me."

"I see." Hank chewed on his lower lip. Peralta was known as a competent, fearless, serious-minded detective. Married for four years, she and her husband, the principal of a high school in Springhill, had no children. They lived in an apartment near the university. Peralta had been talking about buying a small house closer to her husband's school.

He patted Horvath on the arm and went back into the yard. Peralta was sitting on the ground a few feet away from the swing set. Her hands were clasped lightly together in her lap. The front of her blouse was stained with vomit. Bob Rodriguez, her husband, crouched before her, talking to her in a soft monotone. As Hank approached he looked around and stood up.

"Lieutenant Donaghue."

"Hi, Bob." Hank shook his hand. "Can you give us a minute?"

"Sure. No problem." Rodriguez took a few steps back, then caught a gesture from Horvath and moved quickly over to join him at the corner of the yard.

Hank squatted. "What's going on, Detective?"

Peralta said nothing, eyes down.

"Detective! What's going on?"

Her eyes snapped up. "Donaghue. You're here."

"I'm here. What's going on? What are you doing right now?"

Peralta frowned again, licking her lips. She took a deep breath and shook her head. "Taking a break, I guess. Sorry."

"No need to apologize. Listen to me."

She held his gaze. Her eyes were bloodshot and her eyelids were red.

"The scene's secured," Hank said. "The task force is catching the case, so we're off it as of now. Understand?"

She nodded.

"Give me your duty weapon." He held out his hand. When she hesitated, he flicked his hand as though impatient. "Duty weapon, Peralta. Now."

Very slowly she leaned over and removed her sidearm from its holster on her belt. She dropped the magazine into her free hand and gave it to Hank. He put it in his jacket pocket. She ejected the round in the chamber. Hank put it into the same pocket. She then turned the disarmed gun in her hand and offered it to Hank, stock-first. He dropped it into his other jacket pocket and held out his hand again. "Back-up."

"Not carrying it today, Lieutenant."

"You sure?"

She pulled up her pant leg to show him a bare calf and ankle. "Left it at home today."

"My back's killing me. Let's stand up." Hank stood up and, when she remained sitting, he held out his hand once more. "Stand up, Amelda."

She let him help her to her feet.

"Go home with Bob and take the weekend off. We'll talk on Monday morning. All right?"

"I'm done, Hank. That's it. I'm done."

"We'll talk about it Monday."

"No. I want a life, Hank. I can't stand this anymore. I'm not going to be another Stainer. I want a life." She unclipped the badge and identification card on her belt and dropped them into his hand. "I'm done."

He walked her over to Horvath, who led her between the buildings to the street.

Hank gave Rodriguez Peralta's badge and ID card. "Take her home. She's on leave until Monday." He put his hand on Rodriguez's arm before he could turn away. "She isn't carrying her back-up weapon."

"I don't know anything about that."

"Your first priority when you get her home is to find it and secure it, understand?"

"I don't think she's—"

"When she's over the hump she'll be fine," Hank pressed, "but right now you need to make sure you've got all the bases covered. Secure all weapons in your home, and stay with her. She should see a doctor right now, she might need something to get her through the rest of the day. Burnouts are nothing to fool around with."

"Will this go on her record, Lieutenant? Will it affect her career?"

"I wouldn't be worried about that right now. Just get her looked at and get her home. Lock up any firearms you have so she can't get at

39

them. It's an important precaution."

Rodriguez nodded and hurried after his wife.

On the little scrap of lawn in front of the duplex, Hank and Horvath watched Peralta reach out to take her husband's hand as they walked away, down the middle of the street. Rodriguez pulled her close as they passed the clusters of staring young men.

"I feel awful," Horvath said. "I should have done something. Seen it coming."

Hank shook his head. "She's never been the kind to talk a lot about herself. There's no way you'd know."

"I'm her partner," Horvath said.

"You handled it well," Hank said. "You got her outside and away from the others. How was Carleson about it?"

"He's cool. He's with Jarvis but still one of us, if you know what I mean. He won't trash her behind her back."

"I want you to come with me over to Jarrett Tower and help Stainer execute the warrants."

"Sounds good to me." Horvath looked down at his feet. "But first I need to pick up another pair of shoes."

Hank smiled faintly.

They turned their backs on 1437 King Street and walked away.

6

They were met in the lobby of Jarrett Tower by Midtown district Sergeant John Graham, a stocky, square-jawed cop with the demeanor of a Marine Corps gunnery sergeant. He explained that officers were currently deployed on all floors of the building occupied by Jarrett Corporation staff, including floors one to four and fourteen to twenty-one. The other floors were leased out to other tenants. The top floor, Graham explained, was reserved for the CEO and his executive assistant. It was accessed only by an express elevator requiring a pass code and an escalator that ran between the twentieth and twenty-first floors. The express elevator had been shut down and the escalator was under their control, so Jarrett's floor was sealed off. The uniformed officers would stay put in the building, Graham said, until the lieutenant said otherwise.

Hank nodded.

Graham was known affectionately as Johnny Go. As a patrol officer he'd been saddled with the nickname Johnny Gofer because of his willingness to run errands for other people, but it had been shortened to Johnny Go when he became a sergeant because he was constantly urging the patrol officers in his care to strive for bigger and better things. Hank knew him more by reputation than by experience, as Johnny Go had been Karen's mentor when she was wearing a uniform as a young officer. She never tired of telling stories about him.

"Stains is in the twentieth-floor board room right now," Graham finished, "busting some guy's chops. I just came down from there."

Hank and Horvath rode an elevator to the twentieth floor, where they were met by a redhead in her early fifties. Tall and slender, she wore a pink jacket-and-skirt outfit with a string of white pearls. Her skin was pale and her eyes were blue.

"You're Lieutenant Donaghue," she said, stepping forward and holding out her hand. "I recognize you from the news reports. I'm Marjorie Kelly, Mr. Jarrett's executive assistant. You can call me Peggy."

Hank shook her hand. She had a firm, business-like grip.

"Mr. Parris and several other chief executives are downstairs right now holding a press conference," Kelly explained. "We're announcing that Mr. Parris will assume the responsibilities of interim president and CEO until a permanent succession is finalized. Our stock price is taking a hit right now, and we're trying to control the bleeding."

"I understand," Hank said. "I appreciate your cooperation."

"Your detective's in the board room at the moment with Emory Raskin, our general counsel. Emory had a few concerns about the warrants, but if I'm not mistaken the detective was more interested in his whereabouts this morning. When I left, he was answering a lot more questions than he was asking. If you like, I can show you the way."

"In a moment, thanks." Hank had spotted Tim Byrne coming up the corridor.

"We're well underway," Byrne said, his pig eyes flicking from Peggy Kelly to Hank. "Stainer explained the facts of life to their lawyer. She's in the board room with him right now."

Hank glanced at Kelly, saw her jaw muscles tighten, and realized she was suppressing a smile. "Thanks, Tim."

"We're processing the office and board room on the twenty-first," Byrne went on. "I've explained to Mrs. Kelly we'll need everyone's fingerprints for reference purposes. Might be an issue here on c-level."

"C-level?" Horvath asked, frowning.

"Corporate slang," Byrne explained. "C-level refers to the top level of executives whose titles all begin with a C: CEO, CFO, CIO, COO."

"I believe I saw our security company's fingerprint records listed on your warrant," Kelly said.

"And so you did, but I prefer to take my own, thank you very much. More than once I've seen fingerprint records tampered with to hide something or other."

"I don't understand why you need to fingerprint upstairs to begin with. He was shot near his home, not here."

Kelly's tone was reasonable and her expression genuinely puzzled, and although Byrne was a bristly prick who didn't play well with others, he enjoyed these moments in his life when he discovered a gap in someone's education that he could fill with his own superior knowledge.

"You see, Mrs. Kelly," he said, folding his arms across his chest, "the lieutenant's job involves learning everything he can about the victim's activities over the final few days of his life. He'll want to know when he was last in his office, for example, and whom he saw. He'll construct a timeline and fill it with reference points for every person he interacted with along the line. He'll want a record of all the fingerprints in the office for corroboration, and who knows, maybe we'll find a set of prints that don't belong in there. Maybe someone slipped in and bothered him about something. Maybe the same person showed up again this morning on the bike path and—"

"Tim," Hank interrupted, "where are you with the records from the security company?"

Byrne frowned at the interruption. "Mick's down on the fourteenth right now," he replied, referring to CSI Mickey Marcotte, his computer technology specialist. "The security company's owned by Jarrett but run by a guy named Drussler."

Hank turned to Horvath. "Go down there and see if you can find Mr. Drussler."

"He's waiting in his office," Kelly said. "I gave him instructions to make himself available."

"Thanks," Hank said.

"I'm on my way down," Byrne said to Horvath. "Let's go."

Hank followed Kelly to a set of large cherry wood doors that opened abruptly as they approached. A grim-faced man emerged, threw a look at Hank, and pushed by him down the corridor.

Karen popped her head out, scowling. "That was fun."

"I expect you'll have questions for me as well," Kelly said to her. "We can go upstairs to my office if you like."

"In here," Karen pointed. It was a given in Karen's world that potential suspects should be questioned away from familiar surroundings whenever possible. The board room was as close to neutral territory as she could manage at the moment.

Hank looked at her over Kelly's shoulder. Karen motioned with her chin, turned on her heel, and walked to the end of the long board room table. She pointed at the chair on her right. Kelly obediently sat down. Hank closed the board room door and sat down directly across from Kelly. He shoved his chair back and crossed his legs comfortably, his body language declaring that their questions would be casual and friendly, nothing to worry about. He removed his notebook and pen from his jacket pocket and flipped the pages. He noticed that Karen's notebook was on the table in front of her instead of the top drawer of her desk where it usually sat.

He smiled. "I've been listening to a faint Midwestern accent, Peggy. Ohio?"

"Columbus, yes." Kelly folded her hands on the table.

"Did you go to school there?"

"Ohio State. I did my undergraduate degree there and stayed for my MBA at Fisher."

"Is that right? My sister's an OSU alumna, too. She went there for her medical degree. She's a pathologist in California."

"Very interesting," Kelly said.

Karen leaned forward. "Where were you between six and eight o'clock this morning?"

"I was here, Detective. I arrived at five thirty as always and took the elevator up to the top floor, which your criminologists will confirm from the elevator logs included in the data they get from IT, along with video surveillance footage. I haven't left the building. It's been a horrible day and I've been very, very busy."

"How did you and Jarrett get along?"

Kelly looked down and covered her mouth with her hand. She paused, took a breath, and met Karen's gaze. "Fine."

"Do you want to take a minute?" Hank asked.

She shook her head, lowering her hand. "He was a typical CEO: a Type A personality, very self-centered, highly competitive in just about everything, a touch stubborn." She tightened her lips. "More determined, I suppose, than stubborn. He listened to advice from others and acted on it when he believed it was solid. He was very loyal to the people he kept around him, and he was very good to me. I liked him."

"Any recent arguments between the two of you, Mrs. Kelly?" Hank asked.

She shook her head.

"Are you sure you're all right?"

"I had my little cry already this morning," Kelly said. "I suppose there's more, but not right now. Actually, it's not *Mrs.* Kelly. Kelly's my maiden name. My husband's name is Lamb. Commander David Lamb, United States Navy. We've been married twenty-eight years."

"Any children?"

"A son who's twenty-six and a daughter who's twenty-three."

"So you're saying, Ms. Kelly," Karen said, leaning back, "you got along just fine with Jarrett and had no reason whatsoever to pop him?"

"That's correct," Kelly replied calmly. "No motive, no opportunity. Care to go for strike three?"

"Phht." Karen folded her arms across her chest. "A Navy wife who doesn't have a firearm in the house? Give me a break. Why don't you explain what you do around here? You were Jarrett's secretary, right?"

Kelly shook her head. "No, Mr. Jarrett's secretary is Mary Ann Williams. You'll speak to her later. My title, actually, is chief of staff and executive assistant to the CEO. It might help if I explain my duties."

Karen shrugged, as though bored with it all.

"As chief of staff," she began, directing her words to Karen, "I attend all board and committee meetings. I represent Mr. Jarrett whenever he misses them. When I speak, it's Mr. Jarrett who's speaking. I maintain an information management system that includes all reports tabled before the board and committees and all action items, I analyze these reports and action items for problems, and I inform Mr. Jarrett when I see something that needs his attention. I help the senior executives interact with Mr. Jarrett, which means before they meet with him they often meet with me as a sounding board. I keep track of his state of mind and his focus, and I can tell them if they're about to hit a brick wall or if Mr. Jarrett's interested in what they want to do.

"In addition to all that, as executive assistant I handle the administrative details. I make sure one of the secretaries picks up the dry cleaning and keeps the liquor cabinets stocked, I supervise all the directors' secretaries, the personal trainers, the on-site medical staff, the drivers, and everything else that keeps Mr. Jarrett and the chief officers comfortable and moving forward."

"So if you kept track of his state of mind," Karen said, not caring to hide her skepticism, "how was it the last few days? Was he upset about something? Somebody in particular on his shit list?"

"Nothing unusual. His state of mind has actually been quite good the last few months."

"Why's that? Something going on?"

Kelly hesitated. "It's not something I'm at liberty to discuss."

"Are you talking about his decision to retire?" Hank asked.

"Mrs. Jarrett mentioned it to me this morning."

"She did?"

"I realize it isn't public knowledge. I assume the details were still being ironed out."

Kelly nodded. "The board knows, of course." She glanced at Karen. "The board of directors represents all shareholders of the corporation. The directors understand that shareholders might have a negative reaction, since Mr. Jarrett has run this company based on his personal vision from day one. The input of the board was key because the last thing Mr. Jarrett wanted was a loss of shareholder confidence."

"Who's taking over?"

She hesitated again.

"It'll become public knowledge very soon," Hank reminded her, "but not through us. We need to understand the whole picture if we're going to find out who shot him."

"Mr. Jarrett had decided to sell his majority interest in Jarrett Corporation to his daughter, Diane. He made sure she'd have the support to be chosen as president and CEO."

"Diane Jarrett Benson," Hank said.

"Yes."

"So how'd that go down?" Karen asked.

"It caused a hell of an uproar. Diane's a minor shareholder but she's had no active involvement with the company at all to this point. Mr. Jarrett had, shall we say, a few barriers to overcome before the idea caught fire on this floor. A few egos were bruised and there was initial resistance to the notion of an outsider coming in and taking over."

"Do people still feel that way?" Hank asked.

"No, I don't really think so. Diane met with the board and the chief officers, individually and as a group. They tried their best to break her down, but she's extremely bright and runs a very successful investment firm with her husband, David Benson. It didn't take them long to realize she's her father's daughter."

"Sound like you think so, too."

"Diane's a friend of mine. I have enormous respect for her."

"Hang on a sec," Karen said. "Did your boss suddenly get cold feet? Did he change his mind and decide he couldn't give all this up, after all?"

"Not at all. Once he'd made the decision, it was like he was suddenly twenty years younger. All he could talk about was St. Lucia, the boat he was going to buy, the friends he knew down there, how cheap the property was, and how great it was as a tax haven. He couldn't wait."

Karen wondered if someone might have killed Jarrett to stop the transition, but it didn't make sense to her since Jarrett retired and Jarrett dead would have the same basic outcome—a new president and CEO—so she decided to switch gears. "From the sounds of it you know these executive characters pretty well."

"Yes, I suppose you could say I do."

Hank was writing something in his notebook, eyes down, so she pressed on. "Okay, let's start with Raskin. Did you see him come in this morning?"

Kelly shook her head. "I saw him first about ten thirty. We were watching the TV in the large board room. It was the first he'd heard about it."

"Large board room?"

"This is the small board room. There's a larger one on the other side of the floor."

Karen looked around for a moment. For a small board room, it had about the same square footage as the apartment in which she'd lived before moving in with her fiancé, Sandy Alexander, last year. She had trouble understanding why they'd need a larger one. "So you can't vouch for him any earlier than that."

"That's his usual time to get in. He follows a workout regimen every morning, something he started after a heart attack about five years ago, and Mr. Jarrett made sure the daily schedule could accommodate him. He was never required for anything before eleven o'clock."

"He's the head of the legal section for the company, right?"

"He's our general counsel, yes. He's in charge of our legal department, which oversees all litigation, contracts, and dispute management as well as our patents, intellectual property, and everything else."

"So let me get this straight, you can't corroborate Raskin's story that he was," Karen glanced down at her notes, "at the Rollins Total Fitness Club between six and seven this morning, as he says?"

"No, but they're an exclusive club, and they take security seriously. People don't walk in off the street. I expect you'll be able to verify that he was there this morning."

Hank stirred. "Let's talk about security for a moment." He glanced at his notes. "The company that handles everything for Jarrett Corporation, CD Security, is run by Craig Drussler. I'm curious first of all about the arrangements Jarrett had for his own personal security. What can you tell us about that?"

Kelly leaned back and sighed. "Oh, that was an ongoing bone of contention. It was something we all argued with Mr. Jarrett about at one time or another, I can tell you that."

She glanced at Karen. "Mr. Jarrett liked to play games with them, give them the slip, or just order them off. The contract calls for constant, unbroken surveillance of Mr. Jarrett, and we tried many times to convince him of the wisdom of that arrangement, but in vain. Mr. Jarrett valued his privacy, and I'm afraid he thought he was invulnerable. He knew a few people who'd been kidnap victims, but he always said they were in situations they shouldn't have been in, to begin with, and should have known better."

"What kind of a guy is Craig Drussler?"

Kelly thought for a moment. "He's a younger man, has a family. Owns an expensive house, his children attend a private school, all of which became possible when Mr. Jarrett bought out his company and installed him here in Jarrett Tower."

"What was his attitude toward Jarrett? I'm thinking in particular about Jarrett's tendency to screw around with his operations."

"He was frustrated, I suppose."

"Ms. Kelly. Peggy." Karen stood up and walked around to Kelly's side of the table. She eased down onto the corner, leaned on her left fist, and put her right hand into the pocket of her trousers, brushing aside the edge of her jacket as she did so. The movement revealed the gold badge clipped to her belt and the holstered SIG Sauer P226 on her hip.

"The lieutenant and I have been in this business for a long time. We're not a couple of rookie dingbats digging for shit just for the fun of it. You're obviously a sharp woman with a lot on the ball. You've got the moxie to wear the one color redheads should never wear, and you're making it work. You've got a lot of juice around here, and it shows. You've got an opinion on this Drussler guy. The lieutenant and I would love to hear it."

Hank watched with interest as Kelly stared into Karen's cold blue eyes and saw the hardness there. The two women maintained eye contact for a long moment before Hank saw the lines at the corners of Kelly's eyes deepen in amusement. He'd watched enough faces over the years to know the woman had made a decision to like Karen. Because it was not something that happened every day, it told him something interesting about Peggy Kelly.

"It could take a while," she said.

"We'd be happy with the *Reader's Digest* version for now."

"All right." Kelly sat back. "Mr. Jarrett and I often had this kind of conversation. He valued my take on the people he dealt with."

Karen slid off the corner of the table. "So, go."

"Craig Drussler's a former sheriff but he only served one term. When he lost the next election he formed his own company, CD Security, specializing in executive protection. He worked the connections he'd made in office and started getting contracts. We offered him a subcontract to do a short-term assignment for us, and liked what he did. We gave him more work, and eventually he came to the attention of Mr. Jarrett himself. He and Emory took Craig to lunch and made him an extremely lucrative offer to buy out his company and set him up as the sole provider of all our security solutions, world-wide. Needless to say, Craig jumped at the opportunity. I guess it didn't occur to him until it was too late that it meant when Mr. Jarrett wanted to override his procedures, he had no choice but to sit there and take it."

"So he played Drussler like a fish," Karen said, sitting down.

"Pretty much."

"And Drussler was too interested in climbing the ladder to figure it out until it was too late."

"I suppose you could say that."

"And it pissed him off afterwards? Made him resentful?"

"No. What you need to understand is that Craig's a very decent person underneath it all. It's true in hindsight he clearly regretted his decision to sell his company to Mr. Jarrett, but it made him very, very comfortable financially, and eventually he seemed to come to terms with the compromise. His girls attend the best private school in the city, and I've seen pictures of his condo in the Bahamas. It's beautiful. He's very devoted to his family, he's faithful to his wife—we checked—and he'd do anything for his friends. He's a reasonably nice guy who's reached his ceiling. Was he resentful that Mr. Jarrett made a shambles of his protection protocols? No. Was he frustrated? Oh, yes. I spent twenty minutes with him this morning, Detective, after we heard the news.

He's devastated. He was in tears, literally. He knows his reputation's been destroyed, and he's taking it very personally. He was loyal to Mr. Jarrett the way we all were."

"Okay." Karen leaned back in her chair, watching Kelly. "Tell us about Walter Parris. What does he do around here?"

"Walter's the chief financial officer for the corporation, which means he's responsible to the board for all financial and accounting matters."

"He's the numbers guy. The money guy."

"Yes. He controls cash flow, he monitors our financial performance, manages the budget, works with our bankers and other investors, all that sort of thing."

"Makes him a pretty important guy around here."

"Very. Especially now, since he's going to be interim president and CEO."

"There's that. How'd he take the news that Jarrett was stepping down and his daughter was taking over?"

"For the first few days none of us took it very well, but Walter adjusted very quickly. He's a key figure in all this because he decides what Mr. Jarrett's holdings are actually worth and what Diane would have to pay in order to acquire them. Both sides questioned his numbers very vigorously, but that's par for the course. He must have had a few personal talks with Mr. Jarrett because Walter never questioned Mr. Jarrett's decision to retire."

"Bottom line, do you think he had anything to do with his boss's murder?"

"No. Not in a million years."

"What do you know about his son?"

"Brett?" Kelly's expression softened. "Oh, dear. Such a handful for Walter and Lisa. A very confused young man."

"Ever seen him worked up, out of control, or violent?"

Kelly shook her head. "Walter doesn't talk about it, but I understand it's schizophrenia. Mr. Jarrett preferred that we give Walter some space in that regard. I'm not really qualified to talk about it. There was an incident at a Christmas party one time, though, when he thought one of our divisional heads was Richard Holland. He got very upset about it, I remember, and accused the poor man of stalking him. Walter was mortified."

Karen leaned casually on an elbow. "Tell me about Holland."

"A rapid riser. Mr. Jarrett had a lot of time for him."

"What does he do around here?"

"He's vice-president of corporate and regulatory affairs, which handles government liaison in the United States and all other countries where we do business. So, current and proposed regulations for pharmaceuticals, our participation in emergency preparedness, international approval processes, things like that."

"Sounds important."

"He's built an effective network in a very short time."

Karen looked at her. "You don't sound particularly enamored of our Mr. Holland."

"I'm not."

"Because...."

Kelly moved back from the table and swiveled her chair to face Karen. "Let me put it to you this way. I told you Craig is basically a decent man underneath his ambition and his love of money. I can't say the same thing about Richard Holland, unfortunately."

"Oh?"

"His late father worked for Mr. Jarrett in the early days. Before my time, of course, but I know that Mr. Jarrett kept in touch with the widow and her son. After graduation, Richard showed up here, and Mr. Jarrett found a job for him."

"What was that all about?"

"I don't know. I asked the same question. Mr. Jarrett said I didn't need to worry about it, so I took the hint."

"You think there was something hinky in their relationship?"

"I think Mr. Jarrett probably felt bad about Gerald Holland's passing and likely made a promise to look after the boy's welfare. I also think Richard has taken advantage of Mr. Jarrett's generosity to an extreme."

"You don't think he deserves to be a VP around here?"

"He's clever, but I think he's over-achieving at this point."

Karen studied her for a moment before nodding. "All right." She glanced at Hank. "We'll probably want to talk to him sooner, as opposed to later. Is he here right now? At the press conference?"

Kelly shook her head. "He had a meeting with several important contacts this afternoon at the Woodfern Golf and Country Club." She glanced at her watch. "Mr. Parris told him to keep the meeting, rather than reschedule it. He's likely still there. Would you like me to call and

51

tell him to wait there for you?"

"No thanks," Hank said, "that won't be necessary. If you could give us his cell number, we'll call him ourselves."

Kelly recited the number from memory. Hank wrote it down.

"Now, as for that timeline Mr. Byrne mentioned," he went on, "we'll need you to put together everything you have from his schedule, everyone he met, plus everyone you're aware of that he had contact with who wasn't on the schedule. Go back a week for starters. We need to get a sense of his routine to see if there were any deviations from it that need explaining."

"Understood. I'll have it for you right away."

"Thanks very much for your time, Ms. Kelly. We may have some other questions for you later."

When she didn't respond, Hank looked up from his notebook. Kelly's face was turned away from them. Tears were streaming down her cheeks.

7

They left through a rear entrance at the bottom of the emergency staircase to avoid the backpack journalists hanging around the front of the building. A short alley took them into a small parking lot behind Jarrett Tower. The parking lot was set off by a low cement wall topped with black tube railing. The parking spaces were filled with vehicles. Horvath was waiting for them, sitting on the railing, the heels of his wingtip brogues hooked for balance under the lower tube. When he raised the cigarette to his mouth, Hank saw his hand tremble slightly.

"I thought you quit," Karen said, putting her boot up on the lower railing beside him.

Horvath blew smoke toward the tiny patch of blue sky visible between the towers. "So did I."

"You're going to get your ass dirty on that railing."

Horvath stared at his cigarette.

"What did Drussler have to say?" Hank asked.

"He's pretty shook up," replied Horvath. He figures this'll finish him in the business."

"Good guess," Karen said.

"A cousin of mine works in executive protection." Horvath looked at her. "He tried to get me to come in with him when I graduated, but I was stuck on being a cop, so I didn't. He likes to talk to me about the work whenever we see each other, family gatherings, funerals, you know. He doesn't have a lot of people he can talk to, I guess, so I'm it. And I'm a good listener. At least that's what my girlfriend says. Anyway, I've actually picked up a fair bit about the business. Know what the most important commandment is?"

He tossed the cigarette aside and hopped down from the railing. "Protect the client. Drussler's right: he's finished. He let the client poke holes in his protection and didn't properly cover the risks. He's screwed."

"What happened this morning?" Hank asked.

"Same thing as every morning for the last month and a half

since Jarrett started using the bike path. In the winter he apparently stayed indoors in his private gym, but once the weather got better he started going out. They had an ongoing fight about it. At first, Drussler had someone jog along with him, but that lasted only a couple of days before Jarrett raised the roof. Then Drussler had the guy tag along in a car, but Jarrett didn't like that either and it wasn't really workable anyway since the path winds in and out of the trees and there wasn't one hundred percent line of sight on the client at all times. Then Drussler tried clandestine protection, but it was like Jarrett had radar or something. He kept spotting them and busting their ass. He obviously enjoyed playing games with it."

"Sounds like a nightmare client," Hank said.

Horvath nodded. "Thought he was Superman."

"Why waste the money?" Karen frowned. "Why bother with security at all if you're just going to fuck around with it and leave yourself open?"

"Drussler's company provides the full range for Jarrett Corporation. They secure this building and their other properties around the world, they run background checks on employees, they supply the pilots and crew for their executive jets and the guards that protect Jarrett's home and look after the other senior executives when they travel, the whole nine yards. It's a huge contract, and protecting the Jarretts themselves is just a small part of it."

"So I take it they'd backed off on Jarrett's morning routine," Hank said.

Horvath shrugged. "They decided to live with a half-hour window every morning. He left the grounds and went for his bike ride, they picked him up when he came back, then stayed with him for the rest of the day. Jarrett kept telling Drussler he wanted at least that much privacy in his life."

"No way you back off on that," Karen muttered.

Horvath looked at her. "Drussler showed me a purchase order he'd signed off on yesterday morning. It was still on his desk. They were going to set up wireless video surveillance all along the bike path, in the trees and whatever, and have the car trawl along just out of Jarrett's sight. It was their next best shot."

"Too late," Karen said, unimpressed. "Somebody else got their shot in first."

"Where was Drussler this morning?" Hank asked.

"At home, having breakfast with his family."

"I'd like you to go back and write your report on King Street," Hank said. "Let's wash our hands of it so you can work this case full time with Karen." He turned to her. "You and I are going to talk to Richard Holland."

"Where's Peralta?" Karen asked. "Still at the crime scene? How come Jarvis is poking his nose in?"

"Keep it simple," Hank said to Horvath. "Understand what I'm saying?"

"Yes, sir."

"What the hell am I missing here?" Karen complained.

"Where are you parked?" Hank asked her, a little sharply. "Let's get moving."

8

"Funny story," Karen said as she floored the accelerator of the unmarked black Crown Victoria Police Interceptor and shot over to the inside northbound lane of Howard Boulevard. "Johnny Go was having a coffee the other day at this little sidewalk place down on Pritchard Street in Little Italy. Across the street he sees one of his guys come out of a shoe store, walking his beat. As he heads up the street, the guy's firearm suddenly falls off his belt and drops onto the sidewalk behind him. Apparently the holster was one of the swivel types. The swivel broke and the gun fell right out. The guy never even noticed."

"Good lord," Hank said.

"I'm just getting started. A little old lady is walking behind him. Short little thing with the long black dress, big black shoes and a black kerchief over her head, big black purse on her arm. Typical Italian grandmother. She bends down, picks up the gun, and starts after the guy with it, holding it out in front of her."

"Oh, oh."

"You got it. The guy's partner comes out of the next store, sees this short person with a black robe and black headdress trotting after his partner, holding out a gun, and he thinks he's suddenly in the middle of some kind of terrorist action."

"Shit."

"Now I'm thinking, Johnny's gonna tell me the partner drew his weapon and shot the old lady dead." She shook her head. "The guy tackles her from behind, down onto the sidewalk. Bam."

Hank smiled.

"By this time Johnny Go's dodging traffic to get across the street. When he gets there the guy's still lying on top of her, and he's trying to pull the gun out of her hand. She won't let go, and she's yelling, "Is *his*, is *his*!""

Hank started to laugh.

"Johnny gets there and pulls them both up. By this time, the first guy's turned around and walking back, trying to figure out what the hell's going on. The old lady holds out the gun to him and he stops dead, thinking that whatever it is, it ain't over. So he reaches for his sidearm and, what do you know, it ain't there.

"The old lady says, 'Hey you, you droppa you gun! Take it!'"

Hank looked out the window, laughing.

"So the guy takes his gun and Johnny says to the other guy, 'Apologize to the lady for knocking her down.' So the guy apologizes. She hauls off and hits him right in the marbles with her purse."

"Ouch."

"Johnny says to me, 'Lesson Number One, Stains, be aware of your firearm at all times. Lesson Number Two, make sure your equipment never lets you down. Check it before and after every shift.' And Lesson Number Three?"

Hank looked at her.

"Never judge by appearances."

Hank listened to the silence between them for a block.

"Most of the guys figured Peralta was a lifer, but I knew better," Karen said, throwing a glance over her shoulder and changing lanes. "She was too quiet. Most guys, when they're coming down from the adrenaline high, they want to talk about it, tell jokes, make some noise. Not her. She bottled it all up and pretended it wasn't there. People who take that route, they better be good at unplugging from the emotion or it's going to eat them alive. Peralta couldn't unplug from it, no matter how much she pretended she could." They rocketed through an amber light. "Only a matter of time, Lou."

"You may be right."

"I am." She glanced over at him again. "I know a lifer when I see one."

Hank pretended to be confused. "What? Are you talking about me, now?"

She grinned at him, but it was gone almost as quickly as it had come. "We've got that much in common, my friend. We're both lifers."

Hank said nothing.

"So let me get this straight." She braked for a red light at the corner of Bowley and Woodfern. "This country club we're going to doesn't allow women?"

"Correct." Hank had made two calls as they were leaving Jarrett Tower, the first to Richard Holland, who assured him he'd wait in the grill room of the Woodfern Golf and Country Club until Hank arrived, and the second to the general manager of the club, Tate Bernhardt. Hank was well known to Bernhardt as a long-standing member of Woodfern whose family had been prominent members for several generations. Just the same, Bernhardt expressed strong misgivings when it was explained to him that Hank would be accompanied into the club by a female detective. Karen had listened with amusement as Hank smoothed the man's ruffled feathers. When Hank put away his phone she'd had a pretty good crack on the tip of her tongue, but Hank had switched subjects to explain what had happened to Amelda Peralta in Chinatown, and the joke disappeared. Now she was ready to change the subject back to cavemen and their private caves.

"No women at all?"

"None at all. No female members, no female employees, no female guests."

"Unbelievable." She turned onto Woodfern Avenue. The entrance of the country club was only two blocks away.

Hank was flipping through the pages of his notebook. "According to DMV, Holland drives a 2011 Ferrari 599 GTO, Maryland tag two juliet tango bravo forty-six."

"Nice ride. Silver?"

"Silver."

Brett Parris had told them he'd seen Holland running to a silver sports car. He didn't know what kind of car it was and hadn't seen the license plates.

"Probably has a navigation system that can tell you everywhere it's been."

"Could be."

They reached a t-intersection that marked the end of Woodfern Avenue. The entrance of the country club was straight ahead. Karen drove through the massive stone gate and started up the driveway. They passed a short spur on the right in which a yellow and black car sat nose-out.

"Rent-a-cops," she remarked.

She parked in the half-empty parking lot. As they walked toward the club house, Karen amused herself by pointing out cars. "Porsche. Lexus. Lamborghini. Horvath would love this place. He's such a wannabe."

She spotted Holland's Ferrari. "Wow. Nice."

Hank stared in through the driver-side window. "Look at this stuff. I'd have no idea how to drive it. What are all those round things for?"

Karen shielded her eyes from the sun as she bent down on the passenger side. "They're just control knobs and air vents, Lou. Just like any other car. Your problem is, you're car illiterate."

"Car illiterate?"

She walked around the car and patted him on the shoulder. "It's okay. You can still have a full and productive life."

They were met at the door by a man in his middle forties wearing a navy blazer and gray trousers. He held out his hand to Hank. "Lieutenant Donaghue? Good to see you again. Mr. Holland's waiting for you in the grill room."

Hank shook his hand. "Thanks. This is Detective Stainer. Mr. Tate Bernhardt."

Without so much as a glance at Karen, Bernhardt swiveled on his heel. "This way, please."

Karen showed Hank a sardonic grin as they fell into line behind Bernhardt. They walked through an open lounge with comfortable furniture and a two-sided fireplace. Karen noticed that people were staring at her. A uniformed waiter missed a step and juggled an armload of folded white towels.

The grill room came equipped with a maitre d' who nodded at Bernhardt. He took one look at Karen and turned away, disappearing somewhere into the back.

There were men scattered about at six or seven tables in the grill room, in groups of twos and fours. Bernhardt led them to the bar, which was deserted. Hank and Karen sat on stools. The bartender took one look at them and walked away.

"Here's Mr. Holland," Bernhardt said. "I'll be outside in the corridor when you're finished your meeting."

As Bernhardt left, Richard Holland slid onto the bar stool next to Karen and grinned at them. "Lieutenant Donaghue and Detective Stainer, I take it." He held out his hand to Karen, who shook it, then he reached behind her to shake Hank's hand. "This is something of a historic event, and all for little old me. I'm flattered."

He was thirty-eight years old, about five feet ten inches tall, and one hundred and eighty pounds. He had well-groomed, mousy blond hair, smooth chubby cheeks, and small blue eyes that glittered at Karen with amusement. He wore a pale blue golf shirt and tan trousers.

He had a large, expensive watch, a ruby ring on his right hand, a gold bracelet on his right wrist, and a gold chain around his neck.

"When I got your call," he said to Hank, "we were just starting the eighteenth." He nodded at the table where his fellow golfers were trying very hard not to stare. "It's actually fun to see a babe intrude on forbidden territory."

Karen turned on her stool and tapped him sharply on the sternum with her index finger. "Don't *babe* me, pal. We've got some questions you need to answer pronto, so skip the bullshit."

Holland's smile faded. "It's not bullshit; it's a huge deal here. They don't even allow women to turn their cars around in the driveway. I think you're the first female to set foot on this property since 1964 or something, and that time was purely by accident. Some broad got lost and stopped to ask for directions. They threw her out."

Karen moved her face close to Holland's. "I'm not interested in little boys and their tree house rules. Where were you this morning when your boss was getting smoked?"

"With a friend. I spent the night."

"When did you leave?"

"About eight thirty. I slept in a bit."

"This friend have a name?"

"Oh boy, she's going to be mad at me. Melissa Grove. I suppose you want her address and phone number."

"Please," Hank said, his notebook out.

Holland recited the address and phone number. Hank wrote it down.

"Did you have breakfast with her before you left?" Karen snapped.

"I don't eat breakfast."

"Okay, smart boy. Tell us what you do at Jarrett Corporation."

"I'm vice-president of corporate and regulatory affairs."

"So you handle all the government liaison stuff, is that it?"

"That's it," Holland agreed, "and a lot more. For example, I'm the chairman of our public policy advisory committee that works on public health issues like the availability of certain vaccines we produce, emergency preparedness on a state and national scale, environmental protection, and a boatload of other stuff."

"How long have you been with the company?"

"Twelve years. I started as an advertising account manager in

2000. I'm not counting 1999, when I interned at Jarrett while I was finishing my MBA."

"Impressive," Karen said, obviously not impressed at all. "Aren't you a little young to be a vice-president of a big company like this?"

"I'm the youngest corporate officer by seven years, but I've never believed there's a correlation between age and ability. Take a look at my golf buddies over there."

Karen focused her cop stare on the table where three sets of eyes hastily swiveled to the ceiling or the view through the sliding French doors on the far side of the room. "Looks like a collection of deadbeat losers to me."

Holland chuckled. "You're a good judge of character. The guy with the red hair, he's fifty-two. He's the director of operational support for the state emergency management agency. The guy with the goatee, he's fifty-six. He thinks he's an aspiring novelist but he's really a complete knob who happened to marry into money. Big money, a lot of which is invested in Jarrett. And the guy with the white hair, he's sixty. He's a director with a federal agency I won't name here. A raging alcoholic whose sickness I feed with a case of single malt scotch every month to make sure that Jarrett Corporation stays involved at the federal level."

He shrugged. "Next Friday it'll be another set of losers with another set of hidden agendas, all of them older, all of them thinking I'm some wet-behind-the-ears kid they can take for a ride. I beat them at golf and I beat them in here over iced tea and burgers afterwards. It's just another game, and it's one that I'm really, really good at."

"Okay," Karen said, "I get it. You're good. This place is floating with money. I'm wowed by it all. What kind of relationship did you have with Jarrett?"

"H.J.?" Holland casually leaned his elbow on the bar. "It was good. He hand-picked me for the vice-presidency. The board passed me over the first time it came open because H.J. was away in Europe and no one mentioned to him I was the best candidate for the job, but the guy they picked didn't last very long and H.J. made sure the board didn't make the same mistake twice."

"So you're saying you had a good relationship with him."

"That's what I'm saying. He was my mentor and I was his protégé. I like to think there was a closeness there."

"A closeness. Really."

Holland stared back at her.

"Any fights with him lately, disagreements, anything like that?"

Holland glanced down at his right hand for an instant, then looked at her. "No. Nothing important. He didn't like a marketing strategy we submitted to him a couple of weeks ago, tore it all to shreds and threatened to have security throw us out into the street naked. Typical H.J. So I'd been giving him a few alternative things to look at over the last week. He seemed to like this stuff better. But you don't take any of that sort of thing personally if you're going to survive at this level. You stay on an even keel. When he doesn't like something, he lets you know. But if he does like something, he also lets you know, and you just take the good with the bad, and maintain your focus. It's the only way to weather the storms and get where you want to go. Long story short, he gave me shit a couple of weeks ago but I already had him back more or less where I wanted him, so there's nothing worth mentioning."

Karen stared at him. "What kind of car do you drive?"

"Something that costs a little more than your Ford Escort, I'm sure."

"For your information, pal," Karen leaned her elbow on the bar, "I drive a 1979 Firebird Esprit, the Redbird edition with the 301 four-barrel, stock, and I'd rather drive it than any of those over-priced pieces of euro-crap I saw out there in the parking lot."

Holland raised his eyebrows. "My apologies. A respectable choice, but you have to admit it's still a long way from my ride, which is a 2011 Ferrari 599 GTO, with a v-12, 612 horsepower that cost me three hundred and eighty grand, and I'd rather drive *it*, believe me, than anything else parked out there today."

"We're talking about that silver one I saw sandwiched between a Porsche and a Mercedes?"

"Not literally sandwiched, I hope," Holland joked, "but yeah, it's silver."

"Got the navigation system with it, Richard? I couldn't see it there."

"Do me a favor," Holland said, his good humor evaporating. "Look but don't touch, okay? That's a really expensive piece of machinery. And to answer your question, no, it doesn't have the navigation system.

It was screwed up when I bought the car, so I had them take it out. I don't need GPS, believe me. I *know* where I am at all times."

Karen shrugged. "Explain something else to me, then. How come you're here playing golf with your pals instead of attending the big press conference to circle the wagons at Jarrett Tower?"

"Believe me, I'd much rather be there," replied Holland, "but Parris thinks these three turds are important right now, that we need to keep our key government contacts calm and reassured, so I obeyed our new acting CEO's orders and played golf instead of getting network face time like the rest of them." He glanced over at the table. "All they could talk about was the shooting, the idiots."

"When did you hear he'd been killed?"

"About nine fifteen. My EA called."

"You don't seem all that broken up about it."

"You have no idea what I'm feeling, Detective, so I'll thank you not to presume."

"One more question for you," Karen said in a bored tone of voice. "How *do* you get along with Walter Parris?"

Holland shrugged. "Okay, I guess. We have the odd debate about expenditures and so on, but he's a professional guy and I can respect that. If you're thinking that he killed H.J., then you're way off base. H.J.'s more likely to have been shot by one of Santa's elves than by Walter Parris."

"You're probably right." Karen eased off the stool as Hank closed his notebook and put it away. "Nice, harmless family man. His son is an interesting guy. Know him?"

"Brett? Only slightly. He has some kind of condition." Holland stood up as well. "At our company Christmas party one year he thought one of our directors was me in disguise. He got upset and they had to leave."

"Sounds pretty strange," Karen said.

"Yeah. Then a few weeks ago he was at the tower taking pictures. Walter asked us all if we minded. I said, hell, no, maybe we can use a few of them in next year's annual report. Anyway, the guy started insisting my executive assistant was me. And one of Walter's senior staffers, and a couple other people. They were all me, in disguise. It was completely bizarre. I understand he does that sort of thing all the time."

"Did it bother you?"

"It weirded me out. But like I say, I don't take stuff personally."

He tapped his temple lightly. "Too focused."

"When was the last time you saw him?"

"Brett? That day at the tower, a couple weeks ago."

"All right." Karen stepped away from the bar. "We appreciate your time."

"You don't think Brett did it, do you?"

Karen frowned, as though her intelligence had been insulted. "We're just asking questions, Mr. Holland, about a bunch of people. Have a nice day, and enjoy your little boys' club."

Bernhardt walked them out and shook Hank's hand, ignoring Karen again. They got into the Crown Vic. Karen buckled in and started the engine.

"We should come here more often," she said. "I like the ambience."

Hank laughed.

"I really, really can't stand that guy." She gripped the steering wheel tightly, backing out of the parking space.

"Who, Bernhardt?" Hank knew she was referring to Holland but wanted to chafe her a little.

"Funny man. I don't care if he's alibied, he's a goddamned liar and he thinks way too much of himself."

"He's a Type A super-executive. Typical self-centered bulldozer."

"Sure enough, but I'm not buying his bullshit. I think Brett Parris really did see him running from the scene. I'd bet money he's our shooter."

"Brett Parris is not going to be a reliable eyewitness, and anyway, it's far too early for that kind of assumption."

"It's never too early to lock onto a fucking piece of slime like that." She threw the transmission into Park, unbuckled her seat belt, and took out her cell phone.

"I don't know," Hank said. "I thought he was kind of nice. I may go golfing with him."

"Yeah, well, I may just shoot you both." She opened the door and got out.

Hank watched her walk back up the row of parking spaces, passing Holland's Ferrari without a glance. The Porsche that had been parked to the left of it was now gone, leaving an empty space. She walked past that space and stopped at a car farther down. She held up her phone, took a photo, then looked around, spotted another car that interested her on the opposite side and took its picture, came back, took a shot of Holland's Ferrari, getting a clear view of it from the side, thanks to the empty space next to it, then took a picture of the Mercedes beside it. She came back to the Crown Vic and got in.

"I love cars," she said, buckling up again. "I get it from Del. I should e-mail him these shots and ask him to guess which one I just bought. He'll have a stroke."

Del was Delbert Stainer, her older brother, the auto mechanic in Houston who'd fixed up and sold her the Redbird she'd just bragged about to Richard Holland.

"A car photo array," Hank said.

"Why not? Parris may be psychotic but that doesn't mean he's stupid. So he's not into cars and doesn't know a Ferrari from a Volkswagen. Big deal. Doesn't mean he can't identify a car from memory if he sees a picture of it."

Karen rolled through the big gateway and turned right, onto Howard Boulevard.

"He's not going to work as a witness," Hank said. "The state's attorney's not going to be interested. He's going to wish Brett Parris didn't exist."

"Yeah, well, he exists and I'm starting to believe him."

Hank's cell phone vibrated. He took it out, looked at the display, and thumbed the button. "Hello, there."

"Hello yourself," replied Anna Haynes Donaghue. "Am I calling at a bad time?"

"No, not at all," Hank said. "We're just driving back downtown. How are you doing?"

"Not bad for an old girl. I understand you've been spending a lot of your time up here in the Park lately."

"Too true."

"I saw you on the news at noon. You looked very good. Better than your chief did this afternoon, I daresay. Once a Fed, always a Fed."

"Thanks, Mother. I guess."

"The politics will be fierce on this one, dear. One of the more high-profile homicides in state history. Everyone will be trying to get a finger in the pie. Makes me wish I was still on the job." She held the phone away from her mouth to sneeze. "Sorry. Roberts just got himself a cat. He neglected to ask me first if I was allergic."

Roberts was James Roberts, Anna's friend and companion. General James Roberts, United States Army, Retired. Now a military consultant, he spent most of his time out of the country on contract as an adviser to heads of state with more money than brains, according to Anna.

"He should have gotten one of those hairless cats," Hank said. "They're hypoallergenic."

"They're aliens from another planet, poor things, but that's not why I called. There's something happening tomorrow night I need you to attend."

"I'm going out with the boys to shoot pool and steal a few cars."

"It's the fundraiser for the Mercer Foundation," she went on, ignoring him. "I thought Constance would probably want to reschedule it, given what happened today, but she feels it's even more important now than ever, so we'll all be there. You, too."

The Mercer Foundation was a non-profit organization created by Constance ten years ago in her father's memory to raise money for a mental health center providing support and services to people with severe mental health issues. They delivered education and awareness programs, operated an advocacy network for improved medical insurance coverage, and provided shelter, maintenance programs, and short-term funding to people in distress. The Foundation's annual event was notoriously politician-heavy, and Hank preferred just to mail them a check. Unfortunately, he'd lost track of when it was coming and hadn't arranged a suitable excuse.

"I need to spend a lot of time on this case," he tried.

"Nonsense. Jarrett won't be any deader if you take an evening off. You can bring that new girlfriend of yours. It's about time I met her, and this will be neutral ground, as it were."

"She's just a friend, Mother."

"That's not what I hear. I'll send a car for you at six o'clock. Black tie, Henry, but I suppose as usual you'll insist on wearing a suit instead of formal evening wear."

"I only have the one dinner jacket, Mother, and it doesn't fit. I'm a cop; nobody expects a cop to dress well. Besides, didn't Alan Flusser write that a solid navy suit, a white shirt, navy tie, and white pocket scarf are an acceptable alternative?"

"Only if the occasion's black-tie optional."

"Sigh. Then I guess I'll just have to be a rule-breaker, Mother."

"I don't see why. You look very handsome when you dress well. See you there."

"All right." Hank closed the phone and stared at it, reluctant to dial Meredith's number and ask her to go to a high-profile gala fundraiser on such short notice.

Karen looked over at him and shook her head in disgust.

"Mamma's boy."

9

Hank loved the city at night. He walked down Cooper Street at a few minutes before 9:00 P.M., on his way to meet Martinez at Phil's Diner, a block from departmental headquarters. The cigar in his mouth was a Partagas petit corona, good for walking. He'd lit it after leaving the restaurant where he'd had dinner. He was taking his time, enjoying the night. Martinez would be early, waiting for him, but she always showed up early for meetings, and waiting was not a problem for her. She always had an abundance of things to occupy her mind no matter where she was, and Hank knew she put her time to good use without even appearing to move a muscle.

The hot night air moved around him in a steady current. A bus passed in the street, its brightly-lit windows filled with heads and shoulders facing forward, bored, tired. A motorcycle accelerated around it into the inside lane. Cars followed. Downtown traffic. He looked up and saw lights moving in the sky above the buildings. A plane leaving the airport in Springhill.

He waited at an intersection for the light to change. Sirens began a few blocks away and klaxons sounded as emergency vehicles rushed toward him. Fire and EMS. When the light turned green he waited until they had passed, then he crossed the intersection, throwing the remainder of the cigar down a sewer grate.

Martinez sat at a table for one at the rear of Phil's Deli. Tonight she wore a navy business suit, white blouse, and black pumps. She sipped coffee from a tall cup with a corrugated paper sleeve, watching him edge down the narrow aisle toward her. He grabbed a stool and dragged it into the aisle.

Martinez held up her cup. "Coffee?"

"No, thanks." Hank sat down and put his foot up on the bottom rung of the stool. "How's Peralta?"

Martinez reached into the pocket of her jacket and put Peralta's badge on the table between them. "I tried, for over an hour. I said she could have forty-eight hours, think it over, but she blew it off. Her mind's made up."

Hank touched the badge, spun it around so that he could read the number, then spun it back. "I'm not surprised. I saw it in her eyes. Will she be all right?"

"I think so. She doesn't want an exit interview with anyone, doesn't want to talk to any of us, but she has a doctor's appointment on Monday and her husband's sticking close to her, so I think she'll be okay. There's a lot of stuff she has to work through. It's going to take time."

She picked up the badge and put it back into her pocket. "She kept saying she didn't want to end up like Stainer. She wanted a life away from the job. She didn't want to be the kind of person who could shoot someone in the head and walk away from it, like it was nothing."

Hank looked out the window as a police cruiser hurried by, lights flashing. "I understand where she's coming from," he said, "but it's not exactly fair to Karen."

Martinez shrugged. "It's out of our hands. The bottom line is, we're down another detective at the worst possible time."

"At least we don't have to work Chinatown for a while."

"Yeah, I hear you." She set her cup down. "He's a butthead. I'm real sorry Carleson decided to go with him, but I can see it. It's a good move."

Hank waited.

"The chief's calling the Jarrett case a task force in public," she said, "but he's not funding it like one. We've got a small budget coming out of his discretionary dollars. I talked him into letting us bring in one detective on a temporary basis, specifically for Jarrett. What's your plan?"

"I want Horvath working with Karen on it."

"Kaplan and Belknap will have to catch everything else for the time being, then."

"Can I borrow someone from another unit to help cover Homicide, short term?"

"What're you thinking?"

"What about Higgins, in Robbery?"

"I was thinking of Peet in Arson." Martinez pursed her lips. It was her way of smiling without smiling. "Arson's a little quieter right now, thank God. Would you rather have Higgins?"

"Yeah. He's older, more experienced. He can swing between

Kaplan and Belknap and it won't bother him."

"All right. I'll let Murchison know tonight, and we'll get him on board tomorrow." Jim Murchison was the supervisory lieutenant in Robbery, also reporting directly to Martinez.

"Thanks."

"No problem. But you still get another body for Jarrett right now."

Hank folded his hands on the table. "I'd like to bring in a detective from Cold Case. Maureen Truly."

"Don't know the name. Why her?"

"A hunch, I guess. I looked through her file this afternoon."

"And?"

"Just the minimum street experience in uniform and not a lot of field investigation either, I admit, but she's done well in Cold Case. Five closures in four years through new DNA evidence and reworking the files."

Martinez shrugged. "It's CCU we're talking about here."

"I know, but she's got a good rapport with Criminalistics and a knack for collating and analyzing information, from what I can see. Her career path probably points to Intelligence, but I think I can use her on this. It's a big case, the suspect pool is wide and deep up front, and she can help everyone stay focused."

"I thought that was your job."

"My job is to make sure the right people are doing the right things at the right time, Ann."

She pursed her lips again. "One of the many things I learned from you along the way."

"I want Stainer and Horvath at the front end and Truly at the back end."

"And you in the middle."

"I'll be everywhere on this one."

"Roger that." Martinez looked away as two young people, a male and a female, obviously students, came into the deli and leaned on the counter to talk to the kid up front at the cash register. "We're both in the cross hairs on this one. We blow it, we're both toast."

"Then we won't blow it."

She sighed, watching the kids. "Ever wish you were still that young, Hank? Back in school, full of piss and vinegar?"

"No. Never."

70

She laughed lightly. "Not one to look back, are you? I've always admired that. No regrets, no second guessing. Always in control of the moment."

He looked at her profile and involuntarily remembered other times and other places he'd studied the hook in her nose, the large, dark, almond-shaped eyes, the arching eyebrows, the loose black curls. Time moved on; you moved with it. How you felt about it was irrelevant, in the long run. She was wrong about him, but there was no percentage in correcting her. Not anymore.

Abruptly he stood up and put the stool back where he'd found it. "We've got your back, Ann. We'll close it for you."

"Thanks." She reached out and touched his arm.

"For what it's worth? I've got yours, too. Always."

10

Twelve hours later, a few minutes after 9:00 A.M., Melissa Grove opened the door of her penthouse suite and politely let them in after examining their badges and identification. Following her into an expensively-furnished seating area, they immediately understood that this was a place of business rather than Melissa Grove's home. When she invited them to sit down, Hank chose a leather love seat while Karen waved her hand and turned away, looking around. Melissa settled on the edge of a chair across from Hank and folded her hands in her lap.

"How may I help you?"

She was a tall, slender brunette. She wore a cerise-colored kimono wrap dress and matching spaghetti-strap shoes with stiletto heels. Her makeup was a little heavy, and her bust was impossibly large for someone with such a narrow waist, but she was working hard to project a demure girl-next-door image.

Hank took out his notebook, opened it on his knee, and made a little production of finding his Cross pen, twisting it to expose the ball point, and noting the date and time on a fresh page.

"Do you know a man named Richard Holland, Ms. Grove?"

"Richard?" She showed him flawless white teeth. "Oh, yes."

"How would you describe your relationship with him?"

She giggled. "We're good friends."

"I see. When was the last time you saw him?"

"Yesterday morning. Well, Wednesday night." She pretended to be flustered. "He stayed over."

"Here?"

"Yes, of course."

"What time did he leave?"

"I guess about eight thirty."

"After he had breakfast?"

"Just a cup of coffee. He doesn't eat breakfast."

Karen had finished her little tour of the room. She'd found a black plastic holder containing business cards, and now she held up one of the cards between two fingers. "This yours? 'Melissa Grove, Business Consultant, Corona Services, Inc.?'"

"Yes, that's me, all right."

Karen locked eyes with her. "Corona Services? Don't make me go look it up, hon."

"It's a company I formed as a vehicle for my business. It helps if my clients think I'm part of a large organization."

"So what's a business consultant do for her clients? I mean, in your case."

"We look after whatever services our clients request."

"I'll bet. You sure Holland was here Thursday morning?"

"Positive."

"And you'll swear to that on a stack of Bibles in court?"

Melissa's smile faltered, but she managed to maintain eye contact. "If I have to."

"You may." Karen tucked the business card into her pocket and took out one of her own. She walked over to Melissa's chair and held it out. "Here's mine, darlin'. See," she pointed, "it says 'homicide detective.' That's what *I* do. Somebody put a bullet into Holland's boss's brain yesterday. Maybe you heard about it. G'wan, take it."

Melissa reluctantly took the business card.

"How'd he seem?" Hank asked. "Holland, I mean."

"He was fine. Normal."

"Normal." Karen considered the word as though it were unfamiliar to her. "Okay. What did you guys talk about while he was having his breakfast coffee?"

Melissa shrugged. "I don't really remember. Stuff."

"Stuff. The morning news?"

"I don't listen to the news. It's very depressing. I try to maintain a very positive equilibrium."

"What time did he leave here, yesterday morning?" Hank asked.

"About eight thirty, as I told you."

Hank put away his notebook and pen. He stood up.

"Is that everything?" Melissa asked, her voice rising.

"For now,'" Karen said. "Hang onto that card. If you think of something else you'd like to tell us, give me a call."

She nodded, put the business card into the pocket of her kimono dress, and showed them to the door.

73

At the elevator, Hank punched the Down button.

"That was interesting," Karen said. "Holland bought himself a little GFE. Convenient."

"Hmm?"

"Girlfriend experience. She's a courtesan. A night with her would cost half your pay check. Thirty-six triple Ds, size five shoes, no tatts, perfect skin, perfect teeth, no visible track marks. The best."

The elevator door opened and Hank stepped aside to allow Karen to precede him into the lobby. "Yeah, but did he pay for the night, in which case he's telling the truth, or did he just pay for the alibi, in which case he's lying?"

"That's the five-dollar question." Karen looked around the lobby as they crossed to the big glass doors at the front entrance. "Somehow I think we'll have a fight on our hands if we try to get a warrant for surveillance video from this place. That's high-end service up there, and I'll just bet it gets high-end traffic."

"You might be right."

The heat hit them in a wave as they left the front lobby and walked down the sidewalk to the Crown Vic. When they got in, Karen started the engine and cranked up the air conditioning.

"As far as I'm concerned," she said, "Holland's alibi was bought and paid for, and he's a lying son of a bitch."

Hank buckled up.

"Come on, Lou. My gut's telling me Brett Parris was right on the money."

"We're going to need a hell of a lot more than a gut feeling."

"Understood. I'm not a fucking rookie." She threw the car into gear and pulled away from the curb. She drove in silence for a block before looking over at him.

"You just watch me," she said. "I'm going to peel that bastard Holland like an onion."

11

The body of Herbert Joseph Jarrett had already been the subject of intense scrutiny at the Glendale Forensic Medical Center for several hours on Friday morning before Hank arrived at 1:00 P.M. to attend the autopsy. It had undergone the normal external examination, including complete photography, clothed and unclothed, weighing and measuring, fingerprinting, fingernail scraping, washing, and a thorough visual examination noting every feature, no matter how small and innocuous. Dr. Sarah Chalmers, assistant medical examiner, presided over this stage of the proceedings, assisted by Harry Shaniwatru, the diener of Thai descent who boxed professionally in the flyweight class in his spare time. Harry was the most trusted of the attendants on staff at the center, and so it was a foregone conclusion he would be the one called in to assist.

After Chalmers pronounced this phase of the external examination complete, Harry then wheeled the corpse down the hall for full-body computed tomography, at which point Dr. Jim Easton joined Chalmers and the head radiologist, Dr. Paul Oldfield, to pore over the resultant imagery while Harry patiently moved the body next door for x-rays. Easton was of the belt-and-suspenders persuasion when it came to the death investigation of the fifth-richest person in the state and didn't think twice about the expense of running both the CT scan and the x-rays. It was crucial that he be able to answer every possible question that would be raised in this case, and he needed to be able to say he'd left no stone unturned.

As a result, when Hank walked into the main autopsy theater at three minutes after one o'clock, tying his protective gown behind his back, Easton and Chalmers already had a very good sense of what they would find when they dissected the body.

"Ready for the big show?" Easton eyed Hank over the gold wire frames of his glasses. His voice was slightly distorted behind the mask that covered the lower half of his face.

"Ready when you are, Jim," replied Hank, putting on a pair of latex gloves.

"We've already covered the virtual dimension," Easton said, "and I'm prepared to cut you a break. The deceased sustained a single gunshot wound to the left temple, and other than the expected injury to the back of his head where it struck the ground when he fell, there's nothing else of note. This, in and of itself, should be of interest to you, I'd think."

"No signs of a struggle or a fight, nothing defensive."

"Exactly."

"You're suggesting the shooter deliberately brought the gun to the scene with the intention of using it?"

"I suggest nothing. I'm a scientist, pure and simple. I leave the speculation to you. And so, being the considerate person that I am, I've decided to start our dissection with the head so you can get your hands on the bullet and get the hell out of here. Sarah, show him the CT images while Harry and I get started."

Chalmers led Hank over to a MacBook set up on a trolley close to the autopsy station to enable the pathologists to consult still images from the CT scan as they proceeded with the dissection. "The x-rays are there," Chalmers said, pointing to the x-ray view box mounted on the wall near the head of the dissection table.

A strand of her wavy red hair threatened to escape from beneath her hair net onto her high, freckled cheekbone. Her soft blue eyes stared at Hank.

"Great." He leaned over for a closer look at the image of the head that was currently displayed on the laptop screen. "I expected to see you busy at one of the other tables when I came in."

"I was scheduled to do the Chee autopsies today, but we agreed it was better to move them back and have an extra pair of eyes on this one." She sighed. "When I called Detective Carleson to let him know, Lieutenant Jarvis was pretty upset. I could hear him yelling in the background."

"He'll get over it," Hank said.

"He'll have to," Easton said over his shoulder, watching Harry excise the entrance wound and surrounding tissue and place it into a container with fixative. "If he tries to get into a political pissing match over his place in line versus this case he's going to get his ass kicked."

At that moment the door opened and a man in a dark suit walked in. He hadn't bothered to put on the protective gear that all observers were required to wear when attending an autopsy. He passed the other empty dissection tables in a confident stride, head up, arms swinging, eyes fixed on Easton.

"Speaking of politics," Hank murmured. He glanced up at the observation booth and saw another arrival, Glendale State's Attorney Warren Exler, peering down at them.

"Sir," Easton called out to the approaching intruder, "I'm very honored to have you here today but I'll have to ask you to leave my autopsy theater immediately. We're about to begin and I can't have unnecessary bodies getting in the way, living or dead."

The man stopped and folded his arms, his eyes avoiding the corpse lying naked on the dissection table in front of him. "You're Easton, I take it? I'm Attorney General Johnson S. Perry."

"Of course you are. Now get the hell out of my autopsy theater."

Perry was a young-looking fifty-year-old who'd run unopposed in the last state election and was making a name for himself as a relentless prosecutor of organized crime elements in Maryland. He was known as an aggressive, savvy politician with an excellent chance of becoming governor in the near future.

"H.J. Jarrett was my friend," Perry said. "I flew down from Annapolis expressly to assure his family, his company's shareholders, and the public that this outrage will not go unpunished." It was obviously a speech he planned to deliver again, very shortly, to the press.

Easton looked up at Exler in the observation booth and calmly flipped down his face shield. "Warren, as you know, there's a serious risk of infection to anyone in an autopsy theater who's not properly dressed. On top of that, no one is allowed to attend a procedure without the permission of the medical examiner or the prosecutor in charge." He turned to Perry. "Since I am he, in both cases, I'm ordering you the hell out of my theater right now before I have to call security and have you marched out at gunpoint."

"Really," Perry said, "I think I need to—"

Easton motioned with his double-gloved hand. "Harry."

"Yes, Dr. Easton." With precise, practiced movements the diener used his scalpel to make a long, deep incision from behind one ear to the other ear of the corpse, passing over the crown of the bald head. Setting the scalpel aside, he grasped the lower edge of the skin and, with some effort and the assistance of a knife, began to pull the skin down from the top of the skull over the face to expose the front of the skull. It made a disgusting sound and produced a distinct odor that had an immediate effect on Attorney General Perry.

"Unh," he said, turning away.

Harry then peeled away the back flap of skin so that the entire top of the skull was visible. He picked up an electric saw and tested it to make sure it was working.

Easton had had his fun, so Hank moved around the dissection table. "Mr. Attorney General, why don't we go up into the viewing gallery."

Perry suddenly turned and hurried from the theater, his hand over his mouth. Hank followed, stripping off his latex gloves. Outside the theater, he navigated around the mess Perry had left on the floor in his frantic search for the washroom. Hank pushed open the door and found the politician crouching in an open stall, wiping his mouth with toilet paper. It took several minutes before Perry had recovered enough to flush the toilet and emerge, his face pasty and drawn. He walked to the sink, washed his hands and face, and wiped at the stains on his jacket with a handful of paper towels.

"You're Donaghue," he said finally, while washing his hands.

"Yes, sir."

He dried his hands, stuffed the wadded paper towels into the trash bin, and held out his hand. "Johnson Perry. Call me John."

Hank shook his hand.

"I've met your mother." Perry turned to the mirror and finger-combed his hair, making an effort to pull himself together. "Quite a woman, even though she is a Republican. We should go up to the observation room. Chief Bennett's meeting us there."

Hank led the way to the viewing gallery, a long, narrow room that looked down onto the main autopsy theater, affording a clear view of everything happening below. A monitor provided a direct feed from the video camera mounted above Easton's autopsy station, while a microphone caught the whining of Harry's saw and the crunching of bone as the diener cut through the vault of the corpse's skull to get at the brain within.

"Maybe you could turn it down, Lieutenant," Exler said, looking at Perry, who stood before the glass window rubbing his face with his hands.

Hank punched the mute button. The door opened behind them,

and Chief Bennett walked in.

"Very sorry I'm late, gentlemen," he said, heading straight for Perry with his hand extended, "but I was on the phone with the mayor, who sends his regards."

Perry turned around and shook Bennett's hand. "Thanks."

Bennett shook Exler's hand. "Warren, whatever you and Mr. Perry need from the GPD, just say the word."

"I'm sure Lieutenant Donaghue can look after us." Exler glanced at Hank.

"Yes, of course." Bennett said. "He has a great deal of experience as an investigator. I'm completely confident he'll nail our UNSUB in record time. Won't you, Lieutenant?"

"We'll do our best, sir," Hank replied. "It helps that Mr. Exler's made ASA DiOrio available around the clock for our warrants. That's a big assist."

Exler nodded. "I wanted to make sure the lieutenant and his team had immediate access so there's no time lost because of procedure. And thanks to you, Mr. Attorney General, for making Judge Brown available whenever we need him."

"No problem," Perry said, not interested in the round of mutual back-patting Bennett had started.

"It's important to take advantage of any breaks in the case as soon as they happen," Bennett said. "These windows have a way of opening and closing very quickly. It'll be crucial to have our warrants signed off right away."

"They have to be clean," Perry said to Hank. "Watertight. We'll bend over backwards to help you do your job, but we can't go to trial on this and have crucial evidence thrown out because of loosey-goosey warrants. Don't waste Brown's time with wishful thinking, and don't send Exler into court with a case made of sugar cubes. We need to nail the bastard who did this, clean and hard."

"Understood." Hank glanced down into the autopsy theater and saw Chalmers looking up at him. She pointed to her ear and mouth. Hank walked over to the monitor and punched the audio button. Chalmers said something to Easton, who nodded without interrupting what he was doing.

"Hank," he said, "you'll probably want to be down here for this." He gently lifted the brain out of the skull and set it down into the pan of a scale suspended above the head of the dissection table.

The brain was soaked with blood. Harry noted the weight, moved it onto a tray, photographed it from several angles, and then began very carefully to clean it.

"Gentlemen, you may want to leave the audio on," Easton said, looking up at the gallery, "so you can hear me. I'll walk you through the cause of death and get you your bullet. I realize there's a fair bit of blood right now, but you gentlemen will probably find this very interesting just the same, not to mention very important. Since you're here, as witnesses, you might as well pay attention."

As Hank left the gallery, Exler turned to Perry. "Mr. Attorney General?"

"Leave it," Perry said, glancing at the monitor.

Easton looked up as Hank entered the autopsy theater and crossed the floor in long strides, pulling on a fresh pair of latex gloves. He tipped up his eye shield and nodded. "Thank you, Lieutenant."

"No problem," Hank murmured. "We wouldn't want you to screw up your own political ambitions now, would we, Jim?"

"I'll remember you when I become governor."

"I thought you were just shooting for CME."

"A mere stepping stone." Easton's desire to become chief medical examiner of Maryland was as well known as his lack of tact and political discretion.

"Let me show you what we've got," he said, turning to the body on the table with its ruined head. "The bullet struck the deceased in the left temple, the area which we refer to as the pterion. Also known as 'God's little joke,' this is the weakest part of the skull. The round penetrated the parietal bone just above the sphenoparietal suture," he pointed with a double-gloved little finger, "where the bone is thin and pointed. Penetration created several small linear fractures and produced bone fragments which created their own secondary tracks. The middle meningeal artery received extensive damage and created a massive subdural hematoma that resulted in traumatic pressure to the brain. That accounts for the blood you see slopped all over my dissection table. It also contributed in large part to the death of the victim, the blood loss and the resultant pressure on the brain within the skull being a lethal combination. So cause of death will be described as a specific combination of factors resulting from the single gunshot wound to the left temple.

"Now, the lieutenant is understandably fixated on the bullet itself, because it'll no doubt be a key piece of evidence in his case, and while I'm retrieving it for him I'll explain why today is his lucky day."

Harry had finished cleaning much of the blood from the surface of the brain, and Easton now bent over it, scalpel in hand. "What we have is a penetrating head injury, meaning that the round penetrated the parietal bone, as I said, and entered the brain here," he pointed with the scalpel, "creating the primary wound track as it traveled through in this direction," he moved the scalpel diagonally above the surface of the brain, "and coming to rest right here," he pointed, "almost exactly a centimeter from the surface. Up here," he moved his scalpel back to the entrance wound, "penetration of the parietal bone created numerous bone fragments that generated secondary wound tracks, as I mentioned." He moved the scalpel. "See here, Hank? And here and here in particular. They helped shred the artery right at the point of impact and also created additional damage to this portion of the brain. Quite a little mess.

"But back to our round, and the question of range of fire. I should mention, to begin with, that the entrance wound and surrounding skin tissue, which we've recovered and preserved for further reference, showed no searing, soot deposition, or powder tattooing, only the typical abrasion ring I'd expect to see in these situations. I can safely say that we're dealing with a distant range wound, or in other words a shot that was fired from a distance of more than two feet. It's highly unlikely, therefore, that the wound was self-inflicted. I should add that the abrasion ring," he glanced up at the gallery, "which is, you may recall, the rim of flattened, abraded tissue around the entrance wound, was almost exactly concentric, meaning the shot struck the head at an angle very close to perpendicular."

"In other words," Hank supplied, "his head was turned away from the shooter and in profile. He might have been turning away to walk back to his bicycle, figuring their conversation was over. Something like that."

"Assume away," Easton said. "You'll notice, as well, that there isn't an exit wound. We're not dealing with a perforating injury, a through and through, but a penetrating injury, as I already said, even though the round entered at the weakest part of the skull where it would be met with the least resistance." He bent over the brain and began to extract the bullet. "You know where I'm going with this, right, Hank?"

"I've got an idea."

"Then let me," he worked his forceps closer to the bullet, "add it all up for our guests. A penetrating wound and not through and through, even though the bullet entered the skull at its weakest point, a relatively small temporary cavity, which I haven't mentioned yet but is notable because of the relatively small amount of shockwave damage to nearby brain tissue seen on the imaging, a reasonably intact bullet, as we could also see from the imaging, with only some deformation even though it did pass through bone, deflecting in a twenty-degree angle, by the way, all of which is good for the lieutenant because the rifling should be visible for analysis ... Harry?"

The diener extended a plastic evidence bag. Easton pulled out the round and dropped it into the bag. Harry sealed the top and held it up for Hank to see.

"In other words, a standard velocity .22, if I'm not mistaken. As we always say, shot placement is everything. It's not necessarily the caliber of the round that'll kill you but the placement of the shot. In this case, I'd say the shooter couldn't have picked a better spot. More lucky than good, I suppose, but there you go."

Harry took a pen and scribbled on the tear-off receipt at the top of the bag. On the form printed on the side of the bag he then wrote the victim's name, a description of the evidence, date and time of recovery, recovered by, and the first two lines of the chain of custody table. Easton initialed the bag on the first line and gave the pen back to Harry, who put his initials on the second line, tore off the receipt at the top, and handed the evidence bag to Hank, who wrote his own initials next to his name on the third line of the chain of custody table and held the bag up for a closer look.

"Not bad." He could see it was indeed a .22 long rifle bullet. It was plain lead and not copper-plated, which meant it was standard velocity rather than a high velocity load, as Easton had predicted. A very common cartridge throughout the years. His eyesight wasn't good enough to see the rifling marks, but Easton was again correct when he said that the bullet was in good enough shape for the lab to complete an accurate analysis. His lucky day, indeed.

"Now bug out," said Easton, "and take our guests with you so we can get back to work." He looked up at the gallery. "Based on our virtual autopsy, I'm sure we won't find anything else of significance directly related to the death of the victim, and anything we *might* find we'll bring to the lieutenant's attention right away. I think his time would be better spent following the evidence he's now got in his hands instead of standing around here as a redundant witness, don't you?" Easton turned around to Chalmers. "Doctor, if you'd like to get the trunk opened up, we can move this thing along."

Hank gratefully began to peel off his gloves and gown. Evidence bag in hand, he left the autopsy theater, edged around the janitor who was mopping the hallway floor with a strong-smelling disinfectant, and went into the viewing gallery. Attorney General Perry was alone, staring down into the theater, hands clasped behind his back. At the sound of the door opening and closing, he turned and nodded at Hank.

"Sorry for the bluster earlier, Hank. I was out of line. I apologize."

"These things put a lot of stress on everyone."

Perry looked at the evidence bag in Hank's hand. "Our first break in the case, wouldn't you say?"

Hank held up the bag so that Perry could take a closer look. "Dr. Easton's right. A standard velocity .22, which explains why it didn't exit the skull. We should be able to see enough of the rifling to be able to find a match if it's already in the system, or at the very least match it down the road if we find the murder weapon." He put the bag in his jacket pocket. "It's a break."

Perry's eyes wandered back down to the dissection table. "I had no idea it would be so dehumanizing. I've never been at one of these before. Never had to. Wasn't ever in my career path. I thought I was coming to pay my respects to H.J., or something." He turned back and met Hank's eyes. "I don't know what I thought. But that's not H.J. down there. It's some piece of meat."

Hank waited.

"I don't know how you do it, Hank. I'm a lawyer and a politician. I do my job in big offices, courtrooms, government offices, board rooms, conference centers. We deal with autopsy results all the time, sure, but not like this. How the hell do you do this for a living?"

"You get used to it."

"I can't imagine that. Frankly, I'm surprised you didn't follow in your parents' footsteps and make a name for yourself in the courtroom. You must be a hard person to be able to deal with this kind of thing every day." He frowned. "Don't get me wrong. I'm aware of your incredible record as a police officer. I'm just trying to understand how the hell you do it. *Why* you do it, given your background."

Hank hesitated, then saw that the man was struggling to deal with the horror of what he'd blundered into and was genuinely desperate for help. "Someone has to do it, John. Someone who cares about the outcome."

"Of course, but surely you could have been just as effective, or even more effective, as a prosecuting attorney. Above all this." He looked down into the theater and quickly turned his head again.

"My mother," Hank said, "God bless her, likes to remind me on a regular basis of the difference between the law and morality. Those of us inside the system, she always says, don't have the luxury of moral opinions about right or wrong. We serve a legal system that operates within a well-worked set of rules. As civil servants, our job is to apply the rules, catch the violators, and apply the penalties dictated by the rules. Period."

He took a breath, talking more to keep Perry's mind off what was happening below than anything else. "The people who make the laws, politicians such as you, for example, can have a moral agenda when it comes to amending laws or making new ones, but lawyers, cops, and judges can't, according to her. The law is what it is, she likes to say, and it's our job to deal with that. Know what I'm saying?"

"Of course."

"Sure you do," Hank said easily. "You got your law degree from Harvard. But the thing I like to say in response to my mother is that at street level, her point of view isn't all that popular. At street level, there's a hunger for a different kind of morality. An eye for an eye. A punishment that fits the crime. The street can be remarkably Dantesque, that way. A hell in which you ultimately get back what you give."

He saw Perry frown, trying to make sense of what he was saying.

"As a cop, I've spent my career in the middle of it all, dealing with the street's version of what's right and what's wrong, while at the same time trying to work within the rules as a cog in the legal system. I'm pulled in both directions every day. To be there, to do this job for a living, I *have* to have a tough skin. I realized very early in my life I could do it. Things that bothered other people didn't bother me. To put it in a nutshell, I do this not only because I want to, but also because I *can*."

The door opened and Exler stuck his head inside. "The press is waiting for a brief statement, Mr. Attorney General, then we should get you back to the airport."

Perry held out his hand to Hank. "Thanks very much."

"You're welcome," Hank said, relieved to have been rescued from a conversation that was making him feel very uncomfortable.

"Give my regards to your mother," Perry said, squeezing his hand tightly.

"I will, sir."

Perry glanced once more at the window behind him. "Do what you have to do."

12

Karen didn't like psychiatrists very much.

As a teenager, she'd been interviewed by several psychiatrists responsible for her mother's care back home in Fort Worth, and they weren't exactly her favorite category of people. One had made an effort to be kind and understanding, others were formal and impersonal, and one in particular had been an aggressive son of a bitch who thought she was hiding more than she was telling and was determined to intimidate it out of her. Even at that age, though, she'd had enough insight into human behavior to understand that the nice one was putting on an act to make her feel relaxed and cooperative, and she'd had enough self-possession to stand up to the bully and tell him to go fish.

As she fought her way through heavy downtown traffic toward the office of Dr. Sally Caldwell, she remembered that the supposed objective of most of the interviews had been to collect whatever information they could about her mother's behavior before her institutionalization. *We know about her leaving home last month, when they found her on the highway, but were there other times before that when she disappeared? Maybe just for the day? Times when you didn't know where she was? And what would she say when she came back? Did she cry very often? Did she yell at you and hit you? Did she blame you for everything? Did she say you should have been a boy instead of a girl?*

A few of the interviews had been a bungled attempt to explore her own feelings about her mother's illness. They were short and sweet. No matter how fake nice they were, or how aggressive, there was no possible way she'd say a word about what was going on inside *her* head. It was none of their goddamned business.

She was sitting through the third consecutive red light at the same intersection. Irritated, she flicked on the Crown Vic's flashing grill lights and mounted the sidewalk, knocking aside a metal garbage can as she maneuvered into an alley. She drove down the alley between the dumpsters, crates, and abandoned store fixtures to the next block over, where she blipped her siren, forced her way back into traffic, and bulled into the far lane. Someone blew their horn behind her and she threw a glance into the rear view mirror, hoping to see a raised fist or middle finger, but was disappointed.

She killed the lights and took a deep breath.

Celebrity psychiatrists were even worse than the regular kind, as far as she was concerned. Not only were they psychiatrists, which was bad enough, but they were attention-seekers who loved to show up on television hawking their latest book or self-help video or some such waste of time and money. And Dr. Sally Caldwell, unfortunately, was a very hot commodity in the celebrity-psychiatrist racket right now.

In her mid-fifties, Caldwell was originally from Milwaukee. Her hometown origin still lingered in her accent and played well on television, lending her a certain charm that appealed to people. Karen had glanced through Caldwell's book on body language and thought she'd covered it off fairly well, but she'd looked at another on weight loss and self-esteem and found it to be completely self-serving. Karen had her doubts as to how useful Caldwell was going to be on something as off-beat as this Fregoli thing.

In Caldwell's waiting room, Karen badged the receptionist and cooled her heels while The Famous One finished up whatever the hell it was she was currently doing that was So Damned Important. In the waiting room with her were a woman who wouldn't meet her eyes and a teenaged girl who wore some kind of private school uniform. Karen had not missed the interest the girl had shown in Karen's sidearm, which peeked out when she brushed back her jacket to return her badge to her belt. As Karen paced back and forth the woman spoke quietly to the girl, who picked up a magazine from the table beside her instead of responding.

An inner door opened and the receptionist appeared.

"Detective Stainer? Please come this way."

Karen followed her through a doorway into an inner office. Dr. Sally Caldwell sat at a large glass desk that held only a large flat panel computer monitor and a china tea cup and saucer. She looked up from her monitor, flashed Karen a smile, and stood up. As she came around the desk, hand extended, Karen saw that Caldwell was half a foot taller than she was, perhaps five foot ten, and large framed, carrying more weight than Karen but without looking heavy. Her hair was colored platinum blond and cut in a shoulder-length bob style with a medium curl. She wore an expensive-looking blood-red jacket-and-skirt combination with white pantyhose and black pumps, all of which apparently tried to suggest a little-girl innocence.

"Detective Karen Stainer, Homicide," Karen said, flashing her badge.

"Very glad to meet you." Caldwell gave her a quick, soft handshake. "Won't you please sit down?" She led the way to an arrangement of leather chairs in one corner of the office. "The tea's fresh. Would you care for some?"

Karen shook her head. "I won't take much of your time. I understand you made a house call on Brett Parris last night after his day of fun. We've done the disclosure authorization thing, right? So I need you to explain the situation to me. I need to know how reliable he is as a witness. Whether or not I can trust what he said he saw yesterday morning."

They sat down. Caldwell crossed her legs and nodded sympathetically. "I understand your concern. It was a very upsetting situation for Brett."

"How was he doing last night when you saw him?"

"He was agitated, of course. I was there for nearly an hour."

Karen had spent more time with the guy yesterday than that, so the fact that he was agitated wasn't exactly a news bulletin. "Was he freaked out? Delusional? Was he doing the guys-in-disguise thing with you?"

"He was agitated, as I said. He was rational, otherwise. You must remember that he's a paranoid schizophrenic, so the first thing I assessed was his behavior in that context. He wasn't displaying any symptoms such as hallucinations or thought disorder, he spoke fairly coherently despite being upset, and his attention stayed reasonably focused on us throughout. He was mostly upset because he insisted he'd seen Richard Holland and no one would believe him."

"You said 'us.' Do you mean you and his father?"

"No. Brett's APRN was there with me."

"APRN."

"Advanced practice registered nurse," Caldwell explained. "Mona Jensen. She's a PMH-APRN, actually. Psychiatric mental health APRN."

Karen was uninterested in the alphabet soup. She knew what a psychiatric nurse was, and found it informative that Brett Parris had retained one. Probably to help look after his home care.

"Fine. You and the nurse. And he seemed okay, you say. Other than being wound up about whether or not people believed him. Did you sedate him?"

Caldwell shook her head. "We talked him through it. Mona works with him every day, so there was a basis for breaking through the anxiety and bringing him back to a state of relative calm without sedation."

"Okay, fine." The fact that Brett hadn't needed to be sedated was good news. "So what's the deal with this Fregoli condition of his?"

"Fregoli syndrome is actually quite rare," Caldwell said. "It's a form of delusional misidentification syndrome, or DMS, where the patient believes they're being persecuted by someone who disguises himself as other people. It's named after Leopoldo Fregoli, an Italian actor who was famous a hundred years ago for being a quick-change artist."

"Okay. He has these delusions that other people are Richard Holland, and he's paranoid Holland's stalking him. As I understand it, Holland bullied him when they were in school." She leaned forward. "What I need you to do is help me with how this thing works. Does he get it all the time? Just sometimes? Does something trigger these delusions, or are they random?"

Caldwell spread her hands. "As I mentioned, it's a rather rare condition, and unfortunately we don't know a lot about it. Part of our efforts over the years has been to try to separate it from other DMSes such as Capgras syndrome, where the patient believes that a number of people known to him have been replaced by identical imposters. Both Capgras and Fregoli are included in the category of schizophrenia. That may not mean much to you, Detective—"

"I know about schizophrenia," Karen interrupted shortly. "Just tell me how the Fregoli delusions work."

"Sorry. I do tend to get into lecture mode quite easily. The point I was making is that we don't have a solid understanding of Fregoli syndrome as a whole, because there are still so few cases, and we can't say definitively what causes it. If we understood its origins we could probably better predict a patient's behavior and how to treat it. In a low percentage of cases, the patient had some other drastic condition such as Alzheimer's dementia, epilepsy, or a stroke, but not in most. Brain scans have shown some kind of atrophy or damage in perhaps half the known cases, often on the right side of the brain, but not in others. The only consistent factor we can point to right now is an underlying psychosis. In Brett's case, he has already been diagnosed as a paranoid schizophrenic, as I've said, and he's being treated as such, which is how it works with Fregoli subjects. We treat the underlying disorder and it seems to keep the Fregoli symptoms under control."

"So he's on meds for schizophrenia and that controls this other thing."

"Correct. But like most psychotic symptoms, his Fregoli-related delusions come and go. If he skipped his medication that would likely trigger a recurrence of the symptoms, which I understand happened on a regular basis when he was away at school. But he assures me he's very conscientious now about following his regimen, and Mona confirms it."

Karen chewed on the inside of her cheek for a moment. "Here's the thing. Brett Parris says he saw Richard Holland running away from our crime scene moments after Jarrett was shot. I know damned well the state's attorney can't use him as a witness because he'd get torn to shreds on the stand by the defense because he's a schizophrenic with all this other bizarre stuff going on. Everybody tells me he's just blowing smoke when he says it was Holland he saw and that I should ignore it, but I look into the guy's eyes and I listen to the sound of his voice when he tells me it was Holland, and I believe him, damn it. I think he's telling the truth. I mean, I think that's really who he saw. So here's my question. Could you tell last night whether he was telling the truth or whether it was another one of these Fregoli delusions?"

Caldwell shook her head. "Not to any degree of certainty that would be useful to you in your investigation. Generally speaking, these patients are absolutely convinced by their delusion and can appear completely truthful. I've examined Brett several times under such conditions and it's remarkable how certain he is."

Hiding her disappointment, Karen took out a business card, put it on the table, and stood up. "If you think of anything else you think I need to know, I'd appreciate if you'd call me. My cell number's there. I can be reached twenty-four seven."

"I can't make any promises."

"Sure." Halfway to the door, Karen stopped and turned around. "Let me ask you something else. Has Brett Parris ever shown any signs of being violent, or talked about wanting to kill someone?"

"Not at all," replied Caldwell. "You may be laboring under the false belief that paranoid schizophrenics are intrinsically violent. If anything, they mostly want to be left alone, which is very true in Brett's case. If you're thinking that he might have killed Mr. Jarrett, I'd tell you you're wasting your time. It's not in him. Not under *any* circumstances."

"All right." Karen reached the door and turned around again. "There's a girl out in the waiting room. I'm guessing she's your next patient."

Caldwell said nothing, looking at her.

"She showed a real interest in this when I put away my badge." Karen moved her jacket to show her gun. "I'm no psychiatrist, but that sort of thing kinda jumps out at me. I thought you might be interested."

"Thank you, Detective," Caldwell said coolly.

Karen stared back. "You're welcome."

13

Hank's phone went directly to voice mail when Karen called. As she left him a message explaining her next steps, Karen remembered he was attending the Jarrett autopsy. One of Easton's firm rules was that everyone attending a procedure in his Little Kingdom must turn off their electronic devices before approaching The Presence or suffer the consequences, up to and including permanent banishment. It was one of the very few times Karen could think of when Hank was not reachable by phone.

Traffic on the main artery from Midtown to Granger Park was fairly heavy, so she obeyed the posted speed limits through necessity rather than by choice. It was already two o'clock in the afternoon, as a result, when she pulled up in front of the big iron gate and got out to punch the button on the intercom box.

"Parris residence," a female voice responded.

"Detective Stainer, GPD. Here to see Brett Parris."

"Thank you, Detective Stainer. One moment please."

Damned polite, for sure. She wondered whether or not it was a computer-generated voice. Could an actual person sound that inhumanly friendly? She stared through the bars of the wrought-iron gate at the mansion at the end of the long, looping driveway. Christ, these people lived well. A minute dragged along. She examined the gate and wondered whether she could shoot her way in if she had to, but it was obviously electronic and she wasn't sure where to put her bullet.

"Detective, this is Walter Parris," the intercom finally spat. "May I ask the nature of your business with Brett?"

"Yeah, howdy, Mr. Parris. Just wanted a quick chat with him. Is he home?"

"He is, but perhaps it's something I could help you with instead."

Jesus fucking *Christ*. "Just a few easy questions, Mr. Parris. Nothing to worry about. Nothing I need a warrant for, or whatever." She made an effort to swallow her frustration. "Look, believe it or not,

I'm on his side. I just came from his shrink, Dr. Caldwell, and she filled me in on stuff. I don't want to upset him, just confirm a few things."

One steamboat, two steamboats, three steamboats—

The gate clicked softly and popped open. "Please close the gate behind you before you drive up, Detective."

"Okey doke, Mr. Parris," she drawled, hoping it would grate on his nerves. "I'm beholdin' to yuh."

The front door of the mansion opened as she walked up the front steps. A woman in a maid's uniform smiled as Karen stepped into the front hallway. "Mr. Parris is waiting through the first door on your right, Detective."

Damned if she wasn't an actual human being, after all.

Walter Parris gestured her to a chair. "If you don't mind waiting, Detective, Brett is busy at the moment. It's a regular appointment, but he should be finished in a few minutes."

"His APRN? Mona Jensen?"

"Yes. I assume Dr. Caldwell filled you in on his home care program."

"She mentioned it." Karen sat down and crossed her legs, running a hand over her thigh. Her dark blue jeans were nearly new and spotless but these people, damn them, made her feel like she spent all her time pushing a shopping cart piled high with dumpster pickings. "How's he been lately? The last few weeks, I mean."

"I'm not sure how to answer that question," Walter replied, not trying to hide his irritation. "He's schizophrenic. One of the principles by which schizophrenics live their lives is that there'll be ups and downs, and there's no step-by-step process to recovery. Tomorrow might be a good day or it might be a bad day. If it's a good day, he tries to build on it. If it's a bad day, he tries to learn something from it. You say you're on his side. You could start by not making foolish assumptions or over-simplifying his condition."

"I'm not making any assumptions," Karen grated, "I'm just asking how he's been doing lately. Jesus. How about his ratio of good to bad days over the last two weeks, then? Think you could answer my question that way? Fifty-fifty? Sixty-forty? Seventy-thirty?"

A noise in the doorway behind Karen drew Walter's attention. "All done, Mona?"

Karen stood up and turned around. Mona Jensen was a middle-aged woman with short, mousy hair, broad, flat cheekbones, and brown eyes. She was about three inches taller than Karen and fifty pounds heavier. She wore a white long-sleeved blouse, knee-length navy skirt, and thick black shoes. Karen thought she looked like a school cafeteria cook the kids would suspect of serving boiled children for lunch. Karen held out her hand.

"I'm Detective Karen Stainer, GPD. You're Mona Jensen, I take it? Brett's APRN?"

"Yes, I am." Jensen shifted a black briefcase to shake hands with Karen. Her grip was firm, but her voice was surprisingly gentle and soft. She glanced over Karen's shoulder at Walter.

"Detective Stainer's investigating Mr. Jarrett's death. She wants to ask Brett more questions, but I really don't see—"

"Brett's a witness in a homicide investigation," Karen said to Jensen, cutting Walter off, "and we routinely have follow-up questions for witnesses as an investigation moves along. Nothing that should upset him. How's he doing today?"

Jensen said nothing, looking again over Karen's shoulder at Walter.

Karen moved out from between the two of them. She threw Walter a look, hands on her hips, and said to Jensen, "I asked a simple question, and all I need is a simple answer. How's he *feeling* today?"

Jensen's eyes flicked from Walter to Karen. "I'm not at liberty to have this kind of conversation with you, Officer."

"It's Detective. Okay? Not Officer. Detective. Stainer. You're not at liberty. Sure. No problem. We covered the disclosure thing with Caldwell, and I talked to her before I came here. How about we cover that off with you right now and get on to the part where you cooperate with the police in a murder investigation."

Jensen looked once more at Walter, who hesitated.

"Christ almighty, Parris," Karen snarled, "if it's okay with his shrink why in hell wouldn't it be okay with his nurse? I'm not going to strap him to a fucking rack and torture him, for chrissakes, we're just going to have a little conversation. How about we move this fucking thing along a bit?"

"I'll thank you to remember you're in my home on my sufferance," Walter replied. "Belligerence and foul language certainly won't help your cause." He looked at Jensen. "Answer her questions. Within reason."

"Only if Brett's willing," Jensen said. "Wouldn't you think?"

"Let's go ask him," Karen said, heading for the door. "Where's he at?"

"In his rooms," Walter said. "Mona, show her the way."

Karen and Jensen trudged side by side up the wide staircase.

"You got this gig on a referral from Caldwell, correct?"

"Yes." At the top of the stairs Jensen gestured to the left. "Down here."

At the end of the hallway they stopped at a closed door. Jensen raised a hand to knock.

"Just a second," Karen said. "I can do the knocking and talking."

"I'd like to be present."

"Sure enough, no problem. Just don't try to answer questions for him, understand?"

"Of course. I wouldn't dream of it."

Karen looked at her for a long moment. Then she rapped sharply on the door with her knuckle.

"Brett? It's Detective Karen Stainer, with Mona Jensen. Can we come in and talk for a few minutes?"

Silence. Then a faint voice: "Just a minute."

They waited for several moments.

The door opened. Brett Parris looked out through the crack. "Oh, hello. What are you doing here?" His eyes were focused on her chest, but Karen didn't take offense, as she might have otherwise, because she understood it was an eye contact problem typical of schizophrenics.

"I came to see how you're doing, champ. And I brought something for you to look at, if you don't mind. Is it okay if we come in and I ask you a couple of things?"

"Do I have to?"

"No, you don't have to, of course not. It's up to you. I've got a couple of pics to show you, though, if you're interested. I took them myself with my phone. I want you to tell me what you think."

"Okay." He opened the door and looked at Jensen. "Are you coming in, too?"

"Yes, if it's okay, Brett. I was just about to leave, but the detective thought I might want to tag along, so here I am again."

He stepped back and waved them both in. Karen walked into a small sitting room with two doors on the facing wall and another door on the right. The furniture was less pretentious than downstairs, older and more comfortable. There were several framed color photographs on the walls, including a nice picture of sunflowers, another of a sewer drain with oil-tinted water flowing into it, and a sunset between office towers.

"Nice," she nodded at the photographs. "Did you take them?"

"Yes."

"I like them. Good stuff."

"Thanks." He pointed at the door on Karen's right. "The bathroom's there, if you need to use it."

"I'm fine, thanks."

"Okay." He stood there awkwardly, waiting for her to explain what she wanted from him. He was tall and thin. His wavy brown hair was a little tousled, as though he'd been running a hand through it. His face was long and bony, his complexion was very pale, and his forehead was creased in a slight frown. His gold-framed glasses sat halfway down his thin, pointed nose. He wore a pale yellow shirt under a red sleeveless sweater, khakis, and moccasins. The sleeves of his shirt were turned up on his forearms, which were slightly freckled and covered with brown hair.

"I thought this would be your bedroom," Karen said, looking around the room. "Do you have a bunch of rooms up here?"

"Yes." He pointed at one of the doors behind him. "That's my studio. It has the best light in the house." He pointed at the other door. "My bedroom's there. I have a whole little suite here. Everything except a kitchen, since the kitchen's downstairs. Obviously. But she knows that. Something else to say instead." He glanced toward Jensen. "Sorry."

"That's all right, Brett," Jensen said lightly. "Let's sit down for a minute."

She lowered herself into a blue swivel armchair, settling her briefcase against her calf. Brett perched on the end of the couch closest to her. Karen thought it was probably their usual seating arrangement. She hoped it wouldn't affect her ability to steer the conversation where she needed it to go. Sitting on the couch with Brett was out of the question, so she chose a chair across from him, on the other side of a coffee table littered with magazines and photo prints. She sat down, sliding forward onto the edge of the cushion.

"How are you feeling today, Brett? Better?"

"I'm good, thanks."

96

"That's great. Terrific. I won't keep you. I know we went back and forth yesterday on what happened, and I really appreciate your help. I know you told us everything you could think of then, but I just wondered if you might remember something else today, after getting a good night's sleep, and all. Did you think of anything else?"

"I thought about it a lot," Brett said to his hands, which were clasped tightly in his lap.

"Yeah." The corners of Karen's mouth moved very slightly as she thought of similar conversations with her mother. At the crime scene yesterday she'd leaned on him very heavily and had verbally roughed him up, not knowing any better. He'd pissed her off with what she'd thought at the time was faked dopiness, and she'd been a little slow to pick up on his condition. After the sidebar with Walter in Hank's office, she'd shifted gears and asked her questions differently. He'd been upset, though, and Walter and their lawyer were very defensive, so the interview hadn't gotten as far as she'd wished. She wanted another crack at that brain of his, dysfunctional and unpredictable as it was, and although she'd never shown her mother an ounce of patience, she needed to show it now to this guy.

"I've thought a lot about it, too." She slid back in her chair and crossed her legs, resting her hands lightly on her knee, then remembered the change in body language would likely be lost on him, as it was with many schizophrenics. What the hell, Jensen might pick up on it and be that much less likely to feel over-protective of her client.

"I wonder if you'd mind describing to me, one more time, what happened. It might help me figure out a few things. I imagine you already told Mona about it. She probably said that talking it through would help you deal with it and learn from it."

"Yes, that's right." He sounded a little surprised.

"I'm the same way. It's part of my job, actually. Talking about something several times is important with a cop because sometimes small details come out that didn't come out the first time. If you describe to me all over again what happened, you might think of something new. It could help."

"Okay." He closed his eyes. "I heard the shot. You want me to start there?"

"Sure."

"I heard the shot. It was like a pop. I guess maybe it sounded weird—no, different—and I wanted to see what it was. It sounded like a balloon breaking. So I walked over there. Richard ran by me with a gun in his hand. I took his picture. Three frames. He saw me and stopped. He said, 'What the fuck are you doing?' and ran up to me. He grabbed the camera out of my hand before I could move. Then he kind of put his leg behind me and knocked me down. He pointed the gun at my face and moved it like he was shooting me. Pantomimed it. Then he ran across the lawn and got in his car and drove away."

A gun in his hand. Karen took a deep breath. Something new, that he hadn't mentioned before. "What did the gun look like, Brett?"

"I don't know. Like a gun. I don't know anything about them, so that's all. It looked like a gun. Sorry."

"That's okay, not a problem." Karen unholstered her gun and held it flat on her palm, muzzle pointing away. "Can I show you something?"

"Okay." He opened his eyes.

"Did it look like this?"

He frowned. "Sorry. No. Not like that."

"Okay, no problem. Just a sec." She put away her SIG, took out her cell phone, launched the browser, and ran a quick Google search. "Here." She reached across the coffee table and put the phone down in front of him. "Did it look like that?"

He picked up the phone, looked at the photo she'd selected, and shook his head. "No." He put it back down on the coffee table.

"Okay." She picked up the phone and looked at the photo, which was of a Smith and Wesson M66 revolver. "Between the two of them, which one was it more like?"

"It wasn't a revolver," Brett said, "because it didn't have a cylinder. It was the other kind, with a magazine. What do you call that? An automatic?"

Karen grinned. "Sorry, champ. My bad. Feel free to kick my ass any time. Figuratively speaking. So it was a semi-automatic but it didn't look like my SIG. Bigger? Smaller? Different color?"

"I don't remember. Sorry. It looked like a starter's pistol or a target pistol, I guess. Brown."

"A brown target pistol." The grin went away. "Hmm. Interesting. Anything else you can tell me about it?"

"No."

"Okay. But that's good. That's very good. I like it." She worked with the phone again. "Can I show you my pics now?"

"All right."

"Great." She put the phone back down on the coffee table. "I took those yesterday. They're in a table, six in all, but you can look up close at each one. Go ahead and check them out. They're six different pictures of cars. I want you to tell me if any of them look like the car you saw leave the scene yesterday at the bike path."

"Richard's car, you mean." Brett picked up the phone.

"Well, let's not put a name to it just now. Look at the cars and tell me if you saw one of them yesterday at the bike path when Mr. Jarrett was shot."

He took a moment studying the photos. "My memory's not the best. I do exercises with Mona that help, but it's still not very good." He shook his head. "Not this first one. It wasn't a red Corvette." He moved his finger on the touch screen. "Not this one, it's silver but it's too small. And this one's gray." His eyes lifted toward Jensen. "Last night, didn't I say it was silver? Or did I say it was gray? No, it was silver."

"Take your time," Karen said, trying to hide her disappointment.

He thumbed to the fourth photo. "This silver sports car. It's Richard's car. I don't know what kind it is." He looked at Karen, making eye contact very briefly, as though by accident. "I saw him get into this car yesterday and drive away after shooting Mr. Jarrett." His eyes returned to the phone. "It's his car. This is the one I saw."

"There's two more," Karen said. "Take a look at them."

"Okay." He looked. "No, this is black. A nice car. A friend of mine has one like that." His fingers moved. "No, this is white." He put the phone down on the coffee table. "Sorry. It was that other one, the silver one. What kind is it? It looks expensive."

"It's a Ferrari," Karen said, retrieving her phone. "Costs a freaking fortune." She turned it off and slipped it into her jacket pocket. "How come you know what car Richard Holland has?"

"I've seen it before."

"When?"

"Around."

She'd pretty much beaten this horse to death, she decided. "Brett, when you found Mr. Jarrett, did you touch him at all?"

"No."

"You didn't maybe try to see if he was still alive, or try to move him?"

"No, he was dead. His eyes were open and staring. He was dead. I didn't touch him."

"But you took pictures of him with your cell phone."

"I thought I should, in case somebody needed them to prove afterwards he was dead right then. By the time stamp."

"Okay." Karen stood up. "Thanks for your help. I really appreciate it."

"You're welcome."

She started for the door and turned back. "Oh, one other thing. Could you do me a favor?"

"Okay."

"I'd like to ask Mona here a few questions about your memory and stuff. I'd like to get her take on how you're doing, but she needs your permission to answer my questions because it's your private information. I need to know about your schizophrenia and your Fregoli syndrome stuff, how you're treating it, and how it's going. That kind of thing. You remember we went through this yesterday and you gave us permission to talk to Dr. Caldwell. Can you give me the same permission to talk to Mona about it now?"

He stood next to Jensen, looking down at her. "I don't think it's a problem. Do you think it's okay?"

"It's your decision, Brett," Jensen said.

He turned back to Karen. "Sure, it's okay."

"You're sure."

"Yes."

"Okay." She took out a business card and put it down on a little table just inside the door. "That's my card. Call me anytime if there's anything else you want to talk about."

"Thank you."

"No problem, champ. See you later."

Karen and Jensen left the house and walked across the driveway to a small patio with an arrangement of white cast iron lawn furniture beneath a blue and white sun umbrella. Karen had expected to be accosted either by Walter Parris or by Brett's mother, Lisa Gregg Parris, whom she hadn't yet met, but they'd seen no one but the animatronic maid who'd politely opened the front door for them on their way out.

As if reading her thoughts, Jensen smiled as she sat down in a chair. "They're all getting ready for a fundraising event downtown tonight. That's one reason why Mr. Parris was a little stressed. Mrs.

Parris doesn't do very well at those sorts of things, and he's very protective of her as well as of Brett. You caught him on a bad day."

"A bad week." Karen sat down across from her. She remembered Hank promising his mother he would attend some bash or other tonight, and she wondered if it was the same thing. "The life of the rich and famous."

Jensen reached into her black briefcase and took out a pack of cigarettes. "Do you mind?"

"No, go right ahead."

Jensen lit a cigarette, inhaling deeply and exhaling slowly. "What can I tell you about Brett?"

"Well, a bunch of stuff, but let's start with what you do. Caldwell didn't tell me any of the details, but let me guess. As his APRN you're probably more hands-on with him than she is. You've probably developed a whole program for him, and you probably do all the day-to-day work with him on it."

"Yes, that's right. How much do you know about schizophrenia, Detective Stainer?"

"My mother's been living in an institution in Texas with it since I was twelve. I know a helluva lot more about it than I want to, believe me."

"I see." Jensen exhaled another long stream of smoke. "Is she a paranoid schizophrenic?"

"Disorganized. With some hallucinations and delusions, now and then, but disorganized, not paranoid like Brett."

"That's also a very difficult subtype. Well, with Brett, as you'd expect, his treatment includes both medication and therapy. On the meds side, I administer them twice a day, to make sure he takes them, and I monitor for side effects. Anti-psychotics can have some particularly nasty ones, so I watch for those. I also do regular blood and urine tests for alcohol, drugs, and nutrition, I monitor his personal hygiene, his sleep patterns, and the like. On the therapy side, I do things a little differently than your average bear."

"I'm all ears."

"Good. A typical cop would be bored to tears right now. Your experience with your mother has had benefits for you that maybe you haven't completely realized."

Karen bit her tongue.

"Which is a segue into the type of therapy I'm using with Brett.

Have you heard of positive psychology?"

"No." It sounded to her like a contradiction in terms.

"I'm working on my Ph.D. right now, and that's my area of specialization. Positive psychology. It's rooted in the theories and practices of Carl Rogers and Eric Fromm, taking a humanistic view of happiness and well-being. It's a psychology of positive human functioning that tries to nurture talent and make life more fulfilling. It doesn't replace traditional approaches, and on that note I should mention that Brett sees Dr. Caldwell once a month for an hour of psychoanalysis, and he sees me once a week in my office for an hour of therapy based on Carl Rogers's client-centered therapy, where I practice active listening with him. It encourages him to verbalize his thoughts and feelings. I thought he actually did very well with you."

She removed a small red pocket ashtray from her skirt, opened the lid, and tapped ash from her cigarette. "In our daily interactions, Brett and I concentrate on techniques related directly to positive psychology. You're likely aware that flattened affect is common among schizophrenic patients, and you could see that Brett doesn't show a lot of emotional range, but he's had problems with depression. What I'm trying to do is train him to recognize things he can do that give him pleasure, to spend his time doing those things, and so increase his overall level of happiness. It sounds simple enough but it actually isn't, not even for someone like you or me, so imagine how important it might be to someone like Brett.

"I borrowed a technique from Mihaly Csikszentmihalyi, who developed the concept of flow. His idea was that people are the most happy when they're in a state of flow, when they're completely absorbed in something they're doing. Maybe painting a picture, playing music, writing a book, whatever, a person becomes so involved that the world seems to disappear, time passes without them being aware of it, and all their cares and problems slip away."

She smiled. "So the idea is to be able to have periods of time in your day when you can do something that lifts you into this flow state, the overall effect being to increase your level of happiness for that day, and every day, really."

She put the cigarette into the corner of her mouth and squinted at Karen through the smoke. "The technique I borrowed charts the patient's emotional states at various times during the day. They wear something called a flow timer. For Brett it was a simple Casio sports watch with five different alarm settings. I programmed the alarm in the morning to vibrate at five random times during the day. He carried a notebook in his pocket, and when the alarm went off he wrote down what he was doing and how he felt. Basic experience sampling. The next morning I'd set it to different times and he'd do it again."

"I'm sure that went well," Karen said.

Jensen exhaled smoke and laughed. "It drove him nuts, but he tries very hard to cooperate. He did his best. We ran it for two weeks, then stopped for a week. I started it up again, hoping for another week's worth of data, but he quit on me after a day. He said it was so intrusive it was making him unhappy, which is not an outcome we want, so I let it go at that. I'm still analyzing the data, but I've already identified a few things to use."

"Like what?"

"Well, for example, his photography. He works at it as a freelance professional, but he also takes pictures out of interest, for his own enjoyment. It's a good way for him to start his day. He's an early riser—sleep patterns are another challenge—so he goes for a walk early in the morning and takes his camera with him. It's not only for the exercise, then, but also to take pictures. Sometimes he does serious work, and sometimes he just plays with it."

"Okay. I get it." Karen shifted. "You saw him later in the day, after we sent him home."

"In the evening."

"How was he?"

"Very upset, naturally."

"So he told you what happened? Finding Jarrett? Seeing Holland run away from the scene?"

"Yes."

"He told you Holland knocked him down and took his camera?"

"Yes."

"Did he mention the gun to you?"

"No. Maybe because he was still so upset."

"Have you seen him before when he's had one of these Fregoli delusions?"

"Yes, I have."

"Was this another one of them?"

Jensen grimaced and stubbed out her cigarette in the little red pocket ashtray. "I can't say for sure. It's—"

"Before, though, you could tell for sure?"

"Yes. He thought his father was Richard Holland."

"Okay. Tell me about that one."

"I was with him at the time." Jensen put the ashtray back in her pocket. "We were in the middle of something, I forget what, nothing important, and Mr. Parris came into the room. In itself, that's not unusual. Unless I say otherwise beforehand, it's understood our sessions here at the house are interruptible. This time, though, Brett became extremely upset and insisted his father was Holland."

"How upset? To the point that he had to be sedated?"

"Unfortunately. He threw a few things around the room, was yelling, and was very angry that I didn't believe him when he said his father was Richard Holland. I was able to calm him enough to convince him to take the sedative, but he was so close to the edge I had no other choice. Otherwise it would have been necessary to hospitalize him, which has happened in the past."

"So it sounds like he was different yesterday."

"Yes, I suppose you could say that. I know you're trying to establish whether or not he was delusional yesterday when he said he saw Richard Holland running away, but it's just not possible with any degree of confidence. According to his file, there've been other times when he wasn't upset enough to need hospitalization or even sedation, although he was clearly in the grip of a Fregoli delusion. The problem with all of this is that it's an extremely rare condition. There have been so few cases, there's not enough data to make generalizations. We can't point to a set of definitive behaviors that will tell us yes, this is a Fregoli delusion, the way we can with paranoid schizophrenia or other well-known conditions. In the other incidents with Brett we have on record, someone was with him who was able to say that the person Brett identified as Richard Holland was in fact not Holland. Yesterday morning, he was alone. So, basically, it's impossible to say who he actually saw."

"Crap." Karen felt her frustration mount. "His old man's convinced he was delusional."

"He's not a trained psychologist," Jensen said, "but on the other hand, he has a great deal of practical experience with his son. I'd be inclined to believe him."

Karen compressed her lips, frustrated. "All right. He was able to tell me what car he saw, from the photo array I showed him on my phone, and identify it as Holland's car. Can I at least rely on that?"

"I'm sorry." Jensen shook her head. "Again, it's impossible to say for sure. Brett's memory isn't very good. It goes with the territory, as I probably don't need to tell you as someone familiar with schizophrenia. Did he pick the car that actually does belong to Richard Holland?"

"He sure as fuck did." Karen stood up. "I gotta ask. Does this Fregoli thing include objects and the like, or just people? Could he look at an antique Studebaker, for example, and say it's a Ferrari?"

"Not that I'm aware of. I haven't noticed it in him so far."

"Well that's one little shred of sunlight, anyway."

Jensen stood up, smoothed her skirt, and cocked her head at Karen. "You know, positive psychology can provide some very effective life coaching for professionals like you. I could recommend a few books on the subject."

"I'm not much of a book reader," Karen replied. "Thanks for your cooperation." She stalked across the lawn on a straight line toward the Crown Vic, and didn't look back.

14

That evening, Hank and Meredith arrived at the Edward C. Barton Art Gallery in his mother's smaller Mercedes. Their driver was Danny, the son of Anna's full-time driver, Earl Day. Danny was a student at State and his major was criminal justice. He was about to begin his junior year. During the drive he peppered Hank with questions about the professors and the courses. Hank answered patiently through Danny's constant interruptions of his conversation with Meredith, who smiled out the window.

They arrived just after 7:00 P.M. and walked together up the wide staircase to the art gallery while the media behind the velvet ropes on either side took their photograph.

Meredith grinned. "I feel like a Hollywood celebrity."

"You look like one," Hank smiled back. She was lovely in a full-length black Dolce & Gabbana evening gown with gold and bronze details and a black bow at the back. In the Mercedes she'd whispered to him, between Danny's questions, that she'd bought it in a second-hand shop in Paris several years ago at a fraction of its original price. Now, as they left the head of the stairs and followed the corridor to the doorway leading into the reception, he watched her move in it and could have sworn it had been made for her. In two weeks she would turn forty-seven years old, but she bounced alongside him now as though she were twenty years younger, her blond hair moving lightly on her shoulders.

The VIP reception had already taken place and the cocktail reception was now underway in the loft, an event space on the second level of the gallery that overlooked the atrium, where dinner would be served in an hour. They joined the crowd and circulated for a few minutes before Hank went over to the bar, coming back with a Rob Roy for her and a Maker's Mark on the rocks for himself.

She was talking to a woman he didn't know, and for no particular reason he decided to stand behind her for a moment. He looked at a lock of honey-colored hair resting lightly on her shoulder, just behind the strap of her dress. The dress was low-cut in back and her hair reached down mid-point on each shoulder blade, but for some reason his eyes, after noticing the light freckles on her skin, settled on this particular lock of hair. He could see how lightly it lay on her skin, so lightly that she probably couldn't feel it.

Involuntarily he thought about the look on Perry's face this afternoon as he struggled to make sense of what was happening to the body of his former friend in Jim Easton's autopsy theater.

I don't know how you do it. Why *you do it.*

Meredith sensed him behind her and turned. He handed her the Rob Roy and smiled.

They found Anna and Roberts in the crowd. Hank performed the introductions. After a few minutes Anna suggested they go down into the atrium early, to avoid the rush. Meredith thought that was fine, as she and Hank had already met the VIPs, including state Senator Bernard Brickland, Congressman Peter Quick, Mayor Darrien Watts, Mary Strong Ferguson, the president of State University, Bill Keating, head coach of the Baltimore Ravens, and Judge Janet Falcone, chief judge of the state court of appeals.

As they found their table and sat down, Hank glanced at his watch and saw that it was still fifteen minutes before eight o'clock. Roberts began to talk about a contract he'd just completed in Costa Rica. Hank listened politely. He liked Roberts. Despite his age, Roberts was still very active and enjoyed a very good reputation in his field. Costa Rica had no army per se, Roberts explained, but they did have a small special forces unit attached to their intelligence area. He'd gone in to help set up a training program and had been impressed with the people he'd met.

Roberts was small, barely five feet eight inches tall, and he was as bald as a cucumber, with a prominent Roman nose and thick lips. As an army general he'd been known for his strict sense of discipline and unsympathetic disposition, but with Anna he was always polite, quiet, and deferential. He had an apartment downtown and was often out of the country, but he and Anna went out together when he was home, and he spent most of his evenings with her, watching CNN or just reading material in preparation for his next contract. He was an ideal companion for Anna in that he made no demands of her and was good company.

While Roberts distracted Hank, Anna subjected Meredith to a brief but intense interrogation, showing the talent for questioning that had been her hallmark as a state's attorney. Meredith smiled throughout, unperturbed.

Trying to follow their conversation as well as pay attention to Roberts, Hank could tell that Anna had already done her homework and was following the ancient precept of all attorneys that one should never ask a question for which one does not already know the answer. She merely wanted to listen to Meredith's responses and make her judgments based on what information Meredith chose to include or omit.

Once the preliminaries were disposed of and Anna had apparently made her decision on Meredith's worthiness as a companion for her son, she got down to the business of passing on what she felt Meredith would need to know about Hank. Roberts continued to keep Hank occupied enough that he was unable to head it off. At first he thought Meredith might not understand Anna's intentions, but very soon he could tell from their body language that both women were enjoying his discomfort. Since there was nothing he could do about it, he sat there and took it.

"He was a wonderful boy," Anna said, easing back in her seat. "He was the baby of the family and had such a perfect disposition as a child. Lord knows I was entitled to have at least one easy one. The others were a bit of a chore, each in their own way."

"All children are," Meredith said, diplomatically.

"My oldest, Thomas, has had an especially difficult time." She sipped at her drink. "He's a very talented musician. A pianist. He doesn't speak to any of us anymore."

"I'm very sorry to hear that." Meredith glanced at Hank, who said nothing.

"I don't blame him at all," Anna went on. "It was his decision to make a clean break with us, and I respect that. There was a lot of fighting, and he felt very isolated. He's a heroin addict, and we really didn't understand his point of view, I'm afraid. He had a difficult time in Vietnam and when he returned with the addiction, we were very upset. *I* was upset. Hank was the wisest of all; he stayed out of it completely. I wish I had."

"Hank," Roberts said suddenly, "did I tell you about the fellow I met once in Argentina who could throw a hand grenade the entire length of a soccer pitch?"

"No, you didn't," Hank lied, fatalistically.

"I daresay," Anna went on, "as intelligent as the others all are, Hank's by far the brightest. As a child, he found schoolwork so easy they skipped him twice, from Grade One to Grade Three, and again from Four to Six. He knew his fractions before most of the other children in his class could spell words of more than one syllable."

"Mother," Hank managed, clipping off the end of one of Roberts's sentences, "Meredith's not interested in ancient history."

"No, it's all right," Meredith said. "I don't mind. It's very interesting."

"He *is* interesting, isn't he?" Anna said, tilting her head to study him with bright eyes. "Imagine him being two years younger than the other boys in his class and still smarter than any of them. For a while, they picked on him. But Henry, that's what I always called him when he was a boy, was big for his age—which he gets from his father—and he was quite athletic, like Robert Junior, so the fights didn't last very long. I had to make a couple of trips to the principal's office to straighten things out, so they'd realize he was only defending himself. They were basing their judgments on the outcome alone, and they thought he was the aggressor."

"Imagine!" Meredith said.

"But after that, things settled into a very nice routine for him. He made friends, played basketball and baseball, and had a summer job caddying at Woodfern. Before you knew it, he'd breezed through high school and was about to enroll in State as a fifteen-year-old freshman."

"Well," Meredith said.

"He's very much like his father was," Anna went on, "tall, shaggy, well-meaning, and very, very bright. Bob and I met on opposite sides of the court room. I was the first female assistant state's attorney here and Bob was a criminal defense attorney. He was from Alliance, Ohio, and you could hear that flat Midwestern twang in his voice right up to the day he died. He was defending a man accused of murdering his mistress and her young son. I liked our case, and I still do to this day, because we had overwhelming circumstantial evidence, but Bob handed me my rear end on a plate. We married four months later."

Meredith smiled, clearly enjoying herself.

"My father," Anna continued, "Charles Goodwin Haynes, was governor of this fair state and my grandfather, Edward Willis Haynes, had the honor of serving as chief judge of the court of appeal.

Bob's father, on the other hand, was a small-town physician in Ohio and his grandfather was a watchmaker. Honorable professions, and completely indispensable to the community in which they lived, but quite a different philosophy of life, if you will. The Donaghues took their status and influence entirely for granted, and I daresay felt a little self-conscious about it, whereas we Hayneses *never* take power and influence for granted. It takes generations to establish and can be lost overnight."

Listening, Hank remembered a baseball game he and his father had attended the summer before he entered college. As they ate hot dogs and drank sodas in the stands, his father said, "Some day you and I will make a trip to Alliance so you can see the other half."

"We could take the Amtrak," Hank said, anxious to show his father that he knew something about the place. "We could fly into Cleveland and go from there."

"We could do that," his father replied. "I'll show you where my grand-dad had his shop. It's a jewelry store now, according to your Aunt Betty. I remember spending Saturday afternoons in the back room with him, just the two of us, watching him work, listening to him tell stories about the old days. I never saw so many pocket watches in my entire life. He had big cabinets filled with movements, watch faces, empty cases, you name it."

"Wow," Hank said.

"Yeah." His father smiled. "I probably mentioned before, the house I grew up in is a bed and breakfast now. My father ran his practice out of rooms at the back. My bedroom was on the third floor, above the rear entrance. Sometimes the patients came around in the middle of the night. I could hear them opening and closing the door."

"We could stay there when we go," Hank suggested.

His father shook his head. "I'd rather stay at a motel and just drive by for a look."

"It would seem strange," Hank ventured, "staying in your old house with a bunch of strangers."

"That's right." His father took a bite of hot dog and chewed. "It's a pretty small town. Just over twenty thousand altogether. It was smaller than that when I was growing up. We didn't have a lot of money, even though Dad was a doctor. Back then, people couldn't always pay their bills, and Dad would take other forms of payment. A fifty-pound bag of potatoes, a barrel of apples, and one time a man repaired our roof to repay him for attending to the birth of his daughter. His wife had complications, and Dad spent almost two days with her, pulling her through.

"Now, Grandfather Haynes was a fine man, make no mistake, but he spent his career building much different relationships than my father did. It can't help but affect your outlook on life when the cement that holds your relationships together is a mixture of politics and money, rather than compassion and empathy. Trust and respect were much more fundamental emotions at my father's level than they are in the board room."

He frowned at Hank. "I'm not making value judgments here, you understand that, right? I'm not saying that the Donaghues are better people than the Hayneses or that our value system is better or anything like that, at all."

He paused as they watched a batter hit a fly ball to right field for the second out of the inning. "I'm just saying, you have to take everything into account when you decide how to conduct yourself in life. It's not always just money and power. You're the richest fifteen-year-old I've ever known, but life is more than just a number printed in a bank book. I've tried to explain that to Robbie, but I don't think he gets it. He thinks I'm a damned bleeding-heart liberal."

Hank nodded, having heard his brother call their father that on more than one occasion. It was something he'd picked up from their mother.

"Anyway," his father grinned, "I'll take you back to the Midwest, some day soon. We have to work on that awful Maryland accent of yours."

It was a promise his father would not live to keep: he passed away from a heart attack when Hank was a sophomore at State.

Anna was now covering Hank's university years, in which he'd completed a bachelor's degree and a master's in the criminology and criminal justice program she'd had a hand in developing as a member of State's board of trustees.

"Then after he finished his law degree and passed the bar exam—as a twenty-two-year-old, I might add—he worked for a year as an ASA under Will Ingletz." She looked up as Mary Strong Ferguson and her husband Jack took their seats across the table. "I was retired by then."

Meredith looked at Hank. "But how did you go from that to

MICHAEL J. McCANN

becoming a policeman?"

Hank said, "It's a long story."

Anna leaned over and touched Meredith on the forearm. "I didn't agree with the decision at all, at the time. I'm afraid we argued rather bitterly about it. It's the only time I ever remember us disagreeing. It took me quite a long time to understand, which is a reflection on me and not him, but Hank has proven his point rather well, I'd say, over the course of his career."

"He's a very good detective," Meredith said.

"He's the best investigator the department's ever seen," Anna replied firmly.

"You looked good on television yesterday morning," Mary Strong Ferguson said, scooting her chair forward. "Much better than your chief in the afternoon, that's for sure."

"Thanks," Hank said.

"You've certainly got your work cut out for you," Jack Ferguson offered. "Any suspects yet?"

"We're working very hard, believe me."

"Mary," Roberts interjected, leaning across the table, "when's that damned football team of yours going to start winning games?"

"It's a tough division," Mary replied, "and we can't offer as many scholarships as some of the larger schools."

"Sounds like an excuse to me."

"Not at all, merely an explanation."

Hank caught Meredith's eye. She leaned back in her seat and smiled a knowing, familiar smile that surprised him a little.

"When are we going to eat?" Anna chirped. "I'm starved."

15

After dinner Anna excused herself to step outside with Roberts for her usual post-prandial cigar. It was her way of avoiding the speeches and the presentations of oversized novelty checks orchestrated by Constance Mercer Parris and her chief aide, Theona Sherman, the administrator of Mercer House.

Mrs. Sherman spoke movingly about some of the people who had been helped by their programs. Mayor Watts offered a ringing endorsement of the foundation's work in helping people off the streets and into better living arrangements where they received the assistance they needed. Coach Keating pledged not only to continue his participation in special events at Mercer House but also to ensure that the Ravens would make a deeper run into the playoffs this upcoming year. The crowd applauded this last pronouncement with great enthusiasm. Constance then reclaimed the podium to urge everyone to participate in the silent auction that would soon be underway upstairs, in the loft.

"Included this year," Constance said, reading from her notes, "are a pair of Ravens seasons tickets" (applause), "a vintage Orioles jersey autographed by Cal Ripken Jr." (more applause), "a selection of paintings and prints by Maryland artists" (belated, light applause), "and a selection of first edition books generously donated by one of our private sponsors, including, in keeping with tonight's theme," she held her notes a little closer, "a first edition of the collected writings of Thomas Paine, published in 1792, which I'm told is worth seven thousand dollars" (applause), "and the first edition of Washington Irving's *Rip Van Winkle* that was illustrated by American artist N.C. Wyeth, appraised at nine hundred dollars" (faint applause, led by Hank).

"Please take advantage as well of the opportunity to view the special collection that the gallery's made available to us tonight. Our theme for this evening, as I mentioned before, is early Americana, in honor of the collection which includes, I'm told, a Gilbert Stuart and a

John Trumbull. In addition, we have some graduate students with us from the department of American History at State who'll be circulating among us during the mingler which, you'll be relieved to hear, begins shortly. These students will be immediately recognizable, since they're dressed in period clothing and are portraying famous early Americans including Alexander Hamilton and Elizabeth Schuyler Hamilton, George and Martha Washington, and James and Dolly Madison. Please feel free to engage them in conversation. They'll answer any questions you might have, within reason of course" (laughter) "about the characters they're playing tonight. I hope you enjoy it."

Hank and Meredith joined the stream of people heading upstairs.

"This is fun," she whispered in his ear as they stood in line to view the items up for bid in the silent auction.

A volunteer stood behind the table on which the books were displayed. He looked young enough to be a college student. "Anything in particular catch your eye?" he asked Hank.

"The Irving."

The young man wore white gloves. He carefully picked up the copy of *Rip Van Winkle* from the pedestal on which it was displayed and held it toward Hank, carefully turning the pages so he could see them. He stopped at one of the color plates.

"It's beautiful," Hank said, admiring the illustration. He glanced at the bidding sheet and saw that no one else had registered a bid. He picked up the pen and wrote down his name, cell phone number, and a bid of a thousand dollars.

"Are you sure you're a cop?" Meredith kidded him as they strolled away.

"Very sure," Hank said.

He fetched them drinks from the bar, a White Russian for Meredith and another Maker's Mark on the rocks for himself, and they mingled for a few minutes until Hank found himself standing next to Mary Strong Ferguson.

"I apologize for Jack if he put you on the spot," she said, sipping what Hank feared was a Grasshopper.

"Not a problem. You're on the Jarrett board; how's everyone holding up?"

"I'll be over here if you're looking for me," Meredith said to Hank, pointing in a random direction.

"Fairly well," Mary responded as Meredith slipped away. "Considering how much work we've got ahead of us. The press conference yesterday went as well as could be expected. At least our stock price has leveled off. It was scary for a while, there."

"There were some big changes coming," Hank said, moving a little closer to her. "Jarrett was going to divest himself of his stake in the company, resign as CEO, and move to the Caribbean. How was everybody taking that news?"

Mary shrugged. "Some people were ready to jump off the roof, but others could see the logic behind it. You're aware he was going to sell to his daughter? The plan was for her to take over as president and CEO."

Hank nodded.

"I was prepared to support it," Mary said. "H.J. was starting to show his age, I'm afraid. He wasn't as aggressive or as sharp. He didn't always have a complete grasp of the details. Things he would have fired other people for in a heartbeat, and there he was, guilty of them himself."

"How well do you know his daughter?"

"Diane? Fairly well, I suppose. She's her father's daughter, I'll say that. She's got a head for business, a grasp of the numbers, and the moxie to make the hard choices. Actually, she's here tonight."

"Oh?"

"Yeah." Mary looked around. "Well, I don't see her, but I was talking to her before dinner. Maybe you can have a word with her."

Hank sampled his drink. "Anyone in particular upset because of the coming changes?"

"You mean someone upset enough to shoot him in the head? I hope I never meet anyone that insane in my lifetime." She frowned. "No, I can't say as I felt anyone was more upset than the situation warranted. Everyone on the board understands that change is a given in business, no matter how hard you try to build in stability and continuity. Succession plans are a must. I haven't the faintest idea who might have shot him." She put a hand on her hip. "Anyway, weren't you thinking it was a mugging? Some random person who took his money and ran away?"

"It's a theory."

"Well," she said, patting his arm, "good luck with it."

Hank turned around and found himself face to face with Walter

Parris.

"I just want to give you fair warning," Parris said abruptly. "I've spoken to your chief about that detective, Stainer. She was at the house this afternoon and upset everyone. I won't have her coming around using foul language and crashing around like a bull in a china shop. I won't put up with it."

"I'm sorry to hear that," Hank said. He'd listened to Karen's voice message, in which she'd told him about her interview with Dr. Caldwell and her intention to follow up with Brett and the nurse, Mona Jensen. He hadn't called her back because he hadn't thought it necessary. "I wish you'd talked to me first, Mr. Parris, before calling Chief Bennett. Detective Stainer's a first-rate investigator. I'm sorry if she upset you, but she's just doing her job."

"I'm not an idiot, Donaghue. It's the *way* she does her job I take issue with, and that's what I told your chief. He said he wasn't going to remove her from the case without talking to you first, so you may have a chance to save her skin, but I'm giving you fair warning. I don't want her at the house again, and I don't want her around Brett, Mona, Dr. Caldwell, or anyone else connected to Brett. Am I making myself clear?"

"Your concern's noted," Hank replied acidly, "but I don't appreciate you making telephone calls over my head, and no *civilian* tells me how to run a police investigation. Am I making *myself* clear?"

Walter reddened. "There's no need to speak to me that way. I—"

Hank moved close, encroaching on his personal space. "Keep your nose clean and your hands where I can see them at all times. Don't give me a reason to look at you any more closely than I have so far. This is a homicide investigation, not a company picnic. I don't give a damn whose feelings get hurt or whose sensibilities are offended. Police business will be conducted as *I* see fit, not according to your preferences."

Walter spun on his heel and walked away.

As he watched Walter disappear in the direction of the bar, Hank pulled at his drink and took a few deep breaths to lower his blood pressure.

He heard his name called from behind him. He turned to look at a lovely Asian woman in a long turquoise evening gown.

"Are you Lieutenant Donaghue?"

"Yes."

"I'm Emily Ong." She held out her hand. "It's an honor to meet you."

"Likewise," Hank replied, switching his drink to shake her hand.

She grinned at him. "I'm Peter Mah's sister. You're famous in our family, Lieutenant. You saved our little baby brother."

Hank put his hand in his pocket. "Your brother has a nose for trouble."

"I know. Boys will be boys. Can you talk to my father for a minute?"

"Your father?"

"Yes, he's just over there." She motioned in the direction of the silent auction tables. "He'd really like to have a few minutes of your time, if you could."

He'd spoken to Jerome Mah once before, several years ago, at a similar public function. "All right." Hank drained his glass and put it on the tray of a passing waiter. "Let's go."

He followed the turquoise evening gown through the crowd until he was standing next to Jerome Mah at the book table. The multi-millionaire importer gave him a broad smile and shook his hand with a quick, soft grip. He resembled a stout little penguin in his flawless tuxedo, white shirt, black cummerbund, and black bow tie. Even his thick hair was a mélange of black and white. He showed Hank a set of crooked teeth and nodded toward the table.

"I see the Irving caught your eye, Lieutenant Donaghue."

"Yes, it's great."

"I found that in a tiny used book store in Concord about twenty years ago. My late wife and I were driving through and we stopped for lunch. It cost me only ten dollars, if you can believe it."

Hank frowned. "You donated these books?"

"I have quite an extensive collection. I heard you shared this interest and I was hoping one of them might catch your attention."

"Someone will probably outbid me."

"I doubt it very much. You're very generous." Mah gestured. "Can we step aside for a moment?"

"I should really see if my mother needs anything," Hank said, turning away.

Mah blinked at the rudeness. "Really, Lieutenant Donaghue,

there's no need to be concerned. Words cannot possibly express how I feel, but I'd like to try, at least."

Hank hesitated.

Mah gestured toward an open space along the railing that overlooked the atrium. "Please."

"All right."

"Emily," Mah said, looking at his daughter.

"A pleasure to have met you, Lieutenant!" She held out her hand again, her head tilted to one side.

Hank sighed inwardly. This family wouldn't quit. He smiled despite himself and shook her hand. He followed Mah away from the auction tables. On their way they passed the bar, and Mah made a sudden detour. "Let me get you something, first."

"I'm fine, thanks."

"You'll like this." Mah pointed and the bartender poured two fingers of amber liquid into two small glasses and left them on the bar in front of Mah, who gestured to Hank to join him.

"I know you're a bourbon enthusiast, but if you haven't tried this before you really should." Mah smiled at him. "It's a single malt whisky from The Glenrothes distillery in the Speyside district of Scotland. You notice he served it neat in tulip glasses rather than in tumblers, on the rocks. The narrow opening of the tulip glass lets us nose it, just like you would a fine wine." As Hank watched, Mah placed two fingers on the base of the glass and swirled it around briskly on the bar, then picked it up by the stem and waved it delicately below his nose. He glanced at Hank. "Go ahead, try it."

Suppressing a sigh, Hank followed Mah's example.

"What do you smell?" Mah asked.

"I don't know. Alcohol. Butterscotch. Vanilla. Something like that."

"Excellent. Exactly. This particular vintage was matured in bourbon casks made of American oak, which lends very distinctive notes of butterscotch, coconut, and vanilla. Now taste it."

Mah sipped it carefully. Hank followed suit, and raised his eyebrows. "It's good."

"Of course it is. Of all the expressions produced by The Glenrothes, this is my favorite. I'd send you a case, but I'm afraid your people in Internal Affairs would jump to the wrong conclusions, so the best I can do is urge you to try it yourself." He moved away from the bar. "Bring it over here."

They left the bar and moved to an empty spot along the railing. Below, the catering staff was busy clearing the tables, which would be moved aside to create a space for dancing when the rock and roll band replaced the string quartet that was currently playing Haydn. They turned around and looked at the crowd behind them. Emily swirled her turquoise dress and waved.

"She's just like her late mother," Mah said. "Her husband's very lucky. And generous to allow her to accompany her father to bun tosses like this one."

"She's your oldest?"

Mah nodded. "She and Meredith are friends. Meredith's late husband, Stephen Liu, was my brother-in-law, as I'm sure you know. My wife's brother."

"Yes." Hank watched as Emily embraced Meredith. The two women held hands for a moment, admiring each other's dress.

Mah leaned against the railing. "Meredith's a very nice person. She was a wonderful wife and mother. I knew that the Lius were upset when I married into their family. Stephen was very intent on assimilating into American society, and he didn't understand me very well. There wasn't much I could do about it, but there were a few times when our households got together, and Meredith was very kind to Emily. Too bad the occasions were so few."

"They didn't like the Triad connection," Hank said.

Mah's eyes glittered in amusement. "I don't belong to the brotherhood, Lieutenant."

"It's been said."

Mah shook his head. "We can talk about that later, if you like." He straightened and faced Hank. "Thank you for saving Peter's life."

"There was gunfire. I knocked him down, we hid behind a couple of dumpsters, I returned fire, one of them shot me as they were getting away. I didn't do anything out of the ordinary that the Mah family should be thanking me for."

"Lieutenant! You covered my son's body with your own while bullets were being fired at him by that maniac Tommy Leung and his hoodlums! You got him safely to cover and returned fire, risking your own life to drive them away before they could kill him. You took a bullet meant for him! It would be very ungracious not to acknowledge the courage of those actions and the debt of gratitude we owe you."

Hank bit his lip. He was the subject of an open investigation by Internal Affairs into corruption within the department, and it wasn't a good idea to be seen on friendly terms with known Triad officials or their multi-millionaire fathers. On the other hand, he *had* saved the life of this man's son.

"You're right," he said. "I apologize."

He saw some of the stress drain from Mah's face. "You'll accept my thanks?"

"I'll accept the sentiment."

"That gives us a starting point." Mah leaned back against the railing again. "Peter's in Paris now."

"I hadn't heard." Hank sipped his whisky. It *was* good. "What's he doing there?"

"Practicing his French. He studied French in college and has an affinity for languages. Also, we thought it was best for him to be away for a while, with all the unrest in Chinatown these days."

Hank nodded.

"He got rid of that little place he was keeping on Lexington Street, and he has a verbal agreement on a six-story building downtown. He and his man there, the chef—"

"Daniel Chun," Hank remembered.

"Yes. They plan to open a new restaurant on the ground floor when they come back. Peter met some old man in Paris, a Cambodian ex-patriot who was a chef in one of the embassies in Phnom Penh before it fell to the Khmer Rouge in 1975. Peter became enthusiastic, I suppose you'd say, about the man's ideas for food. The old man refuses to leave Paris but he did agree to a nice little contract to show Peter's man how it's all done, so Peter has Chun over there to learn everything he can about it."

"That's nice."

"Peter's also setting up an import business to bring in authentic items when they get their restaurant underway. I told him I could do it all through Dicam for him, but he prefers to have his own business instead of using mine."

"I can understand that," Hank said.

"So can I." Mah sighed. "I'll be glad to see him out of Chinatown."

"Geographically speaking."

Mah smiled wanly. "Peter's an adult. He makes his own

choices." He looked away, down at the floor of the atrium. "Some of my friends are very unhappy with the current state of things. Their business is suffering because of this constant disruption."

"Yours, too?"

"Not really. I supply quite a few of the businesses in Chinatown, but it's a tiny fraction of my total activity. I distribute right across the country. I could pull all my trucks out of Chinatown completely and never notice it on my bottom line." Mah touched the tip of his bow tie self-consciously. "The point is, I sympathize with my friends. They need things to stabilize."

"I thought William Chow was the brotherhood's choice."

"There was no other candidate nearly as powerful as Chow. It would have been worse if they'd chosen someone else instead. Chow would've declared war and destroyed everyone in his path."

"Aren't you violating some kind of oath by talking to me about this?" Hank asked. "Aren't you liable to die a death of a thousand cuts or something?"

"Oh, horseshit. I won't say it again. I don't belong to the brotherhood, I haven't taken any oaths, and I don't attend secret meetings in dark rooms and plot how to smuggle heroin into the country or any such garbage. These people are friends of mine, we share the same heritage and language and history, and it upsets me to see them in such difficulty."

Hank said nothing for a moment. He wanted to lecture Mah on the fact that his friends were criminals and their trouble was of their own making. Instead, he changed the subject.

"I understand you're a director of Jarrett Corporation."

Mah nodded. "A terrible thing. You'll find the person responsible?"

"You bet we will. Are you aware of anyone who might've had a motive for killing Jarrett?"

"Not at all. The directors were aware of H.J.'s plans to retire, of course. Those of us who know his daughter weren't especially upset by his decision to pass everything over to her. She might lack her father's vision and instincts, but she's a capable administrator and conservative in her philosophy. The corporation should continue to do well under her leadership." He shifted slightly. "I can't think of anyone within H.J.'s business circle who'd do this. It had to be someone from the outside. I trust you'll track them down."

"We will," Hank repeated. "By the way, where were you yesterday morning between six and seven?"

Mah blinked. "At home. My alarm goes off at six, I have a light yoga routine I follow, then breakfast. I'm at work by seven thirty."

"Can anyone vouch for that?"

"My household staff. My driver. Lieutenant, I'm surprised."

"And you have no knowledge of anyone who may have been hired to kill Jarrett, no knowledge of anyone who may have made such arrangements? Any of your friends, for example? Bearing in mind that it's an offense to lie to a police officer in order to hinder or obstruct him in the course of an active investigation."

Mah stared at Hank for a long moment. "I have no such knowledge," he said finally. "I hope you believe me."

"I don't either believe or disbelieve at this point, Mr. Mah. I'm just asking questions."

At that moment their attention was drawn to the doorway on the far side. Voices were being raised. There seemed to be something happening over there.

"Excuse me." Hank handed Mah his glass and headed toward the disruption.

16

Bonnie Hatcher and The Heartbreaks had just finished their first set at the Overtones Café when a man slid onto the empty barstool next to Karen. He was short, about her age, with completely unremarkable features you'd forget five seconds after looking at him. His hair was trim and neat, his jacket was navy and only a little wrinkled, and the eyes that turned to look at her were kind and faintly amused.

"Buy a guy a drink, darlin'?"

"Fuck off, buddy, I don't pick up weirdoes."

Sandy Alexander laughed and caught the bartender's eye. "Rye and coke." He looked at Karen. "Want something?"

"Draft. Huge." When the bartender turned away, Karen sighed. "Sandy, I think I fucked up today."

"Just today?"

"Funny. I leaned pretty heavy on Walter Parris, threw my weight around. I don't think it was the right thing to do. If he complains, he'll go to the top and Hank'll get in shit because of me."

Their drinks arrived. Sandy sampled his and shrugged. "Donaghue can handle himself. He's a pro. And, he's got your back. If these people make waves, he'll make sure you don't drown."

"I hate these kind of people. Money and privilege. I just wanna pistol whip some common sense into them. Jess a tiny little bit."

"Stains, I keep telling you, that's the kind of attitude's going to keep you from becoming chief of police. But do you listen? No."

"D'you think I need therapy?"

Sandy choked on his drink. "Christ," he managed, "don't feed me straight lines like that."

"I'm serious, Sandy. I interviewed a psychiatric nurse at Parris's place this afternoon who said I should look into some kinda shit called positive psychology. D'you think I'm a wack job? Should I get some kinda help?"

"Would I be marrying you if you were a wack job?" Sandy shook his head. "You're a typical cop, love. Intense, focused, half-nuts, but not a wack job. No more than I am. Really. We're two of a kind, you and I."

She smiled benignly at him. "You don't shoot nearly well enough to be in my class, darlin', but thanks anyway for the thought."

"I always know the right thing to say, don't I?"

"Yeah." She drank deeply from her glass of draft beer, and when she looked at him again the smile was gone. "We're down a detective." She told him about Peralta's meltdown. "I seriously doubt she'll be back."

"It happens. We've both seen cops check out before."

"I know. Thing is, I hear she's been saying stuff like she wants to have a normal life, she doesn't want to be another Stainer. How the fuck am I supposed to take something like that, Sandy? 'Another Stainer.' What the fuck is that?"

"Since when are you so thin-skinned and sensitive? What do you care what somebody says when they're having a nervous breakdown?"

"I know. I know." She looked at him. "I mean, isn't this normal? Aren't we normal? Stop, listen to me," as he started to laugh, "you know what I mean, damn it. Cops are different, yeah yeah, I know, but we're still people and we still have lives. I don't feel like I'm some kind of fucking two-headed monster. Do you? What's so damned wrong with my life that somebody has to go around saying 'I don't wanna be another fucking Stainer, boo fucking hoo,' like I'm a psycho or something? So I'm not married yet and I don't have kids and I don't have this burning fucking desire to run a corner grocery store and join the PTA or some fucking thing. So what? We're getting married, right? We'll be a family, you and me, right? Maybe we'll even have a kid. So we're law enforcement. So fucking what? Can't we still be human fucking beings?"

"Of course we can." He put his hand on her wrist, always a risk with her, but one he felt compelled to take. "We're getting married. You'll have a husband. Maybe a kid, too, although it's probably a good idea to talk about that more, first. You'll have a life with me, and we'll still be law enforcement with our upwardly mobile careers, our godawful crime scenes, our paperwork, and our endless court appearances where we'll have the pleasure of getting filleted by lots of cynical prick defense attorneys. For us, love, that's normal. So, yes. You're normal."

"You think we should talk about it first? Having a kid?"

"I do. Not right now, because now's not a good time, but soon.

A good talk. With wine and grilled shrimp. You know what I mean."

"Okay. Soon. It's been on my mind."

"Karen, listen to me. You're the toughest, meanest, hardest-assed sonofabitch with a badge I ever met, and yet in the same delicious, luscious package you're also the smart, funny, sexy-as-hell woman I happen to love. Every time I look at you I get this funny feeling in my stomach. That little-kid excitement feeling. I'm normal, love. I'm just a normal guy. You're sort of unusual-normal, ow—" he took back his hand as she tried to bend his thumb out of joint "—stop it, you witch, look, just don't pay attention to what Peralta was saying or anybody else, just pay attention to what that little voice in your head is saying. If it's saying, 'kill everyone now before they get you, Karen,' then you're not normal and I'm going to have to take you into custody, but if it's saying, 'gee, Karen, Sandy's really smart and you should listen to everything he says,' then you're normal but I'm still going to have to take you into custody anyway, just for your own good."

"Jesus Christ, what a wiener." She slapped her hand on the bar and stood up. "Let's get the fuck out of here and get something to eat. And after that bullshit, you're paying."

"Oh damn." Sandy got up and smiled fondly at the back of her head as he followed her out onto the street.

17

A small crowd had gathered by the time Hank reached the doorway, a double-width arch that led from the gallery loft into a wide hallway above the main staircase. He shouldered his way through. A reporter and a cameraman were blocking the path of a petite middle-aged woman who had been trying to pass them into the loft. An elderly guest had intervened but had been pushed down by the cameraman. A young woman dressed in period clothing, one of Constance's graduate student volunteers, was helping the old man back to his feet.

Hank held up the wallet containing his identification and badge. "What's going on?"

The camera swung toward him, and the reporter held out her wireless microphone. "You're Hank Donaghue, aren't you?"

"What's going on here?" Hank repeated.

"Mr. Vanderbeek was trying to help Mrs. Benson," the volunteer said. "This camera guy knocked him down. They have no right to be here."

"This is a public building and we have every right to be here," replied the reporter, whom Hank recognized now as Rachel Pierk, a correspondent for WRTZ, the local CBS television affiliate. "All we want is a few answers from Mrs. Benson and we'll be on our way."

"Have you called security?" Hank asked the volunteer.

"Sorry, I didn't have a chance to. I was helping Mr. Vanderbeek."

"Turn that off," Hank told the cameraman. He looked at Mr. Vanderbeek. "Do you want to press charges?"

"I might," the old man replied. "I'm going to have a helluva bruise on my shoulder from where he hit me."

"Did you hit him?" Hank asked the cameraman.

"He gave me a straight arm like he was a football player," Mr. Vanderbeek said, before the cameraman could respond.

Hank looked at Rachel Pierk. "Did you ask anyone for permission to come up here to interview people?"

"We don't need permission. In fact, I'd like a statement from you, too, and I don't need permission for that, either."

"Yes, you do," the volunteer contradicted.

Hank turned to the cameraman. "I take it you were filming when you straight-armed Mr. Vanderbeek." He held out his hand. "It's evidence in an assault investigation. I'll take it now."

The cameraman lowered his camera and looked at Rachel. "This isn't such a good idea. Let's go."

"Hold on, it's not that easy," Hank said. "Mr. Vanderbeek, do you want to press charges?"

The old man glared at the cameraman. "If they clear the hell out of here right now and leave this poor woman alone, I'll forget it happened. Otherwise, kid, I'll see you in court."

Without another word the cameraman turned around and walked away.

Rachel gave Hank a long look and followed her cameraman.

"Are you okay?" Diane Benson asked Mr. Vanderbeek.

"I play squash three days a week with a personal trainer," Mr. Vanderbeek replied confidently. "I'm as fit as a damned fiddle and rarin' to go." He turned on his heel and headed straight for the bar.

Diane looked at Hank. "Thank you."

"You're Diane Jarrett Benson?"

"Yeah. I guess it's not safe to go out to the washroom around here. Where can I sit down?"

"We could go back downstairs into the atrium, if you like. I think they've finished clearing the tables."

"That sounds like a good idea." She led the way through the loft to the staircase at the far side which took them directly down into the atrium. Tables were now arranged along the walls and spread with clean tablecloths. Catering staff flitted back and forth. Already a few people had deserted the loft and settled down at the tables to talk more comfortably. Diane chose a table and caught the attention of a passing server. "Could we have a pot of decaffeinated coffee with cream and sugar?"

"Absolutely," the young man said. He veered off toward the preparation area to get it.

Diane sat down and touched her cheek. "Thanks again. Normally the press don't bother me, but I'm a little tired tonight."

"That's understandable." Hank turned his chair sideways and

sat down so that he was facing the floor of the atrium. "It's been a difficult time."

"I saw you on TV yesterday," she said. "You looked good. Better than the chief."

"Thanks."

"I hope it doesn't take you long to find whoever did this to Dad. I'd like to get my hands on them and strangle them, very slowly." She caught herself. "I shouldn't be saying that to a cop."

"How was your relationship with your father? Or would you rather do this later?"

"No, no, that's all right. That's why I thought we'd sit down. I knew you'd want to talk to me at some point and I'd rather just get it over with. Ask your questions."

Hank crossed his legs and folded his hands on his knee. The server arrived with their coffee. He set the table for them with cups, saucers, silverware, fresh napkins, pitchers of cream, bowls of sugar and artificial sweetener, and a large pot of coffee. He poured a cup for each of them. "Would you like anything else? We still have plenty of pastries."

"No," Diane said. "I'm fine, thanks. Hank?"

Hank shook his head.

"I saw you on TV last night," the server said to Hank.

Don't say it, Hank thought.

"You look smaller on TV."

Hank smiled politely.

"You going to catch the guy that killed that billionaire?"

"Normally I'd enjoy this conversation with you, son," Hank said, "but right now we'd like a little privacy. Maybe later, okay?"

The server blushed. "Oh, sure, I'm very sorry."

Diane managed a thin smile as the server hurried away. "Hero worship. Very cute in young men that age. You were asking about my relationship with Dad. I was about to explain that it wasn't the usual father-daughter thing, but on the whole I'd say it turned out to be fairly positive. I'm not sure how much you know about him."

"Not a great deal."

Diane sipped her coffee. "Mm. Good. I'll have to use this caterer the next time I have something. They're really very good." She set down the cup. "Dad was born and raised in Baltimore. His father worked in a shoe store and his mother died when he was eight or nine. When

Dad was twenty-four he went into partnership with a man named Paul Gibbons to open up a medical supplies distribution business. Gibbons was a former medic in the Korean War, so the story goes, and was selling bandages wholesale or some such thing when Dad met him. About that time Dad married his first wife, Judith Wilson, and they had Ned, my stepbrother. Judith died from an infection a few weeks later."

"That's too bad," Hank said.

"Yes, it was very sad. Not long afterward, Dad learned that one of his suppliers, the Cross Bandage Company, was going to declare bankruptcy because the owner had died and they were close to insolvency. Dad arranged to buy the company for pennies on the dollar. At the last minute Gibbons pulled out, so Dad found additional funding and bought it on his own. He got Cross back on its feet within a year. Within three years he'd bought two other small suppliers, bought out Gibbons's share in their business, and merged everything into The H.J. Jarrett Company. Within the decade he took the company public and exceeded the million dollar mark in personal income."

"Impressive," Hank said.

"Very," Diane agreed. "During that time he met my mother, Kathleen Whitaker, married her, and they had me. I'm forty, by the way. In case you're too polite to ask. Sorry, I keep forgetting you're a cop. I guess you'll ask whatever questions you want to."

She sipped coffee. "My mother was a working girl when they met. She was dancing at a club in Baltimore when she caught Dad's eye. Apparently it didn't take a lot of heavy thought for her to decide to hang up the g-string and marry him. They actually stayed married for twenty years, although she left and went down to Arizona when I was seven. She's still there. I stayed behind because I was in school and Dad refused to allow me to be uprooted. Kathleen didn't really care much, so I stayed here. Thank God."

Hank said nothing, looking at her over the rim of his coffee cup.

"Booze, coke, you name it," she said. "Kathleen's been in and out of rehab so many times they've practically named a wing after her. I feel sorry for her, I really do, but I thank my lucky stars my father put his foot down. Anyway, we were talking about Dad's business. In 1983 he bought a controlling interest in a pharmaceutical company, and in 1995 he bought a medical devices company, and at that point he reorganized into Jarrett Corporation. They have the three business segments: a consumer products segment, including all their health care products; a pharmaceuticals segment; and a medical devices and diagnostics segment. Each segment generates over three hundred million in revenue." She paused. "I heard you went out to talk to Chrissy, so hopefully I don't have to bother with the rest of the domestic biography."

"How do you and she get along?"

"Oh, we're fine." Diane waved her hand. "She plays the dumb blond sometimes but I know she's very bright. At first I thought Dad had gone out of his mind, marrying her, like he was looking for Kathleen Two or something. But it didn't take long to understand, once you got to know her. It was an unusual relationship but very good for Dad, I thought. Very stabilizing."

Hank reached for the coffee pot. "More?"

"Please."

He refilled their cups. Diane drank her coffee black, but Hank added cream and sugar to his while he thought things through.

"Did you ever work for your father?"

Diane snorted. "Never. I knew better than that. I got my degree here at State, business administration, then I started my own businesses right away. I sold clothing wholesale for a while, then office equipment—you know, photocopiers, shredders, blah blah blah—then I unloaded that one and got into the personal computer wave when it was just taking off. I made my first million and got out of hardware altogether.

"I did some day trading for a while and made a few more millions, then I opened an investment counseling business. That's how I met David. He was an investment counselor too, and we started bumping into each other at the same places. We fell in love, got married, and decided we'd be good business partners, so we formed Benson Holdings and, as they say, the rest is history. Today we're handling more than a billion in capital funds and we're beating off the investors with a stick." She looked at him seriously. "Nothing's guaranteed in this economic climate, but our funds are the closest thing to it you're going to find right now. David's got outstanding analytical skills, and my information network's second to none."

Hank stirred his coffee and sampled it. "So tell me about your father's retirement plans. He was going to divest, sell his controlling interest in Jarrett Corporation to you, and retire?"

130

"Yeah, that's right."

"Although originally his holdings were going to be left to your older stepbrother in your father's will, do I have that correct?"

"You do." Diane smiled at him ironically. "It's okay, Lieutenant. You're wondering if something's wrong, if somebody was going to get screwed in the ear by all this, but believe me, everybody was happy with Dad's sudden decision to cut loose and get a tan on that pasty little body of his. Ned has absolutely no interest in being involved with Jarrett Corporation, believe me. He *hates* business with a passion."

"Oh?"

"He's an academic. He teaches American lit at Harvard. A full professor with tenure, a big old house in a trendy part of Cambridge, and a wife and three kids. He's published two books, one on Hawthorne and the other on some guy, what's his name? Bartram?"

"William Bartram?"

"Probably. Anyway, he's got no more interest in running a billion-dollar corporation than Porky Pig would. Dad flew up to Boston to talk to him about it. Dad sells to me, spends the rest of his time in St. Lucia smoking cigars, drinking rum, and enjoying his escape from Maryland's horrible estate taxes, and when he dies all his properties and cash and holdings go into a tax haven set up for Ned, except for what Chrissy gets through their prenup and something for Kathleen. The new will wasn't going to mention me at all except for a nice little business in Bermuda that would pay me back for some of what I was going to have to spend to buy him out, because I'd already have the bulk of my legacy: Jarrett Corporation. Neat, clean, everybody's happy."

"And Ned was okay with this?"

"Of course. You can ask him yourself when he flies in for the funeral, but he was ecstatic. It would have saved him the huge hassle of having to unload Dad's interest in Jarrett, it would have given him an enormous amount of sheltered cash, and he was practically salivating at the thought of getting Dad's holdings, especially in St. Lucia, where it costs about half what comparable property does in Bermuda, by the way."

"And you were happy?"

She sipped her coffee and set the cup down. "Don't get me wrong. It isn't going to be a walk in the park. First, I have to sell my interest in Benson Holdings. David's going to buy a portion to give him a majority interest, and we're looking for another partner to come in with him on the rest, which isn't easy right now. Plus, I have a lot of other holdings I've been slowly liquidating, and the rest I'm going to have to finance, which is tough in the current economic climate, trust me. But it's been coming together and I was going to be able to raise enough to make the buy. I was *very* happy. This is my father's life's work, and he wanted me to have it. Now, while I'm still in my prime. I want it very much."

Hank was now writing in his notebook, which he was never without. "So how does it work instead? Under the existing will?"

"Ned gets Dad's controlling stake in Jarrett, he and I split properties and various holdings, Kathleen gets a token amount to float her through the rest of her bleary days, which wasn't going to change, and Chrissy gets what she was going to get. The only major difference, other than the estate and inheritance taxes, which can't be avoided now, is that once it's probated, Ned's stuck with control of Jarrett Corporation and I'll have to buy it from him instead of Dad."

"Will he sell it to you?"

"In a heartbeat. Ask him. You'll see."

"All right." Hank rubbed his chin thoughtfully. "Let's look at it from another angle. You're going to be walking into Jarrett Corporation as the new head honcho. You've got a board of directors and a roster of executive officers who've been following your father's lead for quite a few years now. You've got a challenge in front of you to win them over to your leadership and your way of doing things. Who's going to have a problem accepting you as the new head of Jarrett Corporation?"

Diane put her elbow on the table and cupped her jaw in her hand. "You've got a way about you, Hank. I like it. You're very polite and careful, but you ask your questions anyway, as a cop should." She shrugged, staring at him. "The board had mixed feelings about Dad but he made them a ton of money and nobody complained about that. And they knew Ned was going to sell to me no matter what, and I'd be walking in the front door one way or another. No matter what."

"Even if someone came up with a better offer?"

"Even if someone came up with a better offer. Look, Ned's the kind of person who really can't appreciate the difference between five hundred million dollars and seven hundred and fifty million dollars. Either way, it's a lot more money than he could spend in six lifetimes. He and his attorney came down during the negotiations to attend a couple of sessions and get a clear understanding of how the changes were going to work. He made it abundantly clear he had no problem with any of it and supported me one hundred percent. He also made it clear he didn't understand ninety percent of what we were talking about, and didn't want to. If anyone thought that by killing Dad they could get Ned to sell Jarrett Corporation to them instead of me, they'd have to be delusional."

"All right. What about the executive officers of Jarrett Corporation? How were they taking it all?"

"I really can't say for sure. Walter was fine with me. We were having some problems with the books and I didn't really agree with some of the decisions he'd made in terms of revenue recognition and so on that would take several hours to explain, but the bottom line is that we have a different understanding of what my father's stake in the company's worth, and we need to get it straightened out before the transaction can go through because it's a difference of millions and I don't have a lot of wiggle room."

"How was he, in these negotiations?"

"Good. Firm, stubborn, pig-headed, but gracious. We both knew we'd eventually reach common ground."

"What about the other executive officers?"

Diane shrugged. "Olive Chin doesn't strike me as someone who'd kill the boss to take over the company. Jane Anne Marshall, the CIO, is actually a friend of mine, and we'd talked a bit about what I was going to do when I came in. She had a few ideas as well that I thought were pretty good. Emory Raskin's the general counsel, and I don't really know him all that well. He's very much my father's man. Period. Richard Holland's a little pipsqueak whose days in Jarrett might be numbered once I get hold of him, but other than that, I really can't say. I don't see any of them getting so upset about me taking over that they'd shoot Dad. I mean, they're civilized people. Civilized people don't shoot people to change the direction in which corporations evolve. Do they?"

"I don't know," Hank said, his pen moving across the page while his eyes remained on her.

"Look," she said, "I haven't really answered your first question. Dad wasn't the kind of person who got all excited about the presents his children bought him for Father's Day. He never said 'I love you.' He always made it clear he approved of Ned and was proud of his academic accomplishments. You should have seen the book launch he threw for

Ned's second one, the thing on what's-his-name."

"William Bartram."

"Yeah. You'd think Ned was John Grisham or something. I mean, who's going to buy that one off the rack next to the checkout line in the drug store? Nobody knows who this Bartram guy was, let alone care if they did know."

"He was an eighteenth-century naturalist and writer," Hank said, to see how she would respond. "His best-known work was *Travels in North and South Carolina, Georgia, East and West Florida.*"

She grinned at him. "Well, there you are. He's got one fan, at least. Make sure you ask him for an autographed copy. He's got cartons of the damned things in his basement. He'd be glad to give you one."

"You're not impressed?"

"He's a little nerd who wears bow ties and mumbles to himself, but he's a very nice man just the same. We don't do the brother-and-sister thing, but he's never said an unkind word about Kathleen and he's always been a perfect gentleman around me. As I said, he supports me one hundred percent." She sighed. "I've gone off track again, Hank. Sorry."

"That's quite all right."

"I told you about Dad's relationship with Ned. With me, it was a little different. He wasn't really happy about having a child with Kathleen, when it came down to it. But I remember as a little girl I worked very hard to please him, and I guess he saw it, which was why he put his foot down and kept me here when Kathleen went to Arizona. Ned didn't need to do anything, really, to win Dad's approval, but I had to work like hell just to make sure I didn't lose it. So I worked very hard. I got good grades in school and I behaved like a little princess whenever he was around. Just the same, I think it was only when he saw my grade point average at State that he really became aware of me as a person in his life."

Hank listened, watching her.

"It sounds odd, I suppose." She shrugged. "Maybe you've had similar experiences, since your parents were rich and successful, too. But anyway, he started asking to read my term papers before I submitted them. He tore some of them to shreds, but not in a mean way. Always impersonally, so I wouldn't feel like he was attacking me for being a stupid idiot, but in a way that forced me to think about the concepts from angles I'd never considered before. He wouldn't look at rewrites, it was up to me either to get it or not get it, but I could sense there was this tacit approval that was slowly growing.

"After I graduated and started my businesses, he continued to show a restrained interest. A couple of times over the years he'd talk to me, just the two of us, to get a sense of where I was in the game, whether I was growing and learning. A few times I asked him questions and he answered them. But see, if I'd come to work for him, it would've been very different. Oh, yeah. I would've felt smothered and he wouldn't have been able to deal with me objectively. He probably would've ended up firing me because I can be pretty stubborn myself."

"Did he ever give you advice?"

"Only once. I was talking to him about whether or not I should marry David."

"And?"

"He advised me to go ahead. It was solid advice. I wouldn't have expected anything less from him."

"He talked to you about taking over the company?"

"Uh huh. At length. Once he'd made the decision, we had quite a few meetings about it. Some alone, several with Walter, and others with our lawyers in the room. At times I could see how anxious he was to get it done. It was like a yoke around his neck that he wanted to unload onto me, and he was hugely relieved that I was more than willing to take it from him. He was finished. He'd played the game all the way to the end, and he knew it was time to leave."

"All right." Hank made a quick notation and looked up. "Where were you yesterday morning between six and seven?"

Diane grimaced uncomfortably. "I was in the car. The driver takes me in to the office for seven. David starts at five, to catch the overseas action, so he was already there. I stay late; he goes home before I do. So I was in the car at the time it would've happened."

"Is the driver an employee of yours?"

"No, we use a service. Consolidated Transportation Services. We have a contract with them. But it's always the same driver. We call him George. That's what his name tag says."

Hank wrote it down. "How did you get the news?"

"Walter called. I was in a meeting, but these days when Walter calls I interrupt what I'm doing, given the importance of what we've been negotiating. I thought he was calling with some numbers I was expecting. I was devastated."

"Any idea who might have done this?"

"None. It's too horrible."

"We'll try to talk to all the corporate officers to see if they have any ideas," Hank said. "Richard Holland, for example, we've already interviewed. You mentioned him earlier but you don't seem too impressed."

"No, I'm not."

"Why's that?"

Diane shook her head. "Too much of a butt kisser for me. Always trying to make it look like he was closer to Dad than he actually was."

"What do you know about his background?"

"His father, Gerald Holland, was in charge of sales at Cross Bandage when Dad bought it. As I remember the story, Dad kept him on for a couple of years but caught him stealing. Instead of calling the police, he fired him. Or let him resign. Something like that. Holland committed suicide. Richard must've been just a baby at the time. I think his mother still lives in town."

"Do you know her name?"

"Uh, yeah. Mary Holland. She lives in Springhill somewhere. I'm not sure where."

"All right." Hank made a final note and put his pen away. "The detectives will see you for a written statement."

"I understand, that's fine."

She stood up. "Please find the person who did this and make them pay for it."

He slipped his notebook into his jacket pocket, stood up, and shook the hand she offered him. "We will."

"I hope so."

He sat back down and watched her walk away. He picked up his cup and saw that it was almost empty. He poured himself another cup, added cream and sugar, stirred, and sipped. She was right, it was good coffee.

More people had come back downstairs while he and Diane had talked. More tables were occupied, and a number of people stood in small groups, chatting.

The collective net worth of this crowd was probably high enough that it would come close to the gross national product of a country whose flag he might actually recognize if he saw it. He thought about

Diane and Walter trading numbers so large it wouldn't seem possible they'd apply to individual people. He thought about Walter Parris, who everyone said was a nice man, and he thought about Brett. He thought about the gap in time between the photos of the corpse Brett had taken with his cell phone and the call to 911. He felt reasonably certain Brett had spent that time waiting for Walter to arrive, rather than waiting for Walter to do something after having been discovered at the scene by his son.

He thought about Brett's condition, the Fregoli delusion that caused him to believe that people were not who they appeared to be. He looked at a nearby group of six people. Four men, two women. They looked very elegant in their evening wear.

Hank wondered what it would be like to be Brett Parris. Suppose he was Brett, and he'd missed his medication for a couple of days. His mind was slipping out of its groove. He was convinced that one of those men over there, say the short one with brown hair, was actually Richard Holland. Holland, who was always after him. Always stalking him. How would he explain it to himself? A copy of Holland's mind had replaced the mind of the brown-haired man? Or that Holland had some kind of supernatural ability to change his shape, to imitate the appearance of someone else? Or just good make-up and different clothing?

Why was Holland doing this to him? Why was he trying to trick him? Why was he standing there pretending to ignore him, pretending to be a stranger, when it was perfectly obvious he was stalking him, that he had it in for him, that he was going to attack him somehow?

Hank could feel the paranoia of it.

They were all of a type, that was for sure. All rich, well-dressed, anxious to show off their success. He could practically track their conversation in his head by rote. Boats, cars, who's in bed with whom, what's a safe shelter these days. You didn't have to be delusional to think they were all interchangeable.

But that was his own rational mind again, making light of it. It was actually quite unsettling, trying to think like a paranoid schizophrenic with delusional misidentification syndrome. It was difficult, and very, very unsettling, to try to think the way Brett Parris must think.

He saw two men come down the stairs and head across the floor, deep in conversation. One man was grinning and the other was waving his hands while telling a story. The grinning man reminded Hank of how his father had looked just before his death: tall, a few pounds overweight, wavy gray hair shot through with lingering brown. It was the second time this evening he'd thought of him.

He felt a powerful desire to talk to his father right now, to have him sit down in the chair Diane Benson had just vacated. He'd pour him a cup of this great coffee and ask him how it was going. Ask him if he thought his youngest son was spending his life doing the right things. Hoping for approval. Hoping he'd say Hank was doing all right. Hoping he'd see a little glint of pride in his eye.

He remembered, as he often did, the last time he saw his father alive. Hank was downstairs in the kitchen, eating breakfast. His first class wasn't until ten. His father hurried through on his way out the door, stuffing a file folder into his briefcase, his head already in the courtroom where he was defending a client accused of the murder of an elderly man. The courtroom in which he would have his fatal heart attack that afternoon.

"Have a good day, Dad," Hank said, watching him fumble with the clasp of his briefcase.

"You too, son." Distracted, not looking up as he spoke, then around the corner and out the door into the garage to his Mercedes.

Gone.

Meredith walked slowly across the atrium floor. She saw he was sitting alone at the table and angled toward him.

"You look lost in thought." She sat down in the chair Diane had just left.

"Mm."

"Emily's having a big party in two weeks for Jerome's sixty-fifth birthday. She asked me to come, and I said I'd think about it. She said, 'bring that handsome policeman of yours.' I think she likes you."

"Lucky me," Hank said.

The server stopped at the table. "Can I get you more coffee, Lieutenant?" He looked at Meredith. "Or something for the lady?"

"I'm fine," Meredith said.

"No, thanks," Hank said. When they were alone again he looked at Meredith. "I'm sorry for being such a lousy date."

"Well, you did say you were definitely a cop," she said. "Can't say I wasn't forewarned."

"That's no excuse. You deserve someone's full and complete

attention. Especially looking the way you do tonight."

"That's very flattering and I love to hear that sort of thing all the time, but I don't need someone to dote on me like I'm an airhead princess, you know."

"Yeah, I know. I'm sorry. I guess I was hoping for something in between. I should be able to juggle everything, and still have a good time with you."

"You aren't having a good time with me?"

He grinned.

"You know," she said, leaning forward on her elbow, her hand under her chin, "I wouldn't want to have to come to this sort of thing all the time, but I must say it's been a pretty fun sandbox to play in."

"I'm glad you've enjoyed it."

"I have." She leaned back and looked out across the floor. "Now I think it's time, Lieutenant Donaghue, for you to take me home."

18

At ten minutes before ten o'clock the next morning, Hank stood in his office doorway and caught Karen's eye as she was locking her firearm in her desk drawer. He motioned with his head and, when she joined him in the office, he closed the door behind her. She dropped into a visitor's chair. He perched on the corner of the desk closest to her.

She looked up at him. "Am I off the case?"

Hank had just come from a meeting in the chief's office. The chief was unhappy. Walter Parris had in fact made his phone call, and it was the kind of call Bennett hated, one that dug the combined wedges of money and politics under his fat butt cheeks and shoved hard, as he colorfully put it. To his credit, when Bennett was finished ranting, he generously allowed Hank ninety seconds to state his case. Hank proposed a compromise in which Stainer remained on the task force but didn't interview people whose net worth exceeded Homicide's annual budget. Bennett blustered a little more, but with Ann Martinez's encouragement, reluctantly agreed. Hank had crossed his fingers, knowing the arrangement wouldn't last long.

"You're on the case," he told Karen, "but with conditions."

"Chuh. Let me guess."

"Come on, Karen. You know damned well all suspects aren't created equal. Situational management. You've taken the course, it's in your jacket, and you don't need to be reminded because I see you use the technique all the time. Subject A responds best to direct pressure, Subject B to indirect pressure, et cetera. Parris was livid, the chief's livid, Martinez put her ass on the line for us, and now I've got the football. Horvath takes the lead in interviews with these people right now and you're going to let him. Okay?"

"Goddammit. Are you asking me to lay off them because they're *rich*? Is that what's going on here?"

"No, I'm asking you to be the river and not the rock, just for a while. These people love a good fight. They spend their entire lives facing down everybody in their path. We'll have a lot better results if we work around them instead of head-butting them."

"Be the river and not the rock. Jesus Christ, Hank."

Hank forced himself to look pissed. "Yeah, well, we all have to make our little sacrifices, and that's yours if you want to stay on this case. Clear?"

"Clear." She stood up and glared at him as he opened the door for her.

He ignored the look and led the way down the hall to a meeting room he'd co-opted as their war room, where the team was waiting. Two large whiteboards on wheels were lined up along one wall. There was a table in the middle of the room with chairs around it. A projector and laptop were set up on it. There was also a table in the corner with a landline telephone, a networked computer and multi-function printer, and a coffee machine.

Everyone helped themselves to coffee. Hank got things underway by reminding them that the media would be dogging their footsteps throughout the investigation, and that, until further notice, all public statements about the case would be coming either from Commander Martinez or from the chief's office.

He went on to thank CSI Mickey Marcotte for sitting in. A thirty-something with brown hair and sideburns, Marcotte would bring them up to speed on the physical evidence gathered to date.

Karen and Horvath would work the case full time until further notice, he explained. Kaplan and Belknap would carry the load on everything else in the unit, and Higgins was coming over from Robbery to assist. Among the three of them, Kaplan, Belknap, and Higgins would have to work all the other open homicide cases until Jarrett was cleared.

"Any open files you have that are active enough to need immediate work," he concluded, "pass them over, and make sure you give these guys a decent briefing."

"And Peralta's not coming back," Karen said.

"Detective Peralta's not coming back," Hank replied.

Karen's eyes moved from Hank to Truly. When they moved back to Hank, they were asking the question.

"Detective Truly's been seconded over from Cold Case to work with us on this," Hank confirmed. "She's going to be the hub for all the information gathered during the investigation. She'll maintain the murder book, she'll gather and collate everything we get, and she'll help us analyze it. Mickey, I'll ask you to work closely with her over the next while to make sure she knows everything coming out of your lab the instant you have it. She'll be the conduit through which everything reaches this team."

"Sounds good," Marcotte said.

Hank looked at Truly. "You'll also pair up with Jim, Karen, or myself as needed for interviews or whatever else. You won't be sitting around shuffling paper. We need everybody working everything, all the time."

"That's fine, Lieutenant," Truly said, from her position at the other end of the whiteboards. She wore a pale blue blouse, a dark blue sleeveless sweater, a black knee-length skirt, and thick-soled black shoes. She'd switched her glasses from the red-framed pair to a black-framed pair that were just as unflattering.

"Detective Truly was kind enough to come in early and set up these whiteboards for us. On this one," Hank pointed to the board closest to him, "we've got the name of every person directly connected to Jarrett in some way or other who could've conceivably had something to do with it. There are more than forty names here right now, but it could easily be a hundred."

"Person or persons unknown," Horvath quipped.

"Yeah. What we're going to do this morning is go through this list and see how many names we need to move over to the second board, which you can see is empty right now. That'll be our suspect list. But first," Hank looked at Marcotte, "we're going to review our timeline for Jarrett on Thursday morning. Mick?"

Marcotte switched on the projector and lifted the lid on his laptop. "This is kind of low tech, but I guess since we're also using whiteboards and dry-erase markers it'll fit right in." He grinned at Hank. "What we *should* have is one of those cool table-top interfaces with the gesture technology, like they have on *Hawaii Five-O*."

"Oh, yeah," Horvath said. "I love that show. I watch it all the time."

"Really?" Marcotte said, launching his presentation software.

Horvath laughed. "Not."

"Oh." Marcotte looked a little crestfallen. "Okay, well, anyway, we've got a basic timeline here showing everything Jarrett did that morning up until he was shot. We've extended the timeline back a week, so we can go through it that far, if you want." He glanced at Truly. "Maureen and I integrated data from Jarrett's office staff, his household staff, CD Security, and statements from the wife and other main witnesses, plus data from his computer activity and his phone records, which include the line in his office at work, the landline at his home, and his personal cell. We printed out a hard copy of the timeline, and Maureen put it into the murder book."

He looked up at the screen. "As you can see, his alarm went off at five on Thursday morning, and his breakfast was served in the sun room, where he usually eats it, at five twenty. Scrambled eggs, Canadian bacon, toast, orange juice, coffee, and his usual medications and vitamins. In the twenty-minute gap between the alarm and breakfast we can assume that he showered, shaved, and dressed in his track suit. He left the sun room at six o'clock. After a trip to the washroom, he went into his study and worked from six oh-five to six twenty-nine on his personal computer, which has remote connectivity to his office. He spent the time reading e-mails from Kelly, Raskin, Holland, and other people at work. A couple of them had attachments which he opened and read. He answered some of the e-mails with very brief responses. One or two sentences. Nothing jumps out, but you can check them and see. At any rate, that's all he did. He didn't have a Twitter or Facebook account, he didn't browse websites, even news sites, and the phone logs show no calls at all, incoming or outgoing. He had no contact with anyone that morning that we can find, other than through the e-mails."

"Is that normal for him?" Hank asked.

"As far as I can tell. We've extended the timeline back a week, as I say, and it seems to be his usual pattern, which agrees with what witnesses have told us. My guess is that when you're that rich, you get to control your environment a lot better than you or I could. You want peace and quiet, you get peace and quiet."

Hank smiled. "Go on."

"Okay. He logged off at six twenty-nine and, according to James Edward Bishop, his personal assistant and driver, arrived downstairs in his gym at six thirty-five, where he ran through a light workout routine until six fifty-three, when CD Security surveillance picks him up coming outside through the back door of the gym with his bicycle. He headed directly for the bike path, and that's all we have."

"How long would it take to ride his bike from there to the crime scene?" Hank asked. "Has anyone timed it?"

"Not yet, but it would've taken him maybe ten minutes," Marcotte replied. "I don't know how fast he usually traveled. I'm an avid biker, myself, and I'd probably make it in five to seven minutes, but then again, I'm not a sixty-eight-year-old man."

"So he gets there," Karen said, "at about seven oh-three and stops to talk to the guy who pops him."

"But we don't know how long they talked," said Horvath, "before the shot was fired."

"True," Karen said. "Could've been long, could've been real short."

"What were the time stamps on the photos taken by the witness, Brett Parris?" Hank asked.

"Good question." Marcotte checked his notes. "The first picture was taken at seven fourteen."

"So the shot was fired some time between about seven and seven fourteen," Horvath said. "A fourteen-minute window."

"Yes," Marcotte said, looking up from his notes. "And we can shave it a little, if we say that Brett Parris would have taken two or three minutes to reach the body. If what he says is true. So possibly between seven and seven twelve. A twelve-minute window."

"All right, thanks," Hank said. "Now how about giving us an overview of the physical evidence, Mick? Start with the crime scene."

"I threw this together quickly this morning," Marcotte said, looking at the projection screen and clicking his mouse, "so it gives you the basics. I can answer any questions you've got, though, so feel free. Take a look at these five or six pics first of all." He flipped slowly through images of the body as it was found in Granger Park on Thursday morning. "These are the ones taken by Brett Parris on his cell. Okay, now here's a side-by-side with the first one taken by us at the scene. I'll spare you the eyestrain; they're essentially identical. Nothing was changed respecting the body between the time Parris took his pictures and the time we got there."

"Doesn't mean the body wasn't touched before the pictures were shot," Karen said.

"Correct," Marcotte said. "It doesn't tell us everything, but it does tell us something. Which can be said for any piece of evidence, can't it? All right, moving along. Here's the bicycle."

Jarrett's bicycle had been found resting on its kickstand on the bike path, facing east, meaning that Jarrett had still been traveling away from the mansion when he'd stopped, presumably to talk to the person who shot him. The murder occurred at a point just under a half mile from the victim's home.

The bicycle, an expensive Raleigh model, was in excellent repair. They'd found four different sets of fingerprints on it. One set belonged to Jarrett, another to James Edward Bishop, and the other two were currently unidentified.

"The bike was serviced a week ago," Marcotte said. "We figure the other two sets belong to people at the bike shop. The technician and whoever delivered it."

Truly walked over to the person of interest whiteboard and picked up a dry-erase marker.

"Call them Bike Shop Number One and Bike Shop Number Two," Hank suggested.

She wrote the two aliases at the bottom of the list entitled "Jarrett Household," then capped the marker and walked back down to the other end.

"Maybe it was Bishop who met him on the path," Horvath said. "Put his hands on the bike to stop Jarrett and keep him from getting away while they had some kind of argument."

Karen snorted. "More likely it's his job to get the damned bike ready for his lord and master to go for his little ride in the morning."

Horvath shrugged amiably. "Could be."

Marcotte then moved through a sequence of shots of Jarrett's wallet. It had been found under a bush, emptied of its contents, thirty-three feet east of the body at the edge of the path. They could see, from its position underneath the low-hanging bush, that it must have been tossed under there, rather than dropped or placed.

"It's up to you guys to figure out what that means," Marcotte said, "if it means anything at all. I can tell you one thing for sure, though. Whoever threw it there wiped it clean first, inside and out. We haven't found a trace of anything of note. Gloved or ungloved, your perp took the time to empty the wallet *and* sanitize it."

"We've got the traces underway on the credit cards?" Hank asked.

"Yes, sir," replied Truly. "If anyone tries to use them, we'll know."

"Great. Don't call me sir."

145

"Sorry."

Marcotte then ran through an assortment of items found at the scene, either on the paved path itself or in the grass on either side, within the perimeter that had been set up at the crime scene. They stared at a variety of cigarette butts, chewing gum wrappers, a hair pin, a red plastic button, an empty pill bottle, the ubiquitous torn condom wrapper, an aluminum pop can, a small plastic child's bracelet, an empty bottle of nose spray, and other assorted junk.

"It's actually a fairly clean park compared to others in the city," Marcotte said. He looked at Hank. "We can run DNA and all the other tests on any of this stuff, Lieutenant," he said, "and we'll get you the results within twenty-four, but Byrne wants to hold off unless there's something specific you want done. None of this stuff showed signs of having been discarded within a day of us collecting it. It's up to you, but Byrne doesn't want to flood the lab with a lot of crap if we don't have to. We're really backlogged as it is."

Hank looked around the room. "Anything jump out?"

Horvath shrugged. Karen made a flatulent sound with her lips. Truly shook her head.

"We'll get back to you on it," Hank said.

Marcotte looked relieved. "That's great. I've skipped the dog dirt and other lowlights. As for the body, we've already gone over his clothing and found nothing that stands out. There are no pets in the house, as I understand it, and we haven't found anything of a dog or cat nature. A stray thread, a few human hairs which we expect to match up with household staff but you never know, dirt and debris from the path and ground. Nothing that jumps up and kicks you in the ass, though.

"Next is the bullet you brought us from Dr. Easton." Marcotte displayed a photo of the round that had been removed from the victim's brain. "It's a standard velocity, plain lead .22 long rifle bullet. These were sold with a lubricant on them to prevent oxidation, but there was virtually none present on this round, meaning it was probably pretty old. The lubricant evaporates after a while. No oxidation to speak of, which tells us it was kept in a dry, enclosed place."

He switched to another view of the bullet. "The rifling has a right-hand twist and we count six lands and grooves, suggesting it was fired through a Beretta, CDM, Smith and Wesson, Ruger, or Rohm. Bev is leaning toward a Ruger." He was referring to CSI Jon Beverley, their firearms expert. "An older model, maybe the Mark I."

"Killed by a plinker," Karen said.

"Placement is everything," Marcotte said, unconsciously echoing Jim Easton.

"Ain't that the truth." Karen drummed her fingers on the table. "When I talked to Brett Parris yesterday, he told me he remembered Holland having a gun in his hand as he ran away to his car. Said it looked like a starter's pistol or a target pistol. Could be the Ruger Mark I."

"Interesting," Marcotte said. "Oh, one more thing before I finish with the crime scene itself. The photo I'm *not* showing you."

"Not showing us," Hank said.

Marcotte grinned. "That's right. The one of the casing from the round that was fired into our vic. We didn't find it."

"Picked up his brass," Karen said.

"That'd be my guess," Marcotte agreed.

"Interesting," Hank said. "He shot Jarrett, policed his brass, found and removed Jarrett's wallet, emptied it, wiped it clean, and threw it under the bush."

"Premeditation?" guessed Horvath. "Preparation?"

"Could be. What else do you have, Mick?"

The crime scene technician briefly summarized the evidence gathered from the mansion and Jarrett Tower, which included photography, fingerprinting, copying inventories, security data and video footage, and the collection of the victim's electronic devices, computers, and personal financial records for analysis. Work on these items was still ongoing, he told them, and reports would be available as soon as possible. Again, though, he stressed, nothing significant had been found at this early date.

When Marcotte had finished, Hank sat down.

"Let's move some names onto the suspect board," he said.

Karen cleared her throat. "Household staff. Jim and I did the interviews yesterday." She looked at Truly.

"I have copies of your reports here, Detective Stainer," Truly said, looking down at a white cardboard file box on the floor.

"You can call me Karen if you want to. I won't bite your fucking head off."

"All right, Karen."

"Again," Horvath said, "nothing was jumping out. No criminal records, no tax problems or messy divorces or any other kind of skeletons in the closet, no red flags at all. Hand-picked staff, all been there for a while, all came across as loyal, competent, and upset that their boss had been killed. Right, Stains?"

"Yeah." Karen shifted. "I got some vibes off Winterbottom, but nothing you could hang your hat on. Otherwise, zip."

"Winterbottom? We could put her on the board," Hank said.

"I wouldn't bother. Not at this point."

They moved on to James Edward Bishop, Jarrett's personal assistant and driver. The fact that his fingerprints were on the bicycle was judged important enough for him to be moved onto the suspect board for further investigation. Truly wrote Bishop's name on the suspect whiteboard and pulled a file from the box. She took out a copy of Bishop's Department of Motor Vehicles photograph and stuck it on the board with a magnetized strip.

After further discussion it was agreed that the rest of the household staff would stay parked where they were for the present, but they added Bike Shop Number One and Bike Shop Number Two to the suspect board since they were unknown commodities who needed to be checked out.

They moved on to Chrissy Jarrett. Hank pointed out that Winterbottom had alibied the widow. Karen confirmed it, based on her follow-up interview, but reminded them of the statistical frequency with which spouses have turned out to be the guilty party.

Horvath stirred. "It's a waste of time looking at her without more to go on. At this point. In my opinion, anyway."

"I tend to agree," Hank said. "We'll leave her where she is, for now. What about the rest of Jarrett's family?"

Truly reported that she'd made inquiries about Ned Jarrett's whereabouts and confirmed he hadn't left Boston in the last three weeks. On Thursday morning when his father was killed, he was sitting at his kitchen table eating breakfast with his wife and youngest daughter while talking on his cell phone to his teaching assistant about the day's assignments. Likewise, Kathleen Jarrett was accounted for—she was in a rehabilitation clinic in Scottsdale, Arizona. Hank had interviewed George, the driver for Consolidated Transportation Services assigned to Diane Jarrett Benson. He was satisfied that Diane's story was solid. He confirmed as well that David Benson also had an alibi.

"Okay," Karen said, "let's talk about the big shots in his company."

Hank sat forward. "Before we do, let's go back a step. Chrissy Jarrett may or may not have had a motive we don't know about yet, but there are two names that should go on the board: Perry Crocker and Cynthia Troy Powell."

Horvath frowned. "Who?"

"The Jarretts had an open marriage. Jarrett apparently had a relationship with the Powell woman some time ago, and Mrs. Jarrett is currently seeing Perry Crocker. She told me she had to talk to him before deciding whether to join Jarrett in St. Lucia when he went down there after retiring. We need to run down both of them."

"Is that Crocker, the IT guy?" Horvath asked.

Hank confirmed that it was. Truly wrote their names on the board but didn't have a file for either of them in her box, and hence no DMV photo to post under their names right away.

They shifted their attention to the next column on the person of interest board, entitled "Jarrett Corp.," running first through the board of directors. Hank stood up, grabbed a marker, and drew a line under Jerome Mah's name on the suspect board.

"I'm racking my brain trying to think of a Triad angle here, but I'm coming up empty. Mickey, did you come across anything during your data mining that would suggest a connection between Jarrett and organized crime?"

"Zero," Marcotte said.

Hank nodded. "Leave it with me, then."

Marcotte explained he'd queried the backgrounds of the other board members as well and found nothing untoward. They moved on to the chief officers, beginning with Emory Raskin.

"He was definitely accounted for," Horvath said. He'd already double-checked Raskin's alibi. "He's in the clear."

Hank looked at Truly. "You've finished running background on the rest of them, I take it?"

She nodded. "Jane Ann Marshall, the CIO, is also clean and clear. Same with Walter Parris and Olive Chin, the VP of HR."

"Did you run Chin through the intelligence databases?" Hank asked, looking at Marcotte, who lifted an eyebrow.

"Not indulging in racial profiling, are we?"

"Did you or didn't you?"

"I did," Marcotte blushed, "with all of them. Chin's third generation Asian-American, born and raised in Chicago. Her father's

149

a university professor of economics and her mother's an architect. No hits or flags, Lieutenant. No ties to organized crime."

"Fine." Hank shifted in his chair. "That leaves us with Richard Holland."

"On the board, Maureen," Karen chirped.

Truly looked at Hank, who nodded.

"Something else Brett Parris did for me yesterday," Karen said, looking at Hank. "I showed him the photo array of the cars in the parking lot at your boy's club and he IDed Holland's car as the one he saw at the scene."

"Whoa," Horvath said. "Really?"

"Really."

Hank held up a hand. "Let's not get too excited. He's not a reliable witness, and we can't use anything coming from him."

Horvath frowned. "We can't?"

"He's a paranoid schizophrenic," Hank said, testily. "He has an ongoing delusion that Richard Holland's persecuting him, and he has a condition in which he mistakenly identifies all different kinds of people as Richard Holland. It could have been the pope he saw running away from Jarrett's body Thursday and he'd still say it was Holland. The fact he also says he saw Holland's car and Holland holding a gun is not going to hold water either. He's useless to us as an eyewitness."

"Come on, Lou," Karen protested. "There's no evidence he was having a delusion on Thursday morning. He saw Holland. I know he did. He's our guy."

"We don't know that. We can't prove it. For all intents and purposes we have no eyewitness who was at the scene at the time of the murder, end of story. Find another way to put Holland's car there on Thursday morning and a gun in his hand and I'll listen, but otherwise we work every other person on this board exactly the same way. Understood?"

Karen's lips thinned. Then she nodded curtly and looked away.

"All right," Hank said, "now, what about Peggy Kelly, Jarrett's EA?"

Horvath shook his head. "No."

Hank looked at Karen, who reluctantly made eye contact and shook her head.

"I agree." Hank took a minute to survey the board. "Anyone

we've missed?"

"Not that I can see," said Horvath.

"Mickey? Did any names pop up you don't see right now?"

"No, sir. Not at the moment."

Hank stood up and walked over to the suspect board, which now had the following names:

> James Edward Bishop
> Bike Shop # 1
> Bike Shop # 2
> Cynthia Troy Powell
> Perry Crocker
> Richard Holland.

"Here's the way we'll divide it," he said. "Jim, you and Karen take Bishop and Holland. Maureen, check out the two bike shop guys and the Powell woman. Mick, would you be willing to pair up with Maureen to do background on Crocker?"

"I should have a few minutes," Marcotte agreed, glancing at Truly.

"Thanks." Hank folded his arms. "That's it for now. Let's get to work."

Horvath jumped out of his chair as though spring-loaded and headed for the door. Truly knelt down beside her file box. Marcotte closed the lid on his laptop and unplugged it from the projector. As Karen walked past, she caught his eye.

"Holland did it. We're wasting time."

This time Hank's irritation was genuine. "Then prove it, goddammit."

19

"C'mon, Jimmy boy," Karen urged, "it'll work. Trust me. Just make it sound like you're really rich and really, really horny."

Horvath looked at his cell phone doubtfully. "The second part I can do, but I don't know about the first part."

"You *expect* her to make time for you. Everybody makes time for you. They make time for your money. Your money gets you everything you want, whenever you want it."

Horvath punched in the number on the business card in front of him and put the phone to his ear. "Corona Services? Yeah, hi, am I speaking to Melissa? This is Kincaid. John Kincaid. Kincaid Industries? Yeah, a mutual friend passed along your card."

Horvath patiently steered his way through the preliminary fencing and small talk, then said, "I'm in town maybe twice a month. But my jet's on standby to fly me out at six today, which is why I just want to meet you before I go. Kind of a get-to-know-you thing."

He listened, then nodded. "I understand completely. But I don't need very long to make up my mind. I never do. And trust me, I'm always very generous in the business arrangements that please me. My bonuses alone have to be seen to be believed."

Horvath listened and laughed, face reddening. "So I heard. Well, seeing *is* believing, isn't it? Four o'clock? Perfect. See you then."

He listened and laughed again. "Yeah, me too." He ended the call and looked at Karen. "Christ, I need a cold shower."

"Down, Rover."

"I have my own private jet, but she wants to look *me* over?"

"Well don't sound all resentful about it, Horvath. Jesus. She's a courtesan. They cater to the high-end crowd. She'll probably get you to fill out application forms and get a blood test done."

"Not a chance. I got my limits."

Karen laughed.

20

Later in the afternoon, Maureen Truly knocked on Hank's doorframe and peeked in. "Excuse me, Lieutenant, do you have a minute?"

"I have several." Hank closed a file folder on his desk and put it into a drawer. "What've you got?"

Truly hesitated. Captain Elspeth Williams, her supervisor back in Cold Case, detested interruptions and repaid them with brusqueness bordering on hostility, but Hank seemed genuinely open and interested in what she might have to say. It was a little disorienting.

"Mickey, CSI Marcotte, that is, and I have been running background on Perry Crocker and we found something interesting."

"Come in, Maureen. Sit down."

She edged into his office and perched on one of his visitor's chairs. "The thing is, Perry Crocker was issued a traffic summons on Thursday morning at seven nineteen A.M. on Beechwood Road. He was southbound between Metcalfe and Salmon Boulevard when he was pulled over for doing seventy in a thirty-five zone."

"Really." Hank leaned back in his chair. "That puts him close to the crime scene and our time frame."

"Eight blocks away. I can go over the background information with you," Truly said, "but the most important thing right at the moment is the fact that he's about to leave the city. His private jet has filed a flight plan for Chicago and is scheduled to depart from Skychaser FBO," she glanced at her wrist watch, "in less than an hour from now."

She watched him unlock his desk drawer and remove his gun. "Do you drive?"

"Yes, sir. My POV's parked downstairs."

"Let's go."

As they waited for the elevator, Truly handed him a slip of paper. "The number for the air traffic manager at the FBO."

"Thanks."

The doors opened and she preceded him into the elevator car.

She kept her eyes down, careful not to allow her expression to betray her thoughts. As they rode down to the sub-basement parking garage, he called the number she'd given him and asked for the manager of the fixed base of operations. When he came on the line, Hank began trying to convince him to suspend the clearance of Perry Crocker's flight until they had a chance to question him.

Truly remembered when they'd first met, a year ago. He and Stainer were meeting with Detective Dennis Waverman in the cubicle next to hers on the sixth floor. Hank ducked his head into her cubicle and asked to borrow her visitor's chair. She looked up from the file she was reading and frowned at the chair.

"They don't usually come back on their own."

He'd promised to return it when he was done, and was careful to do so when his meeting with Waverman was over. She hadn't looked up from her computer monitor.

The next time he was down to see Waverman he poked his head into her cubicle again. She looked up with annoyance. "May I help you?"

"Good morning." He nodded at the nameplate on her desk. "Detective Truly?"

"Yes, I Truly am," she replied, without cracking a smile.

"Clever. I'm Hank Donaghue, Homicide." He stepped forward, and she saw that he held a tray with three cups of coffee in it. He removed one of the cups and put it down in front of her. "Listen, I won't keep you. I had an extra cup of coffee and thought you might like it. Kind of a thank you for the loan of your chair the other day." He waved at her. "Have a good one."

A few minutes later she interrupted his meeting with Waverman, holding up the cup of coffee. "Where did you get this?"

"From the chip trailer two blocks over."

"Chip's Heaven?"

"That's the one."

"It's really good. I'm going to start buying my coffee there every morning if it's always this good."

"It's always that good."

"Thanks very much." Truly returned to her cubicle, humming.

A few weeks later, after she heard that he'd been shot, she left a voice message on his cell. She was upset about his injury and hoped he was okay. When she learned that Jarvis had been chosen to head up the new task force last month and that Hank was replacing him as supervisory lieutenant, she hung out at the chip trailer one morning, waiting for him. When he arrived, he bought her a coffee. She accepted it with a quiet, unsmiling "thank you," then abruptly asked if she could transfer to Homicide to work for him.

When he told her they couldn't bring in anyone new at the moment, she experienced that combination of mortification and relief which she often felt when she took a personal risk and failed. Then he went on to say that she was welcome to come up and talk to him about it further, if she liked, and the embarrassment evaporated. It wasn't a categorical No, it was a conditional No that left the door open. Just a crack.

She dithered for two days, then decided while brushing her teeth on Thursday morning that she would find the nerve to go up to the ninth floor that day. Now here she was, two days later, seconded to Homicide on one of the most important investigations in decades.

She led the way across the sub-basement parking garage to her personally-owned vehicle, a 1982 Land Cruiser. As she started the engine, he climbed into the passenger seat and looked at her.

"Are you serious?"

"Always." Truly tooled out of the parking space and headed up the ramp for the exit.

"I guess I should be grateful it has doors."

"Yes, sir." Truly stopped at the booth, waved her pass card, and rolled out onto the street. "It's a collector's item. Four-speed manual transmission, the front and rear axles have ARB air lockers, it has front and rear integrated rear winches, and there's even an arc welder mounted under the hood for ad hoc repairs. I'm a certified welder."

She stopped talking, not wanting to sound like a complete idiot. He said nothing, watching the street and the sidewalks around them as they drove. She braked for a stop sign and saw him look down. Then he bent down and picked up a book that had slid out from under his seat and tapped him on the heels. It was her copy of the *National Audubon Society Field Guide to North American Fossils*, by Ida Thompson.

"Oh, I'm sorry," she said, reaching for it. "I'll get rid of that for you." She took the book and tossed it over her shoulder into the back.

"Interested in paleontology?" he asked.

"I like to go off-roading, and I do a lot of fossil hunting around the state." She rubbed the steering wheel self-consciously, "You know, places like Calvert Cliffs, Sandy Mile, Henson Creek. My father gave me that book. When I was young. I have better ones than that, more detailed. Are you interested in that sort of thing, Lieutenant? Fossil-hunting?"

"No, sorry. I'm more of an indoorsman than an outdoorsman."

She smiled politely, accelerating through the intersection, thinking of her twenty-acre property near Lothian with its restored saltbox house and outbuildings, her little herd of goats, and her patiently-refurbished metal windmills connected to a generation system that provided power not only to her house and outbuildings but also enabled her to sell electricity back to the grid on good months when she produced a surplus. He'd probably think she was weird if she tried to explain her lifestyle to him. Professionalism, she reminded herself for the hundredth time, was much safer ground on which to operate.

"Perry Crocker's vehicle is a 2009 Mercedes Benz SLR McLaren, silver," she said. "The witness, um, Parris, spoke about having seen a silver sports car leave the scene."

"Correct."

"Yes. And Richard Holland drives a silver Ferrari, so that makes two possibles." She glanced over at him. "Is Detective Stainer upset with me?"

"No, she's upset with humanity. It's a very non-specific attitude, so don't take it personally."

"I won't."

Truly ran him through the basics. Perry Crocker was forty-two years old, stood six feet, two inches tall, and weighed one hundred and eighty-five pounds. He was born and raised in Grosse Pointe, Michigan. His father was a retired vice-president of General Motors and his mother's father had been a vice-president with Chrysler. Crocker had a bachelor of science degree from the University of Michigan and was the president and majority shareholder of CrocComm, a multi-million-dollar corporation specializing in high speed wireless telecommunications. He owned a home at 11145 Waterbury Place in Granger Park as well as other properties in Miami, Grosse Pointe, and San Bernardino, California. He was twice-divorced and had no children. He had no record of military service. He also had no criminal record, although their systems checks had produced a rather long list of traffic violations, mostly for speeding, unsafe lane changes, and illegal parking. He paid his tickets and fines religiously. The McLaren was one of six vehicles currently registered under his name. He'd been nailed for speeding in the McLaren more often than the others. He also owned the Hawker 400XP private jet Hank had successfully prevented from taking off. It was manufactured by Hawker Beechcraft. It had a cruising speed of four hundred and forty-three knots at twenty-three thousand feet and a range of almost two thousand miles, Truly explained. It cost Crocker seven and a half million dollars to purchase, and he flew all over the place in it.

"So on the surface," Hank said, "a typical successful businessman with no red flags."

"No red flags, sir."

"Don't call me sir, all right, Maureen?"

"All right, sir." She felt herself blushing. "Sorry."

They met Crocker in the small VIP lounge of the Skychaser fixed base of operations on the northern edge of Glendale International Airport. Truly recognized him immediately from his DMV photo: a tall, slender, handsome man with well-groomed black hair, brown eyes, a long jaw, and slightly pointed chin. He wore an expensive navy suit, white shirt, red foulard tie, and black cap-toed shoes. He held a cell phone to his ear and was listening to someone with obvious impatience. He caught sight of her and the lieutenant, said something brusque, and put away the phone.

"There better be a damned good reason for this, Detective Donaghue," Crocker groused. "I've got a crucial meeting in Chicago, and if this deal falls through it'll cost millions."

"Murder's a good reason for everyone to make time to talk to the police," Hank replied. "And it's Lieutenant Donaghue. This is Detective Truly. We have a few questions for you, and then you can get on your way. Why don't you start by explaining what you were doing on Beechwood Road at seven nineteen on Thursday morning."

Crocker stared at him. "Are you kidding me? You want to interrogate me about a speeding ticket?"

"I want to know what you were doing eight blocks away from the bike path where H.J. Jarrett was shot to death approximately ten minutes before."

Crocker bit off whatever he was going to say. He touched the knot of his tie and rolled his shoulders. "Chrissy told me you were asking questions about us. Do you seriously believe I had something to do with H.J.'s death?"

"I seriously want to know what you were doing there. If you prefer, I can explain your rights to you and we can do this downtown. Or we can do it here, and you can be on your way if you answer our questions to our satisfaction. Your choice."

"Jesus Christ. You cops are all the same. Goddamned power trippers." Crocker looked around, spotted a comfortable leather armchair, and walked over to it. "Ask your damned questions." He dropped into the chair and turned his eyes to the big window through which they could all see his Hawker 400XP waiting for him on the tarmac.

Truly sat down on the edge of an adjacent chair and took out her notebook. Hank sat down opposite Crocker and took out his notebook and pen, as well.

"I've already asked the first question," he said. "I'm waiting for the answer."

"I live in Granger Park."

"I'm aware of that."

"I was dropping off a gift to a friend on my way to the office. He also lives in Granger Park."

"Name?"

"Stephen Willis."

"Address?"

Crocker reluctantly recited an address that was in the general area of Beechwood Road.

"This friend can vouch for the fact that you were at his home on Thursday morning?"

"No," Crocker replied, disgusted, "he can't. He was at Myrtle Beach. He came back later in the morning. I left the gift on his front step. It was a joke."

"What was the gift?"

"A case of single malt scotch and a box of cigars. Dominican, thank you. Strictly legal."

"You weren't afraid they'd be stolen?"

"You're kidding, right?"

Hank sighed. "How well did you know Jarrett?"

"Not well. Different generations. The people I spend my time with are younger, more vibrant, a lot more interesting."

"Like Jarrett's wife?"

"She's already explained our relationship, Donaghue. I don't have anything to add to that."

"Did you ask Mrs. Jarrett to divorce her husband?"

"Of course not. Chrissy has her life and I have mine. I'm completely satisfied with the way things are." He glared at Hank. "If you think jealousy was a motive for me to shoot her husband, you're even more stupid than you look."

Truly could see that Hank was making an effort to remain patient.

"How's your business doing, Mr. Crocker?" he asked. "These are tough economic times."

"It's doing very well, thanks. It would be doing even better if I could make this meeting in Chicago. We're negotiating to acquire a distribution chain that'll be key to our growth in the next decade. Are we done here?"

"When are you coming back to Glendale?"

"Tonight."

"Do you possess a firearm, Mr. Crocker?"

"Yes, I do. I keep it locked in the safe in my office at home."

"What kind is it?"

"A Colt."

"Do you mind if we take a look in your car?"

"Of course I mind. Are you insane? Don't you understand you need a warrant for that kind of gross intrusion on a person's privacy? Are we done now?"

When Hank glanced at Truly, she shrugged. Crocker hadn't acknowledged her presence the entire time. He was the kind of male who made her skin crawl: too successful, too good-looking, too self-important. A complete solipsist. If she wanted to ask Crocker any questions right now, Hank was giving her the opportunity, but she preferred to have more background on him before trying. She liked to have a few angles of approach in mind before tackling a difficult subject, and at the moment Crocker was a blank wall to her. She shook her head.

Hank put away his notebook and stood up.

"We appreciate your time. We'll be in touch with you again later."

"I sincerely hope not." Crocker threw himself out of the

armchair and left the lounge without a backward glance.

"I want a warrant for his personal finances," Hank said, "his phone records, the gun in his safe, and everything else you can think of, including that damned case of scotch."

"Yes sir," Truly said, standing up.

"Don't call me sir, Maureen."

"Sorry."

21

There was a button next to the door that sounded a discreet chime within the suite when Horvath pressed it. He waited, self-consciously brushing imaginary flecks from his lapels, until the door opened. Melissa Grove leaned casually against the frame, looking him over.

"I'm Kincaid," Horvath said.

She smiled and despite himself Horvath felt his adrenaline spike. She was tall and very well-built. Her dark brown hair cascaded across her shoulders, and the scarlet kimono wrap belted around her narrow waist failed to conceal her disproportionately large bust. She tapped one of her black mules on the carpet and gestured for him to come in, closing the door behind him.

"Welcome," she murmured, giving him a light embrace. "You look fabulous, just as I hoped you would. As dreamy as your voice on the phone."

"Thanks." Horvath held her for a moment, conscious of her fragrance.

She stepped back, lightly gripping him by the elbows for a moment. "I don't normally accept Saturday afternoon appointments on such short notice, but I think I'm going to be very glad I made an exception in your case. Let's sit down for a moment and get to know each other a little better."

"All right." Horvath followed her into a seating area, where he sat down on a beige leather couch while she poured liquid from a ceramic pot into two small cups and handed him one.

"It's green tea," she said. "An excellent source of anti-oxidants."

Horvath looked at it dubiously. "Nothing stronger? To maybe relax us a little?"

"Definitely not. Alcohol dims the experience, John, and we must treat our bodies as temples at all times."

"I get you," Horvath said, dropping his gaze to her chest.

MICHAEL J. McCANN

"Easy, tiger. Plenty of time."

Horvath took an envelope from his inside jacket pocket and handed it to her. She accepted it, ran her thumbnail over the bills inside, then got up and locked it away in a cabinet along the far wall. "You didn't exaggerate when you said your bonuses are generous. Why don't you tell me a little bit about yourself? That way I'll have a better idea what sort of experiences we can share next time you visit."

"Personally, I'd like to know a little more about you," Horvath replied. "What sort of things you'll do for me."

"My, my. Direct, aren't you? I'll do whatever you like, John, as long as you always behave like a gentleman."

"I might have unusual requests."

"Whatever you want," Melissa said. "It's your money." She loosened the tie on her kimono suggestively.

Horvath nodded. "In that case, could you go to the door and let my partner in? She's waiting in the hall."

Melissa leaned back, frowning. "I take couples, John, but I require advance notice."

"That's okay." Horvath stood up. "I'll let her in."

"Really, I'm a little disappointed, John. I'd rather have known in advance you were bringing someone else."

Horvath walked to the door and opened it. Karen walked in, shaking her head. "Tsk tsk, Melissa. What would your boyfriend say?"

Horvath showed Melissa his badge and identification. "Now, where were we?"

Melissa glared up at him. "Oh, really, this is just ridiculous. You're a cop? This is entrapment, pure and simple."

"Not at all," Horvath replied easily. "Entrapment is when you coerce somebody to do something they wouldn't normally do. This is obviously what you normally do, hon, and I didn't have to talk you into anything."

"What's the point? I've never been arrested for anything before."

"Yeah, well, that's about to go down the tubes," Karen said.

"A misdemeanor."

"Which carries a penalty of up to a year in the slammer."

"It'd never get that far."

"Don't be so sure," Horvath said sadly. "I have a confession to make. I'm not a virgin. I've done this before. Bust hookers, I mean."

"I'm not a hooker. I'm a courtesan."

"And a very fine one, at that. Why don't you ask us what we want?"

Melissa covered her face with her hands for a moment. "What do you want?" she asked finally, her voice faint through her long fingers.

"We want you to drop all this bullshit about Richard Holland and tell us the truth. His alibi for Thursday morning was bought and paid for, correct?"

Melissa lowered her hands and wrung them in her lap. "I can't say anything."

"How much did he pay you?" Karen asked. "Enough to make it worth your while to go to jail for him? Look, darlin', it's not just the prostitution thing. When we nail Holland's ass for murder, you'll go down with him. Accessory to murder, lying to police officers in the course of an investigation, obstruction and hindering. You can kiss all this goodbye, starting right now."

Tears began to leak from beneath the long black lashes.

"Oh, for crissakes," Karen said, feigning disgust.

"It's in your best interest to come clean," Horvath said.

"I can't."

"Sure you can. Just tell us when Holland called to set up his alibi, how much he paid for it, all the details."

"I'm afraid."

"You wanna be," Karen snapped.

"No, you don't understand." She blinked away her tears, looking up at Karen. "I'm afraid of *him*. He's sadistic and demands an awful lot of ego-stroking. I'm not sure what he'll do when he finds out I've gone back on our agreement."

"What are you, his shrink or something?"

"Almost." She took a handkerchief from the pocket of her kimono and dabbed at her streaked makeup. "I majored in psychology and I recognize the type. He's a classic narcissist."

"*You* went to college?" Karen asked skeptically.

"I have a graduate degree. I paid my way through five years of school with this business."

"And a whole lot more, from the looks of it. This is a pretty fancy nest."

"Holland told you to lie for him, is that right?" Horvath

prompted. "He paid for an alibi? He told you to tell us he was here with you on Thursday morning when he really wasn't?"

She nodded.

"How much did he pay?"

"Ten thousand dollars."

Horvath glanced at Karen and saw the triumph glittering in her blue eyes. He turned back to Melissa. "That's it? You lied to police officers in the course of a homicide investigation for ten grand?"

"Up front. As a retainer. Another twenty thousand if I was questioned by police and repeated his alibi, which I was and I did. And another fifty thousand if I'm called to testify in court."

"So you stood to make eighty grand just to provide him with an alibi, and you've collected thirty so far?"

Melissa nodded again.

"You need to come with us," Horvath said. "We want a written statement. We can arrange for protection for the next while, if necessary."

"It will be. He has a mean streak when he doesn't get his way."

"Get dressed. We'll wait."

She stood up, clutching the kimono tightly around her.

"I'll need the envelope back," Horvath added. When she hesitated, he gave her a crooked little smile. "It belongs to the taxpayers, Melissa. Give them a break."

She took the envelope from the cabinet and handed it to him. "You know, I liked you better when you weren't a cop. We were getting along so well."

He watched her walk across the carpet to her bedroom, then turned and grinned at Karen.

"All the courtesans tell me that."

22

"Nice dump," CSI Jon Beverley quipped as he passed Hank at the foot of the staircase and trotted up toward the second floor of Perry Crocker's home at 11145 Waterbury Place in Granger Park.

"Any luck, Bev?" Hank called after him.

"No other guns yet, Lieutenant. But the evening's still young."

Two other crime scene technicians followed in Beverley's wake. As they clumped upstairs, equipment in hand, Truly appeared at the top, looking down at Hank.

"We're ready to do the housekeeper's suite, Lieutenant."

Hank turned and lifted an eyebrow at Jeannette Faucher, the Haitian-American woman who stood next to him, arms folded defensively across her chest.

"You have no right to do this," she complained. "I'm an American citizen, just like you. How would you like me to go into your home and do this to you?"

Hank looked at Perry Crocker's lawyer, standing next to her. "Mr. Baggs. We'd rather that she open the door herself, but we can open it ourselves if we have to."

Baggs shifted uneasily. "Mrs. Faucher, as I already explained, their warrant includes your suite in addition to Mr. Crocker's home and vehicles. You asked for my help and I'm glad to give it, but you need to be reasonable. They can only look for firearms or the specific brand of camera stated in the warrant, that's all. It's much better if you cooperate and allow them to conduct their search with as little fuss and damage as possible. A show of goodwill goes a long way in situations like this."

"I'll ask you again what Detective Truly asked you before, Mrs. Faucher," Hank said. "Do you own a firearm and, if so, do you keep it in your suite?"

Faucher glared at Baggs.

"Please," the lawyer said.

"All right, all right, all right. Yes, Mr. Police Man, I got a gun.

For protection, you know? This is a very fancy house and Mr. Crocker, he's away all the time. Maybe somebody try to break in to my room and I have to defend myself. Ever think of that, Mr. Police Man?"

Hearing Truly coming down the stairs behind him, Hank asked, "Where do you keep it, Mrs. Faucher?"

"In the little table next to my bed. Where I can reach it in the middle of the night if someone breaks in and tries to rape me, Mr. Police Man."

"To the best of your knowledge," Truly said, "is it there right now?"

"Sure, it's there. It's always there."

"Would you show me, please?"

Faucher huffed angrily, glared at Hank, and pushed past him to follow Truly upstairs. Her suite of three small rooms, plus a bathroom, was located over Crocker's four-bay garage. It was accessible through a locked door at the end of the hallway on the second floor. While there was also an entrance from ground level on the far side of the garage, Hank and Truly had agreed it would be preferable to enter her living area from Crocker's side. A search of the suite had been included in the warrant signed by Judge Brown only because it was contiguous to Crocker's living area and because it was reasonable to assume that since Crocker possessed a key, he could have entered the suite at any time to hide a murder weapon, should one have been in his possession.

The lawyer had already opened Crocker's safe for them, and Bev had bagged a Colt .45, along with a box of ammunition, but it was clearly not the murder weapon. Hank knew the tests would prove that beyond a shadow of a doubt. They needed to find a gun that fired .22LR ammunition if Crocker was going to remain a viable suspect.

A warrant served earlier on the residence of Stephen Willis had been disappointing. Willis confirmed he'd returned home on Thursday to find a case of scotch and a box of cigars sitting on his doorstep. He'd called Crocker and joked about it, but had no other way of confirming they'd actually been left there by Crocker himself since his home security system, surprisingly, didn't include doorstep video surveillance. He'd removed the six bottles and discarded the case, which had been picked up by city sanitation on Friday, so fingerprint evidence had now been recycled into oblivion. They took the bottles anyway, one of which had already been opened by Willis. He was not pleased, to say the very least.

Baggs's cell phone rang. He answered it, turning away from Hank and wandering down the hall. "Yes, Perry. Yes, they're still here. No, as I said, they've taken it to their compound to do the search there. I've made arrangements for one of your other cars to be there when you arrive. All right, I'll tell him." He ended the call and came back to Hank.

"That was Mr. Crocker, Lieutenant. His departure was delayed, and he doesn't expect to be home for another hour. I told him you've already taken his car from the airport. He was a little upset. Hopefully it can be returned to him as soon as possible."

"Depends on what we find."

"Understood, Lieutenant. My client wishes only to cooperate. He's completely confident that since he hasn't done anything wrong, this will all be cleared up very quickly."

"Sure." Hank glanced at his watch. Karen and Horvath would be executing a similar search warrant right now on Richard Holland's residence and car, as a result of having punctured his alibi this afternoon.

He went upstairs, Baggs following him, and walked down the hallway to Faucher's suite. He found Beverley in the bedroom, holding up a revolver in a plastic evidence bag.

"A .357 Magnum S and W, Lieutenant." Beverley glanced at Baggs and Faucher, making an effort to hide his disappointment.

"Keep looking," Hank said.

"Roger that."

"Now what the hell am I supposed to do to protect myself, Mr. Police Man?" Faucher demanded.

Hank glanced at Baggs, whose cell phone had chimed. The lawyer looked at the display, put the phone away, and left the suite.

"No sign of a camera," Truly said when he returned to Faucher's tiny living room.

"Keep looking," he told her.

"I said I don't got a camera," Faucher complained behind him. "Why would I want to spend my money on something so foolish like that?"

"Keep looking," Hank repeated and went back downstairs.

A uniformed officer met him in the hallway. "Media's outside," he said. "The lawyer's gone out to talk to them."

"Wonderful." Hank looked through the open front door.

Rachel Pierk was interviewing Baggs in Crocker's driveway beneath the spotlight at the corner of the big three-car garage. Hank slipped out onto the verandah and went down the stairs. It was remarkable, he thought, how journalists were able to get wind of search warrants almost as soon as they were signed off by the judge. He wondered who Pierk's source was this time.

"Mr. Crocker is very pleased to be able to cooperate with the police in this very important investigation," Baggs was saying as Hank crossed the lawn. "He'll be more than happy to share any information he might have that will assist them in their efforts to apprehend the person who committed this heinous crime."

"I understand they're searching Mr. Crocker's home and vehicle for the gun used to murder H.J. Jarrett," Pierk said. "Does Perry Crocker admit to owning a gun, and have the police found it in their search?"

"Mr. Crocker has exercised his second amendment rights to defend himself within his home," replied Baggs, "and he has turned over to the police the firearm which he keeps locked away at all times. As I understand it, the police are looking for an entirely different kind of gun than the one Mr. Crocker owns, but as I say, he's more than happy to assist their investigation in any way he can."

At that moment Pierk spotted Hank standing in the shadows, listening to them. She thanked Baggs quickly and moved forward. The cameraman, the same one who'd accompanied her at the art gallery fundraiser, followed behind, continuing to shoot.

"Lieutenant Donaghue, can you comment on the discovery of a firearm in the home of Perry Crocker that may be linked to the Jarrett murder investigation?"

"All statements must be obtained from the office of the chief of police," Hank said.

"Is that a no comment, Lieutenant?"

"Not at all. I'm afraid I can't help you, Ms. Pierk. All statements have to come from the chief's office. End of story."

Pierk turned to her cameraman and drew a finger across her throat. He shut off his camera and lowered it, glowering at Hank.

"Look, Lieutenant," Pierk said, lowering her voice, "I'm sorry about last night. I didn't mean to come off as the aggressive news bitch. Blame it on adrenaline. Can't you help us out a little? Is Crocker a suspect? Do you have something on him?"

"I'm sorry, Ms. Pierk. I can't help you. Check with the chief's office. They'll have some sort of statement for you shortly."

"Can't you just—" She broke off as the cameraman tapped her on the arm.

"They're executing another warrant," he said, looking up from his cell phone, where he'd just been reading a text message. "One of the company veeps."

"Let's go," Pierk said. She glanced at Hank. "'Bye!"

As he watched them jog down the driveway to their van, Hank took out his own cell phone. It crossed his mind that he should call Karen to give her a heads-up, but he resisted the impulse. She was an experienced hand with the media, she knew the gag was on for this one, and he didn't want her thinking he didn't trust her.

Instead, he punched in Ann Martinez's number to let her know she needed to have a statement ready.

Apparently, he mused as the call went through, it was the cameraman who had the good sources.

23

Richard Holland's lawyer was a thin, tired-looking, thirty-something named Alice Marsden. Captain Martinez leaned forward on the table in the interview room and steepled her fingers while Karen watched, chafing, through the one-way glass in the observation room next door.

"Let's go through it again," Martinez suggested. "I think maybe we're missing something here."

"My client is not prepared to answer any more questions at this time," replied Marsden in a monotone. "He's already cooperated, and," she glanced at Holland reproachfully, "without benefit of counsel, I should add. There's nothing more he can help you with."

Holland sat casually with his arms folded across his chest, a bemused smile on his face. The entire thing was apparently a joke to him. The fact that Horvath and a team of crime scene technicians were tearing apart his condo and extremely expensive car was a joke to him. The fact that Melissa Grove was now swearing that Holland had not been with her on Thursday morning at the time of the shooting, in contradiction to their earlier statements, was a joke to him. Richard Holland's world was an incredibly amusing place at the moment, apparently.

Karen's lip curled as she stood next to ASA Leanne DiOrio behind the one-way glass, forced to the sidelines by the chief's edict that she not be allowed to interview The Select Few.

"Cocky sonofabitch," she growled.

DiOrio said nothing, reading a text message on her cell phone.

"Do you own a gun, Mr. Holland?" Martinez pressed.

"He's already told you that he doesn't."

"Have you ever owned a gun, Mr. Holland?"

"No," replied Holland.

"Mr. Holland," Marsden said, turning to him. "Please let me do the talking."

"It's all right, Alice." Holland smiled at her as though she were a cousin for whom he held a special fondness. "I don't mind."

"Have you ever fired a gun before, Mr. Holland?" Martinez put in.

"Sure. Of course. Hasn't everyone?"

"How recently have you fired a gun?"

"Not for years. Back in college, I guess. A couple of us went to a firing range. One guy was a member. We thought it would be fun to try it."

"Was it fun, Mr. Holland?"

"Yeah. I guess it was."

"And yet you never went out and bought your own gun after that?"

"I've never really needed one. And it actually wasn't *that* fun. It was amusing, I suppose. But that was about it."

"You found it amusing." Martinez leaned back, as though disgusted.

Holland grinned. "By the way, did you find a gun at my place?"

Martinez ignored the jab. Hank had already called to report that Horvath's search of Holland's condo had turned up nothing, and that a cursory inspection of the Ferrari had been just as fruitless, but she wasn't about to concede that point to him. "Tell me again, Mr. Holland. Where were you on Thursday morning between six and eight o'clock?"

"He's already answered that question," Marsden said, "and he has nothing else to say on the subject. As I've *already* said. We have nothing more to say, and my client wishes to leave."

"Counselor, I've already explained to you that his alibi has been exploded. We have a sworn statement to the effect that your client was not where he said he was. Now either he tells me a better one or he's going to be charged with obstructing and hindering for lying about his whereabouts *and* for attempting to bribe our witness to repeat that lie, and that's just for starters because we're also going to hold him over for further questioning in our homicide investigation. So which is it?"

"It's weak," Marsden said. "She's a prostitute. It doesn't take a genius to figure out how you got her to change her statement. The entire thing is a house of cards based on your desperation to find a straw dog for this case, and it'll be a pleasure to tear your ridiculous obstructing charge to shreds. Do your worst."

Beside Karen in the observation booth, DiOrio's cell phone rang. She answered it, turning away from the glass.

"Tell me again where you were between six and seven thirty on Thursday morning, Mr. Holland," Martinez suggested.

"He did?" DiOrio said quietly into the phone, behind Karen. "I'm very sorry, sir."

"We're not going to listen to any more," Marsden said, rising. "Come on, Richard."

DiOrio put away her phone and hit the button on the intercom. "Captain Martinez, a word."

Martinez pointed a finger at Marsden. "Sit down. Right now." Glancing at the one-way glass, the captain stood up and left the interview room.

Karen turned around, frowning. "What the hell's going on?"

DiOrio ignored her.

Martinez came through the door of the observation booth. "What is it?"

"Turn him loose, Ann."

"*What*?"

"I just took a call from State's Attorney Exler. He just took a call from Judge Brown. Judge Brown just took a call from Gerald W. Evans, senior partner at Evans, Curry and Bryce, where our friend Alice Marsden is a junior partner. Unfortunately, Judge Brown was asleep when Evans called and was very upset at being disturbed, and Mr. Exler was asleep when Judge Brown called *him*, and he was even more upset to hear that Judge Brown was upset. The judge is upset because we're holding a client of Evans, Curry and Bryce on the word of a prostitute who, as they're now arguing, is changing her story in order to extort money from their client. Since she's admitted she expected money from Holland, and since I also had to admit to Mr. Exler that your search of his premises and car failed to turn up a murder weapon or Brett Parris's camera, I didn't have any ammunition left to fire. Mr. Exler's instructions are crystal clear. Holland walks."

"What the *fuck*!" Karen pounded her fist against the glass and walked out, slamming the door behind her.

In the interview room, Holland and Alice Marsden looked up, startled. Holland's lip curled in a faint smile.

"Damn it, Leanne," Martinez said, "he lied and gave a false alibi. I don't care what they say, I believe the girl. She took money to back his play, yeah, but she's telling the truth."

"You may believe her," DiOrio said, "but a jury won't. They'll crucify her on the stand and make Holland look like a victim. You've got nothing. He walks."

Martinez stared through the glass.

"She's over her head, Ann," DiOrio said after a moment, looking at the door Karen had slammed on her way out. "She's a liability and you need to take her off the case before it goes south on you."

"She'll be all right," Martinez said, unwilling to admit she'd just been thinking the same thing. "We'll manage her."

"It's your neck on the line here. Detectives are a dime a dozen. Commanders, not so much."

"I know." She turned around. "Don't you think I know that?"

"All right." DiOrio held up a hand. "I'm just saying."

"Stainer's a hell of a detective, and Hank has complete faith in her. She's off her game a bit, yeah, but she'll come through for us and we'll nail that son of a bitch." She looked back at Holland. "Her gut's on the money. That bastard did it. I can feel it, just like she does."

DiOrio stuck out her lower lip. "Good luck proving it."

Martinez pushed past her and went out the door to give Richard Holland his good news.

24

Meredith Collier lived on the twenty-eighth floor of a high-rise condominium complex on the waterfront. The building was only six years old, and no expense had been spared in its construction. The corridors on each floor featured expensive carpeting, discreet video security, and original works of art on the walls. Meredith's condo included an open-concept entry area, three large bedrooms, a master bathroom with a Jacuzzi, a powder room for guests, and a large living room with a spectacular view of the river.

Hank sat in a recliner in her living room, sipping coffee as a cargo vessel moved down the river, leaving a silver wake behind it in the late morning sun. He wore black pajama bottoms and an open silk robe that Meredith had given to him last night. There was a pajama top as well, but he wasn't sure where it was at the moment.

She sat in a recliner angled next to his, reading the Sunday morning news on a tablet. She wore a berry-colored cashmere robe that was belted around the middle. Her feet were bare. She put the tablet aside and stretched.

"I should get us something to eat. Would you like something?"

"Don't go to any trouble."

"Don't be silly. I've got some cold grilled salmon in the fridge. I'll scramble some eggs, make some cheesy French toast, with cherry tomatoes and watercress. It'll only take a few minutes."

"Sounds great."

She didn't move.

"Sorry I was so late last night," Hank said.

"Nonsense. You've already apologized."

He set aside his coffee cup. "It's beautiful here. What a view."

"I'm glad you like it."

"I have a view of the city, looking north. I love it, but I love this, too."

"You'll have to show it to me some time."

The ship's horn sounded softly on the water below.

"I'll have to eat and run," he said. "We're going to caucus at one o'clock. We need to pull this thing together."

"Will you go back to your place first?" she asked, thinking about the time.

"No, Karen will pick me up." He'd already called her, while Meredith was in the bathroom, showering. Since Karen lived nearby, it was not a problem for her to pick him up.

Meredith rose and moved behind his chair. She put her hand on the top of his head, her fingers gently moving through his frizzy hair. "You know, you can leave a few things here if you like. Save wearing the same clothing two days in a row."

He tilted his head back. "I'm not sure that's a good idea."

"There's lots of room in my closets," she joked, pretending not to understand.

His eyes creased in affection. "I'm not a nine-to-five guy, Merry."

"That's obvious." Her fingers continued to caress his hair.

"We keep the detectives on shifts and they get paid overtime if they're called in," he went on, "but I don't work shifts and I don't claim overtime. The phone rings and I go. I stay as long as I have to, then I go on to the next one. That's my life. I don't have the right to force that kind of thing on someone else."

"You might want to consider that perhaps someone else might not be bothered by it."

"You look cute upside down."

"I'm told it's my best angle. Don't change the subject."

"I get very focused when I'm in the middle of an investigation. Sometimes I'm hardly aware of anything else."

"I thought your focus was pretty good last night."

He smiled.

She moved around and sat down on the arm of his chair. "I tease you, but I can't imagine what it must be like, doing your job."

"I've been getting that a lot lately." He told her about Perry's impromptu visit to Jarrett's autopsy on Friday, how he'd been unprepared for the stark reality of post-mortem dissection, and how, afterward, he'd pressed Hank about his career choice.

"I tried to explain, but I didn't do a very good job of it."

She waited.

"Some of it involves what Freud called isolation of affect," he

175

said. "A defense mechanism where you respond to unpleasantness or horror by putting your emotions in a box and cutting them off from the rest of your thought processes. I do that. Every cop does, if they want to survive. Compartmentalize your emotional responses to the things you see and keep the lid on very tightly."

"I can understand that."

"The problems come, though, when you do that for too long and you lose touch with your emotions altogether." He watched the ship inch down the river. "You lose all your highs and lows, and end up in the middle where there's little or no emotion at all. Or, just as bad, you have inappropriate emotional responses to normal things."

He told her about John Douglas, the FBI profiler who, in one of his books, described having lashed out at his children for being upset over cut knees and scraped shins when he'd witnessed terrible brutality against other children that they couldn't possibly imagine. And the instance when his wife became upset because she'd badly cut her hand with a knife in the kitchen and he began to muse aloud about blood spatter patterns he'd seen at horrific crime scenes. Douglas had written about these incidents while discussing his divorce and how his career had made a shambles of his personal life.

"You can't interact with people normally any more," he finished. "Or you crash and burn," he said, thinking of Peralta.

"Was it a problem," she asked, "between you and your wife?"

"Marla?" He chuckled, surprised. "No, not at all. We weren't together long enough for anything that deep. She was three years older than I was, and twice as ambitious. She was disappointed I decided to put on a uniform and become a cop, and that was it. Her expectations were a lot higher than that." He shook his head. "Hard to believe it was more than twenty years ago. Ancient history."

"Where is she now?"

"Annapolis. She married a dentist or something. Had some kids, went into private practice. We don't stay in touch."

They listened to the silence for a moment. Meredith stirred. "Do you worry about it? That you'll lose touch with your emotions?"

"I'm an intellectualizer, he smiled. "Another defense mechanism. Allows me to consciously analyze the things I see without becoming anxious. Focus on the facts instead of the emotions." He smiled at her. "Flight into reason, they call it."

"You think that's what you do?"

"To a certain extent."

"I only took first-year psych," she said, "and I wasn't very interested in it except for how it relates to linguistics and culture, especially Asian culture, but I do remember reading that humor is considered the highest of our defense mechanisms. You have a very active sense of humor, Hank. Maybe that helps you."

"Maybe." He reached out and picked up his coffee cup. As he raised it to his lips, his hand quivered slightly. It reminded him immediately of Horvath's hand, trembling as the detective lifted his cigarette to his mouth in the parking lot behind Jarrett Tower on Thursday. Peralta's meltdown had affected all of them, even Karen with her brave talk about law enforcement lifers. They all knew there was a line that, once crossed, could not be re-crossed. Peralta had reached that line and balked. Had he already crossed it? Was he, as Karen had joked, another law enforcement lifer?

Meredith ruffled his frizzy hair once more and stood up. "I'll get us that lunch now."

Turning, he watched her move away toward the kitchen. He remembered the moment at the fundraiser on Friday night when he'd stared at the blond curl on her shoulder. He watched her bare feet heel-and-toe, heel-and-toe across the floor. He remembered the first time she'd ever touched him, lightly on the arm, a year ago when he'd visited her here in this apartment to interview her about Peter Mah and the Triad view of the world. He remembered still feeling the pressure of her fingers on his arm afterward, as he'd ridden down in the elevator. He knew now it had been the beginning of a change within him, a movement through shadows toward anticipated light.

He set the cup back down, forcing his hand to remain steady.

An act of will.

He knew he'd crossed the line a very, very long time ago. What he didn't know, and what he suspected no one else really knew, was exactly what was possible on this side.

Time to find out.

25

Karen stood in front of the suspect whiteboard in the war room at 1:00 P.M. as they went through the list, beginning with James Edward Bishop.

"Jim and I did a thorough review of the surveillance video from the house. That place is seriously wired. A roach couldn't leave the property without being seen. We saw Jarrett leave on his bike, and nobody else. Noo-body. Zippo. As far as we're concerned, Winterbottom, Bishop the butler guy, Chrissy the widow, and the rest of the staff were all inside the house for the entire window in which he would've been shot."

"So they come off the board?" Hank asked.

"They come off the board."

"Sounds good to me," Horvath said.

"I agree," said Truly, standing next to Karen.

As Truly moved the photos back to the person of interest board, Hank asked her about the two young men from the bicycle shop whose fingerprints were found on the bike.

"Bike Shop Number One," she said, pointing, "is Jeremy Olson, aged twenty, works part time at the bike shop doing repairs, and races part time on the trail bike circuit. He's been in Vermont since last Wednesday morning. Bike Shop Number Two," she pointed again, "is Roger Polk, aged thirty-six, runs a delivery service that includes the bike shop. He's divorced and lives with his mother in an apartment in Strathton. He used an ATM a few blocks from his place at six fifty-seven on Thursday morning. He says he didn't get across the bridge into Midtown before seven thirty because of a car accident near the train yard. I checked. It happened."

"Which means he couldn't have been in Granger Park," Horvath said.

"Correct."

"Move them both off the board," Hank said. "How about Cynthia Troy Powell?"

Truly erased the names of the people she'd moved from the board, then looked at the photo of the woman who'd been the last known person to have an affair with H.J. Jarrett. "She had a stroke three weeks ago in St. Louis. She's convalescing right now in a private facility."

"Off she comes."

"Leaves us with two names," Horvath said. "Perry Crocker and Richard Holland."

Hank looked at Truly. "What's the latest on Crocker?"

"The search of his home yielded the Colt from his safe. It's not our murder weapon. Also the .357 Magnum from the housekeeper's bedroom, which is also not our murder weapon. A search of his vehicle gave us nothing remotely of interest other than Mrs. Jarrett's prints, along with his own."

"Okay," Hank said. "What about the navigation system?"

"No luck, once again. It's disconnected and currently not functioning. He has an appointment to have it replaced. The new unit's been on order for a week. Apparently it costs almost a thousand dollars."

"Christ," Karen said, "remind me not to waste money on one of those things."

"Every time we turn around we're in a blind alley," Hank said. His cell phone vibrated. He took it out, looked at the display, and turned away to take the call.

"Other than a possible motive and possible opportunity," Horvath said, "we don't really have anything solid on this guy."

"On the other hand, Holland gave us a phony alibi," Karen said. "Doesn't that—" She broke off at the expression on Hank's face.

"That was Walter Parris," Hank said, putting his phone away. "Brett's in ICU at Angel of Mercy. It was a hit-and-run, about an hour ago."

26

They found Walter Parris in a waiting area outside the intensive care unit at Angel of Mercy Hospital. He introduced them to his wife, Lisa Gregg Parris, a stiff, emotionless woman in a jacket and skirt, white blouse, and pearls. As Hank shook her offered hand, he saw in her eyes the signs of medication.

"We've met before,' he said, releasing her hand.

"Yes. I remember."

"I'm very sorry to hear this news. I know how hard it is."

"Thank you."

Lisa looked at Karen and said nothing.

Hank motioned Walter to one side. "How is he?"

"Unconscious." Walter glanced over his shoulder at his wife, who was returning to her seat against the far wall.

The waiting area was quiet at the moment. Two hospital staff members in scrubs passed behind them, talking quietly. Three people waited silently in the opposite corner of the room for news about another patient. A young woman sat in a seat two away from Walter's wife, hands clasped between her knees, head down.

"We just got home from church when we heard. My wife's very upset. The doctor thinks Brett's suffered a concussion. They're waiting for results from their tests. He had a seizure, but they stabilized him. He's out of immediate danger, but he has a broken leg, a broken pelvis, and a broken wrist. He's lucky to be alive."

"What happened?"

"He was downtown for lunch. With his girlfriend. They got out of the taxi and a car hit him as he was crossing the road. It kept on going."

"His girlfriend was with him when it happened?"

Walter looked at the young woman sitting along the wall two empty seats away from Lisa Gregg Parris. "That's her there."

"What's her name?" Hank asked.

"Leanne. I can't remember her last name. We don't know her

very well."

Karen walked over to the young woman and sat down in the empty seat beside her. "I'm Detective Stainer. You're Leanne?"

The young woman unclasped her hands, put them on her knees, and straightened up. She wore a green plaid short-sleeved blouse and blue jeans. A black purse was wedged between her scuffed pink sneakers. Her thick black hair was shoulder-length and uncombed. Her complexion was dark and her features were Native American. When she looked in Karen's general direction, her eyes were red from crying.

"Yes."

"What's your last name, Leanne?"

"Nephews. Will Brett be okay?"

"We don't know any more than you do. We just got here. You're Brett's girlfriend, is that right?"

"I'm his friend," she replied, glancing uncomfortably toward Walter. "We're in the same support group."

"For schizophrenia," Karen guessed.

"Yes. We're friends, so sometimes we go out together. As friends."

"Sure," Karen said. "I understand. You're just friends."

"Yes." Her eyes remained on the floor. "Brett helps me. When I get down, if I want to stop my meds, if I want to start drinking again."

Hank approached her, Walter trailing behind him, and crouched down. "You were going to lunch together today, is that right?"

"Yes. At The Box Factory. Brett likes seafood."

"Tell us what happened, Leanne."

"The taxi stopped across the road. We got out on my side. Brett started to cross the road. I left my purse in the taxi. I got it and shut the door, and it happened. I—" She screwed up her face and began to cry.

Hank took a handkerchief out of his jacket pocket and gave it to her. She sobbed into it. "Take your time," he said.

"Sorry," she mumbled into the handkerchief.

"Don't apologize," he said, looking at Karen. She tilted her head sideways a fraction. He nodded.

"Support groups are important," Karen said. "They're like a buddy system. You encourage each other, and it gives you someone to talk to who understands what you're going through."

Leanne blew her nose into the handkerchief.

Walter walked away and knelt down in front of his wife.

"He doesn't like me," Leanne murmured.

"That's okay," Karen said, "he doesn't like me either. Can you tell us the rest of what happened?"

"Okay." She took a deep breath and glanced toward Karen. "I don't cry. They say I should. So I guess it's not wrong to."

"No, it's not. Did you see the car that hit him?"

Leanne shook her head. "It happened so fast."

"That's okay. Which way did it come from?"

Leanne thought for a moment, then raised her left hand, the one holding the handkerchief. "From over here."

"You were facing the street, and it came from your left? From behind the taxi?"

Leanne nodded.

"The Box Factory's on Gage," Karen said to Hank. "It's a two-way street. The car was following the taxi."

He nodded.

"Leanne, did you notice anything about the car at all?"

"It was gray. Or blue."

"And it didn't stop?"

She shook her head, staring at the floor.

"Did it slow down?"

"It hit him and kept on going. It went away fast."

"Okay. Did you see the driver?"

"No." She hesitated for a moment. "I ran out. The other cars stopped. I tried to wake him up, but a man said don't touch him. He said he'd called nine-one-one. Then they wouldn't let me go with him in the ambulance. One of the cops brought me here." Her eyes moved to Hank's shoes. "Nobody will tell me if he's going to die."

"He's not going to die," Hank said, "but he's still unconscious. They've stabilized him. Where do you live, Leanne?"

"In a group home. He's going to be okay?"

"He's out of immediate danger, but he may have a concussion. Where did you and Brett meet this morning?"

"He picked me up in the taxi, at my place. We were going to have lunch and then go see a movie."

"Do you have any way to get home? Can someone pick you up? Family?"

She shook her head. "I'm from Piscataway. My dad, he threw me out a long time ago."

"We'll make sure you get a ride back to the group home," Karen said.

Hank stood up and walked over to Walter Parris. "She says a police officer brought her to the hospital."

"Yes." Walter stood up. He took a business card out of his pocket and gave it to Hank. The card belonged to Detective Tom Brannigan, Traffic Investigation Unit, Special Investigations, Glendale Police Department. "I asked him to stay until you had a word with him. I think he's waiting in the cafeteria on the second floor."

"What can you tell me about Brett's whereabouts this morning?"

"He slept in this morning, which was a bit unusual, so he didn't go out for a walk. Mona came over. They did their session. He stayed in his room until about, oh, eleven thirty when a taxi came to pick him up. That's all."

Hank handed the card back to him and walked over to Karen. "There's a TIU detective waiting for us in the cafeteria."

Karen stood up.

"Do I have to leave?" Leanne asked.

"Not if you don't want to," Karen said. "Like I said, we'll make sure someone takes you back to the group home when you're ready."

"Thanks." She held out the handkerchief to Hank, staring at his kneecaps.

"Keep it," he said. "You may want to cry again."

She nodded and pulled it back, squeezing it tightly.

Brannigan was drinking coffee and talking on his cell phone when they found him in the cafeteria. He ended the call and shook hands. "Not much I can tell you right now," he said as they sat down. "So far we've got a black Honda or a white Ford Escort or a gray SUV, and nobody saw the driver. Nobody got the tag number, either. The cab driver didn't see it happen. He was too busy looking over his shoulder at the girl. Any word on the Parris guy?"

"Unconscious but stable," Hank said.

Karen leaned forward. "I'll bet it was a silver sports car. Unbefuckinglievable."

Brannigan looked at her. "You know something?"

"Just a minute," Hank interjected. "Nobody IDed it as a silver sports car, did they?"

Brannigan shifted a newspaper aside and pulled over his

notebook. "Let's see." He flipped a page. "The girlfriend, Leanne Whatshername, Nephews, said she thought it was gray or blue. Another witness, a Gail Henk, was coming out of the restaurant, and said she thought it was a white car, but couldn't say what kind. And a Philip Marconi, who was just going into the restaurant, said he looked back and thought he saw a black passenger van speeding away. Typical. Some of these vehicles may actually have been on the street at the time but had nothing to do with it. Eyewitnesses in hit-and-run cases are notoriously unreliable, folks."

Karen shook her head, seething. "It was Holland. That arrogant sonofabitch was taking out our only witness."

"Witness?" Brannigan frowned. "To what?"

"A homicide we're working," Hank replied, curtly. "Brett Parris was nearby when it happened. He said he saw a silver sports car leave the scene, but—" He held up a hand as Brannigan reacted. "He's not a reliable witness. He's a delusional schizophrenic with a paranoid belief that a certain individual who drives a silver sports car is stalking him. There's no definite connection here."

"The hell there ain't," Karen objected.

"This hit-and-run could be a random thing, completely unconnected," Hank said.

"What's this guy's name you're talking about?" Brannigan asked.

"Richard Holland," Karen said quickly. She rattled off his address and the make, model, and license number of Holland's car from memory.

As Brannigan wrote it down, Hank leaned forward. "Karen, we can't jump to conclusions here. Perry Crocker drives a silver sports car, too. Remember, it was returned to him this morning."

Brannigan looked at him. "Who's this now?"

Hank sighed and recited Crocker's particulars, also from memory. "It's unlikely there's a connection," he repeated as Brannigan wrote it all down.

"Well, you're right there," Karen said with considerable heat, "because it wasn't Crocker. It was Holland. Crocker has no reason to hit-and-run Brett Parris, but Holland sure the fuck does."

"Are there traffic cameras nearby?" Hank asked Brannigan.

"A few blocks away on either side. We were going to check against all these descriptions anyway when we got time. If our guy happened to go through a red light at those intersections or was speeding, we'll know, but if not, we'll be shit out of luck. Anyway, looks like we could start with these two vehicles."

"Just look for Holland's Ferrari, that's all," Karen spat. "You'll find it. The fucker's a cold-blooded killer, and it'd mean nothing to run down a defenseless bastard like Brett Parris."

"Karen," Hank warned.

She smashed her fist on the table and jumped out of her chair. "Don't fucking *Karen* me! You've been fighting me from day one on Holland, goddamn it, and now that poor bastard's up there in a fucking coma! Thanks to you!"

Hank watched in dismay as she stormed out of the cafeteria. He stood up. "Check those cams. ASAP."

"Roger, Lieutenant." Brannigan looked up at him, amused.

Hank went out into the corridor and looked left and right. There was no sign of her. To the right, the corridor ended in a t-intersection. He went down and looked left and right. Nothing. He retraced his steps, passing the cafeteria entrance, and kept on going. There were fewer people in the corridor this way. He passed a doorway into a small chapel and stopped. Karen stood inside the chapel with her back to him, her fists clenched at her sides, her posture rigid.

He went in and closed the door behind him. They were alone in the room.

She turned and bared her teeth. "You are so full of shit it's unbelievable. You're so busy kissing everybody's ass because they're rich and important you can't see the plain facts right in front of your fucking face!" Her voice rose. "You're so fucking busy being one of *them* you've forgotten you're a fucking cop! You're supposed to act like a *cop*, you fucking hypocrite! He shot that old fucker, he ran over the only person who saw him there, and you're fucking letting him get away with it because he's rich, his lawyer's rich, and everybody else in this fucking case is *rich*!"

She smacked a fist into her palm. "It's not fair! I try *so* fucking hard! And look at how that fucking Parris treats that girl downstairs, like she's a piece of shit on the bottom of his fucking shoe because she's native and mentally ill and not some fucking debutante! She can't even call herself the guy's girlfriend because his rich daddy doesn't like it! I'm sick of all of them, and I'm sick of you! Goddamn it all to hell! You're screwing up this fucking case just to please *them*!"

"Karen, that's not fair and you know it."

"Fair? You're telling me *I'm* not being fair? The fucking chief doesn't want me questioning rich people, but *I'm* not being fair? Have you lost your fucking mind?"

"Not that I know of."

"And then you bring in that fucking Truly," she went on, "who couldn't find her ass in the dark with both hands and hasn't made an arrest in her fucking life, and I'm supposed to sit there quietly like a nice little psycho and watch Miss T-Square analyze and disseminate? What the fuck's up with that? You—"

"Don't hold back, Karen. Tell me what you really think."

She stared at him. "Are you making fun of me? Are you making *fun* of me? You fucking *bastard*!"

She stepped forward and pulled back her fist to hit him right square in the mouth.

He didn't move a muscle, waiting.

She locked eyes with him, upper lip quivering, fist cocked.

He held his breath.

Her mouth opened. Her cheek trembled.

Then she threw her arms around him and began to cry into his chest.

27

He held her while she cried. It took a while.

Then she began to talk while she cried but it didn't make any sense, so he continued to hold her until she finally grew quiet.

She held him for a while longer and then let go. "Now *I* need a fucking handkerchief."

Hank took one out of his other pocket and gave it to her. "I always carry a back-up. Something I learned from a very good detective."

She laughed into the handkerchief. The laughter turned into more crying and she walked over to a chair and sat down. He followed, pulled another chair around, and sat down next to her. He watched her wipe her face and blow her nose. Her eyes were closed and her shoulders were slumped. After a moment she took a deep breath, pushed back her shoulders, and sat up straight.

"I'm really, really sorry," she said. "I didn't mean any of that. I don't know what happened."

"It's all right. I could see it was coming."

"It's *not* all right. I care more about you than anybody else alive. Other than Sandy. And maybe Darryl and Del. You're like a brother to me."

"Number Four, with a bullet."

She laughed, wiping her mouth. "Yeah. I guess. But I can't be saying shit like that to you. It's not true, none of it. I'm so, so sorry."

"It's all right. You're upset."

"Yeah."

"Tell me about it. We've got some time."

"I dunno."

"Pretend I'm Father Hank," he kidded. "Tell me what's troubling you, my child. After all, we're in the right place."

She frowned, looking around at the chapel furnishings. "Fuck, I never even noticed. Shows you how out of it I am."

"What's wrong?"

"This case. That smug bastard Holland. Moneybags Parris, who thinks he can pick up the phone and screw my career and, hey, that's okay because he's got money and I don't, which means he's got power and I don't." She looked at him. "I work real hard, Hank. This is my life. I'm not going to stand by while some fucking worm like Parris tries to fuck me over."

"And you don't think Truly belongs with us."

"Shit. Sorry. She's okay. I see why you brought her in for this. I'm not a complete fucking idiot. She's an intel wonk and a lab geek, but she's doing a good job with the info." She tucked hair behind her ear. "I just feel like I'm being pushed aside on this thing. The fucking Powers That Be don't like the way I do my job."

"Don't worry about them," Hank said.

She smiled at him without humor. "Ordinarily I don't give a rat's fucking ass about them, but they're putting the squeeze on me, Hank. I found a home with you in Homicide, and they're messing with it. Martinez cut me a huge break by pulling me out of Family-Related, and she knew what she was doing when she paired me with you. You saved my ass. Hell, you saved my career. I'm not going to give that up without a fight."

"You're not being asked to give it up."

"No, but it could be taken away again, just like that." She snapped her fingers. "I wasn't exactly in love with Family-Related, but it was my job, right? I do my job. I'm damn good at it. But Paup took it away from me because Williams gave me an order that was fucking out of line, and I told her so."

Hank waited. He'd read the reports in her jacket, of course, but wanted to hear about it from her.

"The kid was only six years old," she said. "The father would beat him with a piece of garden hose on the soles of his feet, then lock him in a little closet with no food or water, sometimes for more than a day. The mother wouldn't say anything and neither would the kid. His teacher was concerned, which is how we got it, but the problem was, the father was a lawyer and I couldn't get into the end zone. He started filing complaints and harassment charges and everything else against me he could think of, and I said a few things to him I shouldn't have, which of course gave him the ammunition he needed. Williams, the chickenshit, was intimidated by the guy and ordered me to drop it. I told her to fuck off. We happened to be outside at the time, in front of the main entrance. Paup was walking in just as I really got going on Williams. She stuck her nose in, and the next thing I know I'm on suspension. At my hearing, Williams drags in a lot of other crap on me and I thought for sure I'd get busted back down to uniform and have to spend the rest of my career directing traffic in Bering Heights or some fucking thing, but Martinez spoke up and offered to take me into Homicide.

"I still don't know why she did that. It saved my ass, though. Paup decided not to bust me down from detective, but I had to sit at home for three months watching TV, and my days in Family-Related were over. I didn't really want Homicide, you know? In Family-Related, you've still got a chance to save the kids and put things right, or as right as they'll ever be, but in Homicide it's too late. The victim's dead. It's over. So I didn't want to move, but I had no choice, especially with the service record Williams and Paup were writing for me. So, I know what it feels like to lose my job because of my mouth. I don't want to go down that road again. I don't know what else there is for me than this, Hank. I really don't."

"To get to you," Hank said, "they'll have to go through me. And Ann Martinez isn't Elspeth Williams."

"Yeah, I noticed."

"She likes you. She'll stand up for you." Hank paused. "Look, getting back to Truly, she's a bit of a project. I think she could be a very good cop, but she's got a lot to learn. You could help me bring her along. She'll probably end up in Intelligence, as you say, but we could help her be a better cop before she gets there."

"Might not be a good idea," Karen said. "You wouldn't want her turning into another Stainer, now would you?"

"You really have to let that go. Peralta was drowning, lashing out, trying to survive. You don't usually take that stuff personally."

"Struck a nerve, I guess."

"I can see that."

"I'm just—" She looked around the chapel for a moment before coming back to him. "I can look you in the eyes, right? Like right now? I make eye contact, right? With absolutely no problem?"

"Sure. Of course you do." He smiled. "You've got that cop stare that scares the shit out of people. You probably practice it in the mirror."

"Yeah. That's a good one. But you've noticed it with them,

though, haven't you? With Brett, and with the girl just now? That they can't make eye contact? It's a thing with a lot of schizophrenics. They can't do it. It's not possible. Brett fastens on my rack like it was the buffet at Golden Corral, but he doesn't mean anything by it. My mother would never look at my face, either. Up, down, anywhere but at me. Some of them say that when they look at you, they see your whole body at once, like looking down the wrong end of a kid's telescope, instead of just your face. Some of them, it's just because they know they stare at people funny and they just want to avoid trouble. Whatever. But I don't do that, right? When I look at your face, I'm looking at your damned face, right?"

"Yes. Of course."

She stood up and walked over to a little stand against the wall that held religious brochures and booklets. She began riffling through the brochures without seeing them. "Daddy didn't know what to do anymore. They kept finding her out on the highway, walking along the side of the road. Thinking she was going back home, to her parents' place. Who were both dead. And she'd have these long conversations with nobody, all this crap about learning to ride a horse and being a famous artist and raising canaries for money. None of which she did. Just random stuff. You know, while she's hallucinating that someone's sitting in the chair across from her."

Hank waited.

"If that happens to me," she said, turning around and putting her hand over her holster, "if I get like that, I swear—"

Hank's cell phone vibrated. He kept his eyes on Karen. She nodded and used the handkerchief to wipe her face. He took out the phone and answered it. "Donaghue."

He listened for a moment. "Go ahead."

He listened, then frowned. "Spit it out, Maureen."

He looked at Karen as he listened. She was watching him intently. It went on for a while, until he said, "Anything else? All right, good job. Thanks."

He put the phone away. "Something interesting. Marcotte found a draft e-mail on Jarrett's home computer from Thursday morning. It was one that wasn't sent. It was auto-saved and stored in his Drafts folder. Apparently he didn't notice when he cancelled the message."

"What'd it say?"

"It was to Emory Raskin. It said, quote, 'Did you take care of the Crocker thing? I want you to,' end quote. He started it at six twenty-seven and logged out at six twenty-nine. Marcotte figures he sat there for a minute, trying to decide whether or not to put it in writing, then changed his mind. Probably decided instead to speak to Raskin directly about it, so he shut the computer down but didn't realize the draft had been saved."

"The Crocker thing," Karen repeated. "The little weasel didn't mention any Crocker thing when I was squeezing him on Thursday."

"Then let's go see him again."

Karen didn't move.

"He's your witness, Karen. I'll take notes. Sound like a plan?"

She whacked him on the shoulder, hard. "Fuckin' A, Lou. Let's roll."

28

Emory Raskin's office was on a corner of the twentieth floor of Jarrett Tower, but unlike most corner offices it was sparsely furnished and completely unimposing. Raskin shook their hands and invited them to sit at a tiny, oval table with two cheap-looking chairs on either side. As they sat down, he scooted his chair around his desk to make a third at the table.

"What can I do for you? Got another meeting in ten minutes. Everything's nuts around here right now. All hands on deck."

Karen sat sideways on her chair and crossed her legs as Hank took out his notebook and pen. "You usually work on Sundays?"

"Seven days a week until further notice," Raskin said. "For my bunch, anyway. This is a publicly-trading corporation and share prices are falling. We gotta stabilize the ship as quick as we can. Legal's pulling overtime checking every last thing six times before it gets signed, no matter what it is."

"We won't take too much of your time, then," Karen said. "Just a couple of questions."

"I thought I answered everything the other day, but okay."

"You left one thing out, come to find out. The Crocker thing."

"Crocker thing?"

Karen uncrossed her legs and leaned forward, her forearms across her thighs, hands folded between her knees. She looked at Raskin with cool blue eyes. "Your boss was typing an e-mail to you the morning he was potholed, Emory. 'Did you take care of the Crocker thing?' We want to know what the Crocker thing was, and whether or not you took care of it."

"Didn't get an e-mail from Mr. Jarrett like that. Sorry."

"Of course you didn't. He never sent it. Now answer the question: what was the Crocker thing, and did you take care of it?"

Raskin looked away, out the window. "There're things I took care of for Mr. Jarrett that were off the books. Nothing illegal, mind you. Just off the books."

"You were Jarrett's janitor. That what you're saying?"

"More or less."

"That's interesting, Emory. Very interesting. So what was the Crocker thing, and did you take care of it?"

"I'd rather not talk about it, if you don't mind."

"I do mind, Emory. In case you didn't notice, we're in the middle of a homicide investigation here. It would be a good idea not to withhold information relevant to that investigation, if you know what I mean."

"Off the record."

"Christ. What do you think we are, goddamned reporters? We don't do off the record."

"You're asking me to break a promise of confidentiality I made to Mr. Jarrett a long time ago. I don't talk about this stuff to anybody. Just him and me."

"He's dead," Karen said. "He's not going to fire your ass now, is he?"

"It's not that. It's a matter of professional integrity. He could always trust me never to say a word about any of the things I did for him, this way. Ever."

Karen sat back. "It's too late to care about keeping your promises to him now, Emory. He's dead. Maybe Crocker did it. Maybe this thing you won't talk about was his motive. Maybe if you keep your mouth shut, he'll get away with it. Maybe your loyalty isn't worth jack after all."

Emory bit his lip, looked out the window. "Okay. But I don't see how it could be connected to someone killing him. I don't see how Mr. Crocker could be the one who did it."

"Just tell us the damned story, Emory."

"All right." He rubbed his jaw. "Mr. Crocker had approached me with a proposal for Mr. Jarrett. That sort of thing happened all the time. People came to me with stuff before they talked to Mr. Jarrett. Sensitive stuff, I mean."

"You were the gatekeeper for off-the-table business. They talked to Peggy Kelly about regular stuff, and they talked to you about the hinky stuff."

Raskin nodded. "This was a business proposal, but it was a personal matter. Mr. Crocker wanted to make Mr. Jarrett an offer. A lot of stuff I just turned down myself, if I knew Mr. Jarrett wouldn't like it or be interested in it, but this one I passed on. Mr. Jarrett listened to it and didn't like it one bit, and he got pretty pissed off with me, but it was something I knew he needed to hear."

"Why was that, Emory? Why did he need to hear it?"

"Well, you know. Because of the relationship between Mr. Crocker and Mrs. Jarrett."

"Which you're aware of."

Raskin said nothing, not interested in belaboring the obvious.

"What was the proposal?"

"Mr. Crocker wanted to buy out Mrs. Jarrett's prenuptial agreement."

Karen blinked. "He what?"

"He made Mr. Jarrett a cash offer equivalent to Mrs. Jarrett's prenuptial agreement. He didn't know what the actual amount would be, but that was his offer. Whatever it was worth."

"In exchange for what?"

"That Mr. Jarrett would divorce Mrs. Jarrett."

Karen glanced at Hank, who raised an eyebrow and shook his head. "That's a good one, Emory," she said. "So you passed on Crocker's offer, Jarrett hit the roof and tore your head off. What next?"

"I met with Mr. Crocker to give him Mr. Jarrett's response."

"Which was no."

"Correct."

"So how'd Crocker take it?"

Raskin shrugged. "He's a businessman. It was negotiation. He made a better offer."

"Christ. What was it this time?"

"The cash equivalent of the prenup, plus a twenty-percent interest in his business."

"In CrocComm? Are you kidding me?"

"No, of course not."

"So how did Jarrett take it this time? Blow up in little pieces again?"

"No. He took a while to consider it. I imagine he checked out CrocComm in more detail."

Karen looked at Hank, whose eyes were down as he wrote in his notebook. She shook her head. "You people are from another planet. You know that, right?"

Raskin shifted in his chair, irritated. "Look, Detective, these are very successful business people. At the top of the heap, okay? They're not like you and me. They get offers every day to do things they don't necessarily want to do, but a lifetime's worth of training tells them to look at these things from every angle. 'Act in haste, repent at leisure,' right? Even with very personal stuff, that's how Mr. Jarrett was. He took a step back and checked it out. Due diligence."

"Okay, okay. So he thought about it, and he did his due diligence. I get it. So then what?"

"He instructed me to tell Mr. Crocker the answer was still no, and that it wasn't up for negotiation. Mr. Crocker should just drop it and wait until he, I mean Mr. Jarrett, passed away before trying his luck to get Mrs. Jarrett to marry him. That he intended to stay married to Mrs. Jarrett for the rest of his life."

"Is that how you told it to Crocker? Like that?"

"Yeah, that was the message I gave him. Just like that."

"That he should wait until the old man was dead."

"Yeah."

"Sounds to me like you put the gun in Crocker's hand and invited him to pull the trigger. Doesn't it sound that way to you?"

Raskin shook his head emphatically. "No. I don't like Mr. Crocker, but he wouldn't do something like that. He's not crazy."

"How'd Crocker take it, getting the door slammed in his face like that?"

"He was a bit frustrated. I've seen it before. He gave me a little speech about Mrs. Jarrett and how they loved each other, and all. Then he said Mr. Jarrett was making a mistake."

"Uh oh," Karen said.

Raskin waved a hand in the air. "No no, not like that. He didn't say it like a threat. He was just frustrated. He thought he'd made a really good offer and that Mr. Jarrett should have taken it. Like I said, I've seen that sort of thing before, where people wanted to make a quiet back-door deal with Mr. Jarrett of some kind or another, and when he said no they'd always say the same thing. 'He's making a big mistake.' People don't like being turned down. But Mr. Crocker also told me to tell Mr. Jarrett he respected his decision."

"He said that?"

Raskin nodded.

"Okay, tell me something else. Did Jarrett's wife know all this was going on?"

Raskin raised his eyebrows. "I severely doubt it. Mr. Jarrett wouldn't say anything to her, I'd bet the farm on that, and there's no way she'd hear about it from me. I don't know if Mr. Crocker told her, himself, but I'd bet he didn't. I'd've felt the aftershocks, believe me. She would've raised the roof."

"You think?"

Hank asked, "Exactly when did all this take place, Mr. Raskin?"

"Last couple of months."

"Can you be more specific?"

Raskin tilted his head sideways. "Yeah, sure. Mr. Crocker first approached me the third week of March. The twenty-first, something like that. I had to wait almost a week to meet with Mr. Jarrett because he was in D.C., then New York. There was no urgency to it, you see."

"Important, but not urgent."

"Yeah, you got it."

"So you spoke to him about it, when?"

"That'd be the first week of April. The Tuesday or Wednesday."

"And what about the rest of it?"

"Let's see." Raskin looked out the window. "I gave him Mr. Jarrett's answer sometime near the end of April. Mr. Crocker had been out of the country for a while. I gave Mr. Jarrett his revised offer the first week of May. Then I met with Mr. Crocker the final time two weeks ago, the twenty-eighth of May, to give him Mr. Jarrett's final answer."

"Interesting," said Karen, "but not the end of the story, right? There was something else you were supposed to do, and Jarrett wanted to know if you'd done it yet just before he got himself popped. So what was that last thing, Emory? Did Jarrett change his mind or something? Were you supposed to reopen the bidding with Crocker?"

"I think maybe you misunderstood something," Raskin said. "When I told you Mr. Jarrett took a while to do his due diligence on CrocComm, I didn't mean he was actually thinking about accepting the offer. That never crossed his mind." He turned to Hank. "Mr. Jarrett never explained himself to me, but he didn't need to. I understood him pretty well. He wanted to do his due diligence on CrocComm because he wanted to know why Mr. Crocker'd be willing to give up such a big chunk of it. He wanted to know if there were problems there, or what."

He scratched his ear. "Mr. and Mrs. Jarrett had a tacit understanding, see. They had an open marriage, far as that went, which was in the prenup. Mr. Jarrett insisted I put it in there. But there was also a tacit understanding he'd leave her boyfriends alone. Turned out Mr. Crocker was the only one, in the end, and Mr. Jarrett was as good as his word. He had me run background on him, sure, and all that stuff, but that's as far as it went."

"But then Crocker crossed the line," Karen suggested.

"Yeah, and it really upset Mr. Jarrett. His instructions for me on Monday were to put together a creeping takeover of CrocComm. At least, the start of one."

She frowned. "A creeping takeover?"

"Yeah. It's a gradual buy-up of shares in a publicly-trading company. You pick them up through the open market so you don't have to make a formal offer to shareholders and pay a premium above what they're worth. Plus, you do it slowly, a bit at a time, so you don't draw attention and spike the price. With something like this you gotta be careful not to violate the *Williams Act*, but I've done it before for Mr. Jarrett and I know how to stay in that gray area where the SEC won't have anything to say. The point, though, is that I was supposed to get the ball rolling, get up to a certain percentage, and then Mr. Jarrett was going to have a quiet word with Mr. Crocker about his attitude."

"His attitude."

"Yeah. He didn't have to say anything, but I understood Mr. Jarrett was very disappointed in Mr. Crocker's attitude toward Mrs. Jarrett. He felt it showed a lack of respect for her as a person, and he wasn't going to just let it slide."

"Interesting. So how far did you get?"

"It was underway. I use certain third parties, and I still had a few to get on board. If Mr. Jarrett was doing that e-mail you mentioned, he was likely going to ask me for a status update."

"Did you usually communicate in writing about these things?" Hank asked.

"Good point, Lieutenant. We're always very careful, but in this case we weren't going to go very far with it. Just fire a warning shot across the bow, so to speak. There wouldn't have been anything to worry about from the SEC, so I guess Mr. Jarrett figured it would be okay to send me an e-mail, particularly if we weren't going to have a chance to talk about it, which we weren't, since we were both so busy with his retirement plans and all that stuff, but I guess he changed his mind and that's why he didn't send it."

"Any chance Crocker caught wind of this?" Karen asked.

"No way," Raskin laughed. "I've done this sort of thing for a very long time, Detective Stainer. Nobody catches wind of anything before Mr. Jarrett wants them to. Period." He looked at his watch. "Look, if there's nothing else, I really gotta go to this next meeting."

Down in the Crown Vic, Karen started the engine. "I still say it's Holland, but I'm willing to play along. Let's go have a chat with Crocker." She shifted into reverse and backed out of their parking space. "Unless you'd rather take Truly, since you and her have been working this angle already."

"You're on a roll," he said. "Do your thing."

She grinned back. "Fire in the hole."

29

They caught up to Perry Crocker at slip twenty-one of the Federal Point marina, where he and Chrissy Jarrett were just coming ashore after an afternoon on the water.

Karen's nostrils flared at the scent of salt in the air. She loved the smell. She stepped up to Perry Crocker and badged him. "Detective Stainer, Homicide. Lieutenant Donaghue and I have a few follow-up questions for you, Mr. Crocker."

Crocker glanced at her badge and shifted his eyes to Hank. "Really, Donaghue. I thought you'd have gotten the idea after ransacking my home and confiscating my car that I had nothing to do with your investigation. Can't you just leave us alone? We're trying to put this all behind us."

"Perry's right," Chrissy said to Hank. "Can't you see he didn't have anything to do with it?"

"Mrs. Jarrett," Karen said, "we haven't met. I'm Detective Karen Stainer. I'm very sorry for your loss. Believe me, the lieutenant and I are fully committed to nailing whoever murdered your husband. It's important that we discuss a few details with Mr. Crocker right now. Is there somewhere you could wait for him until we're done?"

Chrissy opened and closed her mouth, looking at Hank.

"Maybe in the Captain's Run," Hank suggested, referring to the seafood restaurant behind them, next to the marina office. "It won't be long."

"All right," Chrissy said. "After all, it's happy hour, isn't it? I'll have a drink, and be happy." She shifted her small handbag to her left hand and held out her right hand to Karen. "Thank you for your sympathies."

Karen shook her hand. "You're welcome, Mrs. Jarrett."

Chrissy gave Hank a long look and brushed past him, walking quickly down the pier.

"Nice boat," Karen said, stepping up next to Crocker. "Must have cost you a fortune."

"My yacht is no concern of yours," Crocker said.

"No, come on," Karen said. "I love boats. I've searched them before. Busted people on them before. Boats and I get along just great. Love the name. *Croc Runner.* How much did you pay for it?"

Crocker looked over the top of her head at Hank. "Donaghue, can we just get this over with?"

"Detective Stainer's conducting this interview," Hank said. "Answer her questions, Mr. Crocker."

"Jesus, you people."

"Play along, Skippy," Karen said. "It won't hurt. Tell me about your boat."

"Oh, for God's sake. It's a fifty-two-foot 2010 Predator. Cherry wood, teak floors, seven-hundred-horsepower Volvo engine, three cabins, all the extras. I paid one point two million for it in March. Okay? Are we done now?"

"See?" Karen smiled. "Not so hard. Next question isn't so hard either. Does Mrs. Jarrett know you tried to buy her from her husband before he got offed?"

"You have to be kidding. This conversation's over." He tried to move around her but Karen shifted, blocking his way.

"I'd love to book you on suspicion. Just keep it up. You'll find the inside of a cell an interesting new experience."

Hank said, "We know about your failed attempt to buy out Mrs. Jarrett's prenuptial agreement. It gives you plenty of motive for murder. Answer Detective Stainer's questions or we *will* take you downtown and book you."

"Does Mrs. Jarrett know about it?" Karen asked again.

"No, no. Christ, no. She'd kill me if she found out." He realized what he'd just said. "Figuratively, I mean. No, it was just a bad idea. A bad idea. I wanted to see if Jarrett would back out of the picture. I didn't know he actually had feelings for her. He refused, so I dropped it."

"It didn't occur to you it was a brainless, thoughtless thing to do? That you can't buy a woman like that, like she was a business or a yacht or something? I'm just curious."

"It was a bad idea," Crocker repeated. "I'm crazy about her. What can I say? Their marriage was like a business deal. I thought, I don't know, maybe he'd go for another deal. I was wrong."

"Did you know that Jarrett had begun a creeping takeover of

your company? That he was buying up CrocComm stock on the q.t.?"

Crocker's face went blank. His eyes shifted out over the water, then slowly back to her. "What's your source? How do you know Jarrett was behind it?"

"You didn't know, did you? You didn't see it happening."

"No," Crocker reluctantly admitted. "But if Jarrett was behind something like that, I can understand why."

"So can we," Hank said.

Crocker rolled his eyes. "I see where you're going. Forget it. I had no idea, so it wasn't a motive for me to kill Jarrett. Forget it, people. You've already taken my computer records and e-mail and every other goddamned thing that wasn't nailed down. You won't find a smoking gun connected to this takeover you're talking about because I had no idea. Dead end. I was clueless. He was coming at me from my blind side. Christ, what a bastard."

"Where were you between eleven and one today?"

"What? I was at sea. Didn't you hear me say we were out on the water?"

"What time did you leave?"

"Shortly before ten. We just got back." Crocker shook his head. "Tomorrow's her husband's funeral, for crying out loud. The governor's supposed to be there, and a lot of other VIPs. Not to mention all the media. She's under huge pressure. I'm trying to take her mind off it."

"You're saying you took your boat out at ten, and the marina can verify that?"

"I got clearance going and coming," Crocker said. "I stayed in U.S. water the whole time, so I didn't report to customs, but the marina's log, inside, will give you the times I called in to them. Why? What's so special about this morning?"

"When Jarrett turned you down on your bonehead offer," Karen said, "what was your reaction? Did you get mad?"

"What? Yes. No. I didn't get mad. I was upset, but not mad. Not angry. Disappointed. It would've made things a lot easier."

"Well, they're pretty easy right now, aren't they?" Karen folded her arms. "What's your beef against Brett Parris?"

"Who? I don't know who that is."

"Brett Parris," Karen repeated. "Don't you like him, or something?"

"I don't know who Brett Parris is," Crocker repeated. "I know who Walter Parris is. Oh, wait. Brett's his son. Why?"

"Somebody ran him down this morning," Karen said. "If we go look at your car in the parking lot, are we going to find damage on the front of it?"

"What next?" Crocker complained. "You're welcome to take a look, please do. You'll see it's in perfect condition. The way it always is. I have no idea what the hell you're talking about, but you're just as far off base as ever." He looked at Hank. "*Now* are we done?"

Hank looked at Karen. Karen rolled her eyes.

"Thank you for your time, Mr. Crocker," Hank said.

"Yeah, whatever." Crocker shook his head and walked away.

They trailed behind, watching him leave the pier and cross the pavement to the restaurant. They walked back to the parking lot and found Crocker's car. It was intact. Completely undamaged.

"Lou," Karen said.

"Yeah, I know." Hank turned away, looking back at the yachts moored at their floating slips along the pier.

"It was Holland. Both times."

He ran a hand through his frizzy hair, his thoughts shifting.

"Listen," she went on, "we can go in and check on Crocker's story with the marina, but I don't see the point. What we *should* do is go talk to Peggy Kelly again. She's a smart lady. I want to know why she doesn't like Holland. She knows stuff she didn't tell us the first time. Let me talk to her again. I'll behave myself."

He looked up at the blue sky, inhaling the warm salty air.

"Holland did it," she said. "C'mon, Lou. He's just over the next hill. The dogs are howlin'. They can smell him. It's time to nail his sorry ass."

Hank looked at her. "Let's go see Kelly."

30

Peggy Kelly lived in a very comfortable Colonial-style house on Stamford Road in Granger Park. The house had four dormer windows on the third floor, six shuttered windows on the second floor, and two large bay windows on the ground floor. Karen rang the front door bell. Kelly let them in and led them through a set of French doors into a sun room that looked out onto the rear of the property. They could smell food cooking. It smelled good. Roast beef.

Kelly had made a pot of coffee. As they sat down, she poured cups for them and offered cream and sugar. When they were settled, Karen opened on a conciliatory note.

"Thanks for meeting with us on short notice. You said your husband's coming home this evening?"

Kelly nodded. She was dressed casually in jeans, moccasins, and a simple jade-colored top. She glanced at a mantle clock on top of a bookcase. "He should be home in about an hour."

"He's driving down from Norfolk?"

"Yes. He'll be with me at the funeral tomorrow."

"This won't take long."

"You said you had some follow-up questions."

"Yeah, about Richard Holland. When we talked about him before, you said he was the son of some guy who used to work with your boss."

"Yes. Gerald Holland."

"Jarrett caught the guy stealing, canned him, and the guy committed suicide. You figured your boss felt sorry about the whole thing and hired Richard Holland after he graduated from college, then helped him up the ladder. Something like that."

"Something like that, yes."

"I got the impression you don't like Holland very much, Ms. Kelly. I think you said he was an over-achiever. How the hell did he make it as a VP? Help me out here. Holland said he's been with the company twelve years. Started as an advertising account manager or something. Is that right?"

"More or less. He worked for us before that as an intern, while he was finishing his MBA, then Mr. Jarrett instructed me to find him something in the company, so I found an opening for him as an account executive in public affairs. Three years later he was promoted to manager of the advertising account unit, and three years after that to general manager after a reorganization of our marketing and advertising section."

"I see. Sounds like he knew what he was doing."

"His primary skill is using other people around him."

"I guess you could say that about most managers, couldn't you?"

"Of course. Managers need to surround themselves with people who are excellent at what they do. The most successful ones, though, are themselves very detail-oriented. Richard lacks that particular skill. He's more just . . . manipulative of other people."

"Okay, so he makes general manager." Karen pinched her nose, thinking. "Then what?"

"In 2010 the vice-president's position came open in corporate and regulatory affairs."

"The one he's in now."

"Correct."

"But if I remember right, someone else got that job first."

"Yes. Mr. Forrestall."

"So what happened to him?"

Kelly looked down at her hands. "He committed suicide. In a hotel room in Baltimore. You may have seen it in the news. The police discovered he had been using male prostitutes up there for quite a few years. His wife was devastated."

"And this was when?"

"October, 2010."

"Forrestall had already been appointed vice-president?" Karen asked.

"Yes, in August."

"And no one had any idea this other stuff was going on?"

Kelly shook her head.

"And there was Holland, in the right place at the right time."

"You could say that," Kelly said. "Oh, he'd lobbied for the job for himself, quite shamelessly, but the board preferred Mr. Forrestall.

After his death, my recommendation was that we begin a new search for candidates, and most of the chief executives backed me on it, but Mr. Jarrett chose instead to insist that Richard be appointed to the job."

"Jarrett insisted."

"Yes."

"Why? Did Holland have something on him? Something he was using to force his way up the ladder?"

"I don't know. I don't think so. But Mr. Jarrett said to me once he thought he saw something of himself in Richard, and he wanted to see if he was right or wrong about it."

"Okay." Karen switched gears. "Let's go back to something. We understand that Holland's mother still lives in town somewhere. Do you know her at all?"

Kelly shook her head. "I've never met her. Her name's Mary Holland. She lives in Springhill."

"You know where in Springhill?"

"Yes. I sent her flowers and a gift every Christmas in Mr. Jarrett's name."

"Really. That's very interesting. Could you give us that address now?"

"It's in my tablet. In my purse in the other room."

"We don't mind waiting."

When Kelly left the room, Karen looked at Hank, who was sipping his coffee. "Right place at the right time, my ass."

"Could be dirty tricks," Hank said, putting his cup down.

"She's still not giving us the lowdown."

"Maybe she doesn't know. Or it's professional caution. Avoidance of slander."

"Someone else must know what was going on, somebody not afraid to spill the beans."

Hank motioned with his chin toward the door. Karen turned and watched Kelly walk back into the sun room, intent on the tablet in her hand, reading glasses perched on the end of her nose.

"You like that thing?" Karen asked.

Kelly looked at her over her glasses. "Pardon me? Oh, yes, I do. I don't know what I'd do without it. Do you have one?"

"Me? No. I wouldn't have a use for it."

Kelly recited Mary Holland's address. Hank wrote it down.

"Thanks," Karen said. "One more thing before we get out of

your hair. Is there someone else in the company we could talk to who might know a little more about Holland from day-to-day experience, working with him?"

"You could try his EA, I suppose."

"Who'd that be?"

"Ellen Moore. I could give you her home coordinates."

Home coordinates. "That'd be great," Karen replied. "How long has she worked for him?"

"Only five or six months. Here it is." Kelly recited the address and telephone number of Ellen Moore.

"What about before that? Someone who maybe worked with him before?"

"Support staff tend not to stay with Richard for very long. I suppose you could see if Celestina might be willing to answer a few questions. She'd know him better than the others."

Celestina Flores, it turned out, had been Holland's secretary in 2003 when he was advertising accounts manager. After two years she became executive assistant of the general manager, Holland's boss, but continued to deal with him on a daily basis. When the section was reorganized and Holland became general manager in 2006, Celestina transferred out of the division rather than remain and have to work for Holland again. She was now the secretary to a manager in the testing area of their skin care division. Kelly gave them her address. They thanked her for her time and left.

Celestina Flores lived across the river in Wilmingford, in a neighborhood Karen and Hank both knew very well. It was a rough area that had seen its share of homicide investigations over the years. Celestina lived in an apartment above Gomes Used Appliances & Repair on Sifton Street. It was a small building, perhaps a family home in a previous lifetime that had been converted into a business on the ground floor, with living quarters above. Most of the businesses on this block, including the used appliance store, looked as though they'd been abandoned for some time. As Karen got out of the Crown Vic, a police cruiser rolled to a stop next to her. The cop in the passenger side lowered the window.

"Can I see some identification?"

Karen showed him her badge as Hank leaned over the roof of the Crown Vic from the passenger side, amused.

"Thanks, Detective," the officer said. "Hour ago there was a b-and-e two blocks over. We've been trawling for suspicious movement. You never know."

"You're looking for someone who looks like a plainclothes cop?"

"No, m'am," the officer flushed. "We saw the Crown Vic and were hoping you could keep your eyes open while you're down here. Just in case."

"Be glad to."

"Thanks." The window went back up and the cruiser rolled away.

"That kind of neighborhood," Hank said.

They went through an open doorway and up a flight of stairs. There was only one door in the short hallway. Karen pounded on it. It was opened almost immediately by a pretty young African-American woman with an enormous head of frizzy hair, tinted, large-framed glasses, tight black t-shirt, and blue jeans. A television set was blaring in the background. The woman waved a lit joint at them and grinned.

"Hi, who y'all looking for?"

Karen grinned back, badging her. "Boo."

"Omigod, it's not what you think!" The young woman backpedaled into the room and threw her joint into a potted plant. "It's just herbs. From the health food store."

"Sure it is," Karen said, making a production of sniffing the air, which was heavy with the pungent smell of marijuana. "We're looking for Celestina Flores. You her?"

"She's in the bathroom. Celestina! It's the police! They're looking for you!"

"Okay if we come in?" Karen asked, walking into the room. Hank followed, moving to her right.

"Yeah, sure. I just have to go do something in my room. I'll be right back." She hurried into the next room and closed the door.

"Out the window," Hank said.

"Down the fire escape." Karen heard a toilet flush from behind another closed door. She walked over and rapped on it with a knuckle. "Celestina Flores? Glendale PD. Can you come out and talk to us for a minute? It's about your place of work. It'll only take a few minutes."

The bathroom door cracked open. Karen held up her badge. "Detective Stainer, Homicide. We're not narks. Are you Celestina?"

The door opened wider on a tiny woman in her mid-twenties.

Her dark, curly hair was shoulder length, her complexion was mottled, and she had prominent dark circles under her eyes. "Yeah. What's this about?"

"Come on out and sit down over here, we'll talk about it." Karen pushed the door open the rest of the way. "This is Lieutenant Donaghue."

Hank held up his badge and identification. Celestina turned off the television set, to their collective relief, and they all sat down in the tiny living room. The place was small and cramped, but the furnishings were solid and well cared-for, as though they'd come from someone's house and were being kept here as a last resort.

"Nice stuff," Karen said, looking around.

"It was all my grandma's," Celestina said. "I was her only relative, so I got all her things when she passed." She looked around. "I kept as much as I could, when I moved from my old place. It was bigger than this. You want coffee or something?"

"No, thanks. We won't be long. When did you move?"

"I guess it was a few years ago, now. I had a nice place downtown that was a real short commute to work but I couldn't afford to keep it after I changed jobs, on account of my salary going down. And, I had to find a roommate. Good ones are hard to find."

"Yeah," Karen glanced at the closed bedroom door, "you got a real keeper there."

"I didn't know she did weed until after she moved in. I hate that stuff. It gives me migraines."

"So throw her out."

"I can't afford to. It's hard to find roommates who'll live in this neighborhood, and I need someone to split the rent with. Even a dump like this is expensive, with the hydro, the phone, Internet, all those things. Plus a security system and insurance for Grandma's stuff. There's a lot of break-ins around here."

"So we heard." Karen folded her hands. "So tell us about changing jobs. You work at Jarrett, don't you?"

"Yeah, that's right. I've been there fourteen years. Got hired right out of high school as a typist, and I've been there ever since."

Karen glanced at Hank, who looked comfortable in an overstuffed armchair with a hand-crocheted antimacassar and arm protectors. He crossed his legs, notebook open on his lap, and tilted up the corners of his mouth at her.

Such a smartass.

"We understand you worked as a secretary for Richard Holland, is that right?"

"Yes, m'am."

"You don't have to call me m'am," Karen said. "We don't give a shit about the weed, although your roommate should maybe think twice about it. What's her name?"

"Adelia Peterson."

"Okay. Tell us about Holland. Exactly when did you work for him?"

"From oh-three to oh-five. Then I got promoted to EA for the general manager, Mr. Simmons. They had this competition, with tests and interviews. I scored a lot higher than anybody else."

"Good for you. But you left that job when Holland became general manager, right? Why was that?"

"I didn't want to work for him anymore."

"No? How come?"

Celestina glanced at Hank, who was listening with a placid expression on his face. "He just wasn't somebody you'd want to work for, that's all."

"Some managers are hard to live with," Hank said. "If you say black, they say white. If you need time for a doctor's appointment or something, they make a big deal about it. Is that how Holland was?"

"Sort of."

"Or maybe," Karen said, looking at Hank, "he had a mean streak. Could be a little nasty. Some bosses are like that."

"True enough," Hank agreed.

"He was mean," Celestina said, "and not just to me."

"Oh?"

"He was phony nice, but if you made a mistake, he could get real nasty about it. Once, when I was his secretary, I cut off somebody on the phone by mistake and he came out of his office and hit me on the back of the head with a rolled-up magazine. Real hard. I didn't see it coming and it really hurt, you know? It triggered a bad migraine that lasted the rest of the day. I was crying in the washroom afterwards but couldn't tell anybody why. I just made something up. If I said it was because of him and it got back, he'd do something else even worse. But people knew. Word got around anyway, because he was mean to all the girls like that."

"Just the women, Celestina?" Karen asked. "He just bullied support staff?"

"Oh, no. He was mean to everybody."

"All right." Karen glanced at Hank, who was listening to Celestina without expression. "Did he ever do anything of a sexual nature to you or anyone else you know?"

"No. Not at all. He wasn't that kind of person."

"He wasn't a sexual predator or a guy who used his position to pressure women, yourself or others, into having sex with him?"

"No."

"But he was violent. He hit you. Did he hit other people, to your knowledge?"

"Yes. There were stories. The secretary who replaced me when I was promoted, I remember one day she had a lot of bad bruises on her arm but she wouldn't talk about it. My friend Florence heard it was Mr. Holland, that she tried to leave a little early for lunch and he grabbed her, twisted her arm and forced her back into her chair and wouldn't let her leave the office until the end of the day. Not even to go to the washroom. Someone said she wet herself in the middle of the afternoon and he wouldn't even let her go clean up. She quit a few days later."

"Christ."

"As soon as Mr. Holland got the promotion to general manager," Celestina said to Hank, "I got out of there. I wasn't going to work for him again. No way. I didn't even stay at the Tower. I found a secretary's job over here at the Wilmingford campus, in skin care. I took a big cut in pay and ended up moving across the river to this place because I couldn't afford the commute anymore, but it was worth it to get away from him. I'm telling you all this stuff now, but you have to keep my name out of it. And Florence's, too. It's about Mr. Jarrett, isn't it? About him being shot."

"That's right," Hank said.

"I thought so. You think he killed Mr. Jarrett."

"What kind of relationship did Holland and Jarrett have?"

"I don't know. I never met Mr. Jarrett. He never came around to our floor back then. But I heard people say later, after I got out of there, that Mr. Jarrett had a soft spot for him, that Mr. Holland was his golden boy. Nobody could understand it. The people who knew what Mr. Holland was like."

Karen sat forward. "Let me ask you about something else. Do

you know who Brett Parris is?"

"Um, yeah. That's Mr. Parris's son. He's got some kind of mental condition. The poor guy."

"You've met him before? You know him?"

"I saw him a couple of times at parties, like at Christmas. He was there one time taking pictures. Seems like a nice guy."

"Know of any back-and-forth between him and Holland?"

"No. Nobody really knew him at work. Sorry."

"That's okay," Karen said.

"Wait. That's who it was," Celestina said suddenly. "I forgot about that."

"Forgot about what?"

"You're making me remember stuff. That Christmas party I was talking about. It was just one of those things happened real quick and nobody else sees it, you know? I forgot it was Brett Parris until just now, because we're talking about him."

"Forgot about what?" Karen repeated.

"I was walking through the crowd, trying to go get my coat to go home. Mr. Holland was one or two people ahead of me, walking this way"—she motioned with her hand to suggest that Holland was crossing her path from left to right—"and the Parris guy, Brett, was walking in front of him, holding his camera in his hand. His right hand, because I could see it. I remember Mr. Holland reached out and hit him from behind on the elbow, like this"—she made a movement with her hand, as though to hit something with the heel of her palm—"and the guy dropped his camera on the floor. It fell hard and a couple people kicked it by accident before he could get it again. He was real upset about it. He was scared his camera was broken. It looked real expensive."

"Son of a bitch," Karen said.

"Yeah. When he got his camera back he looked around, but Mr. Holland had already gone. But I remember Brett looked at some other guy and swore at him for doing it, and called him Holland, like he thought the guy was Mr. Holland. It was weird. That's all I remember. I got out of there pretty soon after that because I hate those things and leave as soon as I can."

"Son of a bitch," Karen said again, looking at Hank. Peggy Kelly had mentioned an incident at a Christmas party, and even Holland himself had joked about it. Brett had gone into one of his paranoid Fregoli delusions about Holland, and Walter Parris had been forced to hustle him out of there. Now here was a witness telling her the thing had been triggered by Holland himself for malicious fun.

Paranoid schizophrenic or not, Brett Parris apparently had good reason to think that Richard Holland was out to get him.

31

The city of Glendale was configured in a hub-and-spoke arrangement, with Midtown district as the downtown hub and the other districts as the spokes radiating out from the center. Springhill district, the southwest spoke, was formerly a separate municipality that had amalgamated with the greater municipality when consolidation was seen by Glendale as a way to increase its tax base and by Springhill as a way to streamline costs.

Springhill still had its own airport, business section, and affluent suburbs. It also had its own decayed industrial core, housing projects, and middle-class suburbs that had fallen on hard times and seen wholesale foreclosures as a result of the economic downturn. As they drove down Harmans Avenue on their way to Mary Holland's address, Hank and Karen saw that for every three houses with a vehicle in the driveway and kids on the front lawn there was another that was abandoned, front lawn uncut and mailbox overflowing with yellowed advertising flyers and unpaid bills.

Fourteen thirty-six Harmans Avenue was a small, two-bedroom bungalow with an attached garage. It had a low-pitched tar-and-gravel roof, a stained stucco exterior, and awning-style windows that were supposed to pivot outward but looked as though they hadn't been opened in decades. Heavy, dark curtains prevented passersby from seeing inside. The grass on the tiny front lawn had recently been mowed, but the paved driveway was cracked and chipped.

It was a far cry from Granger Park and its mansions.

Hank walked up the three cement steps and rapped on the front door. Karen followed, looking around. He turned and caught her eye. She nodded and went back to her survey of the neighborhood.

The front door opened. Hank held up his identification and badge. "I'm Lieutenant Donaghue. This is Detective Stainer. Are you Mrs. Mary Holland?"

"Yes, I am." She ran a hand down the side of her knee-length flowered dress. "What do you want?"

"We're investigating the death of Mr. H.J. Jarrett. We'd like to ask you a few questions, if you don't mind."

"I don't see how I could possibly help you. Did you talk to my son? He works for Jarrett."

Hank saw the resemblance in the small blue eyes and the hair that had once been blond, but Mary's chubby cheeks had collapsed into jowls and slight plumpness had taken a postmenopausal turn into heaviness. "We've talked to your son, but we have a few other questions for you, if you don't mind."

"I don't see how I could help."

"We won't take very much of your time."

She stepped back and gestured them inside. On the left was a doorway into a combined dining room and kitchen. On the right was a small living room with a sofa, armchair, rocking chair, television set, component stereo system with a turntable, cassette tape deck, and speakers, and a small shelving unit with paperback novels on the upper shelves and vinyl long-play records on the lower shelf.

"Please, sit down," she said, moving to the sofa.

"Thanks." Hank sat down in the rocking chair. Karen wandered past the television set and ran her hand carelessly across the top. It was warm. She'd probably turned it off when she heard them at the door.

Hank took out his notebook and pen. "We understand that your late husband, Mr. Gerald Holland, worked for the Jarrett company before his death. Is that right?"

"Yes, it is. If you've been talking to them, you've already heard the story."

"Them?"

"The Jarretts." She waved a dismissive hand. "The Parrises. All of them. It's part of the folklore around there."

"We've heard something about theft from the company. That your husband was forced to leave. Which he did."

"It wasn't that simple. Gerry was a good man." She looked at Karen, who'd picked up a framed photograph from the top of the shelving unit. "We were married at All Saints Episcopal, downtown. That was taken in front of the church right afterwards. The tenth of June, 1968."

"You look pretty," Karen said, putting the picture back down.

"I was twenty. Gerry was twenty-five."

"He worked for Cross Bandage at that time?" Hank asked.

214

"When we were married? Yes. I was a nurse. I'd just finished my courses, and I was working at Angel of Mercy when we met. He was selling bandages and supplies. Two years later he was promoted to sales manager. That's when Jarrett bought the company and Gerry went to work for him."

"This was before Richard was born, I take it," Hank said.

"Yes."

Karen held up another framed photograph, this one of Richard Holland. It was his college graduation photo. "He looks just like you."

"Yes."

Karen put the photograph down. She walked over to the armchair and sat down on the edge of the cushion, folding her hands between her knees.

Hank watched as Mary Holland looked Karen over. He saw her eyes take in Karen's gun, her jeans, her cowboy boots, her tailored jacket. He thought about her one-word responses to the last two statements.

He said, "Did you know your husband was stealing from Jarrett's company, Mrs. Holland?"

"No. Gerry handled all the finances. I mean our finances. But Jarrett had his own accounting system, and it didn't match up to what Gerry was used to with Cross. They accounted for things differently. There were totals Jarrett was looking for that he didn't have to show at Cross, and there were things he'd accounted for at Cross that he couldn't figure out how to show at Jarrett. He used some of the cash that Cross considered discretionary for a down payment on a car for us, and a few other things, like our winter vacation. He shouldn't have, but he said he thought they wouldn't know the difference."

"But they did."

"Yes. Herb told him he could either quit or be arrested and fired. So Gerry quit."

"And took his own life shortly after."

"Yes."

"How old was Richard when this happened?"

"Two."

"It must have been terribly upsetting for you, with a child that young."

She didn't respond.

"How well did you know Mr. Jarrett?"

She brought her eyes slowly around to Hank's. "Herb? He was a hard man. Unforgiving. He took what was his and didn't make compromises."

"Did he attend your husband's funeral?"

"Yes."

"Did you see him after that?"

She shook her head. "Not very often."

"It must have been hard on Richard," Hank said, "growing up without a father."

Her brow creased defensively. "He did all right. He had some problems in school, but then most boys do."

"Poor grades?"

"Oh, no. His grades were always excellent. Top of his class. No, just a few behavioral issues we had to work through."

"Bullying?" Hank guessed.

"Yes."

"He went to Jesper Logan, correct?"

"That's right," she replied.

"What did you do for money after your husband died?"

"I went back to nursing."

"Do you own this house, or rent?"

"Gerry and I bought this house when we were married. It's paid for."

"The reason I ask," Hank said, "is I'm wondering how you could afford to send Richard to Jesper Logan on a nurse's salary with all your other bills to pay as well."

She looked at him, looked at Karen, looked back at him. "Herb helped out."

"Jarrett? He paid for Richard's tuition at Jesper Logan?"

"Yes."

"Why would he do that, Mrs. Holland?"

"He felt ... responsible."

"Responsible for your husband's death, or for Richard?" Karen cut in.

"He wanted to make sure Richard was taken care of. That he had a decent education."

"Why would he give a damn about that, Mrs. Holland?"

Mary Holland shrugged. "He was Richard's father."

Karen looked at Hank. He raised an eyebrow.

"His natural father, you mean?" Karen asked.

"Yes."

"You had an affair with Jarrett? When did it start?"

"In, uh, I guess it was 1972. There was a social event for the company. We went because we were supposed to. He forced himself on me. Told me he liked my looks, and that he'd come around to see me from time to time. He did. Eventually I became pregnant with Richard. After that, he dropped me. The thrill was gone, I imagine. I was just as glad."

"So you're saying Jarrett was Richard's natural father and that's why he paid for his schooling. Because he was the natural father and he was obligated."

"He said he was glad to. That he'd make sure Richard grew up having every opportunity to get ahead in life."

"Do you own a firearm, Mrs. Holland?"

"A what?"

"A gun," Karen repeated, irritated. "Do you own a gun?"

"Well, yes. It was Gerry's. It's still in his desk."

Karen stood up. "We'd like to see it."

"I guess it would be all right." Mary stood up and led them across the hall into the combined kitchen and dining area. "Gerry kept this as a little office," she said, gesturing to the desk and a couple of small, cluttered bookshelves in the corner of the room.

"The gun?" Karen prompted.

"It's in the middle drawer," Mary said.

"May I?" Karen pulled out the chair.

"Yes. The drawer's locked but the key's in the big drawer right in front of you."

Karen sat down. She removed a pair of latex gloves from her jacket pocket and put them on.

"Why are you doing that?" Mary asked.

Saying nothing, Karen pulled out the big drawer and saw a set of two identical keys on a ring in the built-in tray in the drawer. Taking a pen from her pocket, she fished out the keys by the ring, grasped one of the keys by its edges, and tried it in the lock above the three drawers on the right side of the desk. It turned. She slipped the pen inside the handle of the middle drawer and pulled it open. Inside the drawer was a red box with the Ruger logo printed on the lid. She looked at Hank, who nodded. Gingerly she removed the box from the drawer, set it on

217

the desk, and used the tip of the pen to open the lid.

The box was empty.

Karen looked at Mary. "Is this where the gun's usually kept?"

"I don't understand. It should be there."

"Uh huh. When was the last time you saw it?"

"Not for a while, now. I don't bother Gerry's things at all."

"Got any documentation for it, Mrs. Holland? Something with the serial number of the gun on it, for instance?"

"Gerry's files are in the bottom drawer. There might be something there."

Karen used the pen to open the bottom drawer. She looked at a neatly-labeled set of file folders. She used the pen to sort through the tabs until she found one labeled "Ruger." She took hold of the corner of the tab with finger and thumb and gently tugged the file out. She put it on the desk and used the pen to flip it open.

Hank bent over her shoulder, and they looked at an instruction manual for the Ruger Mark 1, Target and Standard Model, a warranty certificate, and a sales receipt dated October 14, 1973, that was made out to Gerald Holland at this address.

"Is this when your husband bought it?" he asked.

"Yes. We'd had a break-in just before. Gerry wanted to make sure we had some protection in the house."

"Who else has access to this desk?"

"No one. Only Richard, but he hates guns." She paused. "I did have a break-in last year. Maybe the person took the gun then."

"Did you report it?" asked Hank.

Mary shook her head. "Several of us were broken into. I talked to one of the neighbors, and she said she wasn't going to report hers, either, because people said it was gang members looking for prescription drugs and guns. If we reported it, she was afraid they'd come back. So we didn't say anything."

"What else did you notice was missing?"

"Some of my mother's jewelry, from my bedroom. My blood pressure pills. A few other things like that."

"Uh huh." Karen had been looking at the other file tabs, and now she pulled out a folder labeled "Richard" that had been misfiled at the back. "This one of your husband's files, too?"

"I put that there."

"Mind if I look at it?"

"I don't see why you'd be interested in Richard."

"Just trying to understand him better," Karen said casually.

"All you'll find there are some doctors' records from when he was in school."

"May I?"

"Yes, but I don't see what this has to do with anything."

Karen opened the file and sorted through the documents, which included several letters, forms, and receipts. She noticed a report from a psychiatrist named Dr. Miles Fort, dated March 3, 1990. It stated that Richard had been diagnosed with narcissistic personality disorder "as defined by the *Diagnostic and Statistical Manual of Mental Disorders,* because he displays a pervasive pattern of grandiosity and a need for admiration, along with an exaggerated sense of self-importance, a preoccupation with fantasies of unlimited success and power, a sense of entitlement, a pronounced tendency to be exploitive of others, and a distinct lack of empathy for others."

"Well, well," Karen said.

"I didn't believe a word of it," Mary said, "and I still don't. It was a waste of money. I'm a nurse, I know what the *DSM* is. If I could've afforded it, I would've paid for a second opinion."

"It was copied to the headmaster of Jesper Logan," Karen said, tapping the report with her pen.

"I didn't have a choice. They were going to expel him. I had to do it to keep him there so he could finish his senior year and graduate. He saw the doctor a few times, then we dropped him when Richard graduated."

"You had to pay for it yourself? Jarrett wouldn't foot the bill, when he was already paying for tuition?"

"Herb didn't know about it. I kept it quiet. I didn't want it to hurt Richard's future, because it was so untrue."

Karen looked at Hank.

"Mrs. Holland," Hank said, "we're going to want to look through the rest of the house. Since your gun's unaccounted for, and because it may match the type of weapon used to kill Mr. Jarrett, we need to verify whether it's here or somewhere else."

"I don't think I want you doing that."

"We'll have a warrant within an hour. It would be simpler if you'd just give us permission, as you did with your husband's desk."

"I want to talk to my lawyer, first. I can do that, can't I?"

"Of course, if you think it's necessary."

"I do. The telephone's in the hall. I'd like some privacy."

"We'll be right here, Mrs. Holland."

"I'll just be a minute."

As soon as she left the room Hank took out his cell and speed-dialed Truly. When she answered, he said without preamble, "Maureen, I want a search warrant on the residence of Mrs. Mary Holland." He recited the address, gave her a description of the home, ran through the grounds for probable cause, and told her to include everything on the other search warrants they'd already executed.

"Right away," Truly said. "By the way, I just got off the phone with Detective Brannigan in TIU."

"Brannigan? What did he have for us?"

"No silver sports cars, unfortunately. No Ferraris, no McLarens. Sorry."

"Neither one?"

"No. He said he'd have a complete list for us later tonight, but they drew a blank on the vehicles you'd mentioned."

"Damn. All right, Maureen. Thanks."

He put away the phone and looked at Karen. "No joy."

"He must have gone a different way, missed their cameras."

"Or it was unrelated."

"Not a chance, Lou. It had to be him."

Hank turned suddenly, realizing he hadn't heard the sound of Mary Holland's voice on the telephone through the open doorway. He hurried out into the hall, Karen right behind him.

The front door stood open. There was no sign of Mary.

"Jesus Christ, Lou," Karen said. "She's dusted on us!"

32

They searched the rest of the tiny bungalow without finding her. They ran out onto the sidewalk, but no one was visible in either direction. They looked behind the house. Nothing. They went back out front. As Hank called for backup, Karen trotted down the street to the nearest intersection, looked around, and trotted back. They met at the end of Mary Holland's cracked driveway.

"No sign, Lou. Want me to check the other way?"

Hank shook his head. "Backup's coming." He turned around and looked at the garage door. "Was there a car in there? Or is she on foot?"

Karen shook her head. "It's full of boxes and junk. No room for a car."

He frowned at the driveway. "It's too short to park a car here, it'd block the sidewalk. Maybe she parked on the street. They're running her name through DMV." He turned around. "What was out here?"

Karen ran her eyes up and down the street, looking at a battered green Ford Escape SUV in front of the Holland house, the Crown Vic in front of the house next door where she'd parked it, a rusty red Dodge Caravan down toward the corner, a dark-colored Malibu hatchback and a gray Honda Civic across the street, and a Jeep Liberty down near the corner on the other side. Her eyes came back to an empty spot across the road from them.

"Sunfire, dark blue or black, about a ninety-eight or so," she said. "Maryland tag, first two letters alpha golf. That's all I got, Lou."

A police cruiser braked to a stop at the end of the driveway. The passenger window hummed down and a sergeant whose name was Cheriski looked out at them. "Evening, folks. Out for a stroll?"

Hank squatted down. "Working late, Sarge?"

"Short-staffed and short-tempered. Good job I love the shift work. Sorry, Lou, I could only manage two cars right away, including this one." He glanced in the side mirror as a second cruiser pulled up to a stop behind them. "Officer Delany will assist in your search of the premises."

It was departmental standard operating procedure that a uniformed officer from the district be present during the execution of all search warrants.

"I'd rather have him out working the grid. We need to find this woman ASAP."

"I hear you, Lieutenant. Remind me to rewrite the SOP for you tomorrow in my spare time. In the meanwhile, if she's moving on foot, Wiesboski and I should be able to spot her."

"She may be driving. Dark Sunfire, about a ninety-eight, Maryland plate beginning alpha golf."

Cheriski called it in. In a moment they heard the confirmation that a black 1998 Pontiac Sunfire, Maryland tag alpha golf bravo six four nine, was registered to Mary Holland, residing at this address. Chereski glanced at Hank and requested a BOLO on it. The Be On The Lookout call went out across the channel moments later.

"See ya," Cheriski said. He raised the window and the cruiser rolled away.

"She moves fast for an old broad," Karen said, as Hank stood up. "Out the door, across the street, into the car and out of sight while we were standing there like boobs."

"We had to check the house first. It gave her just enough time."

"Sure. That makes me feel a lot better. It really does."

"We need to run her car past Brannigan."

Karen stared at him. "Shit, Lou, you're right. They may have caught it on one of the cameras. There's a curveball for you. Maybe Holland used it instead of his precious Ferrari."

"Or Mary Holland might have done it herself."

"Hmm. I'll chew on it."

Hank called Truly and told her to call Detective Brannigan back with the particulars of Mary Holland's vehicle. He should run it immediately against the list of vehicles captured by the traffic cameras in the vicinity of Brett Parris's hit-and-run accident.

Crime scene technicians Jon Beverley and June Allenson arrived to conduct the search of the house. Beverley parked the van in Mary Holland's tiny driveway. It blocked the sidewalk completely, proving Hank's point that it was too short to accommodate Mary's car. A moment later, Truly parked her Land Cruiser in the spot vacated by the Sunfire and walked across the street with their search warrant in her hand.

They went through the desk again, more thoroughly, photographing and printing as they went. No gun, and no ammunition. They processed the other rooms in the house in turn, with the same results. June Allenson went through the kitchen door down the three wooden steps into the garage while Beverley went back out to the van for a stepladder so that he could poke his head through a trapdoor in the bathroom ceiling.

Hank leaned through the door into the garage. "How's it going, Butternut?"

The technician glanced up. "Photographed, but not dusted," she reminded him. "Look, but don't touch." Her nickname had been given to her by her husband, a carpenter, in tribute to her shoulder-length hair, which was the color of his favorite wood. Hank couldn't recall anyone ever calling her by her given name.

"Jesus Christ!" They heard Beverley bellow from the bathroom.

Karen walked into the kitchen, grinning. "Bats."

"I hate bats!" Beverley yelled after her. "I hate them!"

Hank and Karen joined Butternut in the garage, the center of which was filled with stacked cardboard cartons and plastic storage bins. She showed them an open carton filled with sports magazines dating back to 1996.

"The subscription labels have them going to Richard Holland at an address in New Haven. There are others showing his current address. There's baseball cards, science fiction paperbacks, other stuff like that."

"He was using his mother's garage as a storage dump for his old stuff," Karen said.

"Looks like." Butternut sighed. "It'll take all night to go through everything."

Karen wandered down the wall, looking at a workbench cluttered with tools. Next to the workbench was a shelving unit that held a small collection of Bakelite radios, mantel clocks, and old cameras. She looked at a Brownie Target box camera, a Brownie Hawkeye with attached flash, and an Olympus thirty-five millimeter camera. Next to the Olympus was a very new-looking Nikon camera.

"Hold the phone," Karen said. "Come here."

223

Butternut joined her. "Wait. Let me shoot it first."

Karen moved aside, pulling out her notebook. Butternut took a series of photographs of the camera. Karen found the page she was looking for in her notebook. "Brett's camera is a Nikon D4. That's a D4. Could Holland be this dumb?"

"Mm hmm." Butternut gingerly tipped the camera back and stooped down so that she could read the laser-etched plate on the bottom of the camera. She recited the serial number.

"Ladies and gentlemen," Karen said, "we have a winner."

Butternut gently moved the camera around and popped the hinged flap on the right side. "There are two memory card slots on this thing," she said, pointing, "a CF slot and an XQD slot."

"Like I know what that means."

"Almost nobody uses the XQD, but the card's here, anyway. See? In this slot. And here's his CF card. I have to dust for prints first, then it'll be interesting to see if Holland deleted the photos on it."

"Oh man, don't say that. Tell me he didn't delete them."

Butternut smiled at her. "Relax. Doesn't matter. People think that deleting pictures from their memory card destroys them, but it doesn't. It only marks that space on the card as available for overwriting with future photos. So even if he did delete them, I doubt very much he took any other pictures after taking the camera, so your witness's photos will still be on here. Mickey'll get them for you."

Karen turned around, grinning at Hank. "Hot diggety damn. We've got him!"

33

Maureen Truly pulled up a chair and sat down next to Mickey Marcotte. Despite the lateness of the hour the lab was bustling, as evidence from Mary Holland's residence went to the top of the queue for immediate processing. Truly set down a cup of coffee from the cafeteria next to Mickey's laptop and took a sip from hers. It was putrid, but hot. Her coffee had to be hot. Mickey reached out for his without taking his eyes from the laptop's screen. She admired the peripheral vision involved in finding the cup and getting it to his lips without ever looking at it.

"How's it going?" she ventured.

"Almost done. Piece of cake." Mickey slurped. "'Scuse me. I needed that. Callbacks are a bitch, but the OT check's sweet."

Truly looked at Brett Parris's camera, which was connected to Mickey's laptop by a USB cable. "Will you be able to restore the pictures?"

"Are you kidding?" He grinned at her. "This software could find an octet string in a SPARC server in no time at all. Well, that's a bit of an exaggeration, but it's good stuff. The scan's almost done. What it does is retrieve the file and copy it onto the hard drive of my MacBaby, here. That's what I call her. See?" He pointed at a list of file names on the screen. "That's what we've recovered so far, and we're at ninety-one percent complete. I think we've got it all, but we'll find out in a minute."

"Great," Truly said. "Detective Stainer will be very happy."

"She's something else, isn't she? Scary lady."

"She's an incredible detective," Truly replied, with feeling.

Mickey said nothing, looking at the screen. Then he shifted in his chair. "Look, when we're done, you want to go out for breakfast or something?"

The lab was silent for a ten-count.

"I don't think . . . I don't," Truly said. "Sorry."

"Sure. Okay. No problem," Mickey said. "I'm not married, in

case you thought that. I'm divorced. She used to beat me." He grimaced. "Too much information. Sorry."

Truly frowned. "Are you serious?"

Mickey kept his eyes on the screen. Finally, he sighed. "She had this collapsible umbrella. You know, about the size of a nightstick? She used to hit me with it whenever she got mad. Which was pretty much all the time. Once she broke my wrist, and another time a finger when I was trying to fend her off. Eventually, I'd had enough. It's a pretty lame story. I don't know why I said anything. I'm tired, I guess." He took a long pull at his coffee.

"I was kidnapped once," Truly said.

His eyes widened. "What? You were?"

"Yes. I was a freshman at Harvard. He was twenty-eight, just some guy with a low IQ, no job. I was carrying groceries back to my apartment and he caught me off-guard. Kept me for three days tied up in his bedroom. Didn't hurt me, except when he tried to have sex. He didn't know what to do. Anyway, I got away. He's in an institution now. I think he's still there. Hopefully."

"That's terrible," Mickey said.

"It was at the time. It changed my life."

"I can imagine it would."

"Anyway, I. . ."

"Sure. I understand."

"It's nothing," she said, "nothing at all to do with you."

"No, I understand." He stared at the screen, then glanced at her. "What was your major at Harvard?"

"I was going to major in biochem," she said, "because my mother's an MD in Baltimore. That's where I'm from. So I was going to become a doctor, like her. I had a full scholarship, but I withdrew. Later, I came here to State and majored in criminal justice instead."

"Not surprising," Mickey said.

"I guess not. Anyway—"

"Here we go," said Mickey. "Now, let's look at these files in thumbnail view. There. Trees, bike path, a nice bed of irises, more trees. Jesus. Look at that."

Truly stood up and leaned over his shoulder. "My God."

"And this one. Here, let me open it up. Look, it's a close-up. There's the gun."

"A Ruger, all right," Truly said.

"Hot stuff."

"Yes," Truly said. "It is." She took out her cell phone. "I'll call the lieutenant and let him know."

"They're going to be so happy."

She touched him lightly on the shoulder. "Good job, Mickey."

"It's all in the software," he said, turning around to grin at her.

"When we're done," Truly said, "we could maybe get some pancakes down the street."

His grin faded. "You sure?"

"I'm sure," she said.

Her eyes drifted from his to the laptop screen, where Richard Holland stared at her, brandishing a Ruger Mark I pistol with an angry, half-crazed expression on his face.

34

Hank stood in the entry of All Saints Episcopal church wearing his class A dress uniform, hat tucked under his left arm, as Attorney General Perry walked through the big front doors at 11:10 A.M., followed by State's Attorney Warren Exler. Perry paused, taking a moment to let his eyes adjust from the bright sunlight outside, as the plainclothes state trooper accompanying the attorney general peeked through the open doors, saw the line of city police uniforms, and withdrew.

Chief Bennett stepped forward and shook Perry's hand. He introduced Jason Stone, Midtown district commander, "who's in charge of security for the ceremony downtown here," and Ann Martinez, "our new commander of Detective Services, who's in charge of the Jarrett investigation."

Perry shook Hank's hand. Hank introduced Jim Horvath.

Not to be left out, Exler took his turn down the line.

"This is the oldest existing church in Glendale," Bennett said, leading the way through the doorway into the nave. "It was built in eighteen . . ." he looked at Hank for assistance.

"Fifty-two," Hank said.

"It's beautiful." Perry walked up a few rows and leaned against the end of a pew. He looked at Hank, his eyes lingering for a moment on the citation holder above Hank's left breast pocket that displayed his gold badge and numerous citation bars. "You folks were going to brief me on the status of the investigation."

"Yes," Bennett said. "Commander Martinez, if you will?"

Martinez said, "Hank?"

Perry's eyes never left Hank's as the baton was passed down the chain of command.

"We've issued two arrest warrants," Hank said. "Our suspect is Richard Holland, a vice-president with Jarrett Corporation. Last night we recovered the digital camera of Brett Parris, our witness at the scene last Thursday morning, and we were able to extract photographs of Holland running away from the crime scene with a gun in his hand, a gun that appears to be a match for the type of weapon used to shoot Mr. Jarrett. We still haven't recovered the gun, so we're treating Holland as armed and dangerous."

"And the second warrant?" Perry asked.

"For Holland's mother, Mary Holland. The camera was recovered at her residence. In addition, we have reason to believe she may have been responsible for a hit-and-run on Parris yesterday morning. She was photographed one block away right at the time the hit-and-run occurred. It's one of those intersection safety camera systems where the roadway sensor detects speeding and takes two photos, one of them a shot of the driver. It was her, driving her vehicle, with visible damage to the right front headlight and bumper. So we want her both as an accessory on the Jarrett homicide and for failure to remain at the scene on the Parris hit-and-run."

"Why on earth would she run down Brett Parris?"

"We figure Holland confessed to her that he shot Mr. Jarrett and told her that Brett Parris saw him and took his picture. She knows the Parris family and spoke disparagingly of them during our interview. She likely went there yesterday morning, saw Brett come out in a taxi on his way to pick up his girlfriend and take her to lunch, followed the taxi, and hit him when he crossed the street. Thinking she'd eliminated the only witness to her son's homicide."

"Parris is still alive?"

"Thankfully, yes. He regained consciousness last night."

"I understand he doesn't work as a potential witness."

"He has a mental condition that rules him out as a reliable eyewitness, but at least we've got his camera and the photos. They speak for him."

"What about motive?"

"Allegedly he's Jarrett's illegitimate son. It's possible he shot Jarrett after a dispute about Holland's absence from the will and Jarrett's decision to turn over control of the company to his daughter instead of Holland."

"Really?" Perry showed surprise for the first time.

"We only have it from Mary Holland right now," Hank cautioned. "It may have all been fabricated as an attempt to defraud Jarrett. We don't know for sure, yet."

"You spoke to Holland's former psychiatrist," Martinez prompted.

"That's right. We've been building up a historical pattern of behavior for Holland, based on statements from a number of witnesses, including Jarrett's executive assistant, Holland's former secretary, and so on. There's apparently a history of dirty tricks and aberrant behavior in his past. I talked to a psychiatrist named Fort, who saw Holland several times when he was seventeen. Fort diagnosed him then as having narcissistic personality disorder. He hasn't seen Holland since then, so he couldn't comment on his current state of mind, but I asked him to give me some general information about people like him and how they act, so we could predict what he might do next."

"Good," Perry said. "What'd he have to say?"

"He said that adults with the severest form of malignant narcissism have to have what he called a constant narcissistic supply. Meaning a constant supply of attention and praise from people around them. It's like a drug addiction, apparently, and they need more and more all the time. When the supply ends, as it has with Holland, they often react with what's called narcissistic rage, which is a reaction to what they perceive as an injury. In some severe cases it can include physical violence."

"The idea being," Perry guessed, "that this Holland felt entitled to become president and CEO of Jarrett Corporation instead of Diane Benson, and when he found out he wasn't going to get it, he flew into a narcissistic rage and killed Jarrett?"

"That's the general idea," Hank agreed, "although none of this has been confirmed, yet. It's just our working theory at the moment."

Perry's eyes slid to Exler. "We're not getting into diminished capacity here, are we?"

Exler shook his head. "Not if narcissistic personality disorder's the diagnosis when he's brought to trial. It doesn't qualify. It's one of the personality disorders that doesn't involve sufficient cognitive impairment to satisfy the test of legal insanity."

Perry's eyes slid back to Hank. "So where is he?"

"That's the million-dollar question." Hank glanced at Martinez. "It's possible he's left the city, or even the state. I asked Fort what he thought Holland might do. Naturally, he wouldn't speculate. But he did say that people with this disorder often refuse to take no for an answer. Or words to that effect." He folded his arms across his chest. "I think he's still here, and I think he still hasn't given up."

Perry glanced at his watch. "So what's your plan of attack for the day? The governor's due to arrive at twelve forty-five. I'll need to brief him on the level of risk we're looking at."

"We've pulled out all the stops," Chief Bennett said. "Commander Stone has the entire block closed off to traffic, as you saw when you arrived." He turned and pointed. "Since the church is right here on the intersection of Clergy and Simpson, we've got this intersection blocked off both ways, we've got Simpson barricaded down at Concord," he pointed to his right, indicating the intersection behind the church, "and of course this entire block is closed to through vehicular traffic on Clergy," pointing to the front of the church. "We're allowing pedestrian traffic along Clergy across the road, especially in the plaza directly across, since that's where the media's set up, and on this side right up to the department store next door to the church. We have uniforms all the way around the block and across the street in the plaza.

"The private ceremony for the family's getting underway at noon at the funeral home in Granger Park. The district commander up there, Peterson, is providing a motorcade for the hearse and family vehicles when they leave the funeral home to come down here for the service, and later when they go back up there for the burial at the cemetery."

Stone cleared his throat. "The hearse and other vehicles in the procession will be brought through the barricade and parked right in front of the church. Your vehicle, and those of the governor and other key figures who are attending, will be parked in the small parking lot behind the church, where the rector and church staff park. They'll be brought around to the front before you leave, of course. The rest go into the parking garage the next block over."

"And the people coming into the church?"

"No one other than church staff will be admitted before twelve forty-five. We'll have metal detectors set up just inside the door, and we'll also wand them. We've already wanded the church staff who're here now. Everyone will have to show proper photo ID. We've circulated copies of the suspect's DMV photo, so if he shows up, we'll nail him."

Perry looked at Hank.

"I have two detectives up at the funeral home right now," Hank said, "including Detective Stainer, the one who fastened on Holland as a suspect."

"And wouldn't let go," Martinez said.

231

"That's right. Detective Horvath and I will cover this end."

"We have to keep the lid on this." Perry looked at Bennett. "We've got national media here. We'll have the governor and Senator Brickland," he began counting on his fingers, "Representative Mills, three billionaires and God knows how many multi-millionaires, plus What's-His-Name, the guy who used to manage the Mets and the Orioles, the guy with all the books who was Jarrett's buddy. It has to go smoothly and by the numbers or it'll be a disaster on so many different levels we'll all be sleeping under bridges and begging for quarters inside of a week."

Hank's cell phone vibrated. He took it out and answered it.

"Hank, this is Diane Benson. Something just happened and I thought I should let you know."

"Go ahead. I'm listening."

"I just got a call from Richard Holland. David and I are getting ready for the service at Chappell's at noon, and I tried to get rid of him, but he was very upset. I saw on the morning news that he's wanted in connection with Dad's murder. Do you really think he did it?"

"We have some very compelling evidence. What'd he want?"

"That's the thing. He demanded a meeting with me, right now, this morning. He wanted me to agree to step aside and endorse him as the new president and CEO. Wanted me to sign something. I told him, well, basically, I told him to fuck off and turn himself in. I guess I should've agreed to meet with him instead so you could've grabbed him."

Hank was aware that conversation around him had stopped and that all eyes were on him. "No, that's all right, Diane. You did the right thing. You're still at home? How far away are you from the funeral home?"

"Chappell's? It's only about ten minutes from here."

"I'll make arrangements for a patrol car to be dispatched right away, and I'll send Detective Stainer over as well. If Holland shows up before they get there, don't answer the door. Don't let him in. Don't try to speak to him at all. We don't need you to be a decoy or whatever and put yourself at risk. Understand?"

"Whatever you say, Hank. Just don't let this nutcase get away, that's all I ask."

"We won't." He ended the call and looked at Martinez. "Holland telephoned Diane Benson at her home demanding a meeting. We need a car over there, ASAP."

"I'll call Peterson," Bennett said.

"It's okay, Chief. I got it." Martinez already had her cell phone pressed to her ear.

Hank called Karen, told her what had happened, and gave her the address.

"No problem," Karen replied. "Beats sitting around here with my thumb up my ass. You know how much I love funeral parlors."

"Brief Truly. She can call me if she has any concerns."

"Sure, Lou, but she'll be all right. She's cold case, remember? She's used to dead files and doing fuck all."

"I take it she's not within earshot."

"Please. Don't be insulting." Pause. "She's chatting up the funeral director. They make a real nice couple."

Hank ended the call and glanced at his watch: 11:26 A.M.

"Peterson can spare one car," Martinez was telling the others. "Everything else is either tied up with the motorcade and security around the funeral home, or covering the rest of the district." She looked at Perry. "We're strapped for resources right now."

"Detective Stainer'll be there in under five minutes," Hank said. "That's as good as sending in a company of marines."

Stone took them on a tour of the church. He explained the layout and described how access would be controlled. They walked up the center aisle between the pews, looking at the stained glass windows on either side of the nave. At the front, a man wearing jeans and a white t-shirt ignored them, fussing with the microphones on the pulpit. Stone led them through a door into a small room with an altar. It was a private chapel, Stone explained. Another door took them through a passage and down into the sacristy, where the sacraments and vestments were kept. Across the hall was a small office for the use of the rector.

They met the rector, Reverend Tom Baldwin, along with the assistant priest, the deacon, the choirmaster, and the organist. They all were nervous and distracted.

Stone led them down to the end of the passage. "This door leads outside to the rear parking lot," he said, pushing down on the crash bar. He opened the door and they all stepped out into the sunshine. An officer moved aside, touching his hat to acknowledge the uniforms with their silver bars and stars.

They stood in a small rectangular courtyard marked off as a

parking area. It was wide enough to include a row of parking spaces at the back of the church, two rows in the middle, and another row against the back of the building on the opposite side, which was the six-story Warrick Hotel. The lot was accessed from Simpson Street, on their left, through a laneway that ran between the rear of the church and the side of an old three-story building facing out onto Simpson. To their right, enclosing the courtyard on that side, was a brick wall belonging to the four-story department store next door.

"Uniform here," Stone said, pointing to the officer standing next to them, "and another on Simpson at the end of the laneway." He pointed down the laneway to the street. "Only church employees are allowed to enter through this door. Everyone else will have to enter by the front and pass through the security cordon, including the VIPs."

Hank's cell phone vibrated. He glanced at his watch and saw that it was 11:52 A.M. The call display told him it was Truly.

"Donaghue."

"Something's come up," she said. "I thought I should call you."

"Go ahead, Maureen."

"Walter Parris and his wife haven't arrived yet for the private service. They were expected before now. I spoke to a woman who says she knows you. She says she's Mr. Parris's mother, uh, Mrs. Constance Parris. According to her, she called the landline and their cells, and nobody's answering. I tried the numbers as well and they rang to voice mail, which means they're not turned off or disconnected. They're ringing and not being answered. Not unexpected for the landline if they've left the house, but unusual for their cell phones. Apparently neither of them ever turns their cell phone off, because of their son."

"I understand," Hank said. He heard the sounds of traffic in the background. "Are you calling from outside the funeral home?"

"Yes," Truly said. "I'm on the sidewalk. My POV is parked down the street. I think I should go there. It doesn't feel right."

"Stand by." Hank lowered the phone and turned around. Once again, all eyes were on him. He looked at Martinez. "We need a patrol car to check on the Parrises. They haven't shown up at the funeral home and their phones are going unanswered."

Martinez pulled out her cell phone to call Peterson. Attorney General Perry turned to Chief Bennett. "Walter Parris is acting CEO right now. Is it possible Holland's going after him?"

234

"It's possible," Bennett said, looking at Hank.

"I agree. It's possible." Hank looked at Martinez.

She shook her head in frustration and put her hand over her cell. "He's stretched too thin. They're still processing latecomers, and some attendees haven't arrived yet. He says twenty minutes is the best he can do, unless we have positive confirmation it's our suspect."

"We don't," Hank said.

"What about your other detective, Lieutenant?" Bennett said. "You could send her over there to check. She's not really needed at the funeral home, is she?"

Hank hesitated. Martinez was looking at him with an expression that said, *you wanted her, now you have to play her*. He looked at Horvath, who raised his shoulder in a barely perceptible shrug. He put the cell phone to his ear.

"Go," he told Truly. "Proceed with caution. Remember, he's armed and dangerous. I'll divert Karen over there to back you up, and we'll shake loose a patrol car as soon as possible. Call me on arrival with a sitrep before taking any action whatsoever. Got it?"

"Copy that, sir."

He ended the call, feeling as though he were moving pieces across a chessboard in a deadly game with an opponent whose pieces he couldn't see.

He didn't like the feeling at all.

35

Maureen Truly parked her Land Cruiser behind Richard Holland's Ferrari near the front entrance of the Parris home. She drew her gun as she got out from behind the wheel. In front of the Ferrari was Mary Holland's Sunfire. To her right, the closest of the three garage doors was open, and Walter Parris's Lexus poked halfway out. Evidently both suspects were here and had intercepted the Parrises as they were about to leave. Truly figured they were probably still inside the house.

She moved up alongside the Ferrari on the passenger side and peeked in. Nothing, other than a small black travel bag strapped on the narrow shelf behind the passenger seat. She edged alongside the Sunfire and saw the damage. The passenger side headlight assembly was smashed, the fender was damaged, and the plastic bumper was partially shattered and hanging loose from its clips. To her untrained eye, it looked like very recent damage, but she'd leave that to the experts.

She took a step toward the front entrance of the house and stopped as it occurred to her that the Hollands might have entered the home through the garage with the Parrises after having blocked their escape. Gun held at the low ready position, she trotted to the corner of the open garage door and peeked in. No one was visible. She slid between the doorframe and the Lexus and pivoted, pointing her gun at the door leading into the home.

The door was open. Through it, a staircase was visible. No one was in sight.

She walked quietly across the garage to the door and crouched, pointing her gun up the stairs.

No one.

There were eight carpeted stairs, at the top of which was another door, left open at about a twenty-degree angle away from her. Praying the stairs wouldn't creak and give her away, she headed up.

They didn't creak.

At the top of the stairs she peered through the crack into what she guessed was a mud room. Listening, she could hear distant voices. A male voice in a low monotone. A female voice rising and falling. The male voice again.

She leaned against the door and eased it open with her shoulder, looking at a hall tree, a row of hooks with sweaters and jackets, boot trays with assorted footwear. A mud room. When the door reached a forty-five degree angle she slipped through and leveled her weapon.

No one.

From the mud room she looked into the kitchen. The voices were slightly louder but she still couldn't make out the words. She entered the kitchen, peripherally aware of black, expensive-looking appliances, an island and high stools, oak cabinetry. To the left was another doorway. The voices were coming from that direction. She crossed the kitchen and pressed against the wall next to the door.

The voices had fallen silent.

She hesitated, then peeked around the doorframe.

It was a central hallway running left to right. On the right was a staircase leading up to the second floor. On the left was a table and mirror against the wall, suggesting the front entrance. Straight ahead was an open double doorway into another room. She could see the edge of a dining room table and a chair.

She crossed the hallway, glancing left and right, then pressed against the doorframe into the dining room.

"Absolutely not," Walter Parris said. "It's out of the question."

"You're being completely unreasonable, Walter," a second male voice said. "The company's about to take a new direction and you're already on record as not being interested in the CEO position on a permanent basis. All I'm asking is that you endorse me as the old man's replacement, that's all."

"Are you irrational?" Walter Parris asked. "Do you not realize the situation you're in? You're wanted for murder, man. Your career's over!"

"Oh, it's a goddamned frame and you know it! Thanks to Brett."

"Brett has nothing to do with it."

"He has everything to do with it, Walter. Before, it was funny when he'd say some random person was me, but this time he's gone too far. You have to explain to them it's all a big mistake. That he doesn't

237

know what he's talking about."

"I'll do no such thing."

"Christ, they actually had me downtown on Saturday night, did you know that? I answered questions for hours while they ransacked my condo. I've spent the last two nights in a hotel out of town, just trying to stay out of sight until this all blows over. I can't stand it anymore. You've got to get them off my back, and you've got to clear the way for me to take over the company. I won't take no for an answer."

"Go ahead and shoot me if you want, Holland. I won't do any such thing."

"Walter," a female voice spoke up, "please."

"Lisa, stay quiet," Walter said quickly. "Don't get involved."

"She's already involved," Holland said. "Up to her neck, right along with you."

Truly thought about the cell phone in her pocket. She should've called Donaghue before entering the house, but she'd had to confirm they were here, first of all. Which she'd now done. They were in the room beyond the dining room. Probably the living room. Holland obviously had a gun and was holding the Parrises hostage. The best thing would be to withdraw. Go back down into the garage and call Donaghue from there. Wait for assistance. It was the best tactic, because she didn't know what to do on her own.

She took a step backward.

Something very sharp jabbed into the small of her back and an arm went around her neck.

"Going somewhere, hon?" Mary Holland purred in her ear.

36

For Karen, it was a very simple situation to read. Parked in the looping driveway in front of Walter Parris's house was Mary Holland's Sunfire, Richard Holland's Ferrari, and some piece of ex-hippie junk that just had to belong to Truly. Parris's Lexus was parked halfway out of his garage, and the big iron gates down at the end of the driveway had been left open. Simple: the Parrises had been on their way to the funeral home, Parris had opened the gate, probably with a remote in the garage, he'd opened the garage door, started to drive out, and stopped dead when one or more of the Hollands jumped out, waving that ludicrous plinker Holland had used to kill Jarrett.

She called it in to Hank and told him she figured they were all inside having a pow wow. He told her a patrol car was en route and that she should wait. She said thanks, gotta go, talk to you later, and went through the garage into the kitchen.

Voices were coming from the hallway on the left so she crossed the kitchen and slipped through the door. On her right was the staircase up to Brett's suite and the other bedrooms. In front of her was the dining room. The voices were louder. She went into the dining room and saw a door on the right from which the voices were coming. She walked casually through the door, gun-first.

"Well, well," she said, "how come I didn't get invited to this party?"

Mary Holland turned around, using Truly as a shield, knife to her throat. Behind them, Richard Holland pointed his gun in the general direction of Walter Parris, who stood next to him. Lisa Parris sat on a loveseat on Karen's right.

It wasn't a living room, as she'd anticipated, but a kind of recreation room with a full bar, a widescreen television, a music center, and various other entertainment set-ups. Behind Richard and Walter were open French doors that led outside to a patio and, beyond that, an Olympic-sized pool. A great place for a party. Come in here, get your drink, shmooze a bit and listen to the music, then wander out to watch the hunks jump off the diving board and show off their six-packs. A lifestyle she could get used to, without trying too hard.

"Well, hello there, Detective Stainer," Richard said, touching the muzzle of the Ruger to his temple in an ironic salute. "Somehow I'm not surprised you'd show up. But I think you'd better put down that gun and sit over there with Mrs. Parris while I finish my business with Walter."

Karen took a step forward. "You're toast, Holland. Time to pack it in."

"Don't come any closer!" Mary Holland warned, tipping up Truly's chin with the edge of the knife blade.

Karen looked at Truly. She looked odd in uniform, a little stiff and frumpy. Her eyes, though, were very calm. They looked back at Karen with complete trust. It was a little disconcerting.

"Please, Stainer," Richard said, "put that thing down. I need Walter to sign some documents, and then we'll get out of here and let you all go. No fuss, no muss. Sound good?"

"I'm not signing anything," Walter said. "I told you that already. Diane Benson's taking over the company and that's all there is to it. Now get out of here and let us go mourn the loss of our friend."

Richard grinned, holding up a set of car keys in his left hand. "You're not going anywhere, Walter, until you do exactly what I tell you to do."

"I'll do nothing of the kind. It's out of the question."

"Please, Walter," Lisa said.

"Yes, *please*, Walter," Richard mocked.

"It's his due!" Mary Holland said. "His birthright!"

"I don't know what you're talking about," Walter said, "but I can assure you, Mary, your son has no claim to the title of CEO. Never has, and never will."

Karen had to hand it to Walter. He wasn't afraid to be arrogant and condescending even in the most difficult of situations. She admired his courage while sizing up the layout. Mary Holland was almost the same height as Truly. All Karen could see of her was the top right quadrant of her head, her right arm and knife hand, and her right leg from the knee down. It was more than enough real estate for Karen to take her shot, of course, but she couldn't be sure the knife wouldn't twitch up into Truly's throat after impact.

As for Richard, he was about a dozen feet behind his mother

and Truly, head and shoulders visible above them. Another easy shot. She considered moving sideways to get a full view of him, but decided instead she'd rather keep Mary between them, in his line of fire. She couldn't be sure the sonofabitch wouldn't shoot his own mother to get to her, but he obviously wasn't good with guns and probably didn't realize the .22LR fired by the Ruger was such a pathetic load it wouldn't perforate his mother's body and make it all the way to Karen. Hell, it probably wouldn't even make it to Truly.

"My claim," Richard was saying, "is based on my abilities and you know it, Walter. I'm smarter and hungrier than anyone else, Diane Benson included. And that homo Forrestall."

"It doesn't take intelligence to take advantage of the misfortunes of others," Walter said.

"Unless you've created those misfortunes in the first place. Then it does." Holland waved the gun at Walter. "It was fiendish but simple. Ten grand, a private investigator with no scruples, and a gun bought on the street with no questions asked. Forrestall at least understood what he had to do." He waved the gun again. "I'd hoped you'd take the easier road and just sign your name on the dotted line. At least I'm not asking you to off yourself, Walter."

"You're a murdering fraud," Walter said, "and you're going to pay for what you've done."

"He's not a fraud," Mary said. "I had an affair with Herb, Walter. Richard's his child. He's Herb's heir, and the company belongs to him."

"That's ludicrous," Walter said. "You're deluded."

"It's the truth!"

"Actually, Mother," Richard said, "Walter's correct. You *are* deluded. You may have had an affair with him, but I'm not his son."

Mary turned around, trying to see his face while keeping Truly between herself and Karen. "You're his son! He acknowledged it! He paid for your education! He hired you into the company so you could learn everything and some day take over for him."

"Mother, Mother, Mother." Richard gestured with his gun, reminding her that Karen was still pointing her weapon at them.

"Don't Mother me," Mary said. "I worked and slaved my whole life to raise you, got you through all the heartache in high school, saved and scraped for everything, and now it's time for it all to pay off. Walter, sign those documents or I'll slit this woman's throat, I swear to God!"

"I'm not signing anything," Walter said.

"Did you ever ask yourself," Richard said, "why you had to live in that dumpy little house all those years and drive dumpy little cars and pay all your bills by yourself without a single dime from him?"

"I wouldn't take his damned money! I told him that! Only for you. Only for your education so you could become somebody. That was all."

"He wasn't my father," Richard said, almost sadly. "Oh, I believed you, all those years growing up. I believed all your stories. I thought I was the bastard Edmund in *King Lear*: 'Edmund the base shall top the legitimate. I grow, I prosper. Now gods, stand up for bastards!' That was me, all through school, when I got the internship at Jarrett, and when I started working my way up the ladder. That was what drove me, motivated me."

"So it should," Mary said. "You're his son."

"I'm not, Mother. Aren't you listening? He had a DNA test done last year. Took a glass from me at a party and sent it off for testing. Didn't say a word about it until after he announced to us all that he was stepping down and that Diane was the star of the succession plan. I went in to see him privately and confronted him about it. He laughed in my face! He took the report out of his filing cabinet and practically threw it at me. 'Read it and weep,' he said. 'Your DNA's about as closely related to mine as a baboon's. Now piss off and get back to work before I fire your ass right now.' That's what he said to me. Word for word."

"I don't believe it." Mary began to cry. "He was tricking you."

"He spat in a plastic cup for me, Mother. The arrogant fuck. He spat in a cup and handed it to me and told me to have my own test done. So I did. He was right. I'm not his son."

"How could he?" Mary cried. "How could he?"

"So you know the rest, Mother." Richard looked at Karen. "She knows the rest, but you don't. And you won't. I'll get what I want from Walter here and that'll be the end of it."

"Of course I know the rest," Karen said. "You took your old man's gun and confronted Jarrett on the bike path. What you couldn't have by inheritance you'd take by threatening his life, right? Only he laughed at you again, didn't he? He looked at that pathetic vintage popgun of yours and laughed in your face all over again. But you couldn't take it. You felt that rage, didn't you? When things don't go your way? He was turning away in complete contempt, he was going to get back

242

on his bike and ride away, leaving you standing there like an idiot, so you let him have it. A lucky shot, right in the temple. Then you picked up your brass, grabbed his wallet, took the cards out and threw it under the bush to make it look like a robbery, and took off. Didn't you?"

The anger began to boil behind his eyes. "You're signing everyone's death warrant here, Stainer. You should shut up and let sleeping dogs lie."

"Then who should see you but that poor nutcase, Brett Parris. And he takes your picture. So you knocked him down and took his camera. But like the idiot that you are, you left it in your mother's garage right where we could find it. Not very detail-oriented, Holland. That's what they say about you at work, and man, they ain't kidding. We got your fingerprints on the camera and we got your pictures on it, too." She grinned at him. "Surprised? Thought you deleted them? Well, they were still there, and our techies pulled them out. You take good pictures, Holland. Nice and clear. Gun and everything. The jury's gonna love them, right before you get sent away to a lunch date with the needle."

"You son of a bitch," Holland said.

Karen looked at Truly, who was still staring at her with those calm, trusting eyes.

Karen winked.

The corners of Truly's mouth lifted up, very slightly.

Karen stepped toward Mary, who instinctively moved the knife from Truly's throat to point it at Karen.

"Don't come any closer!" Mary cried.

Amateurs.

Karen fired a .40-inch Smith and Wesson round into the underside of Mary's forearm, about an inch from the elbow. It punched through the arm and sent the knife flying through the air away from Truly. Karen fired a second round above them as both women fell to the floor but, damn him, Holland had already begun to move as she'd stepped forward, and the round flew out through the open French doors into nowhere, which was precisely where Richard Holland was at the moment.

Karen knelt down, ignoring Mary's howls, and dragged Truly clear. "Okay?"

"Wow," Truly said. "Wow. That was something. Wow."

"Are you hurt, Maureen?"

"I'm okay. Wow." She twisted around, half-rising from the floor to look behind her. "Did he get away?"

"Maybe. Shut her up. Tie a tourniquet or some fucking thing. I'll be right back."

"Okay. Thanks. You're incredible."

"Shut up, Maureen." Karen stood up.

Walter Parris was on the love seat with his wife, protecting her with his body. She was crying.

"You okay?" Karen asked.

Walter nodded and looked at the open French doors.

Karen bolted through the doors out into the patio, gun-first.

No one.

She looked left and saw a fence that enclosed the pool. She looked right and saw the garage. She went right, running through the open back door into the garage.

The Lexus was gone.

She remembered the keys that Richard had held up, jingling them, when pressuring Walter to sign his idiotic documents. She ran through the garage out into the driveway. The Ferrari was still trapped between the Sunfire and Truly's Land Cruiser, but the Lexus was nowhere in sight.

She punched the air angrily with her gun.

"Goddamn it all to *hell!*"

37

"Lieutenant Donaghue," Chief Bennett said, "the governor would like a few minutes with you."

"Okay," Hank replied, running a hand through his hair.

Bennett glanced at his watch. "We have to make it snappy. The procession's about five minutes away."

Hank followed him through the sacristy, where the rector was giving last-minute instructions to the assistant priest and deacon, and on into the private chapel. When Bennett opened the door into the nave, they were met by a wall of sound from several hundred murmuring voices and background organ music. The first two rows were empty, reserved for the family and friends about to arrive from the funeral home. Bennett led him along the front, past the three steps leading up to the chancel, toward the center aisle.

Hank's roving eyes took in the ushers guarding the reserved front rows, other ushers at the back seating last-minute arrivals, the smattering of police and military uniforms in the congregation, and the VIPs in the row immediately behind the reserved pews, including Attorney General Perry, Mayor Watts, Senator Brickland, and several instantly-recognizable celebrities. He saw his mother, seated between Roberts and Meredith, several rows back.

The governor sat at the end of the VIP row in the center aisle. His white hair was lacquered into the trademark wave across his forehead. He watched Hank with the bright blue eyes of a predator.

Hank heard the noise level drop as he followed Bennett up the center aisle. Bennett introduced him, and the governor shook his hand while remaining seated. Hank smiled broadly. *All's well with the world*, was his message to everyone watching. *No problems.* Just another stiff getting his five minutes of fame.

Hank crouched down in the aisle so that he was on eye level with the governor, whose eyes focused on the badge and citations on his left breast before lifting to establish eye contact.

"What's the situation, Lieutenant?"

"We've apprehended the suspect's mother, sir," Hank said quietly. "She's an accessory, and she's also wanted on a related hit-and-run. We have photographic evidence placing our suspect at the scene with what we believe may be the murder weapon in his hand. The suspect himself is still at large, but we've issued a BOLO and expect to apprehend him soon."

"I understand there was a shooting."

"The suspect's mother was wounded by one of our detectives while threatening another officer with a knife. She's been taken to hospital and is stable. The suspect eluded capture at that time."

The governor's thick white eyebrows twitched as he glanced up. "Chief Bennett assures me we're perfectly safe. I've been told that your fugitive's armed and dangerous. Will he show up here?"

"It's possible," Hank admitted. "He apparently has an unreasonable belief he can still repair the damage to his career." He forced a grin. "It's a case of plan for the worst and hope for the best. If he shows up, we'll be ready for him."

"It's absolutely imperative nothing happen here. This family's already been through enough, and I don't want them exposed to any more violence. Is that clear?"

"Absolutely, sir."

"Good. You're not a Republican like your mother, are you?"

"No sir, I'm not."

"Excellent. I feel even more confident in your abilities now than I did a minute ago. I'd better let you get back to work."

"Yes, sir." Hank shook his hand. As he stood up, his cell phone buzzed. The governor's expression immediately became serious, but Hank smiled in assurance as he took out the phone and looked at the call display. *All's well with the world. No problems.*

"Stand by," he said into the phone. He walked up the center aisle, lowering the phone, and passed the reserved front row at a leisurely pace, Bennett following like a shadow. They stepped into the private chapel. Bennett closed the door behind them.

Hank put the phone to his ear. "What have you got?"

"He's here," Horvath said.

38

"Here's what happened," Commander Aaron Peterson said to Chief Bennett. "After he stole the Lexus from the Parrises, he stopped at a shopping mall several blocks from the funeral home, drove around the back, and took the tags from a vehicle belonging to one of the store managers. He put the tags on the Lexus and drove to the funeral home. He got there just as everyone was coming out. He managed to slip into the procession and drive all the way downtown with it."

They stood in the middle of the street, facing the front entrance of the church, their backs to the cameras at the edge of the plaza that were now providing a live video feed to the networks. In front of them, at the curb, were the hearse and limousines belonging to the funeral home. To their left was the barricaded intersection of Clergy and Simpson Streets, and to their right the barricades in front of the department store next door to the church, in which the ceremony had just begun.

"The thing you have to understand," Peterson went on, glancing at the others in the scrum for support, "is that we were looking for the Parris tags and we didn't have the luxury of time to run every blessed license plate. Plus, the windows on the Lexus are tinted. Once we were underway, our focus was outward, not inward. I had to divert resources elsewhere, first to the Benson residence and then to the Parris residence. We did what we could with what we had available."

Bennett chewed on the inside of his cheek. "All right. Okay. So how did we spot him?"

"One of my officers on the barricade saw him turn off," Stone answered, folding his arms across his chest. "After we admitted the hearse and the limousines, we were screening the other vehicles in the procession as a precaution. Aaron's right," he looked at Peterson, "every other vehicle in the damned procession had tinted glass and the damned medical waiver stickers to boot, so we were asking the drivers to lower their window so we could get a visual on everyone coming through. He must have seen us doing that and turned off a block away.

My officer noticed and sent someone up. We found the Lexus right away and ran the plate, which didn't match. We called the registered owner and put two and two together."

"So where the hell is he now?" Bennett demanded.

"We're operating on the assumption he's on foot and trying to approach the church," Stone said.

Bennett glanced over his shoulder at the plaza. "He might be over there, just another guy in the crowd. Studying the layout, looking for an opening."

"If he is," Stone said, "we'll find him."

Bennett looked at Hank. "You believe Diane Benson's his target?"

Hank nodded. "It makes the most sense, sir. He tried Walter Parris and failed. Mrs. Benson's already blown him off, and he won't take no for an answer a second time."

"And you're saying he just has a handgun? Not a rifle? Not long range, just short range?"

"That's what we believe." He'd had the handgun with him at the Parris house, Karen had assured him there wasn't a weapon in their garage he could have grabbed, and there hadn't been enough time for him to get his hands on another firearm while making his way from the house to the funeral home in addition to switching license plates on the car. It made sense that he was armed only with the Ruger and that he would need to get close to Diane Benson to use it.

"He's desperate," said Ann Martinez, "and he's already made mistakes. He may be deluded, but he's very intelligent and he won't want any more screw-ups. He'll be cautious." She glanced at her watch. It was 1:08 P.M. "He's got about an hour while the ceremony's underway to pick his approach and get into position." She glanced at Hank. "I don't know about the psychology or anything, but I can't see him still believing he can negotiate anything. This has to be revenge, pure and simple. The narcissistic rage thing. Strike out at whoever's fouling up his plans."

"I think that's probably right," Hank said. "It's most likely he'll try to approach her when they're coming out of the church. She'll be right behind the coffin and Mrs. Jarrett, so that'll be his cue."

"You're suggesting we concentrate right here at the front of the church, then?" Bennett asked.

"We need to cover every angle," Hank said, "but this one's the

248

most likely, unless he feels he can penetrate our security and get into the church while the ceremony's still going on."

Bennett turned around and looked at the line of uniforms standing in front of the church entrance. "Can't see it. We've got it sealed, front and back." He looked at Stone. "Do you think we need to clear the plaza?"

Stone shook his head. "Not necessary. If we can intercept him without tipping the media to what's going on, it'd be a hell of a lot better. If he's hiding there now, in the crowd, we'll find him and pull him out. I agree with the lieutenant, he's more likely to find a spot on this side so he can approach the front door of the church when they're coming out."

Bennett nodded. "All right. This is your detail, so lock it down. I have to go back inside. Text me with any updates." He turned and walked away.

Stone looked at Peterson and motioned with his chin. "Go ahead. I'll text you if there are any updates."

Peterson smiled humorlessly and followed Bennett back into the church. Martinez went with him.

Stone looked at Hank. "Lieutenant?"

"Detective Horvath and I will circulate, sir. We may be able to spot him."

"Good hunting."

"Thank you, sir."

39

They started in the plaza across the street. Horvath found the departmental public information officer, who confirmed the media hadn't yet picked up on the search for the fugitive. She had an extra portable radio, which she gave to Horvath so they could maintain contact with Stone's coordinated search.

They circulated through the plaza without spotting Holland. Hank was recognized several times by media personalities who called out to him for a comment. Hank just shook his head with an apologetic smile.

"Must be nice being a media rock star," Horvath quipped.

Hank barely heard him. They'd reached the far end of the plaza. He was looking across Clergy Street at the department store next to the church. "Have you been inside that store before?"

"Nope. Want me to take a look?"

Hank shook his head. "I will. Do me a favor and go down Simpson to Concord and check out the hotel behind the church."

"Walk the beat, huh?" He held out the radio. "Want this?"

"No. Hang on to it. If I need to reach you, I'll use my cell."

They crossed Clergy Street together. Horvath peeled off to the left, walking in front of the church and down to the corner. He turned onto Simpson and disappeared around the corner. Hank walked past the uniformed officers and the metal barricade into the crowd lined up on the sidewalk in front of the department store. Dodging cardboard signs held up by people for and against the governor, the senator, and big business, he wove his way to the front door of the department store. He stopped and turned around, scanning the crowd around him.

No sign of Holland.

He went into the store. It was nearly empty. He walked up to a cashier, held up his badge and identification, and asked to see the manager. When he arrived, Hank asked about side and rear exits. There was a door that led into the narrow space between the store and the church, the manager explained, but it hadn't been opened in years.

There was a rear delivery door, but it led into a courtyard on the other end of the block, away from the church.

Hank showed them Holland's DMV photo. Neither the cashier nor the manager had seen him. Hank asked about store video security and was told it didn't work. The store operated on a very low budget, the manager explained apologetically. Their inventory was the cheapest they could find, staff were paid minimum wage, and if something broke, it usually wasn't fixed unless the insurance company found out about it.

Hank asked to see the side door. The manager led him through the lingerie department to a locked door. The manager opened it and they picked their way through a cluttered stock room to a metal door on the far wall. There were several cardboard cartons stacked in front of the door. The manager moved them aside, chattering about dead inventory and cash flow, then he hunted through the keys on his key ring, found the one he wanted, and unlocked the door. It opened inward, reluctantly, hinges creaking.

Obviously, Holland hadn't come this way. Just the same, Hank stepped out into the passage. It was narrow enough that he could reach out and touch the wall of the church in front of him. He told the manager to close and lock the door behind him, and to make sure no one else tried to come through there. The manager nodded and shut the door.

The passage was dark and cluttered with refuse and weeds. Hank looked to his left, up to Clergy Street. Stone obviously counted on no one being able to enter the passage from the sidewalk because it was behind police security lines. He looked to his right. Much closer, maybe thirty feet away, was the parking lot behind the church.

As he began to move in that direction, he heard a faint popping sound in front of him that echoed off the passage walls.

He pulled out his cell phone and speed-dialed Horvath. "What's happening, Jim?"

"I'm standing in front of the hotel on Concord," Horvath said, sounding a little out of breath. "A woman's been shot."

40

Hank went down to the end of the passage. In a loud voice, he identified himself and held out his badge beyond the corner of the church where the uniformed officer guarding the back door could see it. Then he cautiously looked around the corner. They made eye contact. The officer nodded.

"Okay, I'm talking to the hotel manager and desk clerk right now," Horvath said in his ear. "The vic's apparently a guest in the hotel. She came out to find a taxi, but it's pretty crowded here and it's hard to find one. Looks like she started walking down to the corner and someone shot her from behind. So far no one's saying they saw it happen. Someone ran into the hotel to tell them to call nine-one-one. Nobody can figure out why she was shot. She's still alive, but she's unconscious. Here's EMS now."

Hank looked around the parking lot. It was completely filled with vehicles, but there was no one in sight other than the officer. Presumably the drivers had all gone off for a coffee and a cigarette while the celebrities were inside celebrating H.J. Jarrett's life.

He stepped out of the passage and looked past the officer at the back door of the church, down the laneway to Simpson Street. There was no sign of the uniformed officer who'd been stationed there. Presumably he'd been drawn down to the corner by the sound of the gunfire and the ensuing panic. Something occurred to him.

"Jim, who ran in to get them to call nine-one-one? Male or female?"

"Stand by, I'll ask," Horvath said. After a moment he came back on the line. "Two people, a man and a woman, both came in."

"See if you can find the man. Make sure it wasn't Holland."

"On it, Lieutenant."

Hank ended the call and speed-dialed Martinez. He heard the call answered, heard the faint sound of someone speaking over the public address system inside the church, and knew that Martinez was making her way to the back where she could take the call.

"There's been a shooting," Hank said when she came on the line. "A woman was shot on the sidewalk in front of the Warrick Hotel. It might have been Holland, creating a diversion. I'm at the parking lot behind the church. I—"

He broke off as a door at the rear of the hotel, across the parking lot, began to open. Over the tops of the limousines and passenger cars, he could just see the top two feet of it as it slowly swung out.

Three shots were fired, and the uniformed officer standing guard in front of the church door folded to the ground.

"Officer down!" Hank yelled into the phone. "Ann—"

A bullet snapped off the wall about six inches above his head.

41

Hank dropped into a crouch and edged along the length of a blue four-door sedan. He took out his gun and quick-peeked around the tail light. No movement. The officer's outstretched arm was visible on the pavement, beyond the last car in the row.

Hank duck-walked into the space between the rows of cars. He started down toward the officer, but a bullet skipped off the pavement about three inches behind his heels. He pitched forward, rolled, and came up behind a Cadillac Escalade. Another bullet skipped between his feet. He looked under the Escalade, through the maze of wheels and low-hanging exhaust systems, and saw a shape on the pavement in the far aisle, nearest the hotel.

Holland was lying down, watching his feet, trying to hit him as he moved.

Hank hastily put the rear wheel of the Escalade between himself and Holland, then stepped up on the passenger-side running board and edged forward, looking over the front windshield.

No luck. He couldn't see Holland from here. He waited for a moment, hoping that Holland would shift into his line of sight. After a moment he heard a scraping noise, but Holland must have moved in the other direction. He stepped down, again behind the rear wheel, and peeked back into the space between the rows.

Nothing.

Hank could now see the top half of the shot officer's body. His hat lay a few feet from his head, his service weapon about six inches from his limp hand. Hank was reluctant to move across the parking lot toward the hotel because he wanted to stay between Holland and the church door, so he moved back behind the Escalade and scuttled down the row, taking refuge behind the rear wheel of a black Mercedes S-class limousine hogging both parking spaces, front and back, in the middle of the lot.

Something tapped along the pavement behind him. Hank held his ground, suspecting that Holland had thrown a stone or something to distract him. He glanced quickly behind him, saw nothing, and scuttled forward to the next car.

Now he had an unobstructed view of the fallen officer. It appeared that the shots had all struck him in the torso, where the soft body armor beneath his uniform shirt had stopped them. The officer's hand moved slightly. It was a good sign, suggesting he'd been stunned by the blows but not wounded. He'd have a hell of a set of bruises, though.

"Checkmate, Donaghue," a voice said behind him.

Hank froze.

"Put your gun down and slide it under the limo."

Hank set his gun down on the pavement and slid it away from him, hating the scraping sound it made as it spun between the tires of the limo. Then he turned around, still crouching.

"You've messed with me for the last time," Holland said. "That's right, get a good look. It'll be the last thing you ever see."

"You don't want to do this," Hank said. "You're throwing away a promising career. There's still time to make restitution."

Holland laughed. He moved the Ruger from Hank's head to his torso. "Head shot or gut shot? Hmm. Probably wearing a vest, like that guy. Head shot it is, then."

"You're out of bullets, Holland. I kept track. You're empty. Put it down."

Holland shook his head. "No, I'm not. This thing holds nine shots. One for the woman—who provided a great distraction, by the way—three for your cop buddy over there, and three at you. That makes seven. One more for you, and one for Diane." He tapped his pants pocket. "I've got the rest of the box here, but I don't think I'll bother. Suicide-by-cop instead. Go out in a blaze of glory."

"You miscounted, Holland. I—"

"You're stalling. Goodbye." Holland pointed the gun at Hank's head.

Hank threw himself sideways as Holland pulled the trigger. He crashed against the back fender of the limo as the round struck the pavement beside him. He hit his head and saw stars, but he heard a volley of shots ring out above him and saw Holland pinwheel backwards, out of his sight.

He scrambled to his knees and stood up, rubbing his forehead. Holland lay spread-eagled on the pavement, a neat grouping of three entry wounds in the middle of his chest leaking blood steadily into his shirt.

Ann Martinez stared at Holland's body, her weapon still outstretched. Commander Stone ran forward, kicked Holland's gun away, and knelt down, feeling for a pulse.

Martinez lowered her weapon and walked up to Hank as a police cruiser entered the laneway from Simpson Street, lights flashing.

"Are you all right?" she asked.

"I had it under control, Ann. He only had one round left."

"He would have shot you with it, you idiot."

"Probably." Hank grinned at her. "Thanks for your help."

"I told you before," she said. "I'll *always* have your back."

42

The church was now empty, except for the rector and a crew breaking down the audio equipment, as Hank walked up the center aisle and out through the open oak doors onto the sidewalk. Across the street, the media were still solidly entrenched in the plaza, most of the networks having assigned separate crews to cover the interment at the cemetery. Word had spread of the shooting of Jarrett's killer in the parking lot behind the church; Chief Bennett and Martinez were already over there holding an ad hoc press conference.

The funeral home vehicles were gone from the curb in front. The coffin, followed by Diane Benson, Ned Jarrett, Chrissy Jarrett, and the rest of Jarrett's family and inner circle, had exited the church without incident. The VIPs had all followed, anxious for media exposure of their own. Most of the spectators had also disappeared, although the steel barricades still remained on the sidewalks and vehicles were still being rerouted away from the block.

There was only a black Mercedes S-Class limousine remaining at the curb as Hank descended the three steps down to the sidewalk. He raised his hand in greeting to Earl Day, his mother's driver, who nodded to him from behind the wheel. The rear passenger-side window was down. Hank squatted and looked in at Roberts, who leaned over from the far side.

"All right, Hank?"

"Yes, thank you, General."

Roberts nodded in approval and straightened, his eyes returning to the perfect-bound report lying open on his lap.

Hank stood up and turned to Meredith and his mother, who were waiting for him on the sidewalk.

"How was the show?"

"If you're talking about the celebration of life," Anna said, "it was damned boring. I nearly fell asleep three times. My ribs are sore from where Roberts kept poking me. But if you're talking about the show that went on outside, I understand it was a little more touch-and-go. You're all right, son?"

"I'm all right."

Meredith's eyes traveled from the scuffs on the knees of his uniform trousers to the red lump on his forehead. "You're hurt."

"Only my pride. I head-butted the back end of Mother's limo. Clumsy."

"But it's over? The threat's over?"

"It's over," Hank nodded.

Anna sighed. "*This* one's over, but the next one's just around the corner. I'd be willing to bet my pension that your phone's going to ring again before the swelling goes down on that bump of yours." She shook her head. "There are more than thirty-five people murdered in this country every day. One-point-two every day in this state. One in this city every day and a half. It's a steady business." She raised an eyebrow at him. "Am I correct, or am I not?"

"Unfortunately," he said, "you are."

"I understand," Meredith said, to both of them. "I get it."

Over her shoulder, he saw a Crown Vic with flashing grill lights edging through the barricade down at the corner.

"I had a quick word with Constance before she left," Anna said as they watched the Crown Vic move up the block toward them. "Walter called her after the ordeal at the house, so she had a word with your chief. Your detective's approval rating is going back up, I'd say."

"Mother," he began, "I hate it when you and your friends—"

"Interfere? Yes, it's terrible, isn't it? We're just a bunch of old workhorses who won't stay in the barn." She turned to Meredith. "Let's not bother with the graveside visit, shall we? How about a bourbon and a cigar in my garden, instead?"

"Well, the bourbon sounds nice," Meredith said, "but I'll pass on the cigar."

"Tell you what," Anna patted her arm mischievously, "you can save it for him, later." She winked at Hank and got into the limo next to Roberts, who closed his report and slipped it into a briefcase at his feet.

Meredith rolled her eyes at Hank and followed Anna into the limousine.

Karen pulled into the space vacated by the limo and exploded out from behind the wheel.

"Damn it, Lou, I missed him, I missed him, I missed him. I

wanted to nail that fucker's ass. God damn it!"

"I'm fine, thanks for asking."

"Yeah, I heard Martinez covered your six. Somebody's gotta. Wish it had been me, though, God *damn* it! I knew it was that bastard. I just knew it!"

"Yeah, you did. It was a good call. How's Truly?"

Karen came up for air, rolling her eyes at him. "Christ, I've got a new fan. She wants to go to the firing range with me now. Wants me to show her how it's done. Like I needed a little four-eyed sidekick."

"Humor her. You're the big sister she never had."

"Oh Christ, just shoot me now."

"Horvath's in front of the Warrick," Hank said. "Holland shot a woman on the sidewalk to create a diversion so he could go through the hotel to the parking lot behind."

"Christ."

"He could probably use a hand."

"Okey doke," she said. "What about you?"

He sighed and ran a hand through his hair, looking at the media circus across the road. "Bennett's expecting me over there to make a statement to the press."

"Ah, fame awaits."

He made a face. "Something like that."

He watched her walk away, disappearing around the corner, and smiled at her confident strut.

Then he brushed at the grit and dirt still clinging to his uniform, and started toward the plaza.

Halfway across the street, his cell phone began to vibrate.

Acknowledgements

I'd like to thank Dr. Ramin Mojtabai, Associate Professor, Department of Mental Health at Johns Hopkins Bloomberg School of Public Health in Baltimore, Maryland, for answering my questions related to Fregoli syndrome and for his articles, "Identifying Misidentifications: A Phenomenological Study" (*Psychopathology*, 1998; 31: 90-95) and "Fregoli Syndrome" (*Australian and New Zealand Journal of Psychiatry* 1994; 28:458-462). Any errors relating to Fregoli syndrome, delusional misidentification syndrome, or schizophrenia are entirely my own.

My research also drew on Frederick A. Jaffe, *A Guide to Pathological Evidence* (Toronto: Carswell, 1976); Vincent J.M. DiMaio, *Gunshot Wounds* (New York: Elsevier, 1985), John Douglas and Mark Olshaker, *Mindhunter* (New York: Scribner, 1995), and Alan Flusser, *Dressing the Man: Mastering the Art of Permanent Fashion* (New York: HarperCollins, 2002).

I'm very fortunate to have a terrific circle of readers who provide invaluable feedback on the manuscript. Thanks to Gwenda Lemoine, Danielle Rapone, and Ani Pulsifer. A special tip of the cap to Margaret Leroux, whose amazing editorial skills and responses to the story, themes, and characters are all very much appreciated.

In particular, I want to thank my editor, business partner, and long-suffering wife, Lynn Clark, whose keen eye misses absolutely nothing. This one was particularly difficult to complete, Lynn, given the circumstances, and your patience and unwavering support kept me going. Thanks, love.

Finally, thanks to Ronnie Cox, Sandrine Tyrbas de Chamberet, and Caroline Hendry of Berry Bros. & Rudd, Ed Bajus of Charton Hobbs Group, Alistair Anderson and staff of the Edrington Group, and Mark Ash, Callum Robertson, Angus Walker, and the real Richard Booth of Frame (Sgt. Booth says thank you) for an incredible experience in Scotland. Blended whisky's for drinking and single malt's for thinking, indeed.

About the Author

Michael J. McCann lives and writes in Oxford Station, Ontario, Canada. A graduate of Trent University in Peterborough, ON, and Queen's University in Kingston, ON, he worked for Carswell Legal Publications as Production Editor of *Criminal Reports (Third Series)* before spending fifteen years with the Canada Border Services Agency as a training specialist, project officer, and program manager at national headquarters in Ottawa. He's married and has one son.

He's the author of *Blood Passage* and *Marcie's Murder*, the first two books in the Donaghue and Stainer Crime Novel series, and *The Ghost Man*, a supernatural thriller.

THE DONAGHUE AND STAINER CRIME NOVEL SERIES

Blood Passage
by Michael J. McCann

ISBN: 978-0-9877087-0-0
(paperback)
978-0-9877087-1-7
(e-book)

Would you believe a little boy who claims to remember the names of the men who killed him in a previous life?

Praise for *Blood Passage*

"Got an hour? Because that's how long it'll take to describe all the great things about this book . . . a great main plot, interesting and not overwhelming subplots, believable characters, true-to-life dialogue, and a satisfying ending."

—*The Masquerade Crew*

"*Blood Passage* is an exciting murder mystery that will keep you turning the pages . . . I especially loved the character of Karen Stainer, a no-nonsense tough woman who is not afraid to get nose to nose with the criminal element, but does have a soft side to her . . . A very tense edge-of-your-seat type of page turner that will keep you guessing to the very end."

—*CelticLady's Reviews*

"Action filled and worthy of its own television show . . . I thoroughly enjoyed this book."

—*Have You Heard Book Reviews*

THE DONAGHUE AND STAINER CRIME NOVEL SERIES

Marcie's Murder
by Michael J. McCann
ISBN: 978-0-9877087-2-4
(paperback)
978-0-9877087-3-1
(e-book)

Hank Donaghue is on vacation when he's jailed on suspicion of having strangled a woman he saw only briefly before her murder. Can Karen Stainer get him released and help him find the real killer before it's too late?

Praise for *Marcie's Murder*

Marcie's Murder "holds the reader with its convincing mysteries. . . . [Donaghue and Stainer] play effectively against type."
—*Toronto Star*

"I highly recommend *Marcie's Murder* . . . as a terrific read. Keep your eyes (and ears) on this writer, because he's going to the top.
—*Catherine Astolfo*

"I really enjoyed watching this novel unfold, especially as Donaghue and Stainer are the perfect team and their witty remarks make for a very fun read. There is an art to writing crime novels, and McCann has perfected it."
—*A Book Vacation*